CIRCLE IN THE DEEP

CIRCLE IN THE DEEP

THE OUTCAST ROYAL™ SERIES BOOK 01

AARON D. SCHNEIDER

MICHAEL ANDERLE

LMBPN

DISRUPTIVE IMAGINATION

Copyright © 2021 LMBPN Publishing
Cover copyright © LMBPN Publishing
A Michael Anderle Production

LMBPN Publishing
PMB 196, 2540 South Maryland Pkwy
Las Vegas, NV 89109

Version 1.00, July 2021
ebook ISBN: 978-1-64971-923-2
Paperback ISBN: 978-1-64971-924-9

THE CIRCLE IN THE DEEP TEAM

Thanks to our Beta Team:

Kelly O'Donnell, John Ashmore, Rachel Beckford

Thanks to our JIT Team:

Dorothy Lloyd
Angel LaVey
Jackey Hankard-Brodie
Peter Manis
Zacc Pelter
Paul Westman

If we've missed anyone, please let us know!

Editor
SkyHunter Editing Team

Are you ugly?
A liar like me?
A user, a lost soul?
Someone you don't know

- *Ugly*, The Exies

I met a traveller from an antique land,
Who said, —"Two vast and trunkless legs of stone
Stand in the desert. . . .

- Ozymandias, Percy Bysshe Shelley

Underface
Underneath my outside face
There's a face that none can see.
A little less smiley,
A little less sure,
But a whole lot more like me.

- *Everything on It*, Shel Silverstein

Dedication: This book is dedicated to my eldest, fierce as a storm, soft as new fallen snow. From the moment I had the honor to hold you in my arms, you've humbled and inspired me, my warrior-princess, my peacekeeping Valkyrie. Steel strong and tender hearted, I could not be more proud of you, and I hope in some way, some day, to make you proud of your ol' Poppa Bear.

— Aaron

*To Family, Friends and
Those Who Love
to Read.
May We All Enjoy Grace
to Live the Life We Are
Called.*

— Michael

ACKNOWLEDGMENTS

This book would not be here without the patient and steady efforts of several people, many of whom I've thanked in previous books, and while their efforts are still appreciated incredibly, I'd thought I'd take a second to acknowledge some other people without whom this book and indeed this entire series would never be possible.

I'm referring to the giants on whose shoulders I now perch so precariously. Lewis and Tolkien, Howard and Lovecraft, King and Butcher, these inspiring titans of the written word who shaped and encouraged me without ever having seen my face or spoken to me (well all but one of you - though I imagine you've forgotten). You are the constellations I chase across the horizon, and without you creating your art and laying it before the hungry, ungracious world I might never have found my way here.

Thank you many times over. May God humor me enough that maybe one day we meet on fairer shores.

PROLOGUE

Khardalis, the Iron Maiden and crown jewel of the Behemon Mountains, lay stripped and broken before her enemies.

The armies of Hasriim the Great already flowed through her streets and the first screams of the harrowed population were soon joined by the ravenous crackle of fire. In the waning night, the mingled voices of victims and flames would rise like an apocalyptic choir to echo across the mountainside.

The city had stood defiant for too long against Hasriim and as such, her humbling would be the subject of dread legends for years to come. Tales would be whispered of how rapine, slaughter, and plunder had left her a shell only fit for vultures and jackals. In cities as far as the fabled courts of Xhulth across the Caged Sea or even far Verenvan, dire stories would be told of the noble houses down to the last babe in arms butchered and hung from the palace Citadel.

Not every word would be true but the message would be clear. Khardalis was broken as was fitting for all who stood against Hasriim the Great.

Yet not one word would be spoken about how it was not

Hasriim, however great he might be, who accomplished the fall of the proud city.

That dubious honor lay with a band that skulked around the gutted barbican of the Goat's Gate.

The fortified gatehouse squatted upon the junction of the city's outer wall. A branch of the interior wall provided, like yawning jaws, access to a rough mountain track into the Behemon Mountains.

The gate's name had been a matter of some debate amongst the learned antiquarians of the city. Some had postulated that it was so named because this was where mountain shepherds used to drive their flocks into the city in antiquity. Others said that anyone exiting from said portal had best be as surefooted as a goat if they planned to travel the treacherous slopes beyond.

A few truly innovative and progressive academics proposed that the appellation of goat was derived as a derogatory term resulting from early conflicts between nomadic and agrarian peoples, but academics often say many silly things and their fellow civilized men indulge such foolishness.

Regardless, those scholars would soon never argue again as they died amongst other civilized men, while the Goat Gate was held by a small detachment of those distinctly less civil.

Moments earlier, they had ensured rapid ingress into the city. Now, they were determined to halt any egress. That is, of course, assuming one couldn't pay.

"That's everything we have," a woman sobbed and clutched a silken shawl around her with one hand while the other pressed a small boy to her hip. The child shivered in the night air and the thin nightgown trembled against his spare frame.

"Not everything, me thinkz," a tall, barrel-chested man rumbled in a basso voice thick with a northern accent. He looked up from perusing the pack he held open with one hand while the other hand rested on the pommel of a sword in a battered scabbard. Seeming all the larger in the coat of scales and gorget worn across his broad body, he loomed over them both.

With thick, scarred fingers, he'd already plucked out the bag of coins and a wineskin that lay at his feet but he now squinted at the woman in the light of the burning city. His pale eyes glimmered in a gaunt face. He sucked his teeth and turned his visage to a skull's rictus grin before he nodded.

"What do you me—" She began to weep but saw the heavy fingers stretched toward her. Fearing the worst, she cried out and tried to draw back but the brute's fingers snagged the opal necklace around her throat.

"You are having theze." The big man chuckled as the child at her side began to cry. "Give me theze and onez in you earz, then it be everything, me thinkz."

"Please…please!" the woman croaked and her eyes bulged as her fingers struggled with the necklace. "Take it, please, but don't hurt us."

After another agonizing moment of fumbling, the necklace came free.

"Hurt?" the brigand asked with a bemused chuckle as he admired the necklace in his fist before he winked at the bawling child. "Why think me do that, eh?"

"Because your face looks like the celestial end of a hell-bound demon," drawled a man from under the gate's shadow. "And that's when you're in a good mood."

The speaker emerged from the belly of the barbican. Bandy limbed and wiry with a horn bow slung over one shoulder, he wore a padded tunic crisscrossed with a leather harness from which hung a long-knife and a quiver of arrows. His voice was even and calm but something in his flinty gaze made mother and child shrink away.

The bowman's black-eyed gaze played across the woman and lingered at every place where her thin nightgown shifted and clung to the soft body beneath. His expression didn't change but his shoulders seemed to roll forward while his advancing steps took on a distinctly predatory gait.

"Perhaps the lady is looking for a guide, hmmm?" he all but purred in the back of his throat. "Someone to see her and her dear son to safety?"

"I can't pay," the woman said with a shiver and hugged herself. "He has everything."

His lips curled to form a cold smile.

"Oh, I'm sure we'll find a way to balance the scales."

"Weren't you—" The big man began to turn to the newcomer but fell silent at the wicked light in his companion's eyes. The shadows on the gaunt face deepened as he looked at the beset mother with a shrug. The necklace fell amongst the other plunder at his feet and he refused to look at the sniffling little boy.

"Earringz first, me thinkz," he grunted flatly and moved his hand to rest it on the pommel of his sword again.

Desperation and fear warred on the woman's face as she struggled to remove the earrings, but a keening scream from deeper within the burning city held her attention for a moment. Something grew hard and remote in her eyes. She handed the earrings over, turned to the "guide," and nodded stiffly, but she held her head high as she met his merciless gaze.

"Very well," she said, her throat so tight she almost whispered. "Get us to safety and you can...can have whatever you want."

As if to illustrate the point, she loosened her grasp on the shawl and straightened to draw her shoulders back. His smile broadened and it was his turn to nod.

"This way, my lady," he said in a throaty invitation as he gestured toward the dark passage leading out of the city.

The big man would not look at either woman or child as they began to shuffle past him. Without turning, he raised his voice to address his companion, his gaze fixed beyond the bloody streets and fire-spattered buildings.

"Be quick about it, Norlen," he called in an ashen voice. "Ax-Wed won't like, me thinkz."

Before the man could respond, a third figure emerged from under the gatehouse and her icy tones froze both men like an arctic gale.

"What won't I like, Brekah?"

He stiffened while Norlen turned jerkily to regard the speaker who stepped from the dark. Their reaction was muted, however, compared to the beleaguered woman who gaped openly.

Had she ever seen such a creature?

The figure that strode forward, in spite of the armor and mail-curtained helm she wore, was ferociously female, but she was a lioness to the domestic feline cowering of the two men. She stood eye to eye with Brekah and her every movement betrayed a strength and agility that pushed beyond mere sinew. One gauntleted hand clutched a flaccid wineskin while the other rested upon the head of an ax on her belt.

Norlen was the quickest to recover and strode quickly to scoop up the wineskin pilfered from the woman's pack.

"We're merely dealing with things," he said with an unctuous smile as he held the wineskin up as an offering. "Nothing you need to worry about."

Eyes like forge-heated copper flashed within the shadow of the helm's sockets as Ax-Wed looked past the wine to where the mother and son gawked at her. She looked at Brekah, who still refused to face her, and glared at Norlen.

"No."

The words were as cold and hard as the grinning edge of the weapon at her belt.

His face spasmed with hatred but he mastered his expression and proffered the wineskin again.

"I don't know what you mean." He chuckled, an almost clucking sound in his dry mouth. "Take the skin and let us get back to it. The others will be back soon and they will probably have many more chickens that need to be plucked."

Her gaze wandered to the wineskin for a moment and her fingers tightened on the limp sack in her hand. With a low sigh that slithered through the metal links that veiled her face, she let the empty skin fall from her grasp as she stepped forward.

"That a girl," Norlen said encouragingly and a genuine grin crept across his face. "There you go. Climb right back—argh!"

His words ended in a choking gag as Ax-Wed stepped past the outheld liquor and seized him by the throat. With an ease that even the larger man would have struggled to display, she dragged the gasping, gargling bowman to one side. His eyes bulging, he clawed feebly at the armored limb that held him in a grasp as hard as the steel it was clad in.

"Brekah," she said without an ounce of strain in her voice. "The pack."

With a grumbling grunt, Brekah ambled around and held the pack out to the woman who stood moon-eyed with her child pressed against her hip.

"Take it," Ax-Wed instructed in a calm, unhurried voice.

The woman hesitated for a moment and her fingers trembled when they stretched toward the pack. Then, with a lurch of resolve, she snatched it from him.

"Go."

Again, the voice was untroubled despite the fact that Norlen now groped with one hand for the blade at his belt.

"Don't," she said and turned a chilling glare upon the bowman, who stilled although one hand still clenched around the arm holding him.

"Go," she repeated and kicked the plundered wineskin toward the woman without turning her gaze from her captive. "Save as much of that as you can. In three days, you should reach a lodge on the north face. If it is empty, fine, but if not, use that wine to barter for assistance. They don't get good wine up there very often."

The woman slung the pack over her shoulder and scuttled forward with the child in tow. She hooked the carrying cords of the vessel with unsteady fingers but her voice was clear as she straightened to address the towering warrior.

"Thank you," she whispered as she began to edge toward the portal. "May the gods bless you."

"Go."

She needed no more encouragement and turned from the ruins of her old life, dragging her son beside her. Before she vanished down the tunnel-like portal, the lad looked over his shoulder long enough to wave a hand in farewell.

Ax-Wed waved in return but something like a shiver passed over her.

When they had moved far enough to satisfy her, she returned her gaze to Norlen, who wheezed through her constricting fingers as he glared at her with undisguised hatred.

With no more effort than if he were the little boy who had fled, she threw him aside. He lost his footing and landed on his backside with a wounded grunt.

"Not a zmart thing, me thinkz." Brekah groaned and rubbed the back of his neck as though he experienced a sudden ache.

"Maybe." She shrugged and let her shoulders sag before she rolled them. "But right isn't always smart."

"Truth." The large man nodded and gestured with his chin at the recovering Norlen. "But him not having zuch ideaz, me thinkz."

The bowman found his feet and snarled obscenities and blasphemies in three different tongues as he unlimbered his bow.

"Don't ever touch me again." He growled belligerently as his fingers brushed the fletching of the arrows at his hip, his bow already freed from his shoulder. "Ever."

Ax-Wed still rested her hand on the head of her weapon and regarded him coldly as his fingers closed around the shaft of an arrow.

"You're a fine shot, Norlen," she said in the same sanguine tone. "But don't be stupid. Not twice in one day."

He tugged the arrow halfway from the quiver and her fingers tightened enough that her gloves creaked slightly.

"Oh, this one isn't for you," he retorted venomously as he rolled the arrow between his fingers so the barbed head clicked against the others. "I think this one will be for your little friend."

She tilted her head enough to look down the passage through the barbican where the woman and her son emerged from the shadow of the wall.

"Don't."

Steel had returned to her voice but this time, he merely sneered.

"It's a far stretch on a small target but you said it." He chuckled cruelly through bared teeth as he drew the arrow completely from the quiver. "I'm a fine shot."

The ax seemed to fly into her hands and one hand grasped high while the other slid toward the bottom of the haft. There was no further word of warning this time but a low, wet snarl rose from deep in the lioness' chest.

Brekah's gaze darted from one to the other, his eyes wide and frightened. His mouth gaped and lips twitched as half-formed admonitions bubbled in the back of his throat.

"W-wait...n-now... Ho-hold..."

An eternal second stretched as poisoned glare met smoldering glower, then Norlen's mouth moved as he raised the shaft to his bow.

"This'll teach y—"

The ax whistled gently before a dull, fleshy thud drew a ragged groan from Brekah. The sound was followed by the heavy thump as Norlen fell on the bloody cobbles. His limbs spasmed and organs voided to leave nothing but a sharp fecal stink in the air.

For a moment, an unnatural silence seemed to settle over that corner of the city as Ax-Wed drew a rag from her belt. Brekah turned away and shook his head.

The lioness had barely begun to clean her blade when he turned to face her, his eyes glittering and huge.

"No need for that, me thinkz," he warned in a hoarse whisper and hooked a thumb over his shoulder.

Almost a dozen wretches in disheveled finery staggered up the abattoir of a street and looked over their shoulders constantly as if harried in their approach. They appeared to be a handful of small families and couples, all wearing or adorned by the kind of casual finery that inspired loathing and avarice in those denied such things. Some seemed to have had time to throw bundles together or retrieve small chests, but others appeared to have only what they wore.

At first, they seemed to be driven by the sight of the burning city but Ax-Wed's gaze settled on the rangy figures arrayed behind them. The light of moon and flame gleamed on battle-greased blades and glinted off hard-worn armor. With cruel laughs and rough threats, they drove their herd toward the Goat Gate, their smiles keen and sharp as they all anticipated a good shearing.

"You run now they won't chaze, me thinkz." Brekah grunted and his gaze slid off her to Norlen's cooling corpse as his nose crinkled. "Too buzy to follow, but you ztay and there'll be more blood, me thinkz."

She squared her shoulders, tucked the stained rag into her belt, and settled both her hands atop the ax head.

"I won't run." She shrugged and nodded toward Norlen's body. "I gave him a chance. It's not my fault he was too stupid to take it."

The man shook his head and stole a glance over his shoulder.

"Norlen more popular than you, me thinkz," he stated matter of factly. "More popular and been two-backing with Targhli for pazt few monthz. She'll want zatizfaction, me thinkz."

Now, it was her turn to shake her head.

"Even if he brought it on himself for wanting his way with a desperate woman?"

Brekah shrugged and turned toward the street again.

"Never bothered her before," he grunted, the words slow and sour. "Won't matter now, me thinkz."

Ax-Wed's chest swelled to answer but her shoulders sagged and she let the retort dissolve into a long, low sigh.

"What will you do?" she asked finally and raised her gaze to confirm that the divested nobles were barely a stone's throw from the gatehouse.

"Watch," he replied over his shoulder. "Tell them what happened if they azk but they won't wazte time azking, me thinkz."

She nodded and forced herself to wait in stillness and silence as the predator-stalked herd approached. Almost in counterpoint to the warrior's poised position, the fallen nobles began to bleat their fearful entreaties.

"Please, have mercy," they pleaded as their gait slowed to a nervous shuffle and they stared in terror at the bared blades behind them. "This is all we have left in the world. Mercy, please!"

Brekah drew a deep breath, coughed a little when the latrine stink of Norlen filled his nostrils, and raised a bellowing cry.

"One line, single file!" he ordered with the certainty and volume of a battle-seasoned commander. "No pushing and no cutting."

"Yeah, no cutting," snickered one of the she-jackals who nipped at the heels of the herd and flicked a red blade before her. "'Less you want us to cut you."

From the looks of things, a few had already received such treatment. Near the head of the forming column was a gray-headed man with craggy features who clutched a crimsoned scrap of velvet to his face. Behind him, a paunchy woman sniffed and winced as she tried to squint around a freshly broken nose that leaked blood down her face.

"Now, now," admonished a tall, lean man who emerged from the circling pack. "We are escorts for these fine people, after all."

His clothing and armor were finer than the others but no less battered and battle-stained. He sauntered toward Brekah through the frightened folk who parted before him. An ivory-hilted sword hung on his belt and a steel-rimmed buckler held lightly in his left hand both seemed parts of his anatomy.

He stopped short when he noticed Norlen's body a pace away from the grisly totem of his head. A face that might have been beautiful were it not so scar-crossed and soot-smeared scowled first at the corpse and then at the blood still clinging to the ax.

"Explain," he ordered between clenched teeth and lowered his free hand to the sword at his belt.

"Well, Jaggor," Brekah began and sucked his teeth again in a death's head grimace.

Before anything further could be said, the blade-brandishing she-jackal uttered a horrible shriek.

"Norlen!" Targhli screeched and shoved through the cowering civilians. "Norlen!"

Her long-bladed knife still in one hand, she threw herself on the ground before her lover's sightless eyes in a perverse imitation of worship. Her hard, wild gaze searched the slack expression and then swung upward toward the towering woman with the bloody ax.

"You! You bitch. I'll kill you!"

The long-knife trembled but the woman didn't rise from her crouch.

Ax-Wed glared at her and her burning gaze determined the measure of the woman in an instant. She dismissed her easily and turned her lioness' gaze to Jaggor.

"We had a disagreement," she said, her voice steady and flat.

The corner of his mouth twitched upward and for a second, cold, reptilian speculation slid behind his eyes. One less share in what was bound to be a prolific haul wasn't something to ignore.

"You'll pay for this." Targhli yowled where she still crouched and the knife quivered in her hand. "I swear it by all the gods and every demon that's earned a name."

Ax-Wed didn't bother to turn her head when she replied.

"There's no need to pester them. I'm standing right here."

The woman screamed like a wild cat but when she did not pounce, all understood what the warrior woman already knew.

"What was the disagreement about?" Jaggor asked and his eyes trailed to the pile of booty at Brekah's feet. More calculations slithered behind his eyes and the rest of the crew seemed to sense it as they began to creep forward between the confused and still terrified flock.

Brekah noticed the change with one sweep of his eyes and took half a step back.

"About a woman," he said quickly, one hand raised in placation while the other remained fixed on his sword. "Norlen was for taking a woman and Ax-Wed disagreez."

Jaggor's fingers tightened around the hilt of his sword.

"So she killed him for having his way with a prisoner?" he asked while the icy arithmetic slid the information on his mental abacus.

"No," the big man said and took another half a step back when he realized some of the band had begun to creep along the flanks. "He intended to kill the woman'z boy or might have, me thinkz."

Targhli rose and bared her teeth along with the long-knife in her hand.

"So she killed Norlen, one of her own, for some war-chaff's whelp." She growled in fury. "It seems to me like she merely wanted a bigger share."

Soft murmurs of assent slid between the mercenaries as they crept closer.

"After all, didn't you hear her say we would have never taken the gate without her?"

Ax-Wed weathered the accusing question without retort, which stoked the discontented current that crackled between the hot-blooded brigands. She rested her hands on her ax and fixed her gaze on Jaggor, their leader, and waited patiently.

Brekah slunk into the shadow of the gate and clear of the encircling band as Jaggor reached the end of his calculations. The leader of the sell-swords stood behind the shrinking circle and with a speculative glance, he assessed the scene with a cool smile.

Ax-Wed read the smile in an instant—one less rival, one less share. With a grimace, she adjusted her footing subtly.

"I suppose I should have known better than to trust a Thulian." Jaggor sighed and expertly feigned self-deprecating resignation. "She couldn't help it, I suppose."

A hate-filled murmur passed through the gathered mercenaries as horrified whispers wove through their captives. All eyes turned to the warrior woman and some of the defeated even squared their shoulders as they stood a little taller.

Yes, a Thulian explained everything, didn't it? No mortal man could defeat Khardalis but Hasriim had not sent mere men but a demon in mortal flesh. There was no shame in defeat when it took one of such a race to conquer them. After all, weren't so many ancient stories full of these monsters from the sea, armored giants who worked foul magic with their very breath?

"That's why its face is covered," a captive muttered. "To hide the streaked hair and the fangs."

Ax-Wed chuckled as the pack of jackals closed in.

Again, the ax was in her hands as though it had sprung there of its own volition.

"You can walk away," she said quietly and smoothly, her gaze still on Jaggor. "You don't have to make Norlen's mistake."

A cruel laugh rose in answer, swirled among the mercenaries like a bitter wind, and made the onlooking refugees shudder. Gory weapons glinted hungrily in the growing light of the fire-swathed city.

She sighed as she set her shoulders and her burning gaze lowered for a single contemplative second.

"When you all wake up in hell, you can talk about what a bad idea this was."

As the first spear thrust lunged toward her heart, she looked up and was already moving.

Her ax a blur of motion, she swatted the impaling point up and away as she drove forward and closed on the first mercenary with the temerity to attack her. The offender scuttled back as she launched a heavy stroke but the swing wasn't meant for him.

Instead, it scythed toward Targhli, who'd prowled forward in search of an opening. For her effort, the singing ax-blade carved across her chest and down through her belly.

The knife tumbled from her fingers and the she-jackal pitched onto her side and gaped like a landed fish.

"I assume the gods were busy," Ax-Wed roared as she drove forward into the next assailant. "And demons know my name."

Disorganized and dismayed, the predators had become prey in the blink of an eye. She vaulted over Targhli and swept the butt of her ax into a face before she caught a sword stroke with the blade. With a sharp twist, she spun the sword away and drove the horn of the ax into the sword bearer's throat. For good measure, she whirled and split the face she'd pummeled previously.

Before the others could grasp that half their numbers had

been felled in a few heartbeats, she pounced. She fell upon a scrambling spearman and cleaved his weapon with one swing and an outstretched arm with another. Jaggor and the remaining two mercenaries shrank back as their comrade spilled his lifeblood across the street in a red rush.

She stood among the remains of her onslaught, the dripping ax still held easily in her strong hands.

"I told you this was a bad idea," she said simply and stalked forward across the gory cobbles.

Jaggor raised sword and buckler together and stepped forward. The bronze-chafed scales of his armor made a soft, serpentine rustle and a simmering pool of vitriol born of wounded pride bubbled in his eyes.

"Those were my warriors." He hissed his outrage like a miser coming up short after his count.

Ax-Wed threw her head back and laughed, a fell sound that might have been beautiful if it weren't so chilling.

"Those weren't warriors." She chuckled and strode forward. "Merely children playing at war."

The leader's nerve failed and his cold facade crumbled as she came for him. His gaze darted around him and he shoved the two remaining pawns toward her, but she swept them to the left and right without even slowing.

As he backpedaled desperately, Jaggor swept his sword before him and slashed the air as if to dare her to close the distance.

"I'm a daughter of the House of Xhulth," she intoned as the ax met his weapon with a shivering stroke. "The Eight Felling Strokes were my birthright, given by the Grim Handmaiden herself."

He punched with his buckler but again, the ax head answered and the disk split as did the hand holding it. The brigand chief staggered back with a sharp cry as he clutched his broken hand. The butt of the ax cracked across his jaw and he landed hard on his knees to look into the face of death itself.

The hot copper eyes glared at him through the sockets of her helm and he could see a cold smile there.

"Don't forget to remind the others," she stated softly. "I warned you this was a bad idea."

He managed half a scream through his broken mouth before the blade found his neck.

Her last enemy still twitched in his death throes when Ax-Wed turned with a cold glare to the huddled herd who'd born witness.

"Shouldn't you be running?"

Without a word, they began to first shuffle, then scurry through the open gate.

She watched them trample the fallen, men and women she'd once broken bread and shed blood with. A part of her knew something should be stirred by the thought but in that moment, she felt only a hard, hollow patch within. She didn't regret what she had done, from beginning to end, although it was not what she would have chosen.

I curse you! I curse you to the Bitter Road. Long may you walk it.

The words echoed from a lifetime ago and her shoulders drooped.

With a single, barely trembling hand, she reached under the curtain of mail veiling her face and loosened the straps of her helm.

A thick braid of black hair streaked with blue fell across her shoulder and for the first time, she turned her unarmored face to the ruin of Khardalis. In the light of the city she'd opened for destruction, her proud and strong features looked on impassively. As the flames flashed and flared, the scars across the left side of her face traced jagged fissures akin to spidery fingers or maybe a lattice of forked lightning.

"Well, I suppose this is merely one more step," she whispered, unwilling to allow the tears welling in her eyes to fall. "Mother knows best, after all."

She stood before the gatehouse for a few moments longer and let the sights and sounds of slaughter and ruin beat against her naked face. This was her road and she accepted it.

Without another word, she replaced her helm, collected what she could from the dead, and set off through the Goat Gate.

CHAPTER ONE

The Gate to the East, Jehadim, loomed large before Ax-Wed as the sun burned toward the edge of the horizon.

With a grimace, she adjusted the pack on her shoulders and estimated the remaining ground she still had to cover and the passage of the sinking orb overhead.

Footsore and loaded as she was, she wouldn't reach her destination until some time after sundown. Beneath the mailed veil over her helm, she sighed a curse in the razored, lilting tongue of Thule. Whether out of superstition or something more reasonable, the city sealed itself tightly for the night. Other eastern cities would close their main gates but still allow a trickle of traffic to pass through smaller posterns manned by the night watch, but she was all too aware that such was not the case in Jehadim.

She sniffed and cleared her throat as she remembered the last time she'd been left outside the gates. It drew another curse from her as she set off again to trudge wearily toward the looming city.

The memory remained vivid—her cradling Noka's head in her lap as each breath grew shallower. She wasn't sure it would have mattered if they'd been able to enter the city and find a physician but he had been so young and soft-spoken. He didn't deserve to die in a beggar's hovel outside the walls like an unmourned outcast.

He was the first sword-brother she'd lost who had meant anything to her but certainly not the last. It had been both easier and lonelier since Khardalis some three years earlier as her fell reputation ensured that she found work but almost always alone. Despite this, she found companions along the way among those who crossed her path, and as surely as she found them, they met with some tragedy or another and she was forced to walk the Ashen Road alone again.

Ax-Wed did not look forward to spending a night in some hovel leaning against the city walls with nothing to keep her company but sagas' worth of bitter memories.

She was so entrapped by her broodings that she remained oblivious to the commotion ahead until she crested the hill and stood face to face with a charging aurochs.

With no time to even think of drawing the ax at her belt, she flung herself to one side and narrowly avoided the impaling tips of the beast's horns. She landed heavily on her stomach—her bulging pack made her clumsier than usual—and as she rolled to her feet, she felt certain that the bovine would be upon her with its horns ready to spit and toss her with one shake of its great head.

When no gouging onslaught came, she looked around with a bemused grunt to see where the beast had gone.

Her head swiveled one way and then the other until she caught sight of the great bull at the base of the hill she'd crested before almost being gored and trampled. It snorted, stamped, and tossed its head in obvious irritation and made a wide circuit around the low patch of sandy earth between the hillocks. For a single tense second, she thought it would return for another charge, but the moment passed as it continued a circular course across the sand. It was only when she watched the creature wheel for another turn that she realized her ax was already in her hands.

After it had repeated this bizarre behavior a few times, the aurochs raised its head, drew in a great snoutful of air, and uttered an indignant bellow before it set off in an agitated trot.

"What in Atlkosh's bones is wrong with it?"

The oath had no sooner escaped her lips than a loud, growling voice yelled, "Don't hurt him!" before something barreled into her knees.

Ax-Wed tumbled halfway down the hill toward the pacing bull with something heavy and determined wrapped about her legs.

"Morah's beak! Get off!" she roared and kicked out as she tried to halt her descent.

One leg pulled free of whatever had captured her limbs and she managed to halt her bruising roll down the hill.

"Leave him alone!" the creature clinging fiercely to her remaining leg commanded.

"I said get off!" With a snarl, she bent her free leg to drive a powerful kick into a wooly lump that looked suspiciously like the back of a skull.

She checked her blow barely in time when the lump moved and a pair of large emerald eyes set in freckled features emerged from under a mop of dark curls. The eyes widened at the sight of her armored boot raised for a kick and they disappeared when the shaggy head buried itself against her knee.

"Please!" the creature bawled and its gruff voice cracked with desperation. "Leave him alone."

Ax-Wed's heart still hammered in her chest as she leveraged the haft of the ax in her hand to scoot herself and her erstwhile passenger a little higher up the hill and tried to gather her thoughts.

"Hezkel two-backing." She growled in exasperation and her gloves creaked slightly as her hold tightened on the ax. It was bad enough that she didn't have a clue what was going on, but being flat on her rump with a creature clinging to her leg and an irate bull a stone's throw away left her feeling more than a little vulnerable, to say the least.

And in her experience, the best answer to vulnerability was violence—and as much of it as possible.

Whether it was from one of her recent encounters, the weariness of her trek across the desert, or forestalled wisdom finally catching up, she managed to fight off the instincts that told her to lash out until things stopped moving.

Ax-Wed took a steadying breath and looked at the lumpy figure still clinging to her legs. Now, she realized, it was shaking uncontrollably.

"Let go of me and we can talk," she managed to say through gritted teeth as she lowered her boot slowly to the hillside.

The brilliant green eyes emerged again and this time, she noticed a large, freckle-dappled nose beneath them pressed against her knee.

"Promise you won't hurt him?" the frightened creature asked with more than a trace of hopefulness in its rough timbre.

She looked down the hill to where the aurochs had stopped to sniff again. Exactly as before, it uttered a frustrated bellow and returned to pacing in angry circles.

"As long as he keeps those horns to himself," she said with a nod of her head to the wide-swept sickles in question. "Then I don't suppose I have any quarrel with him."

The emerald eyes studied her for a second before her leg was released and their owner scuttled away from her to provide her first good look at her would-be attacker.

He—the general proportions and wiry dusting about the face suggested male—was short and stocky and stood no taller than a lad of ten or eleven, although he weighed as much and gripped like a full-grown man. The proportions, along with the bright eyes and facial hair, suggested some breed of dwarf but a young one, probably in that lurching awkward time between childhood and maturity.

"I'm sorry about all that." He grunted as he rose and began to brush the sand from his clothes. "He's scared, is all."

Ax-Wed wasn't certain why the stout fellow made such a fuss about his clothes as they practically blended into the desert. He was clothed in plain but well-made homespun all dyed a dusty beige, with the only ornamentation being crimson stitching worked in a simple herringbone pattern down his right sleeve.

Feeling her gaze upon him, the lad looked up and after a moment of staring at her, his eyes widened and he thrust a hand out.

"Please let me help you," he almost squeaked in his gravelly voice. "To jump on a stranger is one thing but a...uh, that is to say, you are a..."

She looked above the hand to the benighted young dwarf's eyes. His gaze roved over her body with increasing perplexity.

"A woman?" she asked and raised an eyebrow she knew he couldn't see inside her helm.

The bright green eyes bulged to the point where there seemed to be a chance they might pop out and in the next moment, he stared at the sand, his hand still outstretched. Beneath his freckles, his cheeks bloomed crimson.

"I'm so sorry, of course," he muttered to the sand, his voice edged with embarrassment. "A woman, obviously. I don't mean obviously in that your feminine parts are obvious...not that your parts look like male parts—why do I keep saying parts? Oh, Watchful Mount, save me!"

Ax-Wed coughed to quell a snort of laughter and decided she'd better take the lad's hand before he yammered himself breathless. She still had to find out about this business with the aurochs, after all.

"Don't worry about it," she told him briskly and hauled herself upright with the extended hand. To her pleasant surprise, the dwarf kept his footing, a not inconsiderable feat especially given her size, equipment, and the heavy pack she bore.

"Thanks." She nodded at him as she settled the harness of her armor into place and shrugged her pack into a more comfortable position.

"You're welcome," he said softly and dared to look ruefully at her before his gaze fled to considering the hillside and the beast trotting below them. At the sight of the bull, he rubbed and tugged on his large nose in irritated contemplation.

"Were you heading into the city or out of it?" Ax-Wed asked as she turned to look at the sinking sun.

"Huh—what?" the dwarf stammered, shaken from his frustrated musing. "Oh. In—into the city. My *Mehk* is supposed to meet with Vahrem's caravan so we can enter the Azure Gate together."

The lad suddenly turned toward her with beseeching eyes and yanked his nose so hard one might have thought he wanted a trunk.

"She'll be so mad if I make her late." He groaned and glared at his clothes. "Why was I so stupid?"

"Durra!" a shrill voice howled behind them, and both woman and dwarf jumped at the sound. Even the aurochs below paused its strange behavior and flattened its ears at the grating sound.

"Durra!"

"Mount preserve me!" the young dwarf panted as he began to scamper up the hill, then stopped to stare at the bull. "Oh, Stones Below!"

"Durra!"

Ax-Wed was about to ask him what was happening when the drumming thunder of hooves paired with a rattling ruckus distracted her. She looked up the hill at a plume of dust that rose toward the sun and an instant later, the heads of three immense black rams crested the hill. Huge and sleek-coated with great spiraling horns, the beasts might have been something fit for a fable or prophetic myth but as sure as the sand, they trotted forward with their heads high like crowned kings. They moved side by side with precision and unity that parade-ground soldiers might have envied.

"Stones and Spikes." The young dwarf moaned as he stopped and waited for the approaching procession like a man awaiting the gallows.

As they approached, she realized they were all harnessed together to draw a wicker-framed chariot, wherein sat a dwarfess of considerable age. A thick mane of curly hair descended around her broad, bent shoulders, most of it gray going to white except for a few locks as black as coal.

This expanse of hair fell about a face that was tanned with the sun and spotted with age, but her eyes were as bright and green as the young dwarf's and the scowl on her face spoke of a vigorous temper. Her clothes were of much the same make as his except she had the herringbone pattern down both sleeves of her blouse and several bands running down the length of her skirts. In one hand, she held the reins of the chariot lightly and with the other, she gripped a twisted length of bleached wood from which hung several bells of various sizes and materials.

With a sharp tap, she jangled some of the bells and the rams came to a quick but not ungainly stop.

"Durra!" the dwarfess yelled as she leaned against the straining wicker frame. Her ponderous breasts and part of her heavy belly protruded precariously. "You stupid bareface! What is going on?"

The young dwarf hung his head and tucked his hands behind his back as he struggled to form a reply. From where she stood behind him, Ax-Wed noticed his stubby fingers wringing his hands mercilessly.

"The aurochs broke free, *Mehk* Numi," he said and nodded furiously toward the beast at the bottom of the hill. "I think it's because I still had some ash asp blood on my clothes. He scented it and panicked."

The elder dwarf swung her gaze to the rams, who returned her gaze with strange, golden eyes. An understanding seemed to pass between them which seemed vaguely disappointed before she turned her scowl on the waiting youngster.

"I know what happened," she snapped and grasped the protesting wicker supporting her. "What I asked is what you are doing?"

Durra wilted under his elder's glare but managed to sweep a gesture toward Ax-Wed.

"I was chasing the aurochs, trying to catch it, when I ran into this woman," he explained and kept his head low and his voice pitifully hoarse. "At first, I thought she'd been hurt, then that she might hurt him, and then—"

"Then I realized I could help your good nephew," Ax-Wed interjected and took a step forward so she stood beside him. "We were trying to think of a way to get the beast under control when you arrived, wise mother."

To accompany the traditional eastern honorific for noble matrons, she bowed and didn't rise until *Mehk* Numi gave the customary nod.

"I certainly appreciate you trying to help my fool of a nephew," Numi said as she cast an assessing eye over her. "But the silly bareface should have known better than to simply run off like some randy billy chasing a spry nanny."

"I didn't want to lose track of it," he protested and cringed when his aunt turned another immolating glare upon him.

"And I don't want to lose track of my nephew," she retorted and shoved herself away from the side of the chariot with a grunt. "When you have a spooked aurochs, you won't bring it back with nothing but your two hands."

Muttering and grunting, the elder dwarf dismounted and landed heavily but solidly upon her sandaled feet.

"Now, if you and this woman intend to help me straighten this business out by sunset, fetch the halter and rope out of the back of this ol' rumbler," she instructed and began to waddle down the hill. She used the piece of gnarled wood with bells as a walking stick although it seemed far too thin and frail for such a purpose.

"Come on." Durra sighed dejectedly and began to shuffle towards the chariot.

Ax-Wed stood for a moment, utterly perplexed as the old dwarfess continued to amble toward the snorting aurochs. The bells on the staff created a kind of rhythmic chime with each step, and she had a disturbing thought that it almost sounded funereal in tone.

She shook her head, certain that something was missing, and tucked her weapon into the loop on her belt before she followed the younger dwarf.

Her long legs ate up the distance between her and Durra and she joined him at the back of the chariot. He drew out a halter and rope that lay coiled on the floorboards.

"What will she do?" she asked with a nod toward the dwarfess as she took the rope from his hand.

"Settle him," he grunted as he scooped the halter up.

"Should we be down there to help her?" she pressed and felt mounting urgency as each shuffling step brought the beast and elderly dwarf closer together. "I mean, is it safe?"

Durra had turned to descend the hill but stopped and looked at her, his brows knitted together in confusion.

"Have you ever been around Wain Dwarves before?" he asked. Confusion gave way to a knowing look when she shook her head.

"I know there are tribes or clans," she shrugged. "So that's your tribe?"

His brow furrowed even more and he opened his mouth to explain but the chiming steps of the elder became a discordant jangle. Both turned as the dwarfess held her staff over her head and shook it vigorously. The aurochs stood less than half a dozen paces from her with its head raised to study her warily.

"If you've never been around Wain Dwarves, you won't want to miss this," he said softly, his voice almost reverent, and led the way. Shuffling the stout rope in her hands, she followed him down the slope and prayed silently that she wasn't about to see the cantankerous old aunt be gored to death.

They had reached the level ground when the elder stopped shaking the bell-strung staff, threw her head back, and uttered a raw-throated cry almost like a low. As though stung on the haunches, the aurochs reared with a baying bellow and surged forward.

Ax-Wed grasped her weapon reflexively but a hand was there to stay her.

"Wait, please," Durra whispered and quickly withdrew his hand when a dangerous light flashed in her eyes.

Instinct and no small amount of irritation at being grabbed again flashed through her but she mastered it and forced herself to watch events unfold. Once the beast was done with the elder, she knew exactly who she would shove in front of the charging aurochs.

The beast seemed dead set on running the old dwarf down and its massive muscles bunched and flexed as it rushed forward with its huge, horned head lowered. The tips of those horns glinted red in the dying sun as though eager for a more substantial coating of crimson. The last few yards between elder and beast disappeared in the blink of an eye.

In a spray of sand and dust, the aurochs turned the charge into a prance and cavorted almost daintily around *Mehk* Numi.

Ax-Wed couldn't stop a low mutter of amazement from slipping through her lips.

"It's something, isn't it?" Durra nodded with pride. "And one day, I'll learn the charms too."

"That could come in handy," she responded and looked at the rope. "Do we even need this?"

"Do you two think it will be easier to get a lead on this brute before or after sunset?" *Mehk* Numi called over her shoulder as she raised a hand to stroke the auroch's glossy hide.

"The charms don't last forever," her companion explained and raised his voice as he moved toward the now placid bovine. "Coming, *Mehk*."

In answer, the elder dwarf made another lowing sound and the aurochs settled beside her. It was still excited and its great sinews shuddered while it strove to stand motionless at her side.

"Quickly now," the dwarfess ordered as she continued to stroke the shivering colossus. "We've been delayed enough as it is."

Durra approached without the slightest hesitation with the halter in his hands. He made two soft clucking sounds in the back of his throat and the great bull lowered its head enough to allow him to secure the harness. With a wave of his hand, he beckoned Ax-Wed closer and when she reached him after a somewhat halting approach, he took the rope and secured a lead to the halter.

"Tie him to my rumbler," the elder dwarf instructed and pointed up the hill with her peculiar walking stick. "I'd like a word with our new friend."

The young dwarf looked as downcast at being shooed away as the aurochs did at leaving the dwarfess, but both went slowly up the hill to the chariot without complaint.

"Are you headed into Jehadim, then?" Numi asked as she watched her nephew's progress.

"Yes, wise mother," she replied and straightened a little as she fought to shake off the wonder that permeated her. It wasn't the first time she'd seen magic but it was the first time she'd seen it so...pure.

"Do you see a crown on this ol' lump or a jeweled choker

around this waddle?" she asked quickly, tapped her skull, and stroked the folds of her neck with knobby fingers. "You can stop with that wise mother business. Call me Numi or *Mehk* Numi if you insist on being annoyingly formal."

"As you wish, *Mehk* Numi," she replied with a little bow.

The elder dwarf squinted at her and her eyes pinched to slits between the wrinkles. She seemed to be suspicious but on seeing the smile in the coppery eyes within the helm, the dwarfess broke into a gap-toothed smile.

"I think I might get to like you, gell." She chuckled and held her hand out. "Have you got a name worth knowing?"

"Ax-Wed," the warrior answered as she took the outstretched hand.

"Well met, Ax-Wed." Numi nodded and a sly twist in her smile told the Thulian she was making a point of not questioning the epithet. "Would you like to join our little procession to the Azure Gate?"

After a quick look at the bruising horizon, she decided that spending the night with a caravan outside the city would be far better than a night alone. Hospitality being sacrosanct in the East, she might even hope that some food and, gods be merciful, wine could find her.

"It would be my pleasure," she replied warmly. "We're too late to make it into the city but a night among friends doesn't sound too bad."

"Too late?" Numi snorted as she began her shuffling waddle up the hill. "Don't you bet those long, meaty legs o' yours, gell."

Ax-Wed was utterly bemused—something that was becoming an uncomfortably familiar sensation around the Wain Dwarves.

"*Mehk* Numi, Jehadim closes its gates at sundown," she said and fell into step beside the dwarfess. "And we still have a few miles to go yet by my reckoning."

"Not to worry, young one." Numi grunted as they approached the chariot where Durra waited with the secured aurochs. "You don't need to worry yourself about anything but holding on tight."

Without a word, the younger dwarf fell to one knee and held an arm out. Using the arm as a rail and the knee as a step, the old dwarf mounted with minimal fuss. Durra hopped aboard after his elder and shuffled to one side as he nodded encouragingly for Ax-Wed to join him.

The warrior woman forced herself to stride past the watching aurochs and squeeze herself onto a vehicle she was sure was not designed for three, much less one of her size. The wicker gave several rising squeals of protest but everything held fast—to her astonishment—although she was far from comfortable.

"She wasn't joking about holding on tight," the young dwarf muttered at her shoulder.

"What?" she asked but Numi snapped the reins with a braying cackle and things became self-evident.

CHAPTER TWO

Hazarbed Guuhal leaned low enough that Tarkhind could smell the bluegum on the guard commander's breath over the oils perfuming his beard.

"He has come to visit again, my prince," the tall officer whispered before he straightened quickly to match his staff of office.

Prince Tarkhind, the current ruler of Jehadim and son of Prince Turlihnd the Sentinel, choked back a curse as he spluttered into his wine bowl. He tried to play it off as a sniff of his fine aquiline nose but it was a futile gesture at best.

The prince's guests—three men representing major caravans, the very lifeblood of Jehadim— noted the reaction but were too well mannered to comment although they darted a few furtive glances between themselves.

Vipers. He seethed internally as he placed the bowl on the table and dabbed at his mouth and immaculate beard while his mind raced. He felt the pressure of three powerful men who intentionally did not notice his distress but he shrugged it off as his face settled into one of his best smiles. Crafted to seem genuine yet not display his striking good looks—at least too much—it was a gentle, almost self-deprecating expression and he'd refined it to perfection.

"It seems the needs of Jehadim call," he intoned apologetically as he rose slowly from the table where they reclined. "I have been advised that a small matter requires my attention although I am loath to leave you all, if only for a moment."

The words, only lies in part, had enough of a ring of truth that the three merchants saw fit to nod understandingly as they nibbled and sipped the refreshments.

"I'm sure it can't be helped," one of them replied but his cordial smile didn't reach his eyes and he studied his host as though evaluating a stallion on the block. If the prince was any judge, the merchant's eyes indicated that his evaluation was less than complementary.

"My master of revels shall attend you immediately," Tarkhind said before he took his first step away from the table, still facing them. "He is a diverting old fool, at least, and should see you well satisfied until I return."

"If you'd rather..." another merchant began and hauled him back from what would have been an expertly executed withdrawal. "You could always send your seneschal in and we could resolve the details with him. We understand the prince's time is quite valuable."

Prince Tarkhind smelled the trap instantly.

"Our seneschal is seeing to some of our other interests and not immediately available," he replied smoothly, careful to keep the same appeasing smile in place. "And I would never dream of shuffling such esteemed guests and their business to a mere functionary. No, a moment only and we will dine and see your concerns properly addressed."

The answer had the desired effect on two of the men and their chests swelled slightly as they sank easily against their cushions. They were esteemed guests with a prince's word that they would be heard. It was everything men like them loved to hear.

The other man—who'd evaluated the ruler of Jehadim like a piece of horseflesh—seemed less impressed but at least spared them all by not expressing himself. He merely shrugged and took another sip of wine.

"Only a moment," Tarkhind promised with the slightest bow —a master stroke—before he fled the room as quickly as decorum permitted.

"Do you wish me to enter with you, my prince?" Guuhal asked, his fierce gaze fixed on the tall door which opened behind the throne of the Lower Court. His scarred hands tightened around the iron-shod staff as though preparing for an enemy to thrust through the portal.

"No," Tarkhind replied testily, a little flushed and out of breath from the rush down the corridors and stairs of the palace to the subterranean halls where the Lower Court was situated. "Once I've caught my wind, I will go in and deal with this."

The man frowned but he knew better than to argue the matter.

"He's brought two of *Them* with him this time," the guard commander warned and his curled lips made his beard twitch. "I'm amazed we can't smell them from here."

The prince muttered a curse and pressed his thumb and forefinger against his eyelids where a dull ache there threatened to drive the orbs out of his sockets. When he'd taken the throne a decade earlier, he'd been prepared for many of the demands of state, the burden of which he had been preparing for since he was born.

But this... No tutor or training had been offered to prepare him for this.

Because it springs from sins you should never have committed.

The words echoed in his mind but he knew they were not his

own. A chill ran down his spine and he repressed the shiver. Beyond the limits of rational hearing, the rustle of great wings tickled his ears.

"My prince?" Guuhal asked, his voice low and edged with concern.

Tarkhind shook fear's frigid claws off enough to straighten and fix his gaze upon the door before him.

"Once my business is done, have two servants scour the floor," he commanded as he moved to the door, his head held high. "I don't want the stink of them to linger."

The guard commander might have answered but the resounding boom of his sovereign throwing the door open drowned out the sound and the prince swept along the railed walkway to ascend the dais to his throne.

The Lower Court—or the Court of Judgment—sprawled before the throne, a wide, vaulted chamber lit by rings of candles placed around the walls and ceiling. The light reflected and bloomed across the fresco-emblazoned dome overhead, which was supported by parallel rows of columns that divided the entire space into three roughly equal parts.

In the section where the throne stood, the area was occupied primarily by rising aisles of seating where functionaries and scribes would sit around the central throne. They would record and advise the prince as he issued judgments and sentences upon those who had been brought before him. At the moment, the seats were all empty which was just as well. He didn't imagine that any mortal man could offer him any useful advice and he certainly didn't want the present proceedings to be recorded.

The portion farthest from the throne was separated not only by the pillars but also iron grate-work stretched between the stone supports. The far wall, visible through the iron works, was a series of dark corridor entrances which wound to the depths of the palace where dungeons and less conventional prisons held various inmates. The single gate which allowed access between the far section and the rest of the chamber lay ajar, something which filled his chest with a crippling concoction of anger and dread.

In the middle of the central section was a platform where the accused would appear before the prince, his hands and feet shackled to the solid block of stone which legend claimed was the first stone laid when the palace was built. However, instead of an accused prisoner bound and trembling upon that singular rock, He stood there with two of Them cringing and pawing around him like whipped dogs.

All three wore threadbare robes so soiled that their original colors were impossible to determine and although voluminous, the garments could not completely hide the twisted, lesioned creatures within. The fawning underlings stroked their master's filthy robes and poxed feet with sore-riddled claws. Beneath their hoods, distended, dribbling jaws worked jagged teeth and wormy tongues to mewl adorations in slurping voices.

He somehow seemed sinister and powerful despite a hunched spine and twisted legs and appeared utterly disinterested in the mongrel worshippers at his feet. Any trace of his visage was hidden in the shadows of his hood but even in that deep and unnatural darkness, Tarkhind felt an immense and malicious intelligence scrutinizing him. The attentions of the three merchants in the halls above were tiny stars compared to the intensity of the black sun which glared at him from beneath that grimy cowl.

"You will secure more," the faceless figure declared, his voice resonant, deep, and beautiful. "The current quota is insufficient."

Despite feeling like a mouse before a serpent's cold gaze, the prince mustered enough indignation to scoff at the instruction.

"Do you realize what will happen if anyone of any significance catches wind of what I am doing?" he asked acidly and his fingers dug into the arms of his throne. "Even worse, have you ever considered what would happen if the people found out?"

The two curled about their master's feet bared their snarled teeth at him and uttered a bubbling hiss of accusation. He didn't bother to respond to the degenerate creatures but he grasped the throne tighter to hide the tremor in his hands when he saw their wet, hungry eyes gleaming at him.

"Are prince's memories so short?" his visitor asked and the prince's heart quickened as the darkness beneath the hood seemed to permeate the room. "Have you already forgotten what you unearthed?"

The cloying shadows threatened to close in around him and blot out the light which should have surrounded him. His throat was suddenly painfully dry and his tongue felt like a mummified husk plastered in his locked jaws.

"What you awoke with all your scratching, scratching, scratching, scratching."

With each utterance of that final word, Tarkhind heard the grating scrape of shovel, pick, and file upon stony earth as mind-shivering memories were stirred. He tried to drive the assaulting visions away with an effort of will and denial but the scraping continued in the congealing dark and he felt he might come undone.

He yanked his rigid hands from the arms of the throne to cover his face.

"Enough, please," he croaked and hated how small and pathetic his voice sounded in his ears. "I haven't forgotten. Please!"

Even the gibbering worship of Them at His feet hadn't sounded so pathetic.

The scratching receded and he felt the venomous smile under the shadowy cowl as he lowered his arms to wrap them around himself. The chamber was not cold and his finery was thick but he still felt as though his teeth were about to start chattering.

"I am only here to help you, dear prince," the voice assured him, soft, seductive, and as fathomless as the ocean depths. "This is not simply to avert the disaster you almost brought upon yourself but also to one day raise Jehadim above all the earth, resplendent and glorious."

The icy claws of fear still dug into him but when he heard this, an ember of naked ambition bloomed in his heart. He warmed himself over its smoldering, nebulous promise and leaned forward despite his fears to grasp the throne in feverish hands.

"But when?" he asked, unable to master himself enough to sharpen the question into a demand. "When will you have enough?"

The impression of a smile in that potent presence remained but the tone of his voice curled with a warning edge.

"All in good time," He reassured him in the same tone and cadence with which he'd first sworn almost two years earlier. "All things in my good time."

Tarkhind slumped into his throne and his fingers raked ineffectually at the polished stone beneath his fingers. He entertained the idea of pressing for more information but the thought that the scratching sound might emerge again banished the thought immediately.

"Very well," he said and did his best to act as though he were an indulgent lord who succumbed to the minor entreaties of a needy subject. "We will increase the amount provided. How much?"

"Double," said the voice from the darkness as though the word were not a hammer stroke.

Double, the prince thought as his heart began to sink. *Double.*

There was the faintest rustle of feathers in the back of his mind but he drove them away with desperate energy.

"Double it will be," he agreed and let himself lean slowly into the throne as though he were melting. "Is there anything else?"

"No, great prince," He replied, the title said with silk insincerity. "I leave you to see it done knowing you are up to the task."

Tarkhind pinched the bridge of his nose when he felt the grinding ache return with a vengeance.

"I don't see that I have a choice," he muttered softly and immediately felt the smile in the voice again.

"You don't."

With a trailing sigh like the last breath of a dying man, the unnatural shadow evaporated from beneath the deep hood and He was gone. In his place was another of the malformed creatures, its lumpy jaw slack and drooling. The two that had fawned at its feet only moments before rose from their reverential crouch and grasped the staggering vessel, one by each arm.

With malformed tongues muttering something that seemed uncomfortably like language, they dragged the third toward the open gate at the rear of the chamber. Without a backward glance, they hauled their charge through it and drew it closed with a clang.

Tarkhind winced at the sound but did not turn his gaze from watching them slip into the darkness of one of the tunnels leading to his dungeons. Even after the echo of their shuffling steps and wheezing grunts had faded, the prince of Jehadim sat in the candle-bathed Lower Court and stared into the darkness beyond the wrought-iron gate.

"I used to think such things kept us safe," he whispered to himself. "That the stone walls and metal gates could keep out the worst of this world."

When I was a child I thought as a child, recounted the voice in his head that was not his. *When I became a man, I set aside childish ways.*

"It's bad enough I have to contend with those things." He groaned and ground both palms into his aching sockets. "But now you will torment me too?"

You are firstborn of the Line, the voice answered, as unperturbed and undaunted as ever. *I will never leave. I will never forsake.*

The not-quite heard susurration of feathered wings shifted

around him, this time accompanied by the padding of immense paws. The prince felt a presence as weighty and terrifying as malice yet suffused with something even more terrifying —certainty.

Whatever haunted and overshadowed him now was suffused with a surety that was like an unquenchable fire. Nothing could stand before it without seeming determined to be consumed by it and thus only fed its inevitable inevitability.

The prince felt all this and it shook him to his very marrow.

"What curse lies upon my family that I am tormented like this?" Tarkhind sobbed, his head still in his hands. "I have a dynasty to maintain and a city to preserve. I don't need to be haunted twice over."

The only curse upon your head is that which you brought upon yourself, the voice reminded him with infuriating calm. *And if you don't turn aside soon, you will lose something more sacred than a dynasty or precious as a city.*

"What would you have me do?" he snapped and darted his gaze around in a fit of savage temper. "I am doing the only thing I can to prevent this doom and keep my family intact. One misstep and one error could ruin me and thus condemn all of Jehadim. I have no choice!"

Doing what is right is never a misstep, and truth can never be an error.

"It is easy for you to say," the prince all but snarled and his fingers curled into claws. "You are not the ruler of a city."

Neither are you. Only He rules in Jehadim now.

Tarkhind leapt to his feet with a scream of rage and his hands twisted into fists to beat against his chest.

"I am Prince. Prince of Jehadim!" he roared in a shrill, wrath-strained voice. "I rule here. It is my hand that holds the Keys of the East. I am Prince!"

The stirring of great wings beyond what ears could hear was the only answer and he was left alone and panting for breath.

After a long heartbeat, the door behind the throne opened and Guuhal's face peered into the chamber. The *Hazarbed*'s brow was creased with concern and he waited for a moment before he spoke.

"My prince," he said at last and cringed as his voice echoed in the Lower Court. "Is everything well?"

Tarkhind spun on his heel, prepared to chastise the man for daring to ask such an incredibly stupid question but then realized Guuhal had heard his ranting after the gate had shut with a great clash. His inflamed irritation imploded into nothing more than a nervous laugh as he shrugged and put on a disarming smile.

It was warmer and friendlier than the one he'd used with the dinner guests but no less practiced.

"Never better," he said and affected a little laugh as he moved from the throne dais toward the door. "Although it seems collections will have to increase."

The guard commander, who'd begun to move into the room to hold the door open for his master, stiffened for a second. His hand trembled upon his staff of office and for a moment, he looked as though he might drop it.

"Increase, my prince?" he asked and managed to open the door with short, jerky movements.

"Double, to be precise," Tarkhind said and his stomach threatened to rebel as he spoke, although not an ounce of his discomfort reached his face.

"Double?" the warrior repeated and the word almost sounded like a curse.

"Yes, *Hazarbed*," the prince said as he strode past him with a scowl of impatience. "Now please see it done—and don't forget to have this chamber scrubbed."

CHAPTER THREE

It was a sight she had never thought she would see.

The Azure Gate—one of the three great trade gates of Jehadim—stood wide open even though the last light of the sun slipped below the horizon. Despite this, all traffic through was stalled by a large wagon train which seemed to have become wedged within the frame of the portal. A great crowd of people— members of the caravan, she assumed—rushed around to shuffle things from here to there and there to here. Burly men hefted heavy bags from one point to another while sure-handed women lashed ropes and tightened knots. Darting between them were children, some busy helping while others simply did their very best to stay underfoot. To complete the scene of domestic upheaval, the unhappy guards strode around with brass-wrapped cudgels that rattled against wagon beds.

Into this pandemonium rode Ax-Wed, still clinging to the wound wicker rail of *Mehk* Numi's chariot. The great aurochs trotted behind, still on its tether, but behind the now docile beast was a small heard of its kin, hemmed in by three of the wide-framed wains for which the Wain Dwarves were known. Each of the structures was something like the house-wagons the

Vushalan drove in their wanderings except they were open with only poles and a tented stretch of canvas covering to shade them overhead. Each was drawn by a team of huge, burly goats although none quite as magnificent as their leader's kingly sables.

"Ha-ha, I knew Vahrem wouldn't let me down." Numi chortled over the rumble and ruckus. "I swear the man must be half-*dwoon*."

With a chime of her bell-wrapped staff, the black goats slowed to a halt and the entire procession followed suit.

"This looks like a mess," Durra muttered as the debacle at the gates filled any silence that resulted from the chariot's stillness.

Ax-Wed nodded but stopped when she heard the elder dwarf chuckle again.

"Oh, I do believe our horse trader has everything quite well in hand," she commented as she leaned forward to squint at the scene. "Now where is that beautiful rascal?"

"Who is Vahrem?" the Thulian asked, unsure of what she should be looking for. As far as she could tell, no one particularly beautiful or rascally was identifiably in the dusty mess at the gate.

"Caravan master and horse merchant," Durra said. "And *Mehk*'s very good friend."

"Oh, where is he?" Numi fussed petulantly. "Hasn't he seen us?"

She needn't have bothered as half a heartbeat later, a barrel-chested man detached himself from the tangle and jogged toward the chariot. A broad smile flashed in a dark, well-kept beard and the bear of a man raised a beringed hand in greeting. Numi responded with a giggle that would have fit a dwarfess a quarter of her age.

"Oh, get over here, handsome," she demanded and strained over the wicker frame in her precarious way with her arms outstretched.

Ax-Wed was surprised by the figure who strode toward them.

Having done mercenary work in the East for some years,

she'd seen her fair share of caravan masters and not one of them looked like this burly, sweaty creature who approached them. The fact that he was walking was strange enough. Caravan masters were men of considerable wealth and enterprise and came in two types—dashing dandy or gilded socialite— so a gleaming stallion or glittering palanquin was more the order of the day. Yet there he was, on his own two feet and loping toward them with the bowed gait of a man raised in the saddle.

"Numi, my lovely!" the rugged man called in a powerful voice as he slid around the kingly goats and ran a familiar hand over a flank. "I was starting to worry that you wouldn't make it."

"But you waited for me all the same." The elder dwarf beamed at him. "And that's why I love you."

With a spryness that belied his frame, the man sprang onto the central shaft of the chariot and braced himself with one foot on the wicker frame.

"Come to me, my lovely." He chuckled and scooped her up in one brawny, hirsute arm.

Taking the stout dwarven matriarch in his arms like a dainty maid, he bounded off his perch onto the dusty road. At the affectionate display, Ax-Wed's gaze darted from them to Durra, who was red-faced but smiling broadly.

"You've finally grown a proper coat over those naked cheeks," Numi commented approvingly as she brushed her knobby knuckles against Vahrem's oiled beard.

"Do you like it?" he asked and beamed at her still cradled in his arms.

"Oh, if only I were a little younger and you a little shorter," she responded wistfully and her wrinkle-swaddled eyes glistened.

Vahrem laughed heartily as he lowered her to the ground. *Mehk* Numi found her feet easily enough but the peculiar caravan master leaned to one side so he could hold her hand in a gentle but firm grasp.

"Durra, *bruz'tal*," Vahrem called in a thick dwarvish dialect with a cheerful nod. "Your *Mehk* hasn't been too hard on you, has she?"

"Don't listen to a word that little fool says," she declared with an exaggerated growl. "He's a sluggard and liar."

"Master Vahrem, *bruz'tal*," the young dwarf answered with a meek wave. "I look forward to traveling with you again this season."

"And I you," the merchant said with a gentle nod before he turned to look at Ax-Wed for the first time. "And I don't believe I've ever had the pleasure of meeting so fearsome a woman as you."

"She's merely a stray we picked up on the side of the road," Numi said and winked at her. "Not a chatty one but she's made of stout stuff."

"I'll say." He grinned and studied the battered armor and ax the woman wore easily at her belt. "And what name does such an imposing lady go by?"

She vaulted cleanly out of the chariot and landed before the caravan master on steady feet. When she straightened to her full height, she stood half a head taller, a fact the man noticed with an impressed nod. He might also have seen the muscles rippling in her arms as she held a hand out.

"Ax-Wed," she said and squeezed firmly when the hand was taken. To his credit, the merchant had a grasp of iron and in the brief contest, the warrior woman might have even called it an even match.

"Ax-Wed...hmm," Vahrem said thoughtfully as though it sparked a half-recalled memory. She stood in silence, thankful that no one could hear the sudden acceleration of her heartbeat. People having heard of her was almost never a good thing.

"I wouldn't call it a proper name," Numi interjected at the caravan master's side. "But it's not the silliest thing I've ever heard you stilt-walkers call yourselves."

The man nodded but a sharp glance indicated that he didn't agree with the dwarf. He met her gaze levelly and a cold shell formed inside her. She'd become so used to the fearful whispers and the stares of revulsion that she'd developed an instinct to protect herself from them. Ice around one's heart was chilling but it helped to numb the sting of ostracization.

"Well, if it suits the lady, it suits me," Vahrem said and to her utter shock, he broke into another warm smile. "I am pleased to meet you, especially among such fine company."

Before she could stammer a reply, Ax-Wed was interrupted by a sharp-faced man with a gray, wilting goatee who appeared at the merchant's shoulder.

"It would be best if we move things along, master," the man said in a taut, raspy voice. "The guards are no longer amused."

As if on cue, raised voices cut through the bustle and a gate guard, his face flushed, jabbed his finger into the chest of one of the caravan's workmen. A few of the other men began to drift over and ignored the sharp but subtle pleas of the women working beside them. Some of them who saw the trouble brewing responded with sharp-tongued calls to the children.

A knot of guards with their metal-shod clubs in hand began to shoulder through the crowd toward the confrontation and things seemed to be heading downhill fast.

Ax-Wed's hand drifted to her belt.

"Excuse me for one moment, my lovely," Vahrem whispered to Numi and strode toward the brewing storm.

"What's going on?" he bellowed in a voice that threatened to shake the timbers of the Azure Gate. "I told you to clear this mess."

As one, workmen and guards turned to the advancing caravan master. He strode toward them and shook his head with bewildered disgust.

"Can't you see these men are staying past their shift end on our account?" he demanded with a wide sweep of his arm toward the guards. "Come on, now. Move this mess before I move you with a few good kicks."

For a single, trembling second, the violent tension hung in the air and then, to a man, the caravan workers turned on their heels and resumed their efforts with the wagons. In less time than it took for Ax-Wed to take in the sudden rush of work, everything became miraculously unstuck and the laden wagons rolled through the Azure Gate.

The guards stood and gaped as Vahrem approached them and pressed a few coins into each man's hands as the caravan moved into the city. Along with coins, he gave each dumbfounded man an understanding nod and firm pat on the back before he turned to rejoin the group in front of Numi's chariot.

With a broad smile, he took the dwarfess' hand in his and swept a hand toward the waiting streets of Jehadim.

"Shall we?"

It was well and truly dark by the time the entire caravan, including the Wain Dwarves, wound through the streets to their destination inside the city. Their journey through the Silver Quarter had been slow as they had to compete for space with the various merchants and mongers who had closed shop and were heading to their homes in the Copper Quarter.

Every few steps—that was how it seemed, at least—the caravan ground to a halt when some impatient trader cut across their path with his wares piled on a cart. More than once as her frustration deepened, Ax-Wed had considered trying to find a way to make her excuses and separate from the ponderous cavalcade, but the warm attention of the dwarves and Vahrem's good-natured berating of passing merchants connived to convince her to remain with them.

She might have been used to girding her heart with frost but she couldn't deny that it felt pleasant to be made welcome in good company. Her work as a sell-sword and muscle for hire did not often afford her much time around such people. Perhaps—and even more so—it was the opportunity to feel at ease among a family. Her many years of ragged wandering among killers and thieves had not erased the ache of homesickness she felt, but listening to the old dwarf's chatter about nephews and to see parents doting on their children eased the pain somewhat.

All the same, they made slow progress and after her long journey across the desert, she was ready to rest. By the time they reached the edge of the Silver Quarter, she was at the limit of her crumbling patience but mercifully, Vahrem uttered a cheer that was taken up by the rest of the caravan.

"Home at last!" he whooped in a milder but no less thunderous voice than the one he'd used at the gate.

"Home" was a wall-framed stockyard that nestled in the nexus between the Silver, Copper, and Tin Quarters. Located along one of the broad roads which connected the various districts, it was clear that a fair amount of goods could be sorted and distributed throughout the city from the location with relative ease.

A corral gate made of lashed timbers was dragged open by two rangy youths, bare-chested and looking for all the world like they'd rolled around in the packed-dirt yard only moments before.

The merchant ambled forward to the lads with Numi and Ax-Wed in tow, while the rest of the caravan followed to fill the vacant stockyard like water filling a sinkhole.

"Pap said you were coming today," the elder of the two boys declared as he clung to the gate with his brother. Although both were smiling, their limbs trembled as they fought to keep the lashed timbers from swinging free.

"One more reason to listen when your father speaks, eh?" Vahrem nodded sagely as he produced a few coins from his purse

"We made sure there was fresh straw in the stalls and reeds in the barns," the younger added and his eyes gleamed as his gaze settled on the money in the caravan master's hand.

"Did you now?" The man stroked his beard thoughtfully and he watched the two nod so vigorously that they almost lost their hold on the gate. "Well, I suppose that kind of service deserves compensation, doesn't it?"

More coins appeared and the boys' eyes bulged and Ax-Wed wondered if they might even start salivating. Then again, the boys were already wet all over with the sweat that poured off them to create runnels on their gritty bodies. The youngest one had begun to puff with effort and his face assumed a shade that was hard to describe beneath his dappled coating of dirt.

The warrior woman slid her pack from her shoulder, stepped closer, and took hold of the gate.

"I've got it," she said with a grunt and planted her feet.

Both boys looked at her in amazement, struck dumb as they heaved in great breaths of air.

"Thank you, kind sister," Vahrem said and accompanied the traditional honorific with a bow. As he straightened, he cleared his throat loudly and gave the lads a meaningful look, the coins still clasped in one hand.

"Thanks," the eldest said quickly and his fingers curled and uncurled as his hand strayed toward the money.

"Yeah," the younger piped up after a nudge from his brother. "Only a big lady like you could handle something like this. You have to be the biggest woman I've ever met."

Vahrem sputtered a snort while the older boy cuffed his brother, who immediately turned with his fist cocked for a vengeful blow. All she could do was chuckle softly, which made the mail veil tinkle gently.

"Steady now, boys," Vahrem warned in a stern voice as he thrust a coin-laden hand between the brothers. "If you knock these coins out of my hand, who knows if you'll ever find them again."

The imminent brawl was immediately forgotten and both brothers lunged at the proffered coins, which the merchant released with a quickness a lion tamer might show in surrendering a chunk of meat. A fair amount of jostling and muttered curses ensued but the boys reached a hasty agreement over what seemed equal shares.

"Thanks, Master Kal'Stru," both said together and smiles gleamed on their dirty faces.

The merchant made a show of checking to make sure he had all his rings and the fingers inside them before he nodded and held his hand up as if to indicate that he was satisfied with the condition of it.

"Yes, you're quite welcome." He grunted and fixed them both with a firm stare. "Will you boys head home tonight? I can arrange for a wagon to take you or maybe *Mehk* Numi might let you ride in her chariot."

At the mention of the latter, both boys' eyes lit up before they shared a look and a silent understanding passed between them. The younger inclined his head toward the caravan master while he looked pointedly at his brother, who glanced at each of the two adults, lowered his head, and chewed his lip.

"Perhaps they have something else in mind," Ax-Wed suggested and her heart went out to the suddenly shy boy.

"Come on, Julo," the younger pressed after he beamed an appreciative smile at the Thulian.

"Shut up, Jalen," the older brother growled before he turned to Vahrem to stammer, "W-well, I was hoping…well, we was hoping, that we c-could, eh…"

The boy's voice trailed off as the caravan master leaned forward expectantly but after a heartbeat, Jalen proved incapable of suffering his brother's reticence any longer.

"Can we spend the night with the caravan?" he blurted with such force that his brother jumped at the question.

"Spend the night with the caravan, eh?" Vahrem stroked his

beard with one hand as his other settled on his belt. He tilted his head to one side to run a slow scrutiny of the boys while he winked surreptitiously at Ax-Wed and continued the act. Squinting speculatively, he extended a hand to squeeze each of the boys' grimy shoulders in turn.

"Are you strong enough to help us unload?" he asked with convincing gruffness.

Both brothers nodded vigorously and babbled and boasted about how many wagons they would unload. Their voices grew louder as each tried to be heard above the other

The merchant nodded and stooped to give each nose a tug.

"What about these?" he asked. "Can you use these to make sure the food doesn't burn? We have a large group of people to feed tonight and I need some fine fellows to keep a nose busy around the cooking pots. I can't serve scalded soup and burned crusts to hungry people, can I?"

Again with competing exuberance, both Julo and Jalen promised to ensure that only the finest food was served.

Vahrem put on a great show of considering their words, his brow furrowed in concentration before he finally and with pretended reluctance nodded permission.

"All right, all right, you've convinced me," he rumbled before he folded his arms and gave each a stern look that was no performance. "You two behave yourselves and make yourselves useful and you can stay until midday tomorrow. Then I'll have *Mehk* Numi take you home."

Both boys cheered wildly and immediately began a contest regarding the additional duties they now promised to do as a show of gratitude.

"I'll get water for all the animals," Julo declared and gave his brother an imperious look.

"I'll brush them all down," Jalen countered and when his brother shrugged dismissively, he added: "Even the Wain goats!"

The older boy scowled but refused to concede defeat.

"Well, I will stay up all night to watch for thieves," he said and drew his shoulders back so his narrow chest swelled.

"Oh, yes," Jalen cried, a warning note in his voice. "I'll stay up all night too but I'm not gonna watch for silly old thieves. I'm gonna watch for snatchers."

Vahrem and Ax-Wed shared a bemused look.

"You're a liar, Jalen bet'Faru. Everyone knows you're scared to death of snatchers."

"Oh no, I'm not, Julo bet'Faru! You'll see I can do it."

"What are snatchers?" the warrior woman interjected sharply.

Both boys shared a guilty look before they lowered their heads.

"Pap says Crevs problems got Crevs solutions," Julo said, his face downcast. "He said we weren't to speak about it with strangers."

She frowned but the caravan master stepped forward and knelt to look at the boys with a hand on each shoulder.

"Well, I'm certainly no stranger," he said, his voice warm but firm. "I may not live in the Crevice but I was there when you were both blessed with mare's milk as babes. As a matter of fact, it was my mare that gave the milk, so how about you boys be honest with me? What are the snatchers?"

The brothers exchanged another weighty glance before both shrugged in surrender.

"We don't rightly know what they are," Julo confessed and still struggled to look the man in the eye. "No one has ever seen them or at least seen them and been around to tell about it."

"Some says they're ghuls or djinn or even ifreet," Jalen added, his dark eyes huge in his small, grubby face. "Kullah's mom even says she saw a manticore prowling the rooftops and that's what it is, but everyone knows she spends too much time dancing with poppies."

"You don't even know what that means," Julo snapped with a disgusted scowl. "Whatever else anyone says, Pap says they're men but the wickedest kind. He says a man could be a thief for hunger and murder for vengeance, but only the evilest men could do what they do."

"They snatch people," his brother declared, his face a picture of youthful horror. "From the streets or their houses, it don't matter! They snatch 'em and no one ever sees them again."

CHAPTER FOUR

Guuhal hated being with this kind of scum.

If the prince had given him a choice between his current task and wading through city midden heaps, he knew which he would have chosen.

"So it seems his highness has more than whetted his appetite on our wares, then," chuckled a ruffian who went by the moniker Crim. "I should've warned him that once you get a taste, it's hard to stop, eh?"

The guard commander looked down his nose from his considerable height at the wiry man whose stubbled face resembled nothing so much as a hatchet. The officer began to fantasize about how pleasant it would be to spatter the filth's brains across the alley but forced himself to stop. If he grew too familiar with the idea, he wasn't sure he could resist the urge to make his dreams a reality.

"Can you meet the new quota or not?" the *Hazarbed* asked and didn't bother to hide his sneer.

Crim saw the open disgust and it seemed to only make him happier.

"Possibly," he replied slowly and made a show of thinking it over. "That is, of course, dependent upon certain...considerations."

Guuhal let the word dangle between them until the little villain began to squirm. The noise from the streets of Jehadim filled the growing silence between the two men. A block away, two men broke into a raucous bawdy song, which provoked a woman to scream at the two drunkards to do anatomically unadvisable things to one another. Across the street, several dogs squabbled savagely over scraps. A pack of howling teens darted past the alley mouth and continued, oblivious and bellicose, into the dusk-wrapped city.

"You won't get a shekel more than the agreed rate," the guard commander said stiffly and his hands ached to hold his staff of office. With one quick stroke, he'd never have to hear this worm, this parasite, speak again.

"Did I mention money?" Crim exclaimed with an exceptional imitation of moral indignation. "Did I even ask for a single godsdammed qirsh?"

"Lower your voice." Guuhal growled warningly and took a single step to loom over the smaller man.

"Lower my voice?" The villain spat and glared indignantly at him. "You came to me. I don't come to your fancy palace and—"

"Lower your voice!" The *Hazarbed* snarled with suppressed fury and the sound rumbled from deep in his chest.

"Why don't you lower yourself and wrap your noble lips around—"

The guard commander's huge, dark hand launched out with frightening speed. In one smooth movement, it wrapped around Crim's thin neck and pinned him to the alley wall.

"You were chosen because you were useful," he stated coldly as he bent to position his mouth next to the gagging rogue's ear. "Your usefulness requires you to be efficient, consistent, and more than anything, discrete. Do you understand?"

Spittle flecked the corners of the man's mouth and his cocky manner had evaporated, but he still managed to glare as he nodded above the hand that tightened around his throat.

"Good." The word was almost a purr and he flashed brilliant teeth for an instant as he drew his face back to arm's length. "Cease to be useful as described and you will be replaced by someone who can be useful. Is that clear?"

Again, Crim nodded, but his dark eyes burned with loathing.

"Very good," Guuhal said and released his hold with an indulgent nod. "Now, there were considerations you wanted to present."

The little villain coughed and fought to clear his throat as he rubbed at the bruises already welling on his flesh. It took him more than a moment to gather himself and even then, his voice was weak and hoarse.

"We need to expand," he croaked with one hand still nursing his throat. "Across the Tin Quarter. We've picked all the low-hanging fruit from the Crevs and then some."

He paused to swallow, cough, and wince before he continued.

"If we take any more there, it'll be too many to ignore," he explained but refused to look at the officer. "Soon, other groups will notice so we need to spread it thinly across the quarter and even that might not be enough before long."

Guuhal frowned and considered the point.

The ruffian was one very small step above a pit worm but he wasn't stupid and he probably wasn't wrong. Although he despised enabling any group of criminals to operate much less those like Crim, he certainly couldn't fault his reasoning. Jehadim was a big city but not so big that they didn't have to be careful.

"Fine." He sighed and folded his arms across his chest. "Anything else?"

The man's face contorted as he cringed a little, afraid to say what came next.

"To help things stay...explicable, we need to broaden the

target range. The same kind of acquisitions at this rate is also very suspicious."

The guard commander had feared this question more than the last, especially given the prince's instructions, but he knew what he must answer.

"Gods, this makes me sick." He snarled as his hands knotted into fists before his shoulders sagged heavily. "Very well. Fine, yes."

Crim, who'd cowered only seconds before, leaned forward and his lips peeled back from his teeth.

"Truly?" he whispered, almost panting. "Any and all?"

Guuhal refused to look at the slimy creature's grin because he knew that after one glance, he would reshape his face with his bare hands. He took a moment to play the prince's directions in his mind again but he already knew the answer. Not only that, but he also knew what this meant and for the first time in his life, he regretted that he had ever been so ambitious a man as to attain the office he had.

"Yes." He growled belligerently, a hint of warning. "But not another word on that. Do you need any material or equipment to meet the new quota?"

The ruffian's eyes shone bright with avarice, although his grin was checked when he stole a glance at the *Hazarbed*'s dark expression.

"Six or seven more of those little medallions in case the boys get stopped," he said as though it was all very simple. "And two wagons with mules or the like since we'll have to cover more ground."

The guard commander sighed and slid his hand into the heavy cloak he'd wrapped himself in to produce five small clay disks, each stamped with his office's seal and a number.

"You get these and no more," he said and held them out with a scowl. "You should still have some saved from the last group."

Crim's lip curled but he snatched the disks without argument and slid them quickly into his pocket.

"The wagon and mules?" he asked as he looked surreptitiously up and down the alley.

"I'll have two wagons made available outside the Tin Quarter barracks," he said as though the words tasted foul in his mouth. "But you'll have to secure the beasts for them on your own."

The rogue seemed ready to protest but a flash of warning in Guuhal's eyes made his jaws snap shut to forestall any further argument. For a moment, both men stood in uneasy silence, both criminal and commander unhappy yet unable to escape what lay before them.

Crim's cough broke the stillness and he swallowed roughly as he looked toward the entrance to the alley.

"When do we need to start meeting the new quota?" he asked and his gaze slid into the middle distance as he began to devise the necessary schemes.

"Tonight." The *Hazarbed* grunted as he turned to walk up the alley. "Double the previous quota starts tonight."

The other man grunted acknowledgment but his mind had already raced ahead to the particulars of the evening's dark deeds.

"Fair enough," he muttered. "Got to stay useful."

Guuhal sniffed at the weak joke and continued his weary tread up the alley. Like the criminal behind him, the officer's mind was elsewhere, so it was an unpleasant surprise when he stepped on a small pile of fetid filth. He looked down and scowled at the maggots that seethed in the muck that had squelched over his sandal and smeared against his foot.

He kicked the rot away from him, but the smell was in his nose and caked across the bottom of his foot.

With a wry and utterly unamused smile, he remembered the thought about wading through the midden heap.

Yes, that would have been better.

At least that would wash off.

CHAPTER FIVE

The shadows deepened throughout Jehadim, and among those shadows moved darker things than ghuls and djinn. Pap, although not a sagely man by nature, had not been wrong when he'd warned his sons about the kinds of men who now crept through the dark.

In a world without gold's dark glitter or men's darker lusts, they might have been like the tricksters of old stories who humbled the haughty and lifted the lowly. Not living in such a world, however, they were employed by the likes of Crim, a man for whom nothing was sacred and thus not forbidden.

Free from the oppressive presence of the guard commander and back in his lair, he exuded an easy arrogance that could easily be mistaken for unassailable confidence. The night-shrouded city was now woven with webs of shadow. He was the spider-king, seated on a throne he'd built on widow's tears and the bones of his enemies. As his fingers caressed the bruises on his neck, he swore inwardly that one day, the towering fool would join those beneath the webbed throne—and maybe even Prince Tarkhind too.

But for now, he had business to attend to.

His hunting spiders, each one carefully chosen and trained by him, had gathered in one of the empty granaries at the edge of the Copper District. Despite the word going out only a few hours earlier, all had arrived promptly, armed for the night and dressed for the part they were to play.

They had already separated into the teams of two in which they operated. One acted as distraction and hauler while the other was striker and watcher. The former were generally all larger men capable of carrying a limp body for a few blocks without difficulty. They were dressed in the common garb of the Tin Quarter but sometimes accented with splashes of liquor or "evidence" of a false injury. The latter were smaller and clothed similarly, but all were secretly equipped with the tools of the abductor to quickly neutralize and bind their quarry.

Seeing them arrayed before him, Crim felt a swell of pride despite the risks that gnawed at his paranoid mind.

These were the works of his hands and now, they would make him richer than he'd ever dared to dream was possible.

"It seems our newest employer has a healthy appetite," he said with a smile that was all teeth. "We've not only been given a new order to fill but an increased order."

A low, eager murmur passed through the men and women before him.

"Our quota of acquisitions is now double what it was previously."

A series of nervous chuckles rippled amongst those gathered. He could understand. In such a high-risk business, there was a fine line between necessary expansion and fatal overextension.

"I am also happy to report we have two other pieces of good news," he continued, certain that what he was about to say would remove any growing unease. "We now not only have clearance to operate anywhere in the Tin Quarter but we are also authorized to seek any acquisition available."

The chorus of soft jubilation from the abduction teams was

music to his ears. They were motivated and skilled agents set loose to pursue their objectives without the limitations and entanglements that had so frustrated them before. Any concerns he might have harbored about their ability to meet the prince's new demand were washed away by another rush of pride.

"Now," he said with a touch of sternness to catch their attention. "We still need to observe all protocols and precautions. I've acquired two wagons to help with transport, so they should make sure we can make timely deliveries even with a larger order to fill."

It hadn't been quite so easy to find draft beasts, and Guuhal's wagons had been ramshackle assemblies of planks that required much oiling and other finishing touches. In the end, however, he was glad he'd been bold enough to make the request. Having the wagons running delivery rotation while the teams were out making acquisitions would improve things considerably, especially with regard to reducing the exposure of his teams.

"We also have an increase in our stock of passage tokens but as always, please use these sparingly. With an order of this size, we will most likely need them."

Crim met the eyes of each team member to make sure they understood how deadly serious he was about the last point before he raised his hands in a welcoming gesture.

"Are there any questions?"

He was so used to the group standing in silence that he expected to wait for only a single heartbeat before he sent them out, but a purring feminine voice rolled from the group.

"What about exteriors of the Tin Quarter?" asked Masheed, an abduction specialist of particular skill. She was one of his sub-supervisors who usually did double duty and took a double share for both running her own team and coordinating three others. Crim liked to believe that all his specialists were exceptionally loyal through a combination of greed and fear, but out of all of them, the hard-eyed Masheed gave him the most pause.

Careful to control his tone lest others think him disturbed by the question, he looked at her with an imitation of genuine curiosity.

"Did you have something in mind?"

The sharp, mocking smile that flashed on her face irked him more than he would admit to himself, but he stifled the snarl that threatened to curl his lip.

"A contact informed me that a large caravan was coming into the city tonight," she explained. "They will settle for tonight in a stockyard at the edge of the Tin Quarter. Caravans often have very fluid populations and even if some notice a few missing, they won't stay long enough to raise much of a fuss."

Crim, despite his growing dislike for the woman, could see the possible benefits. Even if they only took one or two, it would be that much less pressure on the population of the city. That could be the difference between another week or two of operation before he'd have to renegotiate with the guard commander.

But there were other things to consider.

They were already operating on an unprecedented scale and adding an unknown factor like the composition of a caravan and the personality of its master was tempting fate. He had not formed the organization and network he had by tempting fate unless he had to.

"For now, we will abide strictly by the limits we've been given," he said, his voice flat and emotionless. "Inside the Tin Quarter only. Any other questions?"

Masheed refused to give him the satisfaction of a glare and she wasn't foolish enough to challenge him. After a stretched moment of silence, he nodded and gave his spiders a hungry smile.

"All right, my darlings. Let's get to work."

CHAPTER SIX

"They'll be safe."

Ax-Wed heard Vahrem's words but didn't move from her post.

She watched Julo and Jalen laughing as they munched on honeyed cakes, all talk of snatchers forgotten. Their mouths full of food, they babbled over each other in the company of a group of caravan children around a fire. Some of the children, the brothers included, rubbed their eyes and several mothers and fathers were already busy with sorting out the sleeping accommodations for the motley group.

"Even with these walls, I set men to watch," the caravan master continued and slapped a hand on the solid stones at his back. The fire around which the warrior woman had been invited to take her rest had been lit at the far end of the stockyard so the merchant and a few close associates could sit with their guest. The fact that this was a good distance from the larger fire where the cooking was done was no accident, she decided.

"And any man of them knows that sleeping on watch earns him the whip," a sharp-faced man with the goatee, whose name was Iyshan, added in support of his chief. "I tell you, kind sister, there's no man here who'll trade the skin off his back for a little sleep."

"I'd put money on that," *Mehk* Numi agreed with a cackle, her cheeks rosy from the large wineskin in her lap as she pinched the merchant's thick, hairy arm. "Sweet Vahrem could never bring himself to use the lash on one of his horses, but I've seen him peel a strip or two off a fool or three."

"Maybe you should give me the skin," said Durra, who sat at her left. He received a slap across his outstretched hand in response, which drew laughter from the two men.

Ax-Wed barely noticed the exchange but reluctantly, she turned from her observation as the flock of parents descended upon the children. When she saw Julo and Jalen being chivvied along by a stout matron with three other boys, the itch in the fingers resting on her ax subsided.

"I still don't like it." She grunted as she trudged with an air of resignation to sit between Vahrem and Iyshan. "And I doubt I'll get any sleep tonight."

"I can sympathize," the caravan master agreed as he proffered a plate piled with food to her. "But we've prowled around the whole complex and everything seems in order. It may be little comfort to you but I trust the men I have to keep watch."

"Although having a true sell-sword like yourself around certainly doesn't hurt," Iyshan added with a smile and a meaningful look at the merchant. She grasped his implication but decided she wasn't ready to enter negotiations. After all, she hadn't even tasted their food.

Any mercenary worth their iron knew that more than big words and the flash of coins, how an employer fed his people was most telling. It wasn't simply a matter of knowing what a sell-sword would have to endure under contract to an employer but also an indication of priorities, and wealth ranked second. Good victuals were an investment and one not easily recouped once purchased. A master who provided wholesome food for his servants saw them as worth investing in.

And if Ax-Wed were to judge by what was on her plate, Vahrem Kal'Stru was certainly invested in his caravan.

The fare was not extravagant in its delicacy but lamb, goat cheese, and fried chickpea mash, especially in such quantities, were better than most could hope to eat on all but feast days. As the steam rose from the hunks of lamb, she could smell the crushed rosemary, thyme, and marjoram. Her stomach rumbled fiercely and her mouth began to water.

"You had best feed that beast," Numi commented slyly and slapped her thigh. "Or it'll gobble us all before we ever have to worry about snatchers."

The two men shared a nervous glance before they joined the dwarf in forced laughter.

The warrior woman chuckled as she slipped her hand under the skirt of mail about her face and undid the strap of her helm. It was only after she'd peeled it from her head that she realized the good-natured laughter had died abruptly.

She looked up and saw that all of them were looking at her. Trying not to act as though intentionally hiding anything, she raked a few locks free to hide the scars that forked across the left side of her face. It took effort to force herself to not lower her head as she began to eat, her gaze locked on the fire.

"I knew there was a pretty lass under that ol' bucket." Numi smiled encouragingly at her. "It seems you struck the lads dumb with your good looks, eh?"

"Uh...well, it's...eh, not only that she's beautiful," Vahrem muttered and for the first time, seemed out of his element and unsure.

"Only beautiful?" The dwarfess groaned and rolled her eyes above her apple-red cheeks. "Truly, Vahrem, is that how—"

"She's a bloody Thulian!" Iyshan interjected, his voice a hoarse whisper.

"Iyshan!" The caravan master snarled a reproach before he turned to make a conciliatory bow toward her. "My apologies, my lady. He forgets himself."

"There's nothing to forgive." She shrugged and forced her face to remain neutral although she cursed herself inwardly. "I know that to many, my people are campfire stories."

Damn her vanity. The Thulian realized that by trying to cover her scars, she'd probably made it seem like she was drawing attention to her blue-streaked hair by displaying the natural shining ripples. She might as well have told them to inspect her tresses to see she used no imposter's dye, and amidst her internal berating, she felt the pre-emptive frost creep in.

Everyone knew there was only one kind of creature who was talked about around campfires.

"I thought Thule sank into the sea?" Durra said and looked at his aunt, only to have to duck the hand that swung to cuff him.

If only, the warrior woman thought and stared at the plate of food which suddenly seemed far less appetizing.

"And now seems a perfect time to bring that up, doesn't it?" Numi railed with an incredulous glare. "If it weren't for my dear sister, I swear I would have left you in the dunes three times over."

The young dwarf shrank before his elder's fury, but Vahrem stopped scowling at Iyshan to give Durra a pitying look as he touched the elder dwarf's hand gently.

"Now, Numi, the lad was only trying to explain how we know so little about Thule," he said in a soothing tone and drew the wineskin smoothly away from the old dwarfess. "Weren't you, Durra?"

"He's a fool and a little soft where he needs steel," the *Mehk* responded but her voice softened as she looked at the youngling, who nodded warily. "But he's a good, honest lad when it comes down to it."

"Exactly," the merchant agreed as he put an arm around her

sagging shoulders. "And I think when it comes down to it, you're tired and quite ready to turn in. After all, you know Julo and Jalen will want you to drive them around the city a time or two before you take them home, so you have a full morning tomorrow."

Numi acted as though she might fight the suggestion but eventually, she sank against the caravan master's thick arm, deflated and defeated. She raised her age-bent fingers to stroke his beard again and her reddened eyes glittered wetly in the fire light.

"You're like my good Nur, Stones keep him." She sighed as the first tears began to roll down her cheeks. "He always looked after me too."

Vahrem nodded and bent to kiss the old dwarfess atop her shaggy head. More tears welled in her eyes and with a great sniff, she pulled away and forced herself to rise stiffly.

"Come on, Durra." She groaned and one hand rubbed at her bent back while the other scooped her staff up. "Let's leave the humans to their mutterings."

"Yes, *Mehk*," the lad replied dutifully, but his face suggested that he'd much rather stay for a little muttering.

"I should make sure everything's in order with the watches," Iyshan said and stood quickly. "I'm sorry for giving offense, Lady Ax-Wed."

Now I'm a lady, the warrior woman thought bitterly. *I was merely a fellow traveler before and maybe a friend in the making. No longer, though.*

"There is still nothing to forgive," she answered stiffly and wished she knew some way to put everyone at ease. "But...thank you."

He nodded woodenly and turned to his master.

"Chief," he bowed, his limbs stiff and spine so rigid she was afraid it might crack.

"Thank you, Iyshan," Vahrem said, a heavy note and a meaningful look included in his response. The warrior woman sensed the faintest impression of an understanding pass between the two men before Iyshan turned on his heel and walked away.

"Not to tell you your business," she said softly as she forced herself to eat more of her food. "But you shouldn't be so hard on him on my account."

Vahrem nodded slowly as he watched the man walk away before his gaze slid to the fire.

"Perhaps not." He sighed slowly as he sank into himself a little, rested his arms on his knees, and lowered his chin toward his chest. "But Shepherd help me, although I try, I'm not as patient as I should be."

She stared at this puzzle of a man, her meal momentarily forgotten. A caravan master who walked and more besides fueled her curiosity and she wondered if she might take up with them merely to study this strange creature she'd discovered.

That was, of course, assuming he would have her.

Ax-Wed remembered the look he'd given her when she told him her name at the gate, and now he knew she was a Thulian. She could no more effectively be the kind of thing mothers frightened their children with if she sprouted fangs and scales.

"I'm sure that compared to the great cities of Thule, this must all seem so primitive," the merchant said before the silence could stretch too long. "But I appreciate your patience with us."

She suddenly wished they could talk about anything but thrice-cursed Thule.

"I appreciate you having me," she replied and continued quickly before anything more could be said of her homeland. "Who was Nur?"

To emphasize the question, she jerked her chin toward the wains beside the two corrals that held the wain goats on one side and the aurochs on the other.

He followed the gesture and a wistful smile settled on his face.

"Her eldest son," he said heavily and fiddled with one of the rings on his hands. For the first time, she noticed the bands glittering around the man's fingers. They were not adornments of polished gold and silver as she first guessed but simple and almost crude pieces of hammered tin, copper, and iron.

More and more curious.

"He was friend to my father and like an uncle to me," the merchant continued. "A fine goat trainer and a kind soul."

"Was it quick?" Ax-Wed asked.

Vahrem looked up and spun a ring around a knuckle.

"No such luck." He grunted and his brows furrowed as he glared into the fire with chilling intensity. "I was no older than Julo when slavers raided the caravan and dragged several people off, Nur included."

His lips curled back from his teeth and he spat into the fire.

"By the time we could report the attack and Jehadim sent riders out, Nur was dead," he rumbled from deep in his chest. "He had fought back when one of the jackals had begun to abuse the captives and they dragged him behind their horses to make an example of him."

"Did they catch the slavers?" she asked and immediately regretted it. The man's hands balled into fists and she knew it was a stupid question.

"They found some of the captives who'd managed to escape." He shrugged. "They told us what happened and where to find Nur. The riders were too busy pursuing the slavers—not that it did any good—and by the time my father could reach him, there was hardly anything to lay in the bed of the funeral wain."

Ax-Wed felt a sudden and wholly alien desire to place a hand on his broad shoulder. Why she would do a fool thing like that she couldn't say, but her hand began to stretch of its own volition until she realized there was still grease on her gloves. She drew it back quickly and cursed herself in her mind yet again.

The silence stretched between them and although such things

usually didn't bother her, she squirmed inwardly by the fire as she picked at her plate.

She felt her mother's voice vibrate in corners of her memory, but she shoved the thoughts away. Her mind racing, she tried to think of anything to change the subject from what was undoubtedly a deep wound.

"So is that what you think the snatchers are?" she asked, gave up on her plate, and set it to one side. "Slavers?"

Vahrem shrugged again but made an attempt to rally a smile.

"What makes you think they're not ghuls or djinn, eh?" he replied with a dry chuckle.

He might not laugh so loudly if he'd been farther south, she thought but decided the one thing the night didn't need was such a grisly story. She tried to make herself laugh but all she managed was a faint snort and a smirk.

"Maybe, but who knows?" The merchant groaned as he dragged his hand over his face to tug his beard. "Slavery is expressly forbidden in Jehadim and most of the other eastern cities aren't too keen on it so it wouldn't seem a clever scheme given the limited market."

Unless they weren't taking them to sell, she thought and dismissed the unpleasant thought quickly.

"But I suppose it wouldn't be the first time men were cruel to each other for little profit." He sighed and raised his head sharply to look around before he bent to retrieve Numi's wineskin.

"The old girl won't mind if you finish it," he said and held it out to her. "She likes the strong, sour stuff so I have no stomach for it."

Ax-Wed's hand had closed around the sack before she considered what impression she was making. She told herself it was humanizing for him to see she could enjoy a good drink like any other mortal being, but the justification rang so hollowly that she was embarrassed at the thought.

But it had been a long, dry time in the wasteland and she

knew that when the wine flowed, she could drown the dreams that had chased her across the Eastern Desert.

"Th-thank you." She forced the words out as she swallowed half a dozen weak and obvious justifications.

"Rest easy and make yourself at home, Lady Ax-Wed," the caravan master said as he heaved himself to his feet. "You are among friends and the watch is set. Tomorrow, we'll put our heads together and discuss what the Crow-Child charges to guard a caravan."

She froze with the skin at her lips at the mention of the epithet that had dogged her since Khardalis all those years before.

"And you'd want something like that to walk among your people?" she asked quietly. "You'd trust your lives and those of your children to such a creature?"

Vahrem stretched and looked at the heavens, his dark eyes drinking in the stars overhead.

"The Shepherd cradles and carries what lives he will, kind sister," he said as the touch of a smile crept beneath his beard and he looked at her. "Besides, you've only just met us. Perhaps we're all hiding some dark and dastardly secrets, eh?"

Ax-Wed laughed from the belly for the first time in a very long time.

"Now that would be something of a surprise." She snorted, unable to help herself. "But I'm willing to stay to see what turns up."

The merchant's smile flashed brilliantly in the mixed light of stars and fire.

"I'm so very glad to hear it," he said, a peculiar softness in his deep tones, and suddenly looked away. "Goodnight, sister Ax-Wed."

Somehow, the cold between the stars had trickled between them and she barely had time to say goodnight before he had marched off into the dark.

I curse you...
I curse you...
I curse you...

She tore the cap off the wineskin and something sick and cloying in her savored the hefty weight of the liquor that sloshed within.

"Shut up, Mother," she muttered and ground her teeth before she swallowed the first draught.

"Hezkel two-backing," she swore as she came up for air and the alcohol settled with a burning weight in her stomach.

The caravan master hadn't been lying. It was very strong and very sour.

The perfect potion to drown ghosts with.

CHAPTER SEVEN

Crim was a fool and a coward and Masheed knew it. His hesitancy disguised as caution and wisdom was what held all of them back and she would no longer tolerate his arrogant control.

She wasn't stupid enough to challenge him in front of everyone but as soon as they dispersed from the granary, she'd called her underlings to her. Before she said anything, she stared into their eyes and confronted them with an unspoken test of conviction. Her hard gaze bored like an awl into each of them in turn, but all revealed the same thing.

They were hers.

Their self-declared leader might have trained them and he might pay them but when they were out in the streets, she took care of them. She guarded their backs, ensured that they lived to see another night, and made certain that they made their acquisitions to meet Crim at sunrise for their due compensation. He was their distant nocturnal father who issued commands and doled out rewards, but she was their dark mother who carried them to safety every time they went out.

They trusted her with their lives and tonight was no different than any other. Their loyalty to her complete, they gathered around to hear their matron's will.

"We're getting some acquisitions from that caravan," she told the teams she supervised as they chose their assignments. "We'll pluck two and show the old spider how he's slipping."

Several smiled and a few frowned but all listened with accepting silence.

"Now I don't want simply any acquisitions," she continued and savored the way they hung on her every word. "To show how masterfully this can be done, we will take two together and I want them to be children. That'll show Crim exactly how much his rules are holding us back from real compensation."

This pronouncement was met with far fewer smiles but she'd expected as much. She wasn't merely flouting a situational directive but foundational protocols that Crim had hammered into them from the very beginning of their initiation into this "family business."

Acquisitions were always made singularly to ensure maximum control over compliance and transport. As they typically worked in teams of two, it only made sense that they would keep the numbers squarely in their favor. A skilled and well-planned maneuver against multiple targets in the right circumstance could be accomplished, but it was risky and even when successful, it involved considerable risk in getting the acquisitions to secure transport before they were discovered.

The rule about child acquisitions was similarly rooted in practical concerns. These were by far the most sought after but were only targeted sparingly and usually only under strict selection protocols. While very easy to force compliance upon and transport them, they were both fragile and volatile.

Fragile because the means of compliance, if roughly or overly administered, could damage or even invalidate the acquisition, which brought its own complications. Volatile because while the domestic connections of a mature acquisition only noticed their absence after an extended period of time—sometimes days—children disappearing could, depending on the area, spark a search within minutes. As a result, they were only undertaken when there was a specific viable target and the compensation was commensurate with the special attention required.

Yet Masheed intended to take not one, but two who she would find while in the field without proper approval for a payout that would be the same as if they were mature acquisitions.

Despite their nightly matriarch's words, all of them knew a plan so flagrant was not about compensation but control. By the end of the night, Crim would be faced with a tangible affront to his authority, which would tip the dominoes so confrontation was inevitable. This was the beginning of a coup and as the conspiratorial energy flowed through the group, they responded with darting eyes and half-formed smiles. All of this told Masheed that she had nothing to fear.

Although rightly nervous, they were with her.

"We have five acquisitions to make tonight since the increase, so we'll take the first three from the Tin Quarter itself," she said and affected an unconcerned but erudite air. "After those are loaded on the wagon, we'll move to the caravan in the stockyard. You will all act as secondary assessors while Sohrab and I make the acquisition."

Sohrab, her current transporter and part-time lover, leered at the rest of the clan. While an efficient if unsubtle distractor and as strong as an ox, he couldn't quite understand that no one envied his place beside their daring matron. If anything were to go wrong, it was most likely to be at the outset of this gambit and none of them relished the idea of being in the midst of a situation that had gone awry.

Masheed ignored them and leaned forward to draw their eyes and attention to her.

"Tonight is the night that changes everything," she stated

coldly and her eyes glittered. "We will show everyone that no one and nothing in this city is safe."

CHAPTER EIGHT

The spectral spear point lanced through the wine-soddened mists of her dreaming mind and pierced her breast.

As soon as she felt the phantom steel split the skin, she knew something was wrong, but it wasn't until the tip nipped at the heart hammering in her breast that she understood why.

It didn't happen this way, she thought blearily as the phantasmal crowd below moaned with a single, aching voice. *I deflected that thrust. I almost didn't but I know I did.*

"We wish you hadn't," her father's voice intoned, even deeper and more sepulchral as a dream-shade. "We wish your hand had faltered and he spitted you as you deserved."

She snarled and rage and sorrow choked any rational words, but she could not stoop below the dais to reach him. The ghostly shaft of the spear held her fast.

"We wish you had died that day," her mother added, her voice so sharp and acidic that it stung both her ear and her brain. "We wish our shame had ended with you."

"Morah circles!" the crowd chanted and their voices rose in reflexive exultation. "We welcome her passing shadow."

She grasped the haft of the spear which should not have

protruded from her chest and laughed because she knew what came next. Blood so bright that it glowed with an internal fire rose into her mouth and spattered down her chest.

"No wonder we are damned." She chuckled, unable to shake the horrible humor that recognized that her words had been fitting, no matter what the outcome. "The gods tarried too long."

"I suppose I asked for this." The intimate, silken whisper of her opponent came in reply, his visage a murky blur at the other end of the spear. "One way or another, it had to be this way."

"Morah comes!" the crowd roared, unable to shake the fervor that doomed them.

Her fingers tightened around the haft of the weapon and her words rose to her tongue like the blazing blood that welled inside her as a burning tide.

"It's too late to turn back now." She shrugged and a smile strained at the corners of her mouth as she drew the spear deeper into herself.

The ethereal steel sank into her heart, a cold, merciless fire, and the fiery blood erupted from her like a fountain.

On her hands and knees, Ax-Wed retched a veritable torrent in the stuttering light of embers.

She lurched onto her haunches and recoiled weakly from the putrid puddle that soaked into the soil. It was not the blazing blood from her dreams but by the gods, her throat and nose burned as if it were. She felt a desperate urge to pull away from the stench of the stomach-churned wine but it was all she could do to keep her trembling limbs from betraying her. It seemed certain that if she moved a muscle, she would pitch face-first into her filth.

"Are you ill?" a small voice asked from across the cinders.

Even her shaky arms locked in abashed terror as she raised

her eyes from the vomit to where Jalen stood across from her, his brow furrowed with sincere concern.

"I'm fine," she rasped and paused when her stomach clenched in open rebellion to the declaration. "It's only something I ate. I—"

Despite her efforts, another wave of bilious alcohol heaved up and out so her clenching only made it more painful. She expelled every last thing in her stomach and as if to punctuate its irritation with her, her entire body twisted with a series of dry heaves before she finally felt a release. With a defeated groan, she managed to stand but tottered and collapsed to one side, missing her mess by luck more than anything else.

"You don't look fine," he remarked gravely and his hands fiddled with the drawstrings of his breeches. "Are you sick or something?"

Ax-Wed didn't bother to answer but did manage, with an embarrassing amount of effort, to lean against the wall. The motion made her head swim and left her gulping air down her raw throat, but she was seated upright and had put a little distance between herself and the steaming pool. Shame, guilt, and a considerable amount of alcohol robbed her of coherent thoughts, but at least she could breathe without the searing stench burning her nostrils.

"What are you doing?" another voice asked from the night and a second later, Julo's face appeared, his eyes huge and terrified. "I could throttle you, wandering off like that! If Pap—"

"The big lady's sick," Jalen said and cut his brother off as he pointed to Ax-Wed. "I think she's got the Blight."

Julo recoiled at the mention of the enervating malady but he soon smelled the scent of liquor-infused effluence and saw the pool of evidence shimmering in the firelight.

"It's not the Blight," he said, old enough to recognize what had occurred.

He didn't fully understand the nature or appeal of alcohol yet, but he at least understood that it was compromising for any adult to be found in such a condition. Pap was not a drunkard as a matter of course but the boy was old enough to remember a few feast days when his father had over-indulged. His eldest son was left to help get him to bed as his mother was seven years dead and the new wife wouldn't touch him when he was inebriated.

A swell of pity and dread fascination swept over him as he watched the titanic warrior woman drag in each labored breath while she stared at him with glazed, bloodshot eyes.

"The Pox, then?" Jalen asked and began to tug on the drawstrings now in his agitation. "Or maybe the Flux?"

Julo and Ax-Wed continued to stare at each other until the younger boy grew impatient and punched his brother's arm with his free hand.

"Ouch! Er…no," he replied as he cuffed his brother distractedly. "She doesn't have the Pox or the Flux either."

"The Yax?" Jalen pressed and yanked fiercely on the drawstrings.

"No, it's not…wait, the Yax?" He looked at his little brother with a suspicious squint. "You made that one up."

The other boy shrugged. "It sounds bad, though, doesn't it?"

Julo agreed that it sounded awful and was certainly a suitable name for a horrible disease, but he wasn't about to tell his brother that.

"What are you doing up anyway?"

Jalen seemed locked in a life-or-death struggle with his britches now.

"I had to pee."

"Well, did you go?" he asked but already knew the answer to his question.

His brother shook his head vigorously.

"I heard her saying something," he said and nodded quickly at Ax-Wed. "And then she was puking everywhere and I asked her if she was sick and she said she was fine and—"

"Go pee," Julo said impatiently and pointed down the length of the wall to the latrines.

"And then she said she was fine and I thought she didn't look fine and I wondered if she had the Pox," the little boy continued and twisted savagely at his strings as though they were binding him to his story. "And then you came."

"Janus' balls," he snapped. "Go pee, Jalen!"

His brother scuttled a few steps toward the latrines but halted his retreat to deliver his Parthian shot.

"I'm telling Pap you swore when we get home," he announced.

"And I'm telling him you wet yourself like a baby when I paddled your butt," the elder brother warned and took a menacing step forward. "Go. Pee."

Turning on his heel with an air of righteous indignation, Jalen executed his withdrawal.

Despite her miserable condition, Ax-Wed managed a chuckle.

"Sorry about him," Julo said and lowered his head as his cheeks flushed. "I'll get you some water."

She made to wave the offer off but only managed to flail her arm when she almost lost her balance.

"I'm…uh, f-fine," she stammered and sounded utterly unconvincing, even to herself.

"I know. Jalen told me," he said with a little shake of his head. "But you're also drunk and when Pap gets drunk, water seems to help."

The Thulian wanted to argue but words suddenly seemed very hard to put together. She held one finger up and everything became soft around the edges as she tried to collect herself. In the next moment, he was gone.

"Well," she muttered and eventually succeeded in raising a hand to wipe her mouth. "I can't argue with that, can I?"

What seemed like eons of indeterminate time later, Julo reappeared and hurried to her side with a ladle in his hand. Before she could argue, he'd raised it to her lips and the night-cooled water washed away the acrid film from her mouth. She coughed once and he drew the ladle back as he patted her on the back.

"It will help," he said. "Drink it slowly."

Ax-Wed nodded, followed his advice, and finished what was left in the ladle. Despite any protest she might have raised, the boy wasn't wrong. She already felt better.

"Good boy." She groaned and let her head sag against the wall. "Your Pap's a lucky man."

Julo smiled at the compliment but when he met the woman's eyes, sheer terror filled his gaze and he looked away. In her current condition, she couldn't decide if his fear was caused by her scarred face or the fact that the boy, on the edge of manhood, had looked a woman in the eye. Either way, she found it all inordinately funny.

She began to chuckle but then saw the wounded anger on the boy's face and stopped immediately.

"Thank you, Julo." She sighed and extended an unsteady hand to squeeze his shoulder.

He winced, first from the woman's foul breath and then from the strength of her grasp but did his best to answer her gratitude with a smile.

"Here," he instructed, shifted her hand from his shoulder, and pointed to a half-filled bucket that had appeared beside her leg. "Keep drinking."

Ax-Wed frowned as the boy rose and looked across the darkened stockyard.

"Where are you going?" she asked and let the ladle in her hand sink into the bucket.

"To find Jalen," he explained. "Sometimes, he can't get his breeches tied and he's been gone for a while."

The warrior woman nodded sagely and looked at him with a warm smile.

"You're a good big brother."

Even in the half-light of the dying fire, she could see the blush creep up the boy's ears.

"Keep drinking," he said as he moved toward the latrine. "We'll both come back to check on you before we go to bed."

She nodded and with some effort but less each time, raised the ladle to her lips and took sips of cold water.

How could I be so stupid? The question compelled her to contemplate the congealing evidence of over-indulgence. *What is wrong with me?*

Shame and anger flooded over her in equal measure, leaving her flushed and feeling a sickness that had nothing to do with her stomach. She turned her gaze from the vomit sharply enough to make her neck pop and the world spin and saw the flaccid wineskin laying a few feet away. With a disgusted hiss, she threw the ladle into the bucket beside her with a splash. Tears threatened to trace hot tracks down her face, but she denied them reflexively and desperately willed the icy shell to form around her aching heart.

Did anyone else see?

She looked through bleary eyes and didn't notice any movement in the stockyard. Across the way, she noticed a fire where a few of the men were standing watch but none seemed to be looking at her.

What will they think when Julo or Jalen tell them? What use is a sell-sword who gets vomiting drunk at the first opportunity?

For an instant, her mind entertained what kind of promises could buy the brothers' silence. When nothing came to mind, she wondered what threats might work better.

What is wrong with me?

The light of the fire seemed to shrink and she felt for a moment that the deepening darkness wasn't only in the exterior world.

Is this the curse or is this only me?

The thought scraped and tore at the few tender places left in her but before the damage became too significant, the ice crept in and a practiced and familiar numbness settled in.

It doesn't matter, she told herself and squeezed her eyes shut to will the unshed tears away. *You're damned either way.*

She looked around the tents, wagons, and wains that bore the sleeping members of the caravans all blissfully unaware of her humiliation. Yet, come first light as they stirred to make ready, word would begin to spread and the looks of disgust—or even worse, pity—would spread and hem her in. Their kindness would curdle into fear at what she might do or they would sneer at her weaknesses.

Either way, the answer was clear. She couldn't stay for things to go that way.

It hollowed her out to think of creeping off in the dark like a thief but she knew from experience that facing them the next morning would be worse.

This is your life and this is who you are. They rot out from under you or you ruin them with your weakness. Either way, this is your path. This is your Road.

With a will born of a fatalistic knot of self-hatred, Ax-Wed forced herself to straighten and knocked the bucket over when she took a step. The water spewed across the ground, a narrowing stream of liquid that plunged into the fire embers. With an angry hiss, steam rose and the veil of night descended on the small island of light that had been hers only moments before.

It's just as well, she mused grimly. *Darkness for dark business.*

As quietly as she could, she gathered her things by the light of the stars and the narrow moon and almost lost her balance twice, which made her realize she was still quite drunk. As such, she couldn't bring herself to secure her helm, uncertain that her pounding head could bear it, so it rested gingerly on the dome of her skull. For a moment, she swore she heard the pulse of her head against the lining of the battered skull bucket and was forced to hold very still and let herself adjust to the altered pitch of the pain.

The hammering subsided for a moment but became almost crippling when she dragged her pack closer and tried to haul it onto her back. After she'd almost tumbled for the third time and had to subsequently reseat her helm, she drew her ax and planted its haft in the dusty ground.

With the support of her improvised wooden leg, she managed to get it on her back and raised her eyes to look one last time at the life that could have been hers. Perhaps it was only the wine, but she felt a pain keener than she had when she'd fled Xhultheno, the city of her birth and one of the last great bastions of her people.

She'd left that beautiful, unholy city with her heart breaking but certain that she was right. Now, her heart was breaking and she had no such solace, only the cold certainty that she had no other choice.

Her regrets didn't have the decency to wait for her to make it beyond the wall of the stockyard. As she started to move toward the gate, she began to think about all the lives she'd felt entwined with in only a few hours—Durra, Numi, Vahrem, Iyshan, and the boys.

The boys… Didn't Julo say he would come back?

A chill ran through Ax-Wed as she looked across the dark yard to the shadowed place at the wall where the latrines were.

Why aren't they back yet?

She squinted into the shadows and her stomach twisted anew as a single word crawled across her mind.

"Snatchers," she whispered before she rushed toward the latrine.

CHAPTER NINE

Things were not going as planned.

Masheed handed the second boy to Sohrab as sweat dripped into her eyes and triggered a hiss of pained irritation. As she wiped it away, a huge armored figure stumbled into the latrines.

This was not how she'd envisioned the night's events.

It had seemed so easy at first when she'd crept up the wall and almost immediately saw a child acquisition headed to what she assumed were the latrines for the stockyard. He had been midstream when she'd slid up behind him with a scarf dipped in dreaming bliss. The soporific had worked quickly on the boy, whose startled inhalation for a cry only ensured that he didn't make a sound.

She'd yanked the target's breeches up to avoid getting sprinkled, lowered him to the ground, and bound him securely. Working quickly, she'd fashioned a gag from another scarf, careful that it would silence without smothering him. Her handiwork complete, she'd slid his limp body onto her shoulder and carried him to Sohrab, who'd clambered onto the wall as planned.

It was not without its risks but her coterie of abductors had provided reports on the watchmen's habits and she had devised her plan accordingly. It should have been an easy matter to scoop the boy up and secure him. They would then both scale the wall to make the next acquisition at a secondary location in the stockyard. A large group was situated near the gate and she had been certain she could pluck another child in their sleep with no one any the wiser.

But that had all vanished in an instant when another acquisition—still a child but much larger than the first—had arrived. He'd squinted into the dark and hissed what must have been her quarry's name as he stalked toward the latrines. Sohrab had managed to vanish over the wall with the bound acquisition but finely honed instincts told Masheed to press herself into the shadows before she was seen.

For an instant, she'd considered killing the boy and her fingers played across the dagger at her belt, but she decided that was less than ideal. She wanted to show Crim and the others that her ways were superior and she couldn't do that by dropping a dead child acquisition, which would undoubtedly draw all kinds of attention.

Instead, she'd wound the venom-soaked scarf around one hand and waited for her chance.

It took a few agonizing seconds for him to come within reach as he stumbled and lurched in the dark and whispered the other boy's name a few more times. Masheed almost lost her nerve on the last utterance, certain that someone else in the camp had heard him, but he staggered past her and instinct spurred her to pounce.

This time, it was different. Not only was he bigger and stronger but he was also wary, possibly because he expected foul play or that the previous acquisition was playing a childish prank. As such, he somehow sensed his attacker as she lunged toward him and he twisted away and threw a punch.

The blow skidded painfully off Masheed's ear and her scarf-wrapped hand cupped his mouth but not his nose. She managed to muffle his cry but the heavy fumes could not overwhelm the boy fast enough and his struggles tumbled them both into a midden heap in a tangle of thrashing limbs.

The acquisition was wiry and approaching the strength of a grown man, but she was trained, vicious, and above all, desperate. More than merely her life was on the line and the realization lent her strength. She scrambled on top of him and forced the scarf over his face.

He kicked and punched as she straddled him and at one point, even bit through the scarf to the fingers beneath. But with each passing second, he grew weaker and his efforts slowed. Within a few heartbeats, his limbs flopped against her and after a few more, his entire body went limp.

Panting for breath, she crawled off him and clutched her bloodied hand as she looked frantically around. That had been one of the sloppiest attempts she'd ever engaged in to force compliance from an acquisition and for an instant, she was certain there was no way the entire caravan wasn't about to converge on her in an angry mob.

When the torches didn't flare to life and no enraged cries washed over her, she looked at the boy and fought the urge to give him a hard kick in his pubescent testicles. He'd almost bitten a finger off and when the morning came, she was sure she'd be able to see every bruise she now felt. On top of that, she was smeared in filth. She toyed with the idea of turning him facedown to let him suffocate in nightsoil but ever the mercenary, she decided that would be poor compensation for the struggle she'd endured in his capture.

After all, with the damage his teeth had done, she might have to buy a regenerative tincture to make sure everything healed and was restored to full functionality. No, she would take him to the prince's men and that would suffice for her vengeance. From what she guessed of the royal's intentions, it might have been a mercy to have the boy drown in sodden kak.

Masheed drew a few steadying breaths to master herself and retrieved the strips to bind her acquisition. She checked to make sure the restraints were tight and she hauled him to the wall. After two quick clicks of her tongue, Sohrab appeared and she handed her captive to him.

It should have been over. While it had been more trying than anticipated, two child acquisitions made in utter secrecy would be more than enough to rub in Crim's face. Now, however, this drunken, lurching warrior stumbled in at the last and worst moment.

Fear and frustrated anger surged through Masheed's limbs and she skittered over the wall, hoping against all reason that she hadn't been seen.

She landed catlike on all fours on the other side and her ears strained as she looked at Sohrab, who settled an acquisition on each of his broad shoulders.

"Wait," she mouthed and raised one hand to warn him against moving or speaking. Perhaps the warrior—who even at a single glance had seemed unsteady on her feet—truly was drunk and hadn't noticed them. Crouched against the wall, Masheed prayed to every dark god and all the devils she knew that she would hear the sound of someone relieving themselves.

Instead, what she heard was a slurred snarl and the sound of an armored body trying to clamber over the wall.

"Sssnatcherz!" a throaty feminine voice shouted as a pair of armored gloves curled over the outer edge of the wall. "Damned sssnatcherz!"

"Run!" Masheed snapped at Sohrab as she pushed away from the wall as though it might collapse on her and raced across the street. Two alleys and a sharp right turn from where they stood was the wagon. If they could reach it, they might have a chance to escape the inebriated fool.

"Snatcherz!" the warrior bellowed from where she now stood atop the wall, massive and enraged. Masheed stole a glance over her shoulder and realized that Sohrab was struggling to manage the burdens on his shoulders as he tried to run. She paused for half a moment and considered turning to try to help him but the warrior leapt from the wall with a roar. He dropped both acquisitions in terror and their bodies rolled from his shoulders to the ground like sacks of grain as he looked at the descending comet of leather, iron, and flesh.

His unburdening saved the boys but not him and the warrior pounded into him and knocked him off his feet. The woman floundered for an instant on top of the incapacitated victim before she delivered punches and kicks that reduced the burly man to a pulverized sack of meat. When she looked up from the ugly mess of what was left of Sohrab's head Masheed gasped in shock.

The abductor had a moment of horror in which she imagined a lioness leaping after a pack of scavengers that tried to snatch her cubs. Frozen by this image, she lost a few precious seconds which enabled the warrior woman to throw her head back and roar an accusation.

"Snatcher!"

Her rational mind abandoned her for a moment and she turned to flee but was quickly bowled over by a rush of dark shapes. Knocked to the ground and with her mind broken in terror, she watched events unfold from somewhere distant as if everyone cavorted about like actors on a stage.

Dark figures coalesced into the teams under her direction and even some that weren't. Some distant inkling of awareness told her their presence was a warning but everything seemed so far away that she couldn't rouse herself to form a coherent thought beyond the numbing terror that assailed her.

They came like vultures descending on wings of shadow but like the fetid birds they resembled, each one was batted away with contemptuous ease by the snarling lioness. She maintained a litany of curses beneath the cover of her helm as she swatted them aside with her armored fists and metal-shod feet. With terrible awe, Masheed watched as this seemingly unstoppable engine of vengeance trampled hardened men and women like grass underfoot despite her reeling gait and unsteady hand.

And through it all, the warrior's eyes burned within the rims of her helm and remained fixed on her.

"Snatcher!" she howled, and the mercenary's mind jolted into lucidity with painful clarity. She was still on the ground and had to get up. Her instincts screamed for her to run far away.

She was halfway to a seated position when a merciless weight drove her to the ground. With a gasp, she rolled onto her back and tried to force air into her lungs. The weight settled on her neck and she gagged and looked into Crim's razor-edged scowl.

"You've made quite a mess," he muttered, his voice as cold and flat as a blade before he looked away and spoke in short, sharp commands. "Toad sting—now! Two doses!"

Masheed tried to look at what was happening but his foot pressed her down and she could only listen over the hammering in her chest.

Two heavy impacts preceded a short, trilling hiss which was immediately followed by another. A garbled, wet snarl—almost like something a leopard might make—faded into a low groan and finally, a rattling crash.

For a single instant, there was silence in the street before shouts of alarm issued from inside the stockyard.

"Get her into the cart and tie her up," Crim snapped before he turned an icy smile toward Masheed's horror-filled eyes. "Unbind the children. I have the last acquisition right here."

CHAPTER TEN

Everything burned but she could not even scream as her body betrayed her.

The best Ax-Wed could manage as they loaded her onto a covered wagon was a thin, rasping wheeze with the herculean effort to draw each breath. Her limbs were aflame with an agonizing tension as the venom burned through her and trapped her within a body that was painfully sensate but utterly unresponsive. Even her eyes had begun to dry as her lids infrequently dragged themselves open and shut.

Despite this terrible condition, it was not fear that drove the labored hammer of her beating heart but wrath. This toxin running through her was not unfamiliar. A child of the courts of Xhultheno, she'd been trained from a very young age to recognize toxins of various origins both by their signs and their effects, so she knew this was most likely one of the paralytics extracted from Wallow toads. Her mother had introduced it to her when she was a girl of ten and as she'd lain on the floor of her mother's boudoir, she'd learned to hate the incredible powerlessness as the insidious venom gained control of her.

"You can't fight it once it's inside you," her mother had told her as she wrapped cords of silk around her like a lazy shroud. "But if you are not a fool, you can plan what you will do once you can start wiggling your fingers and toes."

The woman had then dragged her to the full bath and pitched her in.

Now, bound in a wagon that rattled down the streets of Jehadim, she remembered lessons learned as a child bound and drowning in her mother's bath. The toad toxin was potent and fast-acting but it burned through the body quickly and if you could slow your breathing and heartbeat, its effects would diminish far more rapidly.

With this in mind, she forced herself to remain calm in spite of all the truly legendary violence she longed to enact on her captors. Her fury became a cold light in the back of her mind, a terrible dawn that would rise in its own time, and she did her best to allow herself to settle into the wracking pains of her current condition.

At least the wine fog is gone.

A man with a profile so sharp it looked like she could use his face to split wood leaned over her, then looked at one of the abductors who squatted in the wagon bed on top of the woman Ax-Wed had followed over the wall.

"Are you sure this one is tied up tightly?" he asked and tugged at the Thulian's bonds. "We can't have her getting loose before we make delivery."

At the mention of delivery, the woman she had pursued whimpered, which earned her a distracted slap across the face.

"Shut up, Masheed!"

The woman fell silent and she sucked nervously at the lip bloodied by the careless blow.

"I checked 'em myself, boss," the other abductor nodded gravely and raised one hand to prod at the blackening bruise on one side of his face. "We can dose her again if you like. I've got two more."

The ringleader shook his head and drew a frown from the bruised man.

"No, this has been enough of a risk without dropping such a conspicuous corpse," the hatchet-faced man explained and his gaze trailed across her bound body.

It wasn't the first time Ax-Wed had been ogled but it was perhaps the first time she'd had her body inspected with such a cold and detached eye. In Xhultheno, one of her tutors had once introduced her to anatomy through multiple vivisection lessons. The way this man looked at her now reminded her of how her tutor had looked at cadavers.

Even a glutton could look affectionately at a hunk of meat but in those eyes, she was merely a commodity, simple matter through which utility was extracted before it was discarded.

For the first time since she'd followed Masheed over the wall, an icy finger of fear scraped down her spine.

"If the acquisition fails, we could take the leavings to the Grinders," the bruised man suggested, although there was a note of hesitancy in his tone. "It might take them all night but they could make sure no one found anything."

It was increasingly difficult to stay calm when disposing of her remains was discussed, but she fought off the panic that threatened to spike her heart rate by imagining how many pieces she could cut each man into with one stroke. When the wagon rumbled down another side street, she'd reached four but she refused to believe she couldn't do better.

The leader—whose gaze had gone unfocused at his underling's suggestion—refocused and looked at the bruised man with a frigid smile.

"The Grinders, eh?" he asked, although something in his manner seemed unpleasantly disingenuous. "Tell me, are the Grinders part of our little fraternity of acquisitions?"

"No," the bruised man blurted with a reflexive immediacy that spoke of relentless training. "I only thought…"

His voice faltered and he hung his head. The leader watched him with the flat eyes of a lurking spider and he seemed to shrink before that gaze. Ax-Wed couldn't begin to feel pity for the villain but she didn't envy him.

"Say it," the leader said with a silken softness.

The man shuddered and complied.

"Acquisitions never, ever make contact with other actors except for buyers."

The rumble of the wagon over the cobbles was the only sound for a moment before the silken voice spoke again.

"And?"

"Failed acquisitions are still acquisitions," the bruised man said and his voice cracked.

"Good," the leader responded coldly. "Forgetting the rules is what makes you end up like Masheed—doesn't it, darling?"

The mercenary woman shivered and wept silently on the wagon bed as they rolled deeper into the city.

The toxin had almost worn off a few minutes after the wagon crossed a waterway which Ax-Wed guessed was the royal canal that divided the Gold Quarter from the rest of the city. She'd felt her fingers surrender to her imploring will and within seconds, had regained a crude control of her arms. With a subtle flex of her muscles, she tested the strength of her bonds. They were tight but she was certain that with a little time, she could at least work a hand free and maybe her whole arm. If she could do that, she knew the two men in the back of the wagon would both be dead. She'd already determined where they had stowed her dagger and ax.

The warrior woman felt the ringleader's eyes upon her and although she'd barely moved, she held painfully still.

"This is an odd one," he muttered and leaned forward so his

pointed nose hung over her face. She was certain that if he were an inch closer, she could have bitten his nose off despite her bonds and the gag. With a few inches more and a second to struggle with her gag, she could have reached his throat.

But even if I did, I'd still be in no better shape, she told herself and forced the anticipatory tension to slide from her limbs. *He'd be dead but I'd still be bound when his crony stuck my own knife through my eye.*

"What's that, boss?" the bruised man asked. He still hovered over Masheed, but the woman had fallen silent and still and seemed to have either swooned or fallen asleep.

"Have you ever seen an acquisition of these proportions?" the leader remarked. "Not only height or bulk but actual composition."

The other man ran a thumb over his bruise as though trying to remind himself why he shouldn't be impressed.

"I don't think so." He shrugged. "I never had a client call for one so big and there's no profit in making things hard for yourself."

The leader nodded and a small, ugly smile curled his lips.

"The only one who's ever come close was a request from a very particular lady in the palace. She enjoyed humiliating the unwilling and the powerful. The last one I gave her would have been close to this acquisition's size."

His henchman matched his boss's ugly smile but then frowned.

"I don't remember hearing about such a request before," he grunted with hesitant curiosity.

"The client passed before your initiation," the ringleader said and adjusted his position as he extended a hand to Ax-Wed's helm. "It seems she did not properly secure the last acquisition and it throttled her and her husband, poor fool, before the house guards killed—"

"Crim!" An urgent whisper issued from the front of the

wagon. "Crim, you're needed here."

His fingers flattened over the front of the helm and she felt a tremble of irritation pass through the man's body.

"What is it?" he snapped but his gaze remained fixed on her.

"The guards are flagging us down," the driver responded. "It's the *Argbed*. What you want me to do?"

Ax-Wed's ears pricked up at the mention of the title. *Argbed* was a traditional title for a castellan, a rank equal to the *Gondbed* or captains who oversaw a quarter and thus second only to the *Hazarbed*. Given that she was certain they were in the Gold Quarter, the castellan would be from the royal Citadel. The conspiratorial thrill she felt at her dawning comprehension was matched only by the growing unease she felt.

"What else can we do?" Crim growled through gritted teeth even as he forced a smile across his face. "We are merely law-abiding citizens delivering goods to our betters, aren't we?"

"Yes, boss," the driver muttered before he turned to issue a profane command to halt, which the ragged beasts drawing the wagon obeyed.

A surge of hopeful, anxious energy rushed through the Thulian and it took everything she had to stop herself from squirming under her abductor's hand. Either she'd get the guard's attention or she'd use her captor's distraction to get her arm free but this was likely to be her best chance.

Visions of the bloody vengeance she'd planned danced behind her eyes and within the cover of her helm, a grim smile spread slowly.

Crim's eyes narrowed at her as though he might have intuited her thoughts but he removed his hand and slid it inside his ragged coat.

"What are the guards doing?" he asked.

"They approach," the driver whispered, a slight quaver in his tone.

Is he reaching for a weapon? Ax-Wed wondered and felt a pang of dread. She didn't believe an operation like this would be so bold as to fight a guard patrol in the middle of the Golden Quarter, but what if they were willing to kill the two women to avoid being exposed? In Jehadim, the stringent laws against slavery were such that it would be better to be caught with a corpse and a bloody knife than have someone level the accusation of slaver.

Getting the guard's attention isn't an option, she admitted to herself.

Caught between trying desperately to free her arm and not wanting to give Crim an excuse to slit her throat, she continued to hold very still and forced her breath into a slow and even rhythm.

"What's the plan, boss?" the bruised man asked.

The leader's hand emerged from his coat and instead of a blade, he held a small disk. She glimpsed something—a seal or stamp of some kind—along one edge and cuneiform numbering on the other. The clustered triangles and stems denoted the number seventeen.

"Pay our respects, of course," he said in a soft, deadly voice and turned to join the driver.

Masheed's eyes snapped open as the ringleader departed, a painfully fevered light in her eyes. Ax-Wed tried to give the faintest shake of her head while, as surreptitiously as she could, she began to probe and work at the bindings around her arms.

Don't do anything stupid. She wished she could will the words into the desperate woman's brain and held her gaze for an instant before the mercenary's wild gaze roved around the wagon, that of a trapped animal desperate to escape.

"Evening, your honors." Crim's voice carried to them from the front, genial and relaxed. "Well, if it isn't my old friend *Argbed* Alborz. How are you this very early morning?"

"I'm not your friend, Crim," Alborz replied gruffly accompanied by the sound of several heavy sandals striding alongside the wagon. "Another delivery, then?"

Ax-Wed whispered thanks to whatever gods were listening that she hadn't tried to get the guards' attention. From the sound of it, Crim wasn't the only villain running the streets of Jehadim.

She didn't dare to even change the pace of her breathing but set to work on the bonds that trapped her right arm to her side. Mercifully, the bruised man's attention was fixed on the front of the wagon.

"I'm surprised to see you out patrolling this particular area in such force," Crim said, his tone unchanged by either the guard officer's tone or question. "But I'm sure you won't need to tarry much longer once you see this."

There was a creak as Crim shifted on the driver's bench and in the tense stillness, Ax-Wed heard one set of sandaled feet approach the bench and then retreat.

"It's in order, sir," a curt, disciplined voice reported.

"The streets have been crawling with your little spiders," Alborz said and his tone left no doubt as to his opinion on the matter. "What do you have in that wagon that someone wants so very badly?"

There was a single, crackling second of silence and Crim's silken voice cut through the stifling tension in the same instant that the first drops of sweat slicked Ax-Wed's skin. She'd just managed to position one of the lames in her armor to chafe against the ropes.

Keep talking, please.

"My good *Argbed*," Crim responded smoothly. "I'm most astonished that you seem to have forgotten how this works. I give you that piece of clay and we go on our way unmolested and unquestioned."

A gravel-throated laugh answered the statement.

"Imagine that—a little rat like you educating me about how the *Hazarbed*'s seal works." Alborz chuckled before he heaved a weary sigh. "Fine, you can move along but remember that one of these days, I might not care what's stamped on a little piece of pottery."

Ax-Wed was afraid that the bruised man was about to look down and see the cord fraying, but she was so close.

"Oh, *Argbed*, we both know the Citadel will be dust before your vaunted honor crumbles," Crim replied and laughed roughly. "But I suppose if I'm still around when that happens, it will certainly be an interesting day."

"Indeed." The castellan grunted before he raised his voice in a hoarse command. "All right, move along, Crim. And make sure to not get yourself killed before I can drag you to the gallows."

The warrior woman had to bite her lip to stop herself from crying out in frustration when the tough leather refused to part.

I am so close.

"Such is my nightly endeavor, Alborz," the ruffian declared with a flourish of his hand. "A very fine day to you."

With a lurch, the wagon set off again.

"He's getting bolder," the driver growled as they moved into what must have been some kind of tunnel by the sudden cacophony of hooves on stone. "Let's hope you are right about his honor."

"Let's get these delivered," Crim roared and shouted over his shoulder without turning. "Is everything still in order back there?"

"Yes, boss," the bruised man declared with a relieved sigh as he turned his attention to Masheed with a barely audible drawl. "Isn't that right you little—"

At that precise moment, Ax-Wed's bond came apart with a sharp snap.

His head jerked and his eyes widened. She lurched forward with her fingers curled into a powerful claw that snared the man about the throat. The air he'd gathered for a shout stalled in a tight gagging sound and she squeezed with terrible force. His body seemed unsure of whether to fight back or try to escape and one hand clawed at her vambrace while the other pushed against the side of the wagon. As a result, he was successful at neither and spittle began to foam at his lips.

She stared into his eyes as she felt his strength weakening and let him see the futility of his struggle in the face of her furious vengeance. He attempted to rally at the sight and both hands clamped around her wrist, but the violence of that movement only made her fingers bite deeper into his throat.

The man managed to resist for a few more pain-filled seconds before he went limp when something snapped wetly in his throat. His body began to shake and spasm but she dragged him on top of her so his seizing limbs wouldn't thump against the boards of the wagon.

Several heartbeats passed while his body twitched but finally, he was still and she dared to look toward the front of the wagon. Crim and the driver's backs were to her and although it was hard to hear with all the noise in the tunnel, they seemed to try to discuss something.

Her fingers ached and her arm burned from the exertion but she managed to slide the corpse off her and drag herself to where her weapons lay. Although her hands itched for the ax, she took hold of the dagger and with some fiddling, extracted it from the scabbard and set to work on her other bonds.

Some god must be smiling on her but she didn't think she could expect that to last so she sawed furiously at her restraints in defiance of her pained limb.

The timbre of the echoing hooves changed and Ax-Wed knew they must be out of the tunnel and into a larger chamber. The wagon began to slow as the last of the cords parted.

"This is the last two going in tonight," Crim called to someone and in answer, there was a grinding whir as though someone was turning a great iron crank. Somewhere nearby, the sound of stone grating on stone rose to exceed the noise of the slow hoofbeats.

She rose into a crouch and snatched her ax up as the floor-boards lurched under her. The wagon was turning.

Crim and the driver were ahead of her and still oblivious, and she was certain they would fall easily enough, but who else lay beyond the confines of the wagon was a mystery. Looking through the front, she could see stone walls with a few lanterns hanging from iron rings. Were they in a chamber in the palatial Citadel? Did an army of Jehadim's guards wait beyond the patched canvas that blinded her?

A sharp whine sounded beside her and she noticed Masheed for the first time since she'd severed her bonds.

It wouldn't hurt to have someone to watch my back, she thought and attempted to reason with herself even as the thought repelled her.

This thing masquerading as a woman had attempted to abduct two innocent boys for a fate that she now seemed terri-fied to face. The only reason she wasn't free to keep working her wicked ways was because she'd somehow displeased Crim, so she wasn't only a monster but an incompetent one. The thought of freeing her—even to have aid in escaping—galled her beyond measure, but the strange mechanical noises beyond the canvas didn't fill her with confidence.

When the conveyance turned, she thought she glimpsed shadows moving between the lights that glowed through the canvas.

Snarling curses in every language she knew and some she didn't, Ax-Wed bent and began to saw the other woman's bonds.

"Don't make me regret this," she warned in what amounted to a rough growl and expected to hear someone cry out in alarm at any second.

The restraints around Masheed's arms fell free and the woman yanked the gag out. Before she could say anything, the Thulian clapped a hand over her mouth.

"Be quiet and be quick," she said as she pressed the dagger hilt into the woman's hand. "Cut your legs free while I take care of those two. Once they are eliminated, we'll try to drive this wagon out the way we came."

If it is big enough in here, maybe we can turn, she told herself as she let go of the abductor turned abductee. *I merely wish it didn't sound stupider every time I think about it.*

She began to creep toward the front of the wagon when Masheed's hand grasped her wrist beseechingly.

"What?" Ax-Wed snapped as she turned back.

The mercenary's eyes were swollen with terror and brimmed with tears as she looked from the warrior woman to Crim's exposed back and back again. Her split lip quivered as she struggled to force words to form.

"A f-failed acquisition is still an acquisition," she whispered.

"What?" She grunted as she began to pull her arm free.

The dagger drove up between the lames in her armor in search of the meat beneath.

"Crim!" Masheed screamed at the top of her lungs. "Crim, she's free!"

Ax-Wed, with the hilt of her own dagger jutting from the parted lames on her side, thrust back with such force that the ax in her hand punched through the canvas.

"Crim!" the woman wailed and threw her arms around her fellow captive's legs, even though hers remained bound together. "Crim!"

Off-balance and with a dagger point tickling her ribs and a madwoman on her legs, she reeled back and her armored body forced the split canvas to rip apart.

Beyond that was a yawning pit beside which the wagon had drawn up. A sharply sloped stone wall slid into a stygian dark that yawned eagerly before her widening gaze.

"What in all the hells?" she managed as she lost her balance.

She tumbled into the waiting abyss with the mercenary still clinging to her and a manic shriek ripped from her raw throat.

CHAPTER ELEVEN

"I don't care what time it is!" Vahrem roared in a voice like thunder. "You fetch your *Salar* and you fetch him now!"

To the surprise of all present, the caravan master included, the two guards sent to investigate the disturbance at the stockyard responded with quick bows of obeisance and hurried toward the Tin Quarter barracks.

"There's not a chance in the Serpent's Coils that we'll get a *Salar* here." Iyshan growled his disgust. "We'll be lucky if those two idiots come back."

"Don't you think I know that?" the merchant all but snarled in a fury. "But if you'd maintained the watches properly, we wouldn't be here, now would we?"

Iyshan's mouth curled to protest but then his gaze lowered and his shoulders sagged.

"Yes, master," he muttered softly, his head bowed beneath the weight of the merchant's burning glare.

"Vahrem," Numi called admonishingly as she ambled toward the gates of the stockyard.

It was the caravan master's turn to lower his gaze. His calloused hands rose before his face and he curled them into fists that he beat against his thighs. With a shake of his head and a heavy swallow, he turned, calmed himself, and looked at the elder dwarf.

"You're right," he said, his deep voice so tight it was close to cracking. "You're right."

One fist unclenched and he rested a hand on Iyshan's sinew-corded shoulder.

"I'm sorry, old friend," Vahrem said heavily, frustrated tears in his eyes. "Twice in one night, I sin in my anger toward you."

The other man could only manage a single glance at his master before he looked at the ground with a nod.

"Forgive me, please?" he implored, his words pained but sincere. "I know better than to treat you so."

Iyshan nodded again and patted the hairy hand on his shoulder.

"I forgive you," he said. "Shepherd knows we've all been tested tonight."

"And none more than that poor boy," the dwarfess cried and ran a gnarled hand over her face. "Little Jalen doesn't seem to remember anything, which is a mercy, but Julo wouldn't stop crying. It seems he tried to fight one of them and thought he was dying."

With a hiss, she shook her staff and muttered her malediction.

"Spikes find those monsters. Stealing children! Spikes take them to the Pit Without End."

All three fell silent for a moment of dark thoughts and desperate prayers while overhead, the first shades of dawn began to creep across the sky.

"Did you send for the boys' father?" Vahrem said after he'd sucked a breath in between his teeth.

Iyshan nodded and they lapsed into silence again.

"What do you think they'll do with her?" Numi asked, her voice little more than a dry whisper.

Neither man answered but the look they shared spoke

volumes. She shuddered as every dark tale about the seedy dens and foul-hearted villains in Jehadim threatened to overwhelm her.

"I know we just met the lass," Numi said quickly as though afraid either man might cut her off. "But I think we have to do everything we can to try to find her. It seems like the right thing to do. A wandering sell-sword like her has no one to come and rescue her, I'm thinkin'."

"More than likely, she'll be past rescue even if we do find her," Iyshan remarked grimly. His face wore a stony and set expression but a deep well of sorrow lay in his eyes.

"Then we find her faster, damn it!" Numi snapped and rattled her chiming staff. "Or we find her and give the poor thing a proper burial at the very least. She was taken from our camp, by the Mount."

Vahrem rested a bracing hand upon the old dwarf's shoulder and shook his head against the weight of responsibility that lay heavily on him.

"My camp," he said softly. "She was taken from my camp after I told her she was safe. Her care was my responsibility."

"You couldn't have known." Numi was close to tears as she reached for the hand on her shoulder. "These were professional monsters. What could any of us have done?"

He smiled at her as he extracted his hand gently.

"Thank you, Numi," he said and each word fell from his lips like a leaden weight. "But you know the first rule of leadership—it is always your fault. It has to be."

Both dwarfess and man watched the caravan master as he straightened and noted the fierce light in his eye. He gnawed the top of his lip for a moment as his thoughts danced through some wild scheme, then he snapped his gaze to his manservant.

"Fetch Durra," he said in a voice that brooked no discussion before he turned to Numi. "Your sister still has you carrying the clan seal, doesn't she?"

She nodded, her brow furrowed.

"I'll get some parchment and you will help me write a betrothal contract in Wain-cant," he declared as he turned to stride toward the caravan's baggage train. "And we'll need to borrow your chariot."

Numi shook her head as she watched him walk away and struggled before she finally found her voice.

"What exactly are you planning to do?" she shouted after him.

"See an old friend," he called over his shoulder. "And create a diplomatic incident."

Durra was doing a remarkable job of acting exactly as he'd been taught—standing silently in his chariot and looking very irritated and very haughty. His beaky nose raised in disdain and dark eyes flashing with irritation, he was the very picture of piqued entitlement.

This combined with the way he'd been attired in an elaborate and gaudy assemblage of Wain Dwarf garb and jewelry ensured that even a man like *Argbed* Alborz, who was no one's fool, would be utterly convinced that Durra was an irate clan chief.

Standing atop Numi's chariot—which now practically blocked the gate of the Gold Quarter barracks—was the final masterful stroke.

"If this were only a matter of the heart or even of justice, you know I wouldn't be here," Vahrem said, the hastily but precisely forged contract still hanging from one hand. "But this is first and foremost a matter of business. If the chief doesn't get his concubine in short order, the contract is invalidated and that means I don't get my healthy compensation for arranging transport. And if I don't get my compensation..."

Alborz, a man of middling height who looked as tender as old boot leather wrapped around a bar of iron nodded as he took the contract from the merchant.

"Then the prince doesn't get his share for all such commerce," the *Argbed* muttered as he studied the contract with red-rimmed eyes. "I believe the tax for the transport of such persons indentured but not enslaved is a hefty thirty percent?"

The caravan master snorted.

"We both know it is thirty percent for Jehadim and an additional five percent in tribute tax," the caravan master said chidingly. "And we also know I plan to pay every last shekel."

Alobrz held a hand up in a placatory gesture as his gaze darted across the document.

"My apologies, Vahrem," the *Argbed* grunted as he squinted to read the contracts. "But it's been almost two years since we shared the Table together and I know you were here last season purchasing some fine horses."

Vahrem opened his mouth but promptly snapped it shut when Alborz waved away any proffered explanations.

"I don't need you to make excuses but I did fear your feet had strayed from the Watchful Way," he continued, his voice firm but without malice. "And now you simply arrive at my door and ask me to get involved in something that happened in the Tin Quarter."

"I'm sorry about not sharing the Table last year but in point of fact, the abduction happened outside the stockyard along the Fijal side of the Prichan corridor," he corrected and folded his arms. "Which practically makes it the Silver Quarter."

Alborz looked up from perusing the contract to give him a wry glance.

"Even if that were true," he began as he cleared his throat. "If you haven't noticed, this is the Gold Quarter and I am *Argbed* of the Citadel, not *Gondbed* of any quarter—Silver, Gold, Copper, or Tin."

The merchant put on a show of casting a nervous look over

his shoulder at Durra, who responded with flared nostrils and an acidic glare. He would have to mention to his *Mehk* that if the boy had no head for business, he could always take up with a performing troupe.

"Look," he said with a weariness that was hardly an act. "Right now, I can't even get a *Salar* from the Tin Quarter to respond to this. Every second I stand here begging you is one more chance that the clan chief rides out of Jehadim without giving me even a whiff of copper."

"You're begging now, are you?" the other man asked and rubbed his chin as he handed him the contract.

Vahrem met his old friend and fellow convert's eye and with a heavy sigh, sank onto one knee.

"In the name of the Shepherd," he intoned solemnly, his head bowed so his beard rested against his chest. "I'm asking you to bear this burden with me. This woman is very important."

Alborz weighed the sight before him for a moment before he made his decision with a nod.

"All right." He sighed and proffered his hand to the kneeling merchant. "Get up here and tell me what this is all about."

"What?" The caravan master grunted as he rose to his feet. "I don't understand."

"You don't honestly think I'd forget who little Durra was did you?" the *Argbed* remarked dryly before he called past the merchant to the dwarf in the chariot. "Your beard's almost come in, Durra. Well done, lad."

The young dwarf froze halfway through his pantomime of an officious pout and his gaze darted from the guard officer to Vahrem. Alborz chuckled and turned to the merchant, who seemed stricken with a sudden bout of muteness.

"Now this kind of thing seems to align with some of my investigations," the *Argbed* said and folded his arms over the front of his breastplate. "But there is one thing we need to start with."

He tapped a finger on the contract in Vahrem's hand and almost dislodged it from his numb fingers.

"What kind of heathen name is Ax-Wed?"

CHAPTER TWELVE

Tumbling end over end was grueling, and sinking into a lightless world was disconcerting, but doing both at the same time was something the likes of which she'd never experienced.

The fact that she was pursued by Masheed's mad screams was merely an added flavor to the horror. The snatcher clung to her with the tenacity of a hook-clawed parasite and her screeches were barely interrupted by each rolling impact. More than once in the seemingly eternal tumble into the dark, the Thulian tried to close her fingers around the woman, but every impact shattered her coordination and her fingers only managed to rake across her skull and shoulders.

In this sense-destroying plunge, she had enough time to grow introspective and remember the dark stories of her youth of the horrors that lurked beneath the oldest fortresses and temples of the world. Would they be dropped into the heart of a volcanic furnace? Or worse, would they plummet into the waiting maw of a titanic beast? Worse still, they might plunge into a lightless lake filled with blind, needle-mouthed horrors.

Or perhaps worst of all, she'd already fallen into one of the hells where she'd be damned to fall with Masheed for all eternity.

She might have shuddered at that last thought but it would have been hard to tell with all the bouncing.

Regardless, she need not fear as her jolting came to an end with a heavy impact against a wall, followed by a short but truly terrifying plunge and a hard landing on a most unforgiving floor. With this final shock came the sickening sound of bone snapping like wet kindling and the clatter of her helm when it finally came free to roll across the floor.

Ax-Wed lay motionless, her eyes pinched helplessly against the spinning that was now entirely internal, and waited for the agony of a broken bone to seize her. After a second and as her fluids finally began to settle within her, she realized that not only were her bones unbroken but distinct points of light burned on the outer side of her eyelids.

She had little time to appreciate the revelation as she discovered that Masheed was beneath her—the possessor of the broken limbs. The warrior woman's eyes had barely opened when she winced against another aural assault, this one almost beyond human limits. When her fist pounded into the snatcher's face, she suspected she was doing the woman a favor. No one should be awake to make that kind of noise.

With effort, she dragged herself to her feet and her suspicions were confirmed when she studied the gleaming spear of pink bone that stabbed through the woman's breeches above the knee. The bleeding seemed to be minimal for the moment, so the mercenary wasn't in danger of bleeding out immediately, although that might have been a mercy. The odds of the wound not getting infected in some dungeon were unlikely, and any hope of escaping with such a crippling wound was so improbable it was laughable.

Or at least it would have been if one weren't in such agony.

Ax-Wed began to inspect the worked stone chamber beneath the light of guttering torches when she noticed that her hand was painfully empty. With a snarl, her gaze swept frantically around her and she found her ax in the same instant that she realized she and Masheed weren't the only occupants in this room. Two men and one woman huddled under the light of a torch that the woman must have taken off the wall. One of the men grasped her ax in trembling hands and the edge of Thulian sylver danced keen and crimson in the torch's guttering light.

Another figure was sprawled a few feet from her and the sharp angle of her neck told the tale of an unlucky fall from the chute above.

"Give me that!" Ax-Wed snarled at the recoiling three as she began to straighten to her imposing height, then hissed as she clasped a hand to her side. Her dagger had been driven in almost to the hilt. Masheed had barely possessed the strength to drive the blade half an inch into her flesh but gravity and her armored bulk had finished the job as she'd fallen through the dark.

"It looks like you're in no position to give orders," retorted the man behind the one holding her weapon. He appeared to be middle-aged with a jowly face but his shoulders and chest seemed solid if not particularly broad. In her opinion, he might be better suited to wield the weapon than the spare-framed young man—scarcely more than a boy—who grasped it unsteadily. As she glared at them, she saw the terror threaten to turn his growling to a pitiful whine.

"We'll resolve this in one moment," she said through gritted teeth.

She spat and swore as she retrieved a silken rag from her belt while her blood-slicked fingers curled around the dagger.

"Why are we fighting?" the woman asked and her plaintive tone quivered like the light of the torch in her hand. "We're all trapped down here. Shouldn't we help each other?"

"You'd think so." Ax-Wed grunted as she tried to brace herself for what came next. It was probably a foolish risk but with this much steel in her, she wouldn't be able to do anything. It might seal her fate but this at least gave her a chance to die with her ax where it belonged—in her hand.

"You saw what she did," the dog-faced man said and pointed to Masheed's recumbent form. "Do you want her to do the same to us?"

"Look at her hair," the young man cried and gestured to the warrior woman with his stubble-bristled chin. "She's Thulian. It's probably the reason we're down here in the first place."

The warrior woman laughed, a sharp, bitter tune that resounded off the stone walls and made the fearful trio shrink back.

"Oh, of course, that makes perfect sense." She snarled and yanked the dagger from her side with a tight-throated scream. Blood welled but she rammed the silken rag home and her tongue worked through the old charms she'd been taught since childhood. While the lowest order of sorcery, it still tore off her tongue and sliced through her lips so she had to spit a mouthful of blood onto the floor simply to finish it.

Ax-Wed doubled over as the silk kindled with an unholy heat and her wound was seared shut. She forced air through clenched teeth and waited, her knuckles grinding into the steel poleyns armoring her knees. One hand still held her dagger, which dripped her blood onto the floor.

"Did you hear that?" the older man muttered at the young man's back. "Witchery and devil-calling if I ever heard it. Strike now, lad!"

The whiskery youth took one step forward and the ax began to rise in his hands when her eyes flashed at him through a veil of her indigo-streaked hair.

"If you swing, make it count, boy." She grunted as she straightened and brandished her dagger before her. "You'll only have one chance before I find a new home for this."

To the boy's credit—and when she saw him clearly, she knew he was exactly that—he charged toward her with as fierce a cry as he could manage. It was a clumsy, ungainly attack, but he threw himself into the swing.

Ax-Wed let the blow whistle past her before she stepped in and seized his trailing arm above the elbow to check any backswing. Then it was her turn to strike and she drove in hard with the dagger. At the last second, she changed her mind and altered her hold so the flat of the blade slapped hard across his face with a resounding smack.

The young man reeled, a bloody welt across his face, and she used his distraction to move her hand to the haft of the ax. She swept the red, flashing blade toward the youth's face and his hands released the weapon quickly in a desperate attempt to guard his face. With icy control, she pulled the strike short of his sheltering hands and spared him a nasty gash, but she did kick out and plant her heavy boot into his belly.

He toppled and gasped like a fish, while the other two cried out as they shrank back, all their hopes dashed.

Ax-Wed examined her weapon and, satisfied that no great harm had been done, planted the butt on the floor in front of her. She sheathed the dagger at her belt and turned a furious scowl upon the three.

"If that's all done with," she declared with a note of warning in her voice. "Could someone please tell me what is going on?"

All three, even the boy on the floor who clutched his bloody cheek, looked at each other and then at her with dumb expressions. She made a disgusted sound in the back of her throat in reply to their mute answer and moved to retrieve her helm.

When she scooped it up, she noticed it had a few fresh dents, one of which was severe enough that she wasn't sure she could wear it. With some tools and time, she could make it serviceable again but that was assuming she lived to see either.

"Perfect," she muttered and tied it to her belt before she turned to the terrified three. "So do any of you have an idea why we are here?"

Three sets of wide eyes stared at her without answer.

The silence stretched and she was about to repeat the question when a chilling yowl issued from behind her.

She spun with her ax in hand and her gaze settled on a black portal set into the far wall. Uncomfortably familiar sigils were visible on the lintel and posts of the doorway, some of which were smeared with glittering, scarlet handprints.

"What by all the gods is it now?"

"Did you summon a demon?" the young man cried as he clambered to his feet. His hand left his welted cheek to point an accusing finger at her. "Is this your sorcery?"

Ax-Wed gave him a withering look over one shoulder.

Just when I was beginning to like you.

"If it was, would I be preparing to kill whatever comes through that doorway?" she snapped and gestured to the portal with the head of her ax. "Can you please stop worrying about my hair and spend a little more time preparing to fight for our lives?"

Another howl, closer this time, resounded from the black corridor and echoed in the chamber.

The sound galvanized the young man, who looked around quickly, rushed to a wall sconce, and yanked a torch from it.

"Come on," he shouted at the cowering man. "Grab one!"

The older man shrank back, his gaze fixed on the impenetrable darkness of the yawning doorway. His lips stretched over his teeth and his fleshy throat bobbed but no sound came out. In the flickering light, it was evident that his eyes weren't even focused on the portal. He was too busy filling his mind with whatever imagined horrors he could conjure to be of use to anyone, especially himself.

She turned away from him with a dismissive snort and nodded to the young man who stood with the burning brand clutched in both hands.

"Never mind him, boy." She grunted, rolled her shoulders slowly, and willed a strength she didn't feel into the weary muscles. The dagger wound, thankfully, showed no signs of bleeding, but it wouldn't take much to start again. "Some are only fit for dying when it comes time to fight for something."

The Thulian warrior spared a look over her shoulder at the torch-bearing woman and then at the younger man before she nodded at the blood-framed doorway.

"Whatever's coming through that, we have a better chance if we stick together and put some stone at our backs," she said in a firm, commanding tone. "We need to give each other enough room to swing but not so much that we can let someone or something get between us."

When they both nodded but neither moved, she had to stifle a growl of irritation.

"Here and here," she instructed with a sharp command and indicated positions on either side of her. "If we let ourselves get surrounded, we are as good as dead."

The woman took a step forward and Ax-Wed got a better view of the lines creasing her face despite the caked makeup. The cracks in the face paint deepened to crevices as her expression twisted with suspicion and she stopped in her tracks.

"How do you know it's not only one monster?"

She shrugged and her hands tightened around the haft of her ax.

"I don't," she answered. "But if I'm right, you'll get cut off and torn apart if you stand there."

Neither moved to take the positions she'd indicated until a chorus of baying cries filled the chamber. Then, with wide eyes and sweaty hands grasped tightly around the rusted shafts of their torches, they took their places on either side of her. This close, both felt a measure of comfort in the warrior's huge shadow.

Ax-Wed stole a glance at the jowly man who now hunkered down against the bare wall as though he could escape by making himself as small as possible.

Who knows, she thought grimly. *He might last a few minutes longer than we will.*

She hadn't been able to isolate individual voices in that horrible chorus but there was no doubt that they were badly outnumbered.

"What about her?" the whiskery youth asked and pointed toward Masheed's recumbent form.

The fallen snatcher's chest rose and fell steadily but otherwise, there was no movement.

Before she could answer, the sound of rushing, slapping feet began to thrum from the doorway and the volume mounted with each heartbeat.

The mercenary's broken and bound legs stretched beneath her, while blood leaked from a nose pulped by the warrior woman's fist.

"She had better hope she doesn't wake up," Ax-Wed stated grimly.

"We should help her," the young man shouted and broke from the formation. "We can protect her."

She took a single step forward and stretched one hand to drag him back like a straying pup.

"Get back h—"

A flurry of yowling cries, almost sing-song in their mad gibbering, announced the arrival of the creatures in the dark.

They poured into the chamber, a tide of creatures in filthy, threadbare robes that could not hide their inescapable wrongness. Their bodies were twisted and lumpy, with features atrophied or swollen in a wretched caricature of the human form and wrapped in a pallid, suppurating sheathe of grimy skin. They loped and shuffled on bent, mismatched limbs as they swept in, a hooting, shrieking, barking tide of degenerate flesh. Crude, makeshift weapons, some little more than sharpened pieces of stone or wood, were clutched in hands that trembled to bring them to bear.

This will be ugly, Ax-Wed acknowledged as she settled into her fighting stance.

The rush of bodies filled half the chamber in an instant but they slowed before they reached Masheed's motionless form. Their stink was a putrid amalgam of every filth a mortal creature could excrete. Before the wave of foulness, the young man recoiled and staggered back to his place at Ax-Wed's side.

She fought the urge to gag as she faced the gazes of her enemy. Behind their black, wet eyes burned a malign hunger and petty rage that promised no mercy and no gentle death to anything that fell into their jagged, crooked fingers.

"Gods have mercy!" the painted woman cried at her side and thrust the torch out before her as though she tried to banish the collection of horrors like some nightmare vestige.

In answer, a fetid figure with its face hidden beneath a deep hood emerged from the seething mass. The frame seemed to be of the same chaotic, malformed mold as the others but there was a dark and terrible presence in the way it stood as straight as it could and looked evenly at them.

"There are no gods here," declared a voice as deep and terribly beautiful as the ocean. "There is only I and my children."

Ax-Wed's stomach clenched and her knees threatened to tremble but she threw her head back and laughed all the harder for the fear.

"They must take after their mother," she quipped with every semblance of disdain that she did not feel.

The malicious will beneath the hood focused on her and the fear she'd felt before was a mere brushstroke compared to the dark attention paid to her now. It was like a current of despair surged around her, not only from the cowled figure but from the very stones. To her fevered imagination, it was as if the chamber slowly filled with black, icy waters she couldn't see but that would drown her all the same.

I am he, the waters bubbled from a chorus of drowned throats. *Drinker of life, Wallower of souls. I—*"

"Atlacothix?"

The name pushed from her mouth and fought through the horror that locked her jaws together and bound her tongue. It was born on a swelling tide of memories, half-remembered stories read from her father's library. She remembered the smell of musty tomes and the scuffing scratch of parchment pages turning as she beheld blasphemies and wonders graven with ink and quill.

The huge, dark will faltered before the name—or perhaps it was the memories?—and the despairing waters vanished from her mind's eye. The terrible presence retreated to that single voice within the hood and at that realization, a fell smile turned up the corners of her mouth.

"Take them!" the dark voice commanded and the horde of degenerates was unleashed.

CHAPTER THIRTEEN

"What exactly are you asking me, Alborz?"

Guuhal regretted the question as soon as it left his mouth.

When the castellan had requested an audience in his offices the night after the quota had increased, the guard commander had known it was a meeting he would not enjoy. Now, less than a minute into the conversation, he already scrambled to escape.

The *Argbed* was a good man—a friend even—but he was relentless. He had achieved the coveted position as Castellan of the Gold Quarter and thus the prince's Citadel by being a man of singular determination and dogged efficiency. If he'd been a little more politically minded and more secret about his religious predilections, he probably would have been next in line for the *Hazarbed*'s office. While the commander appreciated having such a trustworthy and strong-minded man under his command, by Shizan, the man was not one who could let things go.

"I've said it twice now, sir," Alborz replied, his tone even but uncompromising. "Why are so many individuals—so many criminals—given your permission to pass through the Gold Quarter?"

Guuhal gritted his teeth and tried to force his voice to stay as calm as possible.

"You received another token?" he asked. "Is that what this is about?"

As though waiting for the cue, the *Argbed* produced a string upon which were hung not one but three tokens of the *Hazarbed*'s office. The clay disks had the center of the seal awled through to allow them to be strung on the cord and they gave a soft click-clack as they dangled between them.

"Three last night," the man replied, his voice unchanged in volume or inflection. "It was practically a caravan of wagons that rolled through the quarter last night."

"Isn't patrolling the quarter the business of *Gondbed* Delshad?" he asked, unable to keep the irritation out of his voice as he glared at the tokens.

I told Crim to use them sparingly.

"With respect to the guard captain, we both know that his concerns are elsewhere," Alborz said and his sanguine mask refused to crack despite the loathing he had for the man. The *Argbed* was the son of a lesser noble house and had earned his position by skill and dedication. *Gondbed* Delshad was second cousin to the prince and that was the only reason he held the position he now did.

"So it seems your energies should be spent coordinating with Delshad," the *Hazarbed* countered and secretly wished it could be that easy to get rid of the man who challenged him. "Between the two of you, perhaps, you'll be able to ensure that both the prince's Citadel and the Gold Quarter are secure, as is your charge."

The guard commander saw that Alborz felt the warning in his words but predictably, he pushed forward undaunted.

"It will not do either of us any good to coordinate on an investigation where we are not permitted to make arrests, perform confiscations, or detain for questioning. One of the wagon loads was moving across the canal causeway that leads to the granary basins beneath the palace. How can I secure a fortress when vermin like Crim come and go as they please?"

Guuhal stiffened at the mention of the abduction specialist's name.

"Who is this Crim and what does he have to do with this?"

The lowered brow and clenched jaw before the *Argbed* answered was proof that the man knew the question was a smokescreen. Still, as dutiful as ever, he gave his report.

"Through the weeks, I've learned that the man named Crim is the ringleader of these regular visitors to the Gold Quarter. This is based mostly on the fact that he is most often the one bearing your tokens. According to census records and initial investigations, Crimoush bet'Kamboush is the proprietor of a brothel in the Copper Quarter and a generational resident of Jehadim, which affords him full protection under the law, but even my initial inquiries suggested that negotiable affection is hardly the only thing this man is up to."

An assortment of curses and reproofs ran through the *Hazarbed*'s mind as he listened to Alborz. Some were for himself but most were for Crim. When the *Argbed* concluded his explanation, the silence lengthened between the two men while the guard commander bounced between what lie he could possibly offer and what threats he could level.

And I was fool enough to want good men serving under me, he groaned mentally. *A wicked man would have been far easier to deal with if this had even come up at all.*

His heart began to beat harder and the other man's gaze dug into him like the awl that had punctured the tokens. Guuhal came to his decision in a rush of pent-up frustration.

"Do you have any evidence, *Argbed* Alborz— any actual evidence—to support this breach of conduct?" he snapped and looked down his nose at the officer.

For the first time since they'd known each other, he saw the castellan startled.

"Breach of conduct?" Alborz repeated and his gray eyebrows bunched in confusion. "Wha—"

"You see fit to question me, your superior, as to how I conduct my duties," he continued and in a rush of angry inspiration, snatched the tokens from the man's hand. "These tokens are evidence of my will and permit the bearer and those in his company to pass without being detained, delayed, or questioned. Isn't that correct, *Argbed?*"

Alborz nodded and his mouth opened to answer but snapped shut again when the *Hazarbed* glared at him in warning.

"And knowing this, you understand that it is unacceptable to question me on their use in all but the most dire of circumstances," the commander declared before he turned to cast the tokens on the floor. "You must therefore have some rather compelling evidence to justify questioning how I am performing my duties."

The man stood with his jaw set and ground his teeth as he stared at his superior.

"Go ahead, *Argbed,*" Guuhal pressed. "Tell me the evidence that justifies this insubordination?"

"We have received reports of abduction—"

"Reports are not evidence!" the *Hazarded* railed and channeled the thrill of fear at the mention of abductions to greater fury. "Try again."

"We have multiple sightings—"

"Sightings are not evidence!" Guuhal shouted and a sick feeling curled in his stomach as he did so. At least there was some measure of satisfaction at seeing Alborz wince. "Is there anything else, *Argbed?*"

The castellan's eyes burned with brutal intensity but he closed them and drew a steadying breath. It made him sick to his stomach again to watch it, but the guard commander knew he'd won, at least for the moment.

"No, *Hazarbed,*" the man replied and inclined his head stiffly.

"Then see to your duties," he said and disgust thickened his suddenly weary voice. "And get out of my sight."

CHAPTER FOURTEEN

The first two degenerates to rush directly toward her fell in a spray of blood and their rotted robes and pallid flesh came apart under the caress of her weapon.

Ax-Wed didn't have time to savor the perfect execution of the stroke as she was forced to use a backswing to drive back another three that sprang to take their places. The stinking press of bodies threatened to overwhelm her as they surged forward with a keening howl. Her ax swept left and right to part flesh and splinter bone with each pass but still, they came.

With a wild cry, the stubbled youth and the painted woman joined the fray with their burning bludgeons and a desperate spark of hope was kindled in the dark chamber.

The Thulian buried her ax in the chest of an onrushing brute and a shrieking creature lunged at her, a jagged spar held out like a spear. Before the thrust could find its mark, the painted woman leapt forward with a wild cry. She swung the torch onto the attacker's head and the heavy, corroded brass rim buckled bone as sparks showered over the flapping, filthy robes. The degenerate crumpled and its garments kindled, but the woman continued to scream as she swiped the torch to repel another attacker that targeted her flank. Terror and a desperate will to live granted the small figure a tireless strength to swing the heavy torch relentlessly.

The young man bellowed like a young bull and swept his torch before him to scatter the quick and scorch the slow. One of the filthy mob darted forward and wrapped his twisted fingers around the torch haft and snapped scummy, jagged teeth in the youth's face. He roared his defiance and with a heave disproportionate to his spare frame, threw his enemy down and thrust the torch into it before it could rise. A short, pained wail was followed by silence as the flames engulfed the creature's face and spread across its greasy frame.

With the respite of not being the only target, Ax-Wed stalked the chamber, grim and terrible, and her ax reaped a dreadful toll.

Her weapon sang repeatedly and with each new blow, one or more of the creatures would crumple, often in pieces. Thulian steel honed beyond the craft of mere mortal smiths parted meat like cloth and shivered bones like reeds. The bodies felled and burned by the torches began to fill the room with smoke and soot and she became like the very specter of death materializing out of the mirk as her ax parted another neck or crushed another chest.

It was not a battle or a contest of skilled warriors, only a matter of slaughter. The defenders would have to shed blood by the bucketful or be overrun. It was simple as that.

And blood seemed to be in no short supply.

A degenerate made a clumsy swing with a hunk of statuary in his sore-riddled fist, but the strike only rebounded off her steel lames with a dull clang. Snarling vengeance, Ax-Wed drove the butt of her weapon into the face of a smoke-blinded wretch and looked around before she delivered a killing thrust with the horn of the ax-blade.

At first, the ferocity of the defenders had bought them precious seconds and the dead, burning or otherwise, had slowed the shuffling onslaught. Now, the pallid mob was uncertain and confused. Some even collided with and attacked each other as they fought to stay clear of the torch and flinched at any glint of her sweeping ax.

Can we truly survive this? she wondered, afraid to let herself think of anything more than the next target for her dripping ax. *How much longer before they lose their nerve?*

She'd barely finished the thought when a terrified scream tore through the cacophony.

Afraid that one of her allies had fallen, she whipped her head to track the sound but when she squinted into the eye-watering smoke, she saw them. Almost back-to-back now, their torches swept in wide arcs and they created a circle of burning death for any that came close. The scream came again, even higher and more pained, and this time, she could track it to the side of the room where Masheed lay.

It was hard to see amidst the smoke, but a knot of the debased creatures seemed to have set upon her. There were only flashes of the woman beneath the gathered mass but with growing dread, she realized what they were doing. In unwillingly snatched glimpses, she witnessed the howling, drooling creatures tear and rend the stricken woman. Some seemed intent on satisfying their mindless hunger while others sought satiation of darker, viler passions.

The mercenary might have been a monstrous woman but no one deserved to die in such a way. With a snarled oath, Ax-Wed left the defensive triptych.

"Stay together," she shouted over her shoulder before she drove forward and swept her ax like a scythe felling wheat.

The creatures gave way before her and a few even snapped at and stabbed their comrades in a desperate effort to flee. Those that toppled under her ax but did not expire had their bones and throats crushed beneath her advance. With each step, her fury deepened so her weapon was a blur of gory steel, a sharp, shining comet that trailed particles of bone and strings of viscera.

In moments, she reached those huddled about Masheed and a roar to match that of any lioness erupted from her throat. Even in the midst of their depravity, the degenerates looked at her and found the voice to cry out in fear and despair.

She was a vengeful goddess who moved among them and her every motion and gesture claimed another sacrifice wrought in ruined flesh and fractured bone. With hands smeared and stained with the blood of their victim, they sought to shield themselves and cover their wailing faces but those guilty hands parted before her wrath as easily as the rest of them.

"Grim was the Handmaiden yet sharp was her grin!" Ax-Wed sang in the achingly beautiful and chilling tongue of Thule. "Her song a dirge of hells amidst the battle din!"

The few not felled around Masheed's stricken body began to flee, but the Thulian bounded after them and snatched a life with every step as she continued to sing.

"Bridal bed never to see yet suitors by score! Ax she has wed, now and forevermore!"

When the last of the mercenary's tormentors fell, the back of his skull cloven to his neck, a fresh cry issued from behind her. She swung, smiling as she watched the few degenerates around her scatter and race to the doorway, but the smile vanished in an instant.

The whiskery youth swung his torch drunkenly, his whole body thrown into the movement. The only thing that held him upright were two splintered shafts of wood thrust into his belly by festering attackers. Beyond the reach of the sweeping brand, they drove him back until he struck the far wall. The lengths of wood snapped on impact but when the young man pitched forward, the stakes lodged in his body were driven through his flesh and out his back.

One hand still grasped the torch and he scraped it across the floor as he struggled to drag it closer for another swing.

Ax-Wed screamed in red despair but before she could take revenge, her gaze was pulled across the chamber by an agonized shriek.

Surrounded and flagging, the painted woman drove her torch into the face of an attacker before another degenerate lunged at her back with a sharpened stone raised high.

The warrior woman shouted a warning but it was too late.

Chipped rock gouged through the back of her skull and down her neck to open a cruel, flapping gash. The beset woman, shaken and bleeding, tried to turn to face her new attacker and was rewarded by a series of club-like blows across the side of her face. Blood and pieces of teeth spewed from the gaping wounds and her knees buckled.

The pack of degenerates closed their circle, no doubt determined to harvest whatever vile rewards they could from the poor woman's body.

Ax-Wed fell upon them with a sequence of ax strikes that was almost manic. Relentlessly, the weapon rose and fell until she was spattered from head to foot in blood and her gloves were slick with it.

For a time, there was nothing but deep darkness that rose from within her and all she saw were fleeting wraiths of crimson and vermillion that flitted before her before they vanished into the void.

When the darkness finally subsided and her senses returned, she stood alone in the midst of an abattoir.

The dead degenerates were strewn about the smoky room, their stench somehow even more rancid in death. There was no sign of the young man's body, nor of Masheed and the cowering man with the hanging jowls.

Her limbs began to shake and her breath came in ragged

gasps. She staggered back a step and heard a choked sob rise from beside her armored boot.

The painted woman, one side of her face an utter nightmare of sagging flesh and exposed bone, looked pleadingly at her with her remaining eye. Half a dozen other wounds showed through her torn clothes and blood leaked through ragged punctures and flesh distended around ugly blackening bruises across her chest, belly, groin, and thigh.

Ax-Wed was accustomed to the ruined remains of the battle-field and had known since before she was a woman grown, but this was so much worse. The fruits of war were ugly but this obscene torment was born of acts more loathsome than anything done with sword swing or ax stroke.

A choked sound—almost a word—came from the woman and she was shaken from her dark reflections. The bruised mouth continued to work weakly and with her whole body trembling, the warrior woman sank to her haunches to listen.

"Please," the dying woman rasped wetly from her ruined mouth and extended one hand beseechingly toward her.

Thinking the woman was reaching toward her sorcery-patched side, she fought to keep her voice steady as she spoke softly.

"I'm sorry," she said and forced the words through the lump in her throat. "It won't work. There's...there's too much for me to even start. I'd be more likely to kill us both if I tried."

She hated the answer even though she knew to her very bones that it was the truth. While she knew the petty sorceries taught to all Thulians and a few tricks of her house, besides that, she didn't know of any magic potent enough to mend a body so broken. This knowledge did little to ease the ache in her heart and the helplessness in her hands as she looked at the agony-wracked woman.

Although she'd managed to master her voice, she could do nothing to stop the tears rolling down her face. The glittering, crystal droplets cut tracks across the blood that had spattered her cheeks.

The painted woman continued to reach out, her hand tremulous and clumsy, and she almost took it in her gory grip when she realized what she wanted. A sliver of ice raced toward the Thulian's heart as the woman's fingers pawed at the dagger on her belt.

"P-p-please," she sobbed and tears budded around her remaining eye. "Please."

Ax-Wed's hand seemed to move of its own volition while something deep within her wailed in silence. It was a terrible thing but it was not the first time she'd been asked to deliver Morah's Mercy. The jagged pieces which comprised her heart sliced and caught against each other at the weight of the dagger in her hand but she knew what she would do. The words came to her lips unbidden, the same prayerful incantation she'd whispered over every friend and comrade in arms who had met such a fate.

"Morah, Watcher in the Dark, spread your night-black wings and descend from on high," she intoned as she held the blade parallel to the woman's shivering and ravaged body. "Let your glimmering eye see this soul seeking audience in the Halls of the Victorious Vanquished."

The dagger's tip began to tip downward so the needle-sharp point would hover above the laboring heart.

"Quicken the beating of your wings, oh Sentinel upon the Outer Wall. Rush swiftly now and seize upon the fleeting shade."

As it always did, her hand began to tremble and she steadied the blade with her other hand and forced the final words around her parched tongue.

"Come quickly and let your hold be sure. For we are vapor and shadows, wrapped in ashes and dust."

The dagger plunged and it drove home with ease as it had all those times before. The body trembled, blood welled, and within a few meager seconds, the last breath slid free.

She watched it all unfold, the tracks of her tears already drying, and something that had never happened before swept over her.

A sound—no, it wasn't a sound but the impression of sound—all but submerged her and filled her mind with memories of great wing beats and a powerful, cyclopean voice.

No.

Ax-Wed gasped and recoiled from the body where her dagger still stood upright in the painted woman's corpse.

Her gaze darted around the chamber in search of the source of the voice of denial and huge wings but felt foolish as she did so. She knew she had not heard it but remembered it—all of it—with a clarity that struck her mind like a hammer against an anvil.

But what memory did she have of sun-blotting wings stirring the air and the voice of a god?

For some time, she crouched in the dark, charnel chamber, afraid to stir more memories that were not her own yet knowing that every second spent cowering hastened the return of the degenerates or perhaps even worse, the dark presence that had commanded them.

I must have taken a hit to the head and not realized it, she lied to try to assure herself as she summoned the will to draw the dagger from the dead body. *The dark and the strain are wearing on me—and probably still some of that wine.*

Her denials diligently if not firmly entrenched, she rose after cleaning her dagger, ax, and smeared hands as best she could. She knew she should check her wounded side and felt its dull burning at the edge of her awareness, but she needed to get moving.

The only exit from the room was the darkened doorway, but

she was willing to wager that beyond were corridors and other passages.

And if not, what other choice did she have?

If they came again, they would overrun her in the wide chamber and there would be no one to grant her Morah's Mercy as they glutted themselves on her flesh and debasement.

She snatched one of the few remaining torches from the wall, took one last look at the carnage of the chamber, and then set off into the darkness.

CHAPTER FIFTEEN

The Copper Quarter baked as morning gave way to afternoon, and with the hot desert sun came the end to the day's labors. Men and women who'd toiled since before the sun rose set aside their unfinished projects, stowed their tools, hung their aprons up, and bade their foreman and overseers a good day.

From there, they were bound for Reveler's Row.

The quarter was home to not only the many of the tradesmen operations that saw to the needs of Jehadim and its many visitors but also to the various amenities that kept such tradesmen from taking their skills and joining the next passing caravan to another city. Immediately beyond the yards and workshops where the artisans plied their trades lay street after street that brimmed with the pleasures to sate them on their way home from a hard day's work. Whether it be food, drink, or flesh, the Copper Quarter's Reveler's Row would not disappoint.

Some of the offerings were on gaudy display, be they glistening foods or glistening bodies, but others seemed to choose a different tactic. One such place was the three-storied sandstone structure bearing the name the Silken Nest. Besides the red velvet curtains which draped its many windows like crimson veils, there was nothing to draw the eye besides the large bas relief over the door. Set deep into the stone and chafed in bronze, it displayed a masterful depiction of layered spider webs amidst which could be glimpsed svelte naked bodies. The edge of the relief declared the name of the building in several languages and scripts that wrapped the square image.

One look at the building filled Vahrem with a kind of dizzying dread.

"Let's go over it again," he said to Iyshan as they moved down the street in a meandering path to the building.

"We're glassblowers from Scadish come to Jehadim on invitation from Tobarr Beadsman," his companion said under his breath as he lowered his blushing face to avoid looking at two lithe catamites who dangled from a window two buildings before their destination. "Tobarr recommended the Nestled Slip as our introduction to the ladies of Reveler's Row. We must have the directions wrong but since we are here and we have coin to spend, we might as well see what the Silken Nest has to offer."

"Good, good," the merchant said and fought to keep his tone light and even. He'd executed his fair share of tricky negotiations and faced no few dangers in his travels, but reconnoitering the likes of the Silken Nest was not something he had any experience with.

"And after that?" he asked and paused to make a show of studying his surroundings. If the establishment was indeed a hub for the abductors, he wouldn't be surprised if they had lookouts and runners posted along the street. Seeing them floundering somewhat would lend credence to their story.

"We spend some coin freely on drink, with you doing most of the drinking," Iyshan continued and did his part to gaze around and scratch his chin quizzically. "Then I act as though I am growing bored and demand to see the options for companionship. I ask to see the women first and then the men. If there is one who matches the descriptions of the others taken last night, I choose them and demand to show them to you—and act very drunk."

"When you present the person, I mock you and also act very drunk." Vahrem nodded and his brow furrowed as his heart began to pound in his chest. "We do our best to start a brawl and Alborz's friend *Salar* Parviz will be waiting to swoop in and arrest us while also occupying the brothel."

Iyshan pointed at the Silken Nest and slapped a hand on the caravan master's shoulder as though telling his companion he'd found what they sought.

"If none of them match the description, I say nothing is to my liking," he continued as they moved toward the structure, which seemed to loom even more menacingly as they approached. "I ask if they have anything more interesting for a man with good coin to spend. When they pretend they don't know what I am talking about, I tell them that in Scadish, a discerning and generous man can have whatever he wants. I turn to go and leave a Scadish Eighth Ingot behind. As I collect you, I whisper loudly that I gave them something to think about and tell them we are staying as guests at Tobarr's villa."

Vahrem nodded again, this time more animated as though growing excited as they approached the brothel.

"It seems like we are forgetting something," he said after a moment and grunted in irritation. "But I suppose it's too late now."

"Shepherd guard us." Iyshan swallowed as they stopped under the bas relief.

"And let our feet not go astray," he added and together, they swept through the red silk and into the perfumed twilight beyond.

CHAPTER SIXTEEN

She'd only walked a dozen paces from the chamber she'd first fallen into when she stood in another round chamber with stone walls and guttering torches.

Ax-Wed's nose stung with the fetid smell of the degenerate mob that must have moved through the room mere moments earlier, but other than smears of blood and less wholesome substances, she saw no evidence of occupation. The floors and walls were smooth stone panels fitted closely together—which suggested remarkable craftsmanship—but otherwise, there was no indication as to the function of the chambers and there was no decor beyond the torches in their sconces. The only thing that seemed noteworthy was that all the torches seemed to be lit.

The creatures can't see in the dark, she observed and her fingers tightened reflexively on the torch in her hand. *At least not completely.*

It was a small comfort given her predicament, but the realization bolstered the calm and clarity that had remained since the strange episode in the chamber behind her.

As she felt her mind settle, her gaze swept the shadowed walls of the floor of the room. It took a moment of scrutiny but when she squinted through the guttering torchlight, she realized this second chamber had an additional element to it. Although nothing so much as gaps between the stones, there were two more exits from this chamber, both opposite each other and equidistant to the portal she'd come from.

Left or right? she wondered as she moved into the chamber. One hand held her ax in a shortened grip. For all she knew, the creatures had executed a false retreat to lure her into an ambush. The degenerates themselves seemed capable of such things with their low cunning, but combined with the dark presence that had directed them, it seemed all too likely.

Despite these grim thoughts, however, no ravening mob descended upon her and no hunting pack pounced from the dark. Only the stains and stink provided testimony to the fact that she wasn't utterly alone in this deep place.

Ax-Wed paced the room and it took only a moment to realize which way the retreating creatures had gone. The smell emanating from the right portal was a blow to her nostrils, and if that retch-inducing evidence hadn't been enough, she noticed fresh spatters of blood glinting darkly under her torchlight.

For a moment, she stood motionless and stared into the noxious dark. She wondered if she could catch up to them if she hurried and perhaps overtake them as they shuffled through the narrow corridor where their numbers wouldn't count for much.

For what, though? she asked herself.

Even if she could kill them all before they reached another chamber to surround her in, she was assuming there weren't more coming to reinforce the initial vanguard. She could rush after them only to run into a fresh wave of the creatures. Not only that, but they more than likely knew these passages better than her and could turn the situation against her very quickly.

And for what?

The damning question weighed heavily on her chest as she peered into the black gap between the stones.

The boy is dead, Masheed has to be moments from death if she isn't already, and dogface won't be useful as a corpse.

The cold arithmetic of it chafed her like a frigid collar but she found the sum of it impossible to refute. There was no profit in pursuing them unless she wanted to put in her best effort at dying faster.

"Left it is, then." She sighed and cast one last look down the right-hand passage before she slipped through the left portal.

The passage, like its entrance, was narrow and lightless and so unmarked by any sign of artifice that she might have believed it was the result of an accident rather than intention. It was much longer than the passage connecting the initial room to the second and although hard to discern at first, she eventually realized it had a slight curve and downward slope.

This was hardly a comforting fact as she was fairly certain that up would be the way out but needs must and she was most certainly in need—a point driven home when after a handful of minutes of her padding down the passage, she heard an uncomfortably familiar chorus of howls.

They were coming back for her and it would only take a minute for them to realize she was not in the initial chamber. From there, even a child—and a very stupid one at that—could determine which way she'd gone.

She needed to find a place to hide or barring that, a place to make her stand.

For a moment, she considered dropping the torch behind her and making her stand there in the hope that the cramped passage would only allow them to attack one at a time. Even though her side still burned and she knew she wasn't recovered from the last fight, she knew she could fell any of the creatures that fought her if she faced them singly.

Looking back the way she came and then down the passage ahead of her, Ax-Wed chewed her lip for an instant longer, then swore and hurried down the passage again.

They could as easily have a tunnel that goes around and then what will you do? she asked herself in irritation. *Hope they fight fair instead of creep up behind you and club you into submission?*

The mental berating lasted as long as it took for the next hunting call to sound, which was a few minutes after she'd set off again.

Was there a vengeful tone in the baying cries? She didn't know and frankly had no time for such speculation as she moved through the passage, but something hung in the air besides the stench of the creatures.

Moving as quickly as she dared lest she raise a racket with her armor, harness, and weapons, she focused to determine what exactly she sensed.

Some hint of the dark will she'd experienced before was on the move. It crept ahead of its minions and sought her out in the dark corridors. She remembered the peculiar instant when she had recalled a name from her childhood explorations of her father's library, but there was too much in that experience she didn't understand to trust her life to a confrontation. If whatever was in the darkness was active again, it must not be too concerned about her muttering a name she barely remembered.

The corridor wound along its deepening path until Ax-Wed began to fear that the dark passage would go on until she tumbled into whatever uninhabitable realm lay beyond the tiers of earth. She'd remembered from her tutelage that beneath the rounded shell of earth upon which men walked and burrowed like insects, there was supposed to be a vast reservoir of molten stone and poisonous vapor akin to that which volcanoes belched across unfortunate lands. Her tutors had made clear it was not one of the hells, which were different realities as opposed to different locations, but she remembered thinking a burning ocean of venom seemed close enough to a hell to count. They'd taught her that this place was far deeper than men ever delved but they might not have known of it, she supposed.

Was that where she was bound—to the not-hell hell? How far down would she need to be before she would feel the heat or begin to choke on the toxic fumes seeping from below? If that began to happen, would she have time to turn and head back to face her pursuers? Which was worse, falling into the hands of the degenerates or slowly cooking as she choked on treacherous air?

Thankfully, she was not forced to make such a choice as a moment later, she stumbled into another chamber. Her legs had become so used to the pull of the declining plane beneath her feet that she almost lost her balance on the suddenly level floor. With a muttered oath, she righted herself, held her torch up, and began to peer around the room, hoping she hadn't gone all this way to reach a dead end.

No torches burned in this chamber but it seemed smaller than either of those she'd seen before so it took one sweep of her single torch to determine the layout. The room was square, not round, although it seemed to be layered with the same cunningly made stone tiles and had doorways at the center of each wall. The portals to the left and right of where she'd emerged were fitted with doorways like those connecting the two round rooms above her, while the portal opposite where she'd entered was as small and unadorned as the passage entrance she'd almost missed earlier.

She stood for a moment to consider which way to go next and realized that a bad decision here could see her inescapably lost. All thoughts of cooking in magma were replaced by new imaginings of wandering twisting, barren corridors until she collapsed with a swollen tongue and sunken belly, never to rise again. With a grim frown, she cut off the first swells of panic and moved her torch from left to right in search of any indication of where she should go.

Her gaze settled on a candle on the floor. It was not placed there but appeared to have been dropped. She stepped forward, crouched to prod it with the horn of her ax, and discovered that there was still a point on the wick which gleamed dull red as though just extinguished. A small dribble of cooling wax lay on the floor where it had fallen and it was still soft and pliant.

She reacted with a curious grunt before something pounced on her.

Squatted over the candle as she was, it was a quick trip to the floor as her attacker rode her back down. Despite this, the impact combined with her surprise was enough to knock the torch from her outstretched hand and it rolled across the floor.

In the wild kaleidoscope of red light and shadows, her ambusher lashed out with something sharp and stabbed and hacked at her back, shoulder, and neck. Fortunately, the first two were shod in armor that was proof against the biting point and the latter was saved by her instincts which made her shrug her paulders up to guard the vulnerable flesh.

Ax-Wed drew her arms up to cover her head, suspecting that the attacks would spread, and her forethought saved her with only a nick on the ear before the blade glanced off her armored gloves.

That smarting little cut, though, was enough to break the shock of the initial attack and feeling rather than seeing her attacker, she retaliated.

Sensing the forward heavy stance of her assailant, she bucked upward with her hips and was rewarded when her enemy slewed forward. He clamped down with what must have been his legs like a rider trying to stay on his mount. She used his forward lean and the respite from the stabbing to reach up with her free hand and pull very hard as she curled her body forward. The grip of his legs about her ribs was unequal to her strength and with a high-pitched bark of surprise, he flipped off her back and onto the floor.

He landed with an impact that knocked the breath from his body in a loud wheeze and before he could even begin to recover, she brought the short-hafted ax around to drive the edge down to the exposed throat.

She checked the weapon barely above its intended target when she saw that her attacker was not only not one of the degenerates but also not a he. A slight, almost gaunt girl in an assemblage of rags lay upon the floor and her green eyes glared at Ax-Wed. The Thulian's copper eyes fixed upon that gaze like the storm-tossed waves of the Caged Sea. Fear and fury were mixed to a fever pitch, and she was so bound by their intense stare that she almost missed the knife that was thrust toward her face.

Ax-Wed caught the stabbing hand by the wrist and pinned it to the floor while she held the razor edge of her ax-blade a hairs-breadth from the lass's neck.

"Steady," she said in a low, hard voice.

The girl bared her teeth with a snap and raised her head enough to open a thin cut along her neck.

"Do it!" she hissed with the same maelstrom of terror and rage in her eyes. "End it!"

Long years as a mercenary and surviving so many battlefields willed her hand to descend. There were a hundred reasons to kill her attacker, child or not, but despite experience and reason, she would not and could not.

Not quite sure she wasn't about to get herself killed, she moved the ax-blade from the girl's neck but maintained a firm grasp on the hand holding the knife.

The child watched her every movement with ferocious attention but did not struggle. The fear and anger in her eyes gave way to suspicion and for a few heartbeats, they stared at each other until Ax-Wed held the ax up again.

"I will let go," she said slowly. "Run, and I'll catch you."

The fire in the green eyes returned and this time, anger far outweighed fear.

"Scream or attack me," she continued, "and you won't have to ask me to end it."

The angry light flared but the girl remained silent.

She held her gaze a second longer and let go.

In an instant, the girl's pinched, wiry frame twisted in a catlike motion and landed on all fours but as the warrior woman prepared to pounce, she settled onto her haunches. Another heartbeat passed while they stared at each other and each tried to determine some measure of the other.

They might have sat there in the flickering torch light for some time, studying one another silently, but from somewhere far up the passage, another round of howls fed the awareness of the malign will seeking Ax-Wed.

She half-turned at the sound but was unwilling to take her attention completely off the child. For her diligence, she saw a shiver race through the slender fame that she was willing to bet had nothing to do with the temperature.

"Do you have somewhere to hide?" she asked with one hand still tight around the haft of her ax.

The girl's eyes narrowed into sharp slits but she nodded slowly.

"Is it big enough for two?" she pressed and felt an itch between her shoulder blades as the dark will seemed ready to crawl up her spine from behind.

Again, the child nodded.

"Let's go, then," she said with forced assurance and calm. "And don't forget your candle this time."

The child nodded before she turned and retrieved the candle from the floor.

Ax-Wed waited while the girl rose to her feet and waved a beckoning hand.

"Hurry," the would-be ambusher said and moved like a ghost toward the far wall.

The warrior woman rose, snatched her torch up, and followed.

CHAPTER SEVENTEEN

"So it was a waste of time?" Numi asked from the other side of the screen.

"No, I don't think so," Vahrem said as he and Iyshan set about scrubbing away the cloying perfume of the Silken Nest.

Their clothing had been cast to one side and they'd both sunk into large tubs of almost scalding water which had been prepared upon their request. Their host, Tobarr Beadsman, was an old friend of the merchant's and had been more than willing to accommodate the ruse without asking too many questions, although he wasn't entirely happy about it. Regardless, as was common in those days in the East, he endeavored to see them accommodated in any and every fashion if for nothing else than to maintain his dignity.

And currently, that accommodation was measured by strong soap and a good supply of hot water.

"Explain to me how spending so much time in that whore-house with no one rescued is not a waste of time?" the dwarfess demanded and rapped her jingling staff on the screen hard enough that both men froze. When it did not fall, they cautiously resumed their efforts with scrubbing rag and bristle brush.

"Because they'll make contact with us," Iyshan said as he worked a furious lather over his tan, sinewy arms. "Shepherd spare me, what is this?"

"Anthallia." Vahrem groaned as he worked the bristle brush through the beard on his cheeks until his skin burned. "It's found in the Girdle. You plant patches of it over fresh corpses and it does something to the buds. Then, you press the buds into a syrup that you dry and you sprinkle that resin into a brazier like those they had in the main room."

The other man grunted acknowledgment, then straightened to look at his master.

"Hold on, how do you know that?"

The merchant set the brush aside and plunged his hands into the tub to search blindly.

"I once dealt with a boyar in the Girdle who wanted to pay me in the resin," he explained before finally fishing his wash rag from the soapy depths. "He went into great detail about how valuable it was in some courts if for nothing else than the rarity and effort it took to create the singular scent."

Iyshan nodded and dunked his face into the steaming water. He emerged a moment later, rosy-cheeked and blowing water from his mustache.

"Well, those courts can keep it," he stated in disgust. "It smells like what might happen if sugar cane could pop a squat."

Vahrem began to laugh but as he pressed the rag to his face, he managed to partially snort the wet rough cloth into his nostrils. He tugged the offending fabric away with a splutter and saw the other man's face contorting to prevent a laugh. This naturally had the effect of making the caravan master laugh and in an instant, master and manservant were guffawing together, a wild, relieved expulsion of the combined fear and anxiety that had dominated their recent existence.

Mehk Numi was having none of it.

"You two rascals!" she admonished shrilly and beat upon the

screen until it seemed she would shatter it to kindling. "How do you know they are going to contact you? You never said anything about them promising that."

Even the threat of exposure was not enough to completely quell their amusement but after several snorts, they forced themselves to answer.

"They didn't say so but took the ingot," Iyshan said.

"That merely means they are greedy," the dwarfess argued and stamped her foot. "Not that this scheme is progressing."

"But taking it is a sign that they know what we are asking for and they didn't protest," Vahrem explained. "If they had an inkling of what we intend, they wouldn't have let us leave without at least making an attempt at getting us to take it."

Numi began to pace and her sandaled feet scuffed across the tiled frescos as her staff rapped an anxious beat.

"I still don't like it," she muttered. "How long does that poor girl have to suffer at the hands of those monsters before someone does something?"

"Numi, darling, I know it's hard but we have to be careful," Vahrem told her, his tone sobering. "Being impatient now could ruin any chance of finding her, especially if they panic and try to cover their tracks."

"They have to be on high alert after what happened last night," Iyshan agreed. "Alborz knows this, which is why he wants us to do it this way."

"Well, that's easy for a group of braying, giggling asses like you!" Numi shrieked at the screen. "But some of us have bitter experience with what happens when Jehadim's justice is too slow."

Both men were silent for a moment and the weight of the dwarfess's words seemed to push them deeper in their tubs.

"Ax-Wed is not Nur," Vahrem said at last and the words came out rough but determined. "We will find her and we will make sure this is all set to rights."

The other man grunted his agreement but before anyone could say anything more, the doors to the chamber swung open and the man of the house strode through.

Tobarr Beadman had been a tall and vigorous man in his youth, but with success and its abundant rewards, he'd begun to overflow his natural frame. His oiled, ringleted hair spread over his wide shoulders and his similarly treated beard stretched to rest against his wider belly, and both were festooned with the gem-bright beads of his namesake. The collection of glass jewelry gave a chorus of clicks as he walked to the screen with his silken robe rippling about him.

"Pardon me, wise mother," he muttered as he swept past the dwarfess without a second look. "Vahrem? Are you decent behind there?"

"Not even remotely," the merchant answered and was not in the least surprised when Taborr swept the screen aside.

"A message arrived for you," the glass monger declared and held out a sealed parchment envelope with a flourish. "It seems your little conspiracy is progressing rather rapidly."

"It's not a—" Iyshan began impatiently before Vahrem cut him off with a sharp cough.

"Nice try, Tobarr," the caravan master said with a frown as he took the proffered scroll. "I'm glad you didn't read it first."

"Don't think I didn't consider it." Their host chuckled as he fiddled with one beaded ringlet. "But given how you two returned reeking of Anthallia, I supposed the meddling was too rich for your blood."

"You and me both." Vahrem nodded as he lifted the waxen seal and peered carefully inside. It was more than legend that some criminal elements in Eastern syndicates answered investigations into their business with letters bearing venomous arachnids. While rarely lethal, he was determined to not spend days in bed battling a toxin.

When nothing bounded out to sting him, he released the

breath he hadn't realized he'd been holding. He began to frown as he stared into the envelope and the furrow in his brow only deepened when he realized what he was looking at.

"What is it?" Numi demanded, strode forward, and shouldered past the surprised Tobarr.

"Serpent's sting!" Iyshan swore as he sought to cover himself and sink beneath the water at the same time. The result was mostly a great deal of splashing and the elder dwarf's scornful snort.

"Have no worries on account of my virtue, fishbone," she grunted. "Vahrem, what does it say?"

"I need to see Alborz," he said, his gaze still fixed on the envelope's contents.

Tobarr looked ready to make another attempt to probe but saw the grim lines that had formed in his friend's face and seemed to decide against it.

"I'll have fresh clothes brought up," he said with a raised eyebrow. "Will you need transport or will you take madame dwarf's chariot?"

"Don't be stupid, you tub of guts," Numi roared. "We'll take my chariot. Now get those clothes up here on the double."

The man looked less than impressed but responded with a stiff bow before he turned on his heel and strode out of the room.

"What is it?" Iyshan asked, forgetting his modesty as he leaned halfway out of his tub. "What's in there?"

In answer, the caravan master raised the envelope and tipped its contents slowly into his other hand, careful not to spill it.

A sparkling sediment as fine as sand poured into his palm and formed a small pile. The last of the twinkling grains settled in his hand and he sank into the tub as his brawny shoulders sagged. The other man shook his head and slid into his tub with a groan with both hands over his face.

"I don't understand," the dwarfess said with anger mounting

in her tone. Her sharp gaze darted from one to the other. "Damn you both! What is it?"

Vahrem's cupped hand clenched slowly into a trembling fist and ground gold slipped between his fingers.

"They gave us back our ingot."

CHAPTER EIGHTEEN

The girl could have escaped more than once, she decided when the child immediately displayed her extensive understanding of the area. She scuttled to a wall and with what seemed only a caress between the tiles, opened a panel that allowed access to a narrow tunnel.

Ax-Wed had to bend almost double to enter but once inside, her impromptu guide led her through a web of interconnecting passages. Twice, after a silent pause before what seemed a dead end, they emerged from behind one panel into one of the square chambers, only to scurry to another stone panel where another tunnel access was located.

Such a convoluted journey through a place in which she struggled to move quickly meant she was one fleeing child away from being left utterly lost in the cramped tunnels. The fact that the girl hadn't abandoned her was puzzling, but she chose to take it as a good sign that she might have an ally. Of course, she knew she was taking it on faith that the girl didn't have intentions of leaving her in an even worse location, but the fact that they kept moving provided some assurance.

That combined with the utter absence of the dreadful unseen intelligence and sightless will as it groped after her in the dark was a good reprieve as well. The more time she had to think about everything, the more she had to repress the urge to collapse into a shuddering heap. She possessed a rudimentary understanding of sorcery and thus a crude understanding of the things the mortal races shared existence with and that was enough to chill her to the bone.

To keep herself together, she focused on the physical realities before her. Her back ached and her muscles burned, but that was evidence that she was alive. Following this, she acknowledged that the torch was beginning to burn low but she could still see the girl leading her on, a scuttling collection of ragged cloth. Her ax was still in her hand and her dagger was still on her belt.

The thought of her dagger reminded her of the pain she'd repressed but as soon as she thought of it, the wound in her side demanded attention. She still didn't dare to test her guide by slowing so she secured the ax to her belt as she shuffled forward and slid a hand between the lames of her armor.

When the fingertips of her glove emerged smeared with fresh blood, she heaved a bone-weary sigh.

You should have known it wouldn't hold, she chided herself. *Now you'd better hope it doesn't split any more and you make a real mess.*

If she had enough room to undress and time to rest, she was certain she could tend to it herself, but that felt like asking for a miracle when she was already halfway to the hells. Did she honestly think they would find a cozy corner where she could strip down and tend to her wounds in peace and quiet?

In silence but with flagging strength and fraying nerves, she continued in the dark, followed the girl, and checked her side every so often. The wound seemed to only bleed a trickle but it was steady and besides that, her muscles and joints paid for the contorted journey she was taking. As the time wore on, she soon found she could no longer embrace the pain as a distraction from existential gnawings and while she fought to press through it and even to bury it, she understood that she was fighting a losing battle. She began to stumble as her muscles cramped and seized in defiance of the continued abuse and she knew it was only a matter of time before she fell.

And if they continued, she would fall and not get back up.

Whether her guide sensed this or not, Ax-Wed didn't know, but when she was finally led out of the tunnels she almost cried with relief.

They stepped into a softly lit chamber that she immediately recognized as different than the others. Its walls seemed suffused with a pale blue light and although something about this all seemed familiar, the significance was lost as she immediately set about stretching her tortured body. Mindful of her side, she extended her limbs and unfurled her spine in a slow expansion that left her dizzy but grateful.

"You're not made for tunnels," said a small, almost dainty voice. "There were times I thought I would have to drag you through."

Ax-Wed stared at the girl. Her eyes watered and although it took a minute for them to adjust, she decided that perhaps her guide was not as much of a child as she'd first surmised. The rags hanging on her made it difficult to get a clear view of her silhouette but here and there, hints of a frame on the cusp of womanhood pressed against the tattered layers. Also, the girl's face, while round and dirty, showed a sternness and strength that no child could possess.

"I wasn't sure myself," she admitted. "I'm merely glad I can stand straight."

The corner of the girl's mouth hitched in half a smile and it was only then that she noticed the thin but distinct tracery of fresh scar tissue. In an uninterrupted line that began at her crown and continued down the side of her face and narrowly skirted the corner of her eye and mouth, the scar vanished over the edge of her chin.

A suspicion wormed into her heart and with its germination, a deep anger rose inside her, utterly ignorant of her weariness.

"Where did you get the scar?" she asked bluntly.

The youth's sea-green eyes flashed and she made no attempt to misdirect or confuse her.

"Why does it matter?" she answered. One foot slid behind her as she settled her weight there.

Front foot light, back foot strong, Ax-Wed noted with a hint of respect. *She's ready to run or fight at a turn.*

She held the girl's gaze for a long, trembling moment and her respect for the youth grew when the gaze was met unflinchingly.

While a little brash, this child has some salt in her. Maybe I misjudged her.

Deciding there was only one way to get answers, she settled a hand on the ax head at her belt.

"Did one of those creatures hunting us give it to you?"

The girl's eyes betrayed nothing as she continued to glare in response. "Maybe, maybe not." She sniffed pugnaciously. "Why do you care?"

"Because I know blades," the Thulian said in her flat, almost bored tone. "And I know scars."

The girl threw her another half-smile, but this one was twisted and sneering. "Ha, good for you," she snapped. "I don't see how that means a rat's a—"

"That scar is too straight and too smooth," Ax-Wed explained with a frosty squint. "You don't get that from an accident or fighting. You get it when someone or something has you holding very still and cuts you deep and long and slow."

Something like true terror flared behind the girl's eyes at the words, but the brash hardness that rose to counter it was astonishing in its speed and intensity.

"Am I supposed to be impressed?" she asked in a voice that

seemed too small to contain the venom in her words. "Honestly, are you done showing off or is there another part of this act?"

The Thulian shrugged and hid a wince when she felt a little more blood seep from her wound.

"If those creatures gave you that scar, it means they had you," Ax-Wed said and battled pain, fatigue, and frustration to keep her tone even. "You were helpless and they marked you."

At the word "helpless," the youth's mocking facade was breached for an instant but the terror was soon replaced by the simmering rage she had seen by torchlight when they first met.

"You think you're so clever, huh?" she all but snarled and her lips peeled back in a feral smile. "Is there a point to this or do you simply find the best way to say thank you is to be a real bitch to the person who saved you?"

If I was clever, I would have thought of this earlier, she admitted silently and clenched her jaw for a second as another stab of pain shafted through her side. She needed to tend to her wound without delay but didn't dare to let her guard down yet.

"If they had you like that," she continued and her voice sounded raw even to her. "Why would they let you go? I saw what they did to the others, so why did they spare you? Unless…"

"Unless, what?" The girl scoffed and did her best to act incredibly bored with the conversation but she was too angry to be very convincing.

"Unless you started to work for them," Ax-Wed said with a pitying look at her. "Willing or not, they could be using you as a kind of lure or trap—someone is dumped here who doesn't go down easily and you come along and get them to let their guard down. In return, those creatures let you live."

The youth's eyes narrowed and an incredulous snort issued from the back of her throat.

"Did you even see those gnashers?" she asked. "They're animals. All belly and balls without half a brain between 'em."

"Maybe," she agreed with a nod. "But not whatever leads them. That…Voice from under the hood."

Ax-Wed hated how scared she sounded as she mentioned it, but she saw that the girl wasn't jeering at her. She was too busy looking scared herself.

"Okay," the youth said, her voice on the point of cracking as she licked her lips. "The Voice, yes, but that's not what happened. They didn't give me this."

A dirty finger ran along the scar to emphasize the point.

"If you say so." Ax-Wed grunted and made it clear that she didn't believe her. Another ripple of pain raced across her body and she clenched her jaw and hoped the child didn't see the tremble in her legs.

How much longer until it simply gushes down your side?

"Look, you don't have to believe me," the girl snapped and turned away enough to hide the marred side of her face. "But I'm telling you the truth. I got this before they caught me and pitched me into this place."

Something in the girl's voice—some newfound fragility—nagged at Ax-Wed to reconsider. The Thulian liked to believe that her time as a traveling sell-sword had given her a nose for deceit which, combined with her paranoid-infused childhood, made her difficult to take advantage of. She couldn't dismiss the possibility of deceit but if the child was playing her, it was one of the best performances she'd ever witnessed—and she'd grown up among a people for whom lying was like breathing.

"Convince me," she said quietly and shifted a hand to surreptitiously cover her wounded side.

Silence filled the space between them and she struggled to stay focused. Something hard and frighteningly cold inside her urged her to kill the girl and see to the injury, but she dismissed the thought firmly. It was better to bleed out in this pit than murder a child—even an impudent one—on a suspicion.

Ax-Wed fought to keep her breathing steady although her eyes threatened to lose focus as the girl began to speak.

"Behnam did it," she said and snapped her world into focus. "After Shirein...left, he said he'd been too soft on us and we had to serve more clients and in more ways. Me and Vashthy were the oldest and we tried to stand up to him."

Despite the haze of injuries, the warrior woman understood the words and her righteous anger rallied her strength to attend to the girl's story.

"He killed Vashthy right there—beat her head in against the table," she said. Tears welled in her eyes but refused to fall as her voice deadened. "Then he told the others he would do the same to anyone who didn't hold me down."

A pained breath became a groan, although whether for the girl's tale or her wound, Ax-Wed couldn't have said.

"I tried to fight but there were too many and I've always been small," she said as though explaining the weather. "Then he took a knife from the table—he'd been using it to peel a plum, I think —and did this."

Her finger traced her scar again.

"'They only want you because you're perfect and pure,' he tells them," she said and her voice conveyed a heavy, coarse male tone. "'Now no one wants her and she's merely another mutt in the street.'"

She raised her head and seemed determined to keep her face from being downcast as she spoke around a tightening throat.

"Then he made them strip me and throw me out," she said, her voice brittle and jagged. "The cut had barely started to close when the snatchers caught me one night when I was sleeping on the street."

Ax-Wed nodded and began to rock on unsteady feet.

Did I get more wine without realizing it? Honestly, it wouldn't be the first time I got drunk without knowing it.

The girl looked at her and her eyes narrowed and then widened as she went through several emotions at once.

"Zam's dug!" she swore. "You're hurt!"

Ax-Wed followed the child's gaze groggily and looked down to where her side now glistened with a fresh coat of blood.

That happened fast, she marveled as she sank to one knee.

The girl was at her side instantly and made a valiant if futile effort to support her.

"What can I do?" she asked, her eyes huge and frightened but her voice remarkably calm.

The Thulian's hands settled on her belt and her fingers worked the buckle with automatic efficiency despite their numbness. "Help me...help me get this off," she mumbled as she tossed the belt aside and pawed at her cuirass. "Need...need to...see it."

The effort took several moments and more than once, only a sharp word or a slap from the girl kept her from losing consciousness and pitching forward. Once the cuirass fell to the floor with a slithering rattle, they tugged the arming vest off and finally, the thin, blood-soaked tunic. Now naked from the waist up, she bent and inspected the injury. Something like a red mouth had grown between the ridged muscles of her abdomen. In defiance of her scrutiny, the wound ejected more of her vital fluid as she probed the edges.

"The patch must...eh, must have been flushed out." Ax-Wed panted and her head swung from side to side as she searched for her belt. It was where she'd tossed it, barely out of reach but seeming so very far away.

"Do you need that?" the girl asked as she followed Ax-Wed's gaze. "The belt?"

"The d-dagger and the sssilk ribbon," she slurred as she slid back toward the floor. The stones felt icy on her bare skin but she was beyond caring. She needed to save enough of her strength to try one thing—one last roll of the dice.

Despite her determination, she'd started to fade into the gray that crept along the edges of her vision when she felt something pressed into her hand.

"There's the dagger," the girl said above her, the calm in her voice beginning to crumble. "And there's the silk ribbon."

A sleepy smile pushed at the corners of Ax-Wed's mouth as she began to wind the silk around the dagger.

"Good girl." She sighed and her will railed against the lethargy that threatened to drag her down. "Once I...I do this, I need you to do...do two things because I'll probably p-pass...out."

"What?" the girl asked and a trace of a sob slipped out.

"After the...the incantation, p-pull this out," Ax-Wed instructed and held the dagger up with its silk-wrapped blade. "G-gently, please."

"What?" the child demanded incredulously but when she saw her bleary stare, she nodded quickly. "Very well, and the second thing?"

"T-turn my head t-to one...one side." The Thulian dragged a breath in. "You'll s-see...see why. G-got it?"

The child nodded.

"G-good...good girl," she muttered. "Here goes."

The blade began to descend when the girl's voice rose sharply, shrill and unmistakably young.

"Don't leave me," she pleaded. "Please."

"B-be back...before you know...know it," she assured her as she lowered the dagger so its tip caught on the edge of her wound.

As groggy as she was, she'd thought she was beyond pain but the cruel point proved otherwise. Her muscles tightened with the sudden surge of agony that radiated from the wound but she embraced the pain. Riding the waves of torment that coursed up her nerves, she found the clarity she needed. The words and mental framework of the incantation came into her mind, unnatural traceries ingrained into her psyche.

Her vision cleared and she locked gazes with the girl watching her with huge, tear-filled eyes.

I hope I'm not wrong about you, she thought and drove the dagger in as she let the incantation tear a path from her mouth.

Pain—physical, mental, and even spiritual—ripped through her and her body arched upward as though lightning coursed through her frame.

Lightning would have felt better, she had the time to think before the world vanished into a lightless, numbing void.

CHAPTER NINETEEN

"What exactly are you asking me, *Hazarbed*?" Prince Tarkhind asked, his voice dangerously cold.

Guuhal would have laughed at the role reversal from his conversation the day before had the stakes not been so dire. Instead, he gave the servant who came to refresh the prince's cup a warning look and the experienced retainer responded with the slightest nod of acquiescence. The cup was filled, the carafe left upon the table, and the man vanished.

Besides the two royal guards at the gate to the palatial gardens, the *Hazarbed* and his prince were utterly alone with the horticulture and a bevy of drowsy songbirds.

"It is not my aim to question you or your decisions, my prince," he said and wondered if what he felt was like walking on brittle ice. "But as I seek to do your will, what I don't know can hurt my efforts and thus hinder your plans."

Tarkhind turned his gaze to a copse of trees that were his favorite and his dark gaze roved across the elegant twists and curves of the trunks. The silence stretched, interrupted only by the mostly intermittent birdsong, and the guard commander wondered if he'd been wordlessly dismissed.

His father was no treat but this boy is something else altogether, he thought as his fingers tightened on his staff of office. *And when did he become so old?*

The guard commander's eyes narrowed when he saw the patches of white at the handsome royal's temples and the strands of gray that marred his majestic black mane.

"Who is getting in our way?" the prince asked at last and took a sip without looking away from his trees.

"It is not as simple as that, my prince," Guuhal said quickly and his stomach squirmed at the direction this conversation was taking. "The simple fact is that it is not sustainable. The first round of this new quota and the complications have already started to pile up. We can't keep doing—"

"How long have you served Jehadim?" Tarkhind asked and cut him off abruptly.

The guard commander felt the net underfoot even though he couldn't yet see the cords but he knew there was nothing for him to do but answer.

"Twenty-seven years as a royal guard, my prince," he said. "Twenty-two years under your father and twelve of them as his *Hazarbed*. Five years under you as your *Hazarbed*."

"And before that, you served in my father's armies as a Kushadi lancer, didn't you?"

"Yes, my prince." Guuhal nodded warily. "Only for three years but all of them on campaign or outrider patrols."

Tarkhind held the cup to his lips but did not drink and his breath caused a slight ripple across the hot mint tea.

"Thirty years of service," he said, the cup still perched against his lower lip. "I have difficulty believing you survived this long by not answering a question posed to you by your prince."

He stifled a frustrated growl as he bowed his head.

"My apologies, my prince."

"I want names, Guuhal," his sovereign said and a scowl touched the corners of his mouth. "Not apologies."

The guard commander's teeth ground together as he kept his gaze lowered and wondered how the entire conversation had slid out of his control so quickly. He'd hoped to be able to leverage the disruptions to get the prince to give him more information about what exactly was going on, but it seemed information was only bound to travel in one direction in the court of Prince Tarkhind.

"There are several, my prince, some less deliberately disruptive but all potentially dangerous," he said and decided to attempt a change of tactics. "I didn't wish to entangle you with matters of dignitaries, merchants, royal guards, and criminals when you clearly have much on your plate."

The prince raised an eyebrow as he sipped his tea. Then, with the kind of calm deliberation that made Guuhal increasingly nervous, he placed the cup on the table and turned his gaze upon the *Hazarbed*.

"I admit I'm impressed," the ruler declared in a tone that made it clear he was anything but. "I would never have thought you were the type of man who had the spine to mock his master to his face. Well done, Guuhal, I would never have thought you had it in you."

The guard commander couldn't help recoiling from the accusatory compliment.

"M-mock you?" he said and the incredulity of the situation robbed him of any decorum he'd held onto. "I don't understand."

Tarkhind adjusted the cup on the table by a quarter turn and responded with a smirk which Guuhal would have found infuriating if he wasn't suddenly frightened by the dangerous mood the young prince seemed to be in.

"Oh, don't spoil it now with denial." The ruler of Jehadim sighed wearily. "You see me here sipping tea while I send you scurrying off to do my dirty work. Well, that must be frustrating."

"I do not mock you, my prince," he insisted. "I've served long enough to understand that the burden of rulership is something not easily understood or appreciated by those being ruled."

Tarkhind frowned as he stopped fiddling with his cup and leaned back in his chair with his fingers steepled in front of him. For a moment beyond simple discomfort, he studied the guard commander with his fingers resting against his pursed lips.

"Hmmm, perhaps not," he said at last and his eyes narrowed as he watched Guuhal. "Manipulation then? You get me to commiserate and feel safe so I'll spill everything to you? Then what—you blackmail me or simply turn me over to Hasriim?"

The prince hadn't moved from his seat but Guuhal rocked back as though fleeing a blow.

"My prince, n-no," the *Hazarbed* stammered, his mind reeling as he tried to comprehend the seriousness of the accusations being leveled against him. "I-I only...why would you... You can't possibly believe—"

"You wish to prove your loyalty, then?" Tarkhind asked, his tone still that of a man unimpressed but unperturbed. "Then please stop wasting my time and tell me who is getting in the way of things."

He tightened his hand on his staff until his knuckles whitened and noticed that it had never felt quite so heavy in his hand.

"As you wish, my prince," he said and his head lowered toward his chest. "But I would have you know that these are good people, not—"

"*Hazarbed*," Tarkhind said with a longsuffering breath. "Names."

Guuhal, his stomach and heart almost rebelling in disgust, let the names fall from his mouth like drops of lead.

"*Argbed* Alborz. Vahrem Kal'Stru. A possible Wain Dwarf clan chief connected with Kal'Stru."

The prince nodded slowly and his gaze slid from the beaten guard commander to resume his admiration of the trees.

"What is the problem and how do we know about it?"

The *Hazarbed* took a steadying breath and wished he had something strong to wash the foul taste from his mouth.

"Our associate took someone of significance to the Kal'Stru and the dwarves. They went to the *Argbed* for help, and he seems to have agreed at least in part because he shares in the merchant's deviant religious beliefs. I learned this from an informant I keep in *Argbed*'s command, a guard who was there when Kal'Stru arrived looking for help."

The prince's eyes narrowed as he kept scrutinizing the trees.

"How much have they learned?"

"They know about our associate," the guard commander said. "They made an effort to get him to tip his hand—a soft infiltration ruse, it seems—but he wasn't drawn in. He informed me about it and that is why I came to you, my prince."

Guuhal drew in a shuddering breath and wished he could convince himself that he hadn't sold out good men or that it was out of loyalty and not fear. In time, maybe he would find more convincing arguments but at the moment, he only felt sick and cold.

"I'll need a means of contacting your informant," Tarkhind said after a thoughtful pause. "Please arrange it."

"Yes, my prince," the guard commander nodded and leaned on his staff like an old man.

"That will be all, *Hazarbed*. You are dismissed."

Guuhal opened his mouth, although whether to blather about his innocence or beg for the lives of the men he'd exposed he wasn't sure. In the end, nothing rose from his dry throat and with his head shaking wearily, he closed his mouth and shuffled toward the garden gate.

He would make the necessary arrangements, of course, and then he would find as much liquor as it took to convince himself he wasn't a coward.

That was unworthy of one of the Line.

"Then maybe the Line should have done a better job," Tarkhind grumbled. He sat alone in the garden and nursed the cup of tea. "Or perhaps we should blame you, oh mighty guardian."

The voice that was not a voice responded with a low, sad sigh.

"Either way, I wouldn't be here, feeding that creature in the dark," he continued and tried to stop his hands from shaking when talking about Him. "Maybe I'd even be able to throw off Hasriim's yoke."

Hasriim was the judgment upon your father and his father, the voice intoned like a patient tutor having to repeat instruction for a belligerently disinterested pupil. *You will never escape this doom as long as you continue to make others pay for your choices.*

"What am I supposed to do, eh?" the prince demanded and took comfort in the defiance in his voice, even though he knew the voice was not convinced. "You know what he wants."

I know, the voice said, practically sepulchral in resignation. *And you know there is only one choice in the end.*

He felt the voice seeking to press a vision and a memory into his mind. A huge door opened upon itself and from the widening gap, there streamed a pale light of an unnatural hue. The colored light was not something his mind could accept and as the image entrenched itself, he felt the most brittle parts of him giving way like mooring lines parting with a snap. A manic shriek welled and he shoved the vision from his mind with such force that the cup flew from his hands as he curled forward and his hands grasped his head.

I will not remember what waits down in the dark. That is not my fate.

With a frantic will born of something furious with terror, he forced his brain to recall trivial facts and figures until the image fractured in his memory. Further scattering and seething thoughts formed a dissolving pool to dismiss the troublesome trauma, and he felt the voice give another sigh as it withdrew.

You know that you cannot keep this up much longer, it warned. *Eventually, you will either seek the Door or you will lose everything you are fighting so very desperately to keep.*

"Go away." Tarkhind sobbed and his fingers raked through his graying hair and came away with half a fistful of it. "See, you are killing me!"

The voice's breath fell over his soul and he felt a cooling breeze across his fevered mind. He knew he should have felt grateful for the relief, but he was incapable in that moment.

I will never leave. I will never forsake.

"Because I'm the firstborn of the Line, I know!" he snapped through gritted teeth before his gaze looked upon the graceful willow he loved so much. "I didn't ask for this. I never wanted any of it."

I know you never wanted me, the voice said and there was the tell-tale ruffle of great wings. *But if I had not been with you, think what might have happened when your workers finally breached the chamber? Won't you at least consider this?*

The sound of stone scraping upon metal seemed to sound around him and the blasphemous light pierced through his mind. In an instant, the sun was blotted from the sky and he was plunged below the earth to sit upon his garden seat before the Door. He heard the breath of a hundred thousand demonic pipes calling him to dance.

"No, I won't!" the prince wailed and threw himself from his chair, his hands still wrapped around his head as he beat it against the soft grass of the garden. He had to do something to get the memory out.

"I won't! I won't! I won't!"

The wings beat their silent tattoo but his battle was no longer with the voice. The skin across his brow had begun to break open as he pounded and ground his face against the earth repeatedly

"My prince!"

"I won't!"

There was some commotion beside him and it was not one of those blowing the pipes.

"My prince!"

A hand seized his shoulder and he feared to look into the face of whatever had taken hold of him.

"I won't!"

He tried to tear free from the hand but its grasp was unrelenting.

"My prince, please," the human voice cried and another commotion began at his other side. "Damn it, Gabr, help me before he hurts himself."

"It's poison, mark my words," another human voice declared sagely before a strong hand took hold of his other side. "It was probably slipped into his tea."

"I won't!" Tarkhind roared but the world had already lost its frantic energy. "I won't."

They dragged him—no, carried him—to his chair. He tried to focus and realized that it was his chair in the garden in his palace. The pipes had already begun to fall silent as the night-dark room around the Door crumbled into the sunny world of his garden.

Before his swollen eyes were his favorite willows and their branches drifted lazily in a light breeze.

"Steady now," the first voice soothed and he looked into the face of a royal guard who stood over him. He knew he should know the man's name but in the moment, it didn't seem to matter.

Remembering the other grasp on his opposite arm, he looked into the face of another royal guard he should know.

Shame and anger swept over him like ice water upon his simmering imaginings and he remembered that he was Tarkhind the Prince of Jehadim, Keeper of the Keys to the East. With a snarl, he yanked his arms out of their grip.

"Let go of me," he demanded and made a haphazard attempt to rearrange his clothing and clean the smarting wounds opened across his brow.

"My prince, you are not well," the first guard ventured, the younger and more eager of the two.

"Perhaps it is the heat," the other guard suggested and cast a suspicious glare skyward.

Their innocent and thoughtful ministrations enflamed his anger and shame all the more.

"Return to your posts," he all but snarled as he forced himself to stand and resisted the urge to check that it was springy grass underfoot and not bare stone. "I will not be here much longer."

Both men drew back but they paused before they turned away. Each seemed afraid to speak what they both clearly thought.

"My prince, you are not well," the younger guard repeated. "Perhaps we should seek a physician? I can run and fe—"

"Return to your post," Tarkhind instructed in a cold, imperious tone "Now."

Both royal guards shared a moment of uncomfortable silence but quailed before their liege's fury and moved quickly to the gate.

He stood in the garden, alone again, but he didn't dare to look in any place where shadows might crest and draw his mind to that deep place somewhere beneath his feet.

Instead, he looked skyward to the blueness there and glared until his eyes burned.

Somewhere in a place he would never admit existed, he wished to hear the throb of great feathery wings again.

CHAPTER TWENTY

She was bleeding and it wouldn't stop.

"And it won't stop until you get this right," Mother repeated and an edge of impatience frosted her words. "Now please hurry. We are visiting the Eztali's later and you will need to change."

Her need to change was an understatement.

The deep laceration Mother had opened on her upraised hand had sent rivulets of blood streaming down her arm to stain the wide sleeves of her dress. When she'd clutched the wound, her fingers had naturally been covered, and when her mother swatted the other hand away, she'd unintentionally rested the blood-wetted fingers in her lap and befouled the linen garment even more.

"I hate the Eztali's." She'd groaned as she tried to press the throbbing awareness of the wound from her mind. "Especially cousin Lamachwen. He's never clean and worse, he always stares at me."

Mother snapped and pointed at the scroll open upon the table.

"Get to work before you make more of a mess."

She buried a growl of protest in the back of her throat and

lowered her gaze to the spidery script woven in concentric circles around a central glyph. As she worked around the rings, she recited the words in her head and felt the power building there as an atonal buzzing. She continued through the circles and shifted to tighter assemblies of syllables while the buzzing rose in intensity and frequency until her head ached and her ears rang.

With considerable effort, she ignored the discomfort and took up the silken napkin she would press into the wound.

Like riding the momentum of a flooding river, she felt her mental recitation drawn along with greater speed as the sorcery took on a life of its own. The sigil would be upon her in moments and she knew what would happen.

The sigil, the final expression of the incantation, would tear out of her in a rush of blood and profane energy.

Fearing the force of the unnatural expression that she could already feel coursing through her mind, she tore her eyes away from the scroll. Somewhere between beginning to read and her attempt to break away, she'd forgotten what would happen when she disrupted the energies with such a violent halt.

"You fool!" Mother snarled her irritation as the magic curdled in the air but it was too late.

She screamed as the energies twisted upon themselves within her and threw her to the floor and her chair tumbled back. Her body knotted around itself in spasms so powerful that her joints gave grinding pops. As she thrashed, blood ran freely from her eyes, nose, and ears, while her jaws jerked open with a violent expulsion of bile. Here and there, she saw flashes of sorcerous fire licking off her trembling limbs in eye-stabbing tongues of black, blue, and purple.

Vaguely, she wondered if the magical backlash would be strong enough to kill her and in the back of her mind, she wondered if that was a bad thing.

But despite her wishes, she did not die and moment by

agonizing moment, she felt the energies discharge into the floor and release her from their hold.

"Get up!" Mother ordered, her voice high and cold above her.

The paralyzing spasms eased and she strained to climb to her hands and knees.

"Why do you keep doing this?" The woman groaned but didn't bother to pause for an answer. "Are you determined to shame me with your failures? A Xhulth without sorcery is like a lion with no mane. The others will see your weakness and rip you apart."

"It hurts." She sniffed and failed to keep the tears from beading at the corners of her eyes. "I get scared."

Mother snatched the front of her dress with her steely fingers and drew her nose to nose.

"Life is pain," she stated, her voice like a chorus of serpents. "As the daughter of Xhulth, you can drink that cup or drown in it but by the hells, you will never escape it."

It was that moment, perhaps, when she became determined to prove her wrong.

"What's this now?" Father boomed as he strode into the room, huge and barbarically magnificent in his armor. "My womenfolk at odds?"

Mother threw her on the floor, where she tried to catch herself with her injured hand and another pained scream was dragged out of her.

"Your daughter is being stubborn," the woman declared and one long finger pointed condemningly to her daughter, who sprawled on the floor. "And seems determined to be a coward."

He leaned on his spear and squinted at her as she cowered and cradled her wounded hand in her lap.

"Stubborn, certainly, but coward?" he asked. "That doesn't sound like my little War-Crow."

She looked up and saw him wink and for a second, she stopped shivering.

"Do you want this house to fall around us or do you want to do your duty as her father?" Mother asked with a disgusted snort.

Father frowned and straightened with a low sigh.

"Yes, dear," He grunted and drove his spear through her chest.

It didn't happen this way, she thought in a voice that was not that of the eleven-year-old who kneeled, impaled, upon the vomit and blood-smeared tiles.

"I wish it had," her mother said and looked at her with cold, coppery eyes. "It would have been better this way."

"We would have been spared much," Father agreed, his hand firm upon the haft of the spear. "The House of Xhulth endures what it must but your disgrace was too much."

Her hands, Mother's in miniature, wrapped around the spear haft.

"It's too late to turn back now," she declared in the voice of a grown woman and drew herself up on the spear so it bit deeply into her heart.

Blood, as brilliant as forge flames, spewed from her mouth in an exultant spray.

She awoke with a hacking cough. Her mouth tasted awful and every part of her was aching and cold.

"Janus' scrot!" cried a voice that seemed too small for such language. "You're alive."

Ax-Wed lay on the floor while her mind tried to organize itself after the disorientation and displacement of the dream. She remembered where she was and the events which led to her laying naked from the waist up on the cold stone. When she raised her head to survey her wounded side, the effort proved too much and she let her head sink again.

Yes, she was alive but in that moment, it did not feel like a victory.

The soft rustling of garments intruded and the girl's face—cleaner than she remembered—appeared above her.

"For a while there I wasn't sure," she said, her stormy eyes inscrutable. "I wanted to try to find something to cover you but I was scared you'd wake up and need me."

The taste on Ax-Wed's tongue was gaggingly foul and somehow even that organ seemed swollen and sore, but she forced herself to turn and smile.

"Good girl," she managed to say with a rasp before she coughed again.

Something she hadn't realized was lodged in the back of her throat rose in a jellied mass. With a heave that set her back and made her ribs pop in a crackling chorus, she rolled to one side and let the partially congealed lump of blood slide out of her mouth. It landed on the floor with a wet slap and she grimaced.

Wheezing, Ax-Wed rocked back and let gravity draw her against the stone, where she lay with her eyes half-lidded.

"Don't you go back to sleep," the girl said with equal notes of warning and concern in her voice. "I won't keep playing nurse-maid for someone whose name I don't even know."

The Thulian raised a shaky hand and ran it across her clammy face, although the effort of the gesture was concerningly taxing.

"A nursemaid would have covered me," she said with a shiver and a small smile.

"Live and learn." The girl shrugged. "Now, your name?"

With a pained moan, she folded her arms to cover her breasts and her fingers pressed against the goose-pimpled flesh on her shoulders.

"I'm cold," she observed and turned her half-open gaze on the youth.

"You big baby." The girl snorted and disappeared for a moment.

In her absence, Ax-Wed finally realized that the chamber was lit by a soft blue-toned light, something not unfamiliar to her but nothing like the torches from before. She also noticed that overhead, rather than an expanse of plain stone, designs were carved into the ceiling that were also uncomfortably familiar.

But before she could give them the attention they deserved, the youth appeared with a ratty expanse of dark fabric stretched between her open arms.

"Name?" she said.

"Sadist." She groaned as she tried to think of a way she could get the blanket without unfolding her arms from her shivering body.

"Name?" the youth pressed.

Ax-Wed wondered if she could sweep the girl's legs out from under her and hope she fell on top of her with the blanket between them. Then, she could headbutt the runt in the face and snatch the blanket in her teeth. She was so committed to the idea that she twitched one leg as a test. Her thigh burned and her hips ached with even that small movement.

It wasn't worth the risk. She would have to acquiesce to her tormentor.

"Ax-Wed," she muttered gruffly and glared daggers at the girl.

"What?" her companion asked and her face crinkled with confusion.

"I'm cold." She growled belligerently to emphasize her point.

"What kind of a name is Ax-Wed?" the girl demanded and shook her head slowly.

"It's better than Brat-Bully or Blanket-Torturer," she replied and sniffed disdainfully. "And I'm still cold."

"Fine, fine." the girl sighed with exaggerated patience. "It's nice to meet you Ax-Wed. I'm Zoria."

"I'm still cold," she pointed out and added as an afterthought, "Zoria."

The youth rolled her eyes as she made the eternal noise of adolescent disgust in the back of her throat, but she sank into a crouch to drape the dark expanse of fabric over her erstwhile hostage.

"You are pathetic," she muttered as she tucked it gently around her shivering body. "But I suppose you're better company than my other neighbors."

Ax-Wed chuckled despite her circumstances and was rewarded by another fit of coughing and a mouthful of clotted blood. She wasn't sure how much lined her throat but it was beyond absurd how much she'd already expelled today.

That is if it was still today.

"How long was I out?"

"Time is difficult to tell down here," Zoria said as she settled beside her, careful to avoid the gory lumps. "But if I had to wager a guess, it would be at least a day."

She responded with a low groan. "A day," she repeated and incredulity added a sharp edge to her tone. "You sat and watched me shivering on a cold stone floor for an entire day?"

"I was distraught," the girl protested and her nostrils flared in an adorable expression of indignation. "And it's not like I have some downy bed to lay you on. Where do you think I've been sleeping over the last few months?"

Few months? Ax-Wed's mind reeled at the revelation.

"You've been down here that long?" she asked, unable to keep the awe from her voice. "How?"

"By not being stupid most of the time," Zoria replied and a scowl puckered her features. "That and a few happy accidents have kept me alive in this hellhole."

Months?

The implications were an odd mixture of unsettling and encouraging. Unsettling because it meant she could probably expect the same if she was lucky, but encouraging in that there must be some food and water there. Zoria was quite thin but certainly not emaciated as far as she could tell, so there was a decent chance that food was more than starvation rations but with two of them, it could get complicated.

Besides, she told herself, *I don't plan to be down here for months. I'll meet Morah like the Grimm Handmaiden herself before the week's out while I can still give a good account of myself.*

The dour thought of her falling beneath a ripping, grinding pile of degenerates wasn't the heroic end she'd hoped for, but she didn't plan to creep around the tunnels until her arms wasted away and her back bent. It was better to spend her strength trying to find a way out but if nothing came in a few days, she wasn't sure what she would do.

A thought suddenly struck her and she turned to Zoria with a frown stamped on her face.

"How do you tell time down here?" she asked and the first kernel of hope rose in her mind. If there was some view—maybe a high window or grate that gave a view of the sky—then together, they might have a chance.

The girl lapsed into silence, her expression utterly blank. Staring at her, Ax-Wed had a sneaking suspicion that she shared the expression when she let the ice form around her heart. The armor was coming up and the fortress of mind and soul secured themselves against attack.

"It has to do with the deliveries," she said, her voice flat and almost bored. "Through talking with some of them, I determined that it was six days between each time they dump people into the hole and I've learned to judge the rough spacing of the time to estimate when a day is. I'm getting good enough that I can guess it within the hour of when they'll bring the next people in."

The warrior woman conceded that it made some sense, especially when combined with their meeting.

"That's why you and I ran into each other," she said and nodded. "You knew those creatures would be occupied in another part of this place."

Zoria nodded but said nothing else and her gaze slid downward as if to stare through the floor.

"Why did you stop trying to talk to those who were dropped in?" Ax-Wed asked, having already deduced what had happened to the unfortunates. "I'm not blaming you and only saying it would have been nice to have warning as to what was coming."

The girl shrugged.

"Too dangerous?" she suggested gently as she adjusted her blanket.

Zoria began to nod, paused, and shook her head.

"What then?" she pressed, not sure why she risked alienating the girl with her questions except she felt she needed to get a better understanding of the strange youth.

The girl took several breaths as though gathering herself to speak but each time, she let the breath go with a sigh and the silence stretched between them. After a while, she was about to give up and ask for some water to rinse her throat and mouth when the mechanical, disinterested facade fell and her companion sniffed.

Ax-Wed, whose gaze had wandered to the strangely carved ceiling and walls, returned her focus to the girl and saw more tears brimming there that refused to fall.

"Once I'd learned about the schedule, there was no point," she whispered. "I couldn't save them. Even when I offered to lead some of them into the tunnels to escape, they suspected me and wouldn't come." A short, sharp laugh pushed out of her. "One idiot even thought I was responsible and almost got me killed trying to chase after me."

Zoria's gaze finally met hers and her eyes were like glittering jade through the watery veil.

"Why talk to people who will die screaming a few minutes after you meet them?"

Ax-Wed could see the painful logic of that and she couldn't help but feel part of her heart going out to the girl as she imagined her cowering in the tunnels while she heard the sounds of those creatures descending on their victims. She was lucky she hadn't gone stark raving mad in her months down there from continually hearing the screams mingled with obscene howls, hoots, and grunts.

A shaft of suspicion entered her mind and she studied the girl's vacant, gleaming eyes and began to wonder if the child had truly escaped madness.

"Water…" She coughed and shook Zoria from her absent staring. "Water, child."

The girl blinked rapidly and looked at Ax-Wed with a small but grateful smile on her lips. She nodded and darted away, leaving her to stare at the ceiling.

While she was gone, the Thulian took a moment to force herself onto one elbow and inspected her injury.

She winced at the sight.

Where once there had been a gaping wound, there was now a twisted knot of dark, pulsating flesh. It wasn't that she didn't know the effects of sorcerous healing, but she'd never had to heal a wound this severe before. Like a blistering, malignant tumor, it squatted on her flesh as the obscene cost of the unnatural magic of her people.

As delicately as her trembling hands allowed, she probed along the perimeter of the lump. It clung doggedly along the entire circumference and when she applied a little more pressure when she thought she felt a gap, she was rewarded by a stab of pain. A hissed curse escaped her and for a moment, she could do nothing but freeze propped on one elbow, not daring to move.

"I thought about doing that too," Zoria said as she appeared with a peculiar vessel balanced in her hands. "It swelled inside the wound as soon as I pulled the dagger out and I almost took steel to it on principle."

Ax-Wed thought about covering herself with the blanket

again but she was still scared of moving too much and at the moment, blessed water was so very close.

"Hey," she said, her voice calm but firm. "Is that water for me?"

Zoria's gaze snapped up from the offending growth and looked at the dish in her hands.

"Right, sorry," she muttered absent-mindedly and sank beside Ax-Wed. "It's very cold so not too fast now."

She wasn't joking although the word she might have used would have been icy rather than merely cold. All the same, the Thulian woman's first drink was a long one and she savored the cleansing rush of the liquid sweeping through her blood-crusted mouth. A fresh crop of gooseflesh broke out across her chest and arms but she still enjoyed it as it rolled down her clotted throat.

"Easy now," Zoria warned as she began to draw the vessel back. "Take a breath. It isn't going anywhere."

Ax-Wed might have made a quip about the child's mothering but she was too busy staring longingly at the retreating dish. The water lolled tauntingly in it, almost coy as it sloshed over curling glyphs that rose above the tarnished copper.

Her mournful glance turned into a sudden glare as she realized that she recognized the embossed symbols. Her frailties momentarily forgotten, her hand seized the edge of the receptacle.

"What are you doing?" Zoria demanded as the frigid water slopped and some of it splashed over her legs.

"*Lamt*," the warrior woman said as she bent over the dish and ignored the cold water that lapped at her fingers.

"Have you gone mad?" the girl cried as she made a single, utterly ineffectual tug to retrieve the bowl before she let go. She might as well have tried to pry a crag from a mountain.

"This is *Lamt*," Ax-Wed declared and ran a finger over the spiraling glyph before she traced her finger to another symbol embossed along the outer rim of the dish. "And this... this is *Inax* but inverted, so *Xaneh?*"

If Zoria was being asked she'd have honestly said she didn't have a clue, but the Thulian's furrowed brow assured her the question must be rhetorical. The strange giant of a woman seemed to be lost in her musings, although the child couldn't begin to guess why.

Rising to her knees with a stifled groan Ax-Wed took the vessel in both hands, drained the water in one long gulp, and barely shivered when trickles of chilled water ran down her chin to dapple her breast. Wherever the water fell, a fresh ripple of cold-prickled flesh rose but she didn't even shiver as she held the emptied container before her and her fingers traced the series of symbols.

When she finally spoke, it was in the ancient language of her people, as fierce and musical as jagged chimes in a sea wind.

"*Lamt - Xani - Yjaw - Nyth - Shoth*," she intoned and frowned. "No, that doesn't make any sense."

"I agree," Zoria added irritably, more than a little put out to be so suddenly on the outside looking in as it were. "It doesn't make a damn—"

"Shush," Ax-Wed muttered absently as she began to turn the vessel in her hands.

This did nothing to improve the girl's mood and she practically glared daggers as she folded her arms and waited with a tapping foot.

"*Nyth'Shoth Lamt'Xani Yjawen*," she murmured and the pieces fell into place as the blood drained from her face. "Morah be swift."

Zoria's indignation melted away as she watched dread blanch the warrior woman's features.

"What?" she asked and tried to not sound like a frightened child. "What is it?"

Ax-Wed looked at the bowl as though it was made of scorpions and with unsteady hands, she lowered it to the floor and withdrew her hands as though afraid it might spring after her with a stinging tail or venomous fangs.

"Where did this come from?" she asked, her gaze fixed on it.

The girl looked confused and her gaze darted from the woman to the dish.

"I found it," she said and a defensive edge crept into her voice. "It was simply laying there and—"

"Where?" the Thulian asked and her voice refused to rise even as it impelled the word with dire gravity. Her gaze rose and met Zoria's. "Where did you find it?"

The girl, who'd already seen too much in her young life to be easily frightened, felt fear's numbing, crippling talons trace intimately down her spine.

"Follow me," she said with a rough swallow.

CHAPTER TWENTY-ONE

"I don't like this." Iyshan rumbled disapproval and his long, scarred fingers caressed the hilt of the scimitar at his belt.

Vahrem nodded and decided it was better to not point out that this was at least the fifth time his faithful manservant had made his opinion known. The fact that they now moved armed and accompanied by stout members of the caravan, also armed, was evidence enough that the merchant was suspicious as well.

When the attempted ruse at the Silken Nest had come to nothing, there had been no reason to continue to impose upon Tobbard's hospitality. With sincere thanks and a sincerer hope that he hadn't brought trouble to his friend's door, the company had moved to the stockyard. There, they'd waited for word from Alborz, which had come that evening in the form of one of his men.

"The *Argbed* wants you to come to him at the Tin Quarter barracks," the man had stated brusquely after Vahrem had gone to meet him at the stockyard gate. "I'll conduct you to him."

Before Iyshan had uttered his first misgivings, the merchant had sensed something afoot.

"The Tin Quarter, you said?"

The royal guard nodded, his entire demeanor stiff and sour.

"Not the Citadel?" he had clarified.

"Your friend was taken close to here, wasn't she?" the guard had said and his eyes narrowed to accusing slits. "It makes sense to work with the nearest barracks."

A lifetime of reading men told him that although this man was most certainly from Alborz's command—his face was certainly familiar—he had no intention to go with the guard right then.

"Thank you for the prompt delivery of the message," he had said with an easy smile. "I have a few business matters to finish but I will be there shortly."

The guard had scowled and his hand tightened around the metal-banded rod he bore like a walking stick.

"You're supposed to come with me," he'd replied in a flinty tone.

"I appreciate that but my business ensures that I can pay hefty sums to the prince. Besides, I do know the way," Vahrem had answered smoothly.

The man had left but not without another scowl.

The streets of the Tin Quarter were atypically quiet but that in and of itself wasn't particularly suspicious given the abductions sweeping the quarter. It had at least become apparent that whatever stalked the alleys of Jehadim's poorest quarter preferred its victims isolated, so most sane souls were cloistered in their homes with the doors barred.

"It's almost unrecognizable," commented Asa, a Wain Dwarf who'd volunteered to come with Durra, who had insisted on being present. "The Tin's not the hub of entertainment like the Copper but I've never heard her this quiet."

Vahrem had to agree, but he wasn't sure if he appreciated the stillness and barren streets or not. If something foul was about to happen, he was glad he didn't have to discern foe from bystanders in a crowded street. Still, a street empty of witnesses meant ambushers had no reason to not come in force.

"Stay sharp and stay together," he instructed, one hand curled around the pommel of his whip. "We have only a short way to go."

As it soon proved, it wasn't short enough.

They'd intended to cut as direct a path across the quarter to the barracks without taking any alleys that would leave them bottlenecked. Strolling down a narrow corridor was a good way for them to be picked off by attackers on roofs while men on the ground blocked the exits with wagons or their bodies.

Understanding this, Iyshan and Vahrem had planned to take Drop Street as far as Rakers Avenue and then follow said avenue to the fork where they'd pass through the Handy Market, a wide plaza where the homeless of the city sometimes gathered. There were usually no more than a few small knots of indigents and the occasional roving pack of thieves but given the numbers and arms of the group, they'd trusted that no one would give them trouble.

When they reached the fork where Rakers became Bone and Bite streets, they discovered that they'd underestimated the fear that gripped the quarter.

"Serpent's Sting," Iyshan swore and grasped the hilt of his sword hard enough to make it rattle in its scabbard. Vahrem nodded as he stared wide-eyed at the spectacle before him.

Handy Market was filled to bursting with bedraggled figures huddled together. It seemed every poor and wayward soul in all the city had come to this place in hopes of avoiding the specter that preyed on the lonely and lost. Some hunkered down around crude fires that blackened the worn paving stones of the plaza, while others grouped together in crude rows of sleeping figures. They were a squalid, stinking, sniffling, shuffling herd of humanity but at the very least, for tonight, none of them were alone.

"Where did they all come from?" Durra muttered as he blinked like a dawn-struck owl.

"From every gutter and every back alley," pronounced a deep, soulful voice. "Out from under every bridge and forsaken doorway."

The company from the stockyard jumped and almost drew their weapons as a single figure approached them with a small lantern. The bearer of the small beacon of light was short and dressed in dark, drooping robes whose wide neck pooled around a bald, tattooed head.

"Peace, my children," the man reassured them and raised the light to show his wizened, ink-engraved face. "It is only your good father wishing you welcome and bidding you come as friends."

"I know no father but the Shepherd," Iyshan retorted and settled his scimitar into its sheath. "I need no father but the Shepherd."

The man, clearly a priest of Myrnatt, extended his lantern, which was the gleaming crystal pendant of his office and shined with alchemical light.

"What was that, my child?" he asked and bemusement put a quaver in his potent baritone. "I could not hear you. Do you wish to take your rest amongst this poor congregation? It shall be close quarters but all children of Myrnatt are welcome."

"Thank you, gentle priest," Vahrem said and stepped forward to draw the priest's attention. "We do indeed come as friends but we don't come to rest. We've been summoned to the guard barracks and simply wish to reach our destination quickly. Is there perhaps a path through this…eh, congregation?"

The Myrnattian's deep frown mingled the shadows on his deeply creased face with the dark ink on his skin to create a bewildering and almost ghoulish mask.

"The plaza is thick with those poor children seeking rest," he declared with a doleful shake of his head. "I would not have you disturb them as our shrine has promised to watch over them. Even if I should allow it, you would be hard-pressed to pass through without upsetting them. You would be better served to travel up Bite Street and turn south when you reach Darning."

Asa swore softly and Vahrem sympathized with the short-legged fellow, although he'd expected as much.

"Thank you, kind priest," he said with a nod that wasn't quite a bow. "We'll trouble you no more this night and wish you safety until the dawn."

The company turned to go when the priest advanced another step.

"A blessing from your father before you go, my children," he called after them and the crystal pendant swung in his upraised hand. "For Myrnatt's blessing and guidance tonight."

Iyshan and the other two men from the caravan shuffled back as though the old man had offered them a viper. The two dwarves shared a look and Durra shrugged, which triggered a stifled giggle from Asa.

"Sadly, our errand calls," Vahrem said and turned away again. "Farwell."

"No child is so busy that he has no time for a father's blessing," the priest pressed, his voice softly chiding. "It will take but a moment."

The merchant gritted his teeth and sighed as he shook his head.

"We mean no insult but the men among us are of the Flock and the dwarves follow His Speaker," he explained as quickly as he could without seeming rude. "Such things as you offer are forbidden to us and wasted on the dwarves. We hope you understand."

For second things seemed to rest upon the edge of a knife. Technically, the followers of the Shepherd were recognized both under the laws Jehadim and the Imperial Dictates of the Hasri-iman Dynasty, but none of those of the Flock were under any illusions. One perceived indiscretion against the established sects—especially the favored Myrnattians—could be all it took to raise the accusations and vigilantism of the mob from a shallow and unquiet grave.

Vahrem thought about commanding the company to simply run as he watched the old priest's face in the moonlight, but a vision of the masses behind the priest in pursuit with blood hymns upon their lips made him wait. He'd hate to rob any assassins of their fee by being run down by an angry mob. Maybe once the mob flayed him alive—as was the tradition for "shearing the sheeple"—the assassins could recoup their losses by putting him out of his misery.

The priest's face assumed the ghastly contemplative facade again but when he spoke, it was in a slow, rueful tone.

"Very well, my children. Go," he said and swept one hand before him three times as was the custom for dismissing unwelcome spirits. "I shall pray Myrnatt shows you his bounties and leads you from this path you've chosen."

"You don't choose the Shepherd." Iyshan snorted with an outthrust chin. "He chooses you."

"Thank you for the consideration," Vahrem said with another slight nod and a warning look at his manservant. "We're headed to the barracks now."

The priest walked away and shook his head slowly.

Iyshan sniffed and set off at his master's side, his face etched with disapproval.

"I don't like this."

The caravan master paused long enough to fix him with a burning scowl before he moved forward without comment. The man wilted a little but marched along in silence. The other members of the company seemed to be of similar mind and they settled into a silent and determined trudge up Bite Street.

They might have continued like that to the barracks had the

attack not come two blocks from the intersection of Bite and Darning.

Four men emerged from an alley brandishing meat hooks, cleavers, and mallets, the gory implements of the meat workers' trade. They wore greasy aprons and, to hide their faces, stitched leather masks in which crude holes for mouth and eyes had been cut. Oddly, their flesh appeared to have been smeared with some concealing, congealing pigment so the color of their skin seemed to be unnatural and indistinct hues.

They appeared both grisly and hungry as they prowled forward with weapons that gleamed in the moonlight.

"Vahrem Kal'Stru," the leader said and leveled a flensing knife so long it was practically a sword. "You owe the meat market."

Iyshan's scimitar, a fine blade of Carnyxian steel, slid free and flashed a moonlit warning.

"My master has never done business with you butchers," the manservant declared and stepped to the merchant's side. "Leave now while you can still do so."

The rest of the company drew their arms, none as fine as Iyshan's blade but all of them weapons of war, be it horseman's ax or Wain lance. Only Vahrem, his eyes fierce but his countenance unmoved, kept his blade and whip at his belt.

"I have no quarrel with you," he declared and stood his ground with his hands on his hips. "But if your guild has a claim against me, have them bring it before the magistrate or even the prince. I will pay you then. There is no need for this."

The butchers pantomimed laughter as they gnashed their teeth in a series of dull clacks. In response, a chorus of whoops and jeers rose behind the company. They turned and saw another four men, similarly armed and dressed, exit the alley behind them.

"Form a circle!" Vahrem ordered and armed himself with both his long-bladed knife and his whip in an instant.

Hemmed in on all sides, the company formed a rough circle.

Their gazes darted from one group of the encroaching foe to the other but their hands were kept steady by their leader's steady, booming voice.

"Stay together and watch the man to your left," he instructed and rolled the woven length of the whip out in front of him. "Feet set, eyes up, and into the Shepherd's rest we go."

The whip cracked once, a peal of thunder in the city street.

"Get 'em!" yelled one of the butchers and like a pack of wolves, they began their advance.

CHAPTER TWENTY-TWO

Despite the hot sweat caused by her shuffling trek and the covering which clung to her, she stood before the shadowy chamber and shivered so badly her limbs trembled and her teeth chattered.

"We are a blight," Ax-Wed moaned as her gaze swept over the shadowy bas reliefs carved into the walls. "A cancer."

Zoria stood a few steps away from the quaking giant, her cherubic features crinkled into a fearful frown.

"You did this?" the girl asked, unsure if she should move a little closer to the doorway into the chamber. "Or you know them, at least?"

Despite her apparent horror, the Thulian staggered into the room. She gathered her ragged shawl in one hand and extended the other to trace her fingers across a polished column. Where they touched, ripples of thin, azure light gleamed within the stone and the illumination seemed to defy the otherwise opaque appearance. The growing rings of light spread up and down the pillar but didn't stop when they reached the floor and instead, continued to dance across it.

Here and there, the ripples found veins within the stone and after they had spiraled around these twisted cords, more light came.

"What are you doing?" Zoria demanded as she retreated to the doorway and squinted against the sudden illumination.

Ax-Wed did not speak but with her head bowed, she rested her hand on the stone until the ripples had spread through the whole room. The awakened brilliance made it seem as though they stood in the world above under the light of a pale morning.

The ceiling remained a dark, stony sky but all else was revealed in that false daylight. Both stood silent in dreadful awe.

Upon the walls, the bas reliefs depicted scenes of horrible historic accounts. At the direction of some vast enthroned figure worked in black basalt, warriors wrought in white marble set off across oceans to lands of terrified, shrunken people, now depicted in gray granite. There was no depiction of battles waged between the marble warriors and the granite pygmies, only the images of the bodies of men, women, and children being hewn and fed to carrion crows of gleaming basalt. Upon piles of broken granite bones, the marble warriors raised an edifice of marble—possibly a tower or perhaps a temple. This cyclopean structure dominated the far wall, its gates spread wide to expose a yawning disk of black stone as large as a man.

This stygian circle loomed large in the eyes of both women, as terrible as a lightless sun yet for vastly different reasons. For Zoria, it was the crowning horror of a vast and inscrutable honorific to a heathen history but for Ax-Wed, it was far worse.

"Atlacothix," the Thulian muttered as she shuffled toward the black disk set in the wall. "Now it all makes sense."

The air stirred and like an echo from a deep well, a whisper of the presence that moved among the degenerates drifted around them.

She stood before the night-dark circle with one hand outstretched.

"Don't touch it!" Zoria cried and took a step into the chamber but refused to release her hold on the doorway. The poor girl didn't know exactly why she'd cried out, but the longer she spent in the presence of what seemed terrifyingly like a black eye, the more she feared it was staring back.

Ax-Wed paused and looked stiffly over her shoulder.

"It's only a stone, girl," she said before she rested her hand against the smooth, dark surface. "Evil with memory but harmless."

When the Thulian was not devoured by the night-black edifice and was able to draw her hand away, Zoria finally found the will to draw a breath. She shuffled another few steps into the room and squinted against a brightness she had not seen for months.

At the base of the pillar where she'd found the bowl, she noticed a small pile of what she'd assumed were discarded dishes and eating utensils. She hadn't been wrong about the bowls—many were akin to the one she'd used to fetch water and others that were more elaborately decorated—but what she'd taken for cutlery she now realized were items she was certain no sane person would ever want to put near their mouth. Knives with their edges set with obsidian barbs and forks whose tines ended in cruel, jagged hooks were merely the ones she could recognize in an assortment of tools both bizarre and menacing.

"What is this place?" she asked and her voice sounded loud and breathless, even in her ears.

Ax-Wed turned toward her, silhouetted against the utter dark of the black disk.

"This is a Chamber of Dedication," the Thulian said and her shoulders sagged as she spoke. "Or at least what is left of it."

The girl shook her head and retreated a step.

"That doesn't explain anything," she pointed out and trembling anger crept into her voice. "You need to tell me the whole of it."

The warrior woman looked over her shoulder and drew in a

sharp breath as she did so. Despite that, her companion noticed that she was already moving more easily. Her body had lost some of its stiffness and replaced it with a fluid strength. Given the strange look in her copper eyes, the girl would not have said such a development was not comforting.

"What do you know of Thule?" Ax-Wed asked.

Zoria shrugged and shook her head and looked even younger with the gesture.

"Some haunted place in the Caged Sea," she replied. "Most of it sank when the demons that lived there angered one or more of the gods. It's as made-up or long gone as the sky-castles of Zahnd and Nanujin's Caves of Wonder—the kind of stories I'd tell the little ones at night when Benham wasn't around."

The Thulian smirked, an expression completely bereft of humor.

"If only." She grunted and pointed to the wall where the marble warriors stood before the giant worked in black stone.

"That tells of how the One-Eyed King sent out the warriors of Thule," she explained and her finger traced the panels of graven stone. "They ranged the world over, gathered slaves and sacrifices, and built Gatehouses which were the foothold of the Empire."

The hair on the back of Zoria's neck prickled. She knew the words used meant far more than the simple assembly of syllables implied, but she had no desire to be stripped of her ignorance.

"When the Empire fell, those strongholds that were still intact were supposed to shatter their Gatehouses and return to Thule," Ax-Wed continued and nodded toward the black disk. "But it seems something went wrong. Atlacothix," she muttered and paused when the stirred whispers rose again at the word. "Very wrong."

The girl's gaze swept left and right but there was nothing but the evil room and its masterful commemorations of atrocity.

"Please stop saying that," she snapped as she wrapped her arms around herself. "And why do you keep saying it anyway?"

The warrior woman shook her head and a sad smile spread across her face.

"I keep hoping I'm wrong," she said as she moved toward the door. "I need to get ready."

Zoria gave her a wide berth as she moved out of the room and her horror-hardened gaze scrutinized the woman.

She was bowed as though bearing something heavy on her powerful shoulders. Despite this, she already seemed to move as she had before she'd collapsed from her injury. Whether this was a function of sorcery or the superhuman nature of her people remained unclear but the rate of recovery from such an injury was uncanny.

Was there no end to the wonders and terrors this woman could introduce to her already strange world?

As Ax-Wed stepped through the doorway, the chamber began to darken and the light passed through all the stages of the world above with dizzying speed. Morning brightened to noon and burned to an afternoon that smoldered into dusk before sinking into the night. Only as darkness descended could Zoria see the glimmering veins within the stone like bolts of lightning frozen there.

They faded in the next moment and the room looked as it had before—a darkened chamber with a collection of items piled at the base of a central pillar.

Unfortunately, it seemed that nothing in the world could make her unsee the black eye staring at her from across the room. Even as she crept to the doorway, she felt its awareness of her. Never in her wretched life had she ever felt so small and so naked.

Say it.

She clawed at the stone doorframe until her fingers remembered they were flesh and the skin broke and her nails splintered.

Say it

It willed her to speak its name.

"No," she whispered, her gaze fixed upon the sentinel eye.

Say it.

"No!" she shouted savagely as she tore herself away from the portal and raced after Ax-Wed.

Her mind told her that all she heard was the sound of her footsteps but deeper within, she knew she heard laughter behind her.

It was a long while before either of them spoke and in that time, Ax-Wed began to make her preparations.

She tore a strip from her blood-stiffened undershirt and bound the fleshy bulb tethered to her former wound. With grim resolution, she tightened the binding until her eyes watered and her breath came in low rasps, but the pain subsided when numbing atrophy set in.

This done, she examined her arms and armor. The latter was in good condition aside from the puncture from Masheed's treachery and some superficial damage sustained during the battle with the degenerates. Her ax and dagger were in good order although some of her blood crusted where blade and guard met, but she would worry about picking that out later.

Carefully, she checked the edge of her ax and as always, drew a bead of blood as she ran her thumb along the edge of Thulian sylver.

"So what are we getting ready for?" Zoria said at last, not yet ready to raise her head from where it had sunk onto her knees.

Ax-Wed sucked her thumb for a second before she turned to raise an eyebrow at the girl.

"We?"

The girl's head rose and her gaze met the warrior woman's fiercely.

"What are *we* getting ready for?"

She smirked but gave no answer as she inspected the gore-crusted remains of her shirt. Her brow furrowed in dubious examination as she shook her head slowly.

"I suppose you could go bare-breasted into battle," Zoria suggested and her eyes brightened with a mischievous light. "In fact, I think I heard one of the girls read a story about wild Thulian sisters riding naked into battle."

"Tothian." She grunted as she rubbed the garments between her hands to loosen the worst of the stiffness in a flurry of red motes.

"What?" Zoria asked and watched the drifting crimson cloud in morbid fascination.

"Tothian Sisters," Ax-Wed said and held the shirt up for inspection. "Not Thulian."

"Oh." The girl sniffed, unperturbed by the correction. "I remember they were great warriors, so I simply assumed—"

"Do you remember how their story goes?" the warrior woman asked.

The youth paused for a moment and her face scrunched as she tried to recall the few nights of peace when they did not entertain clients and weren't drugged into a stupor. These were a few bright points in a long litany of darkness but their light was ephemeral and almost dreamlike and as such, of little use for historical recollection.

"No." She sighed and shook her head.

"Dead to the last brazen hussy," Ax-Wed said with a snort that was almost a laugh. "It turns out armor helps."

Zoria, for reasons she didn't understand, scowled in indignation.

"They fought bravely," she protested and although she

wracked her brain, she found nothing of use in her impromptu defense.

"And they died bravely, too," the Thulian said as she slid the red-stained shirt on. "Not for me."

"Don't you plan on dying bravely?" Zoria smirked.

"Not yet," she muttered as she lifted the bottom of her shirt and looked at her garroted polyp. "Not today."

Before the girl could respond, the warrior woman grasped the blackening lump and gave it a sharp twist. With a sound like tearing parchment, the bulb of decaying meat came free. She swore fiercely but held the trophy of her conquest up triumphantly. Thickening fluid too dark to be blood dribbled weakly from the lump in her hand, while her side revealed pink-toned new skin where the tumor had been.

"That's disgusting." Zoria gagged, unable to shift her gaze from the gory chunk. "Couldn't you have warned me?"

Ax-Wed smiled at her prize and tossed it over her shoulder.

"Hey!" the girl cried. "You can't throw your...your...whatever those are around here. I have to live here, you know."

She chuckled and heaved her armor into place.

"If we are a *we*..." The warrior woman sighed as the comforting weight settled over her. "Then you won't live here much longer."

The words struck Zoria like a lightning bolt and her entire body went rigid as she turned wide eyes on her.

"What do you mean?" she asked.

"We'll make a way out of here," she stated as she rose and buckled her belt on, the settled one hand on the sylver head of her weapon. "Or die bravely."

The girl stared but didn't dare to foster that most dangerous of fires—hope.

"But first, we see about provisions," Ax-Wed said as her stomach rumbled. "Even an army of two marches on its stomach."

CHAPTER TWENTY-THREE

One butcher staggered back with a bubbling shriek and raised his hands to the riven remains of his face.

"Stay together!" Vahrem bellowed a moment before the whip cracked again and the braided length peeled skin and meat from a bare arm.

One of the flesh mongers ducked and rushed under the retreating whip, his cleaver raised for a hewing stroke. Iyshan's scimitar cut air and flesh with equal ease and the man crumpled without even a scream.

"Come on!" the manservant snarled and scattered blood with a liquid flourish of his blade. "The Serpent's Coils always have more room. Who else wants to go?"

The assembly of masked thugs wavered for a moment and studied their dead and maimed members. The merchant sensed their weakness and rose from his fighting crouch enough that he could meet the eyes of several men before him.

"I don't know who is paying you," he said, his voice firm but without anger. "But you can't spend silver when you're dead and even gold loses its luster without a hand to hold it or eyes to see it." He nodded to the dead man and the two who shuffled and moaned over their wounds. "Leave now," the caravan master said with absolute authority. "Leave now and we all go about our ways."

The air trembled with the tension.

After an uncomfortable silence, the man with the maimed arm turned to flee and left his flensing blade on the street. His fellows watched his retreat and appeared to be on the edge of fleeing alongside him. As he passed the last man, however—a huge brute with a wiry black beard jutting from under his hood —the tension ruptured. The colossus, with a meat hook in one hand and a hatchet in the other, snared the fleeing man with the hook and threw him down. Still cradling his whip-flayed arm, the injured man tried to shield himself but the hatchet swung in a rush. He begged, then he shrieked, and finally, he was silent.

The bearded giant rose from his work spattered with blood and glared at the men around him. Dark eyes blazed within his hood. He lifted the bloody hatchet and pointed at Vahrem.

"Kill them all!" he commanded in a guttural bellow.

The battle in the street began in earnest.

With the numbers still to their advantage, the flesh mongers attacked in a rush and swung their chopping and slicing implements in wide and heavy arcs. The company from the caravan beat them back. The few injuries among them were only superficial but in avoiding the hewing, tearing strokes, the defensive ring was broken. The defenders were forced back-to-back with the man or dwarf beside them.

"I told you I had a bad feeling about this," Iyshan shouted over his shoulder as his scimitar drove back three of the enemy. The wiry man's curved blade licked across a butcher's knee when he tried to race inside the longer weapon's guard. He collapsed with a cry and his hand clutched his bloodied leg.

His fellows seemed less inclined to follow in their comrades' footsteps.

"Thank you for reminding me." Vahrem grunted as he

reversed his grasp on the stout whip handle to catch a meat hook that plunged toward his face. "I'd almost forgotten."

The man who'd attacked him snarled, his teeth bared like a wild beast as he fought to drive the hook into him. The merchant pivoted on his heel and let the man tumble forward before the sword in his other hand—a thrusting blade that might have almost been an enlarged knife—drove through his foe's ribs.

With no further resistance, the butcher fell free of the blade and painted the street with a series of gasping coughs.

To the left, Asa and Durra warded attackers away with both point and bill of their Wain lances. The former seemed in his element and bellowed wild, braying taunts as the iron tip of his weapon menaced any who came near. Although the younger dwarf was less confident, his grip was firm and his face set as he forced their adversaries to scuttle back from the sweep and thrust of his lance.

When he glanced to the right, the caravan master noticed that the two men he'd brought besides Iyshan were not faring so well. The younger of the two, a fit and handsome man named Siava, had sustained a cut across his brow in the initial attack and he struggled to keep his attackers at bay as blood ran freely over one eye. The elder, a gnarled old scrapper called Heydr, fought like a lion at bay to make up for his flagging comrade, but with each stroke of his red-streaming ax, he gave a little more ground. The blood on him was not only from his enemies, and an injury across one shoulder bled freely.

Striding toward them like an executioner toward the block was the black-bearded giant.

"We need to go right," Vahrem called as he snapped the whip to dissuade another two attackers from their efforts.

"When?" Iyshan shouted and parried a swing before he riposted through the throat of another encroacher.

"Now!" the caravan master roared.

Like a sirocco of steel and braided hide, they spun across the street and scattered foes in their wake like plumes of desert sand. Despite this, he knew they were not moving fast enough and he worked whip and blade furiously while one eye watched his beleaguered men.

The blood-spattered colossus loomed over Siava and the blood-blinded man swung with his horseman's ax raised over-head. That fact alone saved his life when the hatchet descended through his hand and bit into the ax haft. The young man fell to his knees and clutched his hand, now short two fingers and the better part of his thumb, which lay in his blood next to his ax. He choked back a scream as he looked into the face of the cruelly chuckling giant, his eyes wet with pain but not fear as he faced his end with his head raised.

"I am the Shepherd's," he declared and struggled to rise to his feet. "I know his voice."

The giant kicked him squarely in the chest and he fell heavily.

"Hold still, li'l sheep." His adversary laughed and lifted his hatchet. It gleamed in the moonlight. "I have mutton to make."

Haydr, his ax abandoned in the skull of another flesh monger, launched himself onto the hulk like a rabid dog. Biting, raking, kicking, and punching, he drove the colossus back, first by one step then another. He screamed a primal challenge, his veins bulging and sinews straining under his weathered skin, and drove his larger opponent hard. Such was his fury that he seemed to strike everywhere at once.

The meat hook swung upward and caught the old scrapper in the belly.

He screamed pain and rage that made the air tremble and one hand clutched the cruel metal that bit into his flesh while the other continued to swing at his foe. With a savage twist, the colossus buried the hook deeper and both the scrapper's hands grasped the arm holding the hook. With a vicious roar, the giant pulled upward and Haydr's feet rose off the ground and kicked ineffectually as he was hoisted by the hook in his stomach.

The hatchet rose again but this time, began its plunge without taunt or jeer.

A whip-crack gave answer all the same.

A gory welt bloomed across the giant's hand and the hatchet fell from his grasp.

"Watch over Siava!" Vahrem shouted to Iyshan as he closed on the colossus, who still held Heydr squirming on the meat hook.

His manservant spun to meet another two oncoming butchers and his scimitar lashed out in hungry flashes.

The huge man on whom the merchant was now focused seemed confused as to how suddenly the situation had changed, but the dull bewilderment beneath his mask turned to bestial rage when another snap of braided leather drove the meat hook from his hand. Heydr landed with a scream and the blood-dowsed handle of the hook still jutted from his belly.

"I'll pull you apart!" the colossus roared and ignored his previous victim to advance on this new aggressor, his huge hands curled into claws. "Piece by piece."

The whip answered for its wielder as his foe rushed forward, but the brute took the stinging blow across his shoulder when he lunged at the merchant. Vahrem ducked beneath the wide, grasping sweeps and cracked the pommel across the brute's face as he tried to bring his sword to bear.

A roar like that of an enraged bull issued from the butcher and a massive fist knocked the blade from Vahrem's grasp while the other arm snaked around his neck when he tried to dive away. A limb thick with huge blocks of muscle clamped on the merchant's throat and the pressure made him think his head might burst. The titanic crushing force was such that when the bloodied fist arced into his face, he barely noticed. His eyes watered and his nose gave a series of gristly pops, but it all seemed distant.

"I'll stove your head in, runt!" the giant bellowed although, if the truth be told, this latest threat was wasted on the caravan master, who could hear nothing over the grind of his spine and his gagging breath.

Years of hard-earned experience and numerous times in this kind of situation served him well. He tensed his wide shoulders and drove his weight into the throttling headlock. Sweat and blood slicked his head and face but these aided him to slide free and his adversary staggered forward. Before the giant could turn, he leapt onto his back and with an expert flourish, wound the whip coils around his neck.

His enemy roared and one hand clawed at the braided leather that cut into his bullish neck while the other swatted and swung vainly to try to catch hold of his tormentor. Vahrem swung on the man's back with each attempt and strained to retain his hold on both ends of the whip and to keep it taut.

Close to despair and desperation, the butcher threw himself on the ground, hoping to dislodge his strangler on the hard stone. The merchant felt as much as heard his bones pop as he was crushed between the huge man and the unyielding street and for a moment, the world seemed all soft sounds and bright lights.

Still, his grip held firm and when the big man rolled, he rode his back as though breaking in a new stallion.

The giant's attempts grew weaker and while his thrashing flagged, Vahrem had time to locate his short sword, which fortuitously lay within reach. He took both ends of the braid in one raw hand, leaned back, and tried to snatch his weapon. His adversary, sensing the end was nigh, summoned the last of his strength against him but the caravan master's fingers found the sword hilt.

After a single thrust through the side of the huge man's head, he tumbled onto the street with a pained groan.

Ignoring his injured hands and the taste of so much blood pouring from his nose, Vahrem staggered to his feet, yanked his sword from the man's skull, and looked around. The fight was over and the bloodied street had suddenly fallen silent.

In the eerie stillness, he swept his gaze over the dead and dying scattered like broken dolls across the street. Most were the butchers but not all.

Siava knelt beside Heydr, a dripping rag pressed to his injured hand. The old scrapper lay motionless. He was still breathing but each labored breath saw a fresh rush of blood join the pool around him. In the moonlight, so much blood looked almost black, a pool of liquid shadow that spread beneath the man.

Iyshan wiped the blood from his scimitar and scowled at his surroundings as though he expected the dead to rise and begin another attack.

"The dwarves?" The merchant choked and spat a gobbet of blood that he hadn't noticed had filled his mouth. That punch must have hit him harder than he thought.

The other man pointed with his chin and he followed the gesture to where Asa limped toward them while Durra braced him under one arm.

"The whoreson dove for my leg." The dwarf chuckled and nodded at his stained trouser leg. "I spitted him but he put one of those hooks through my foot all the same."

"We'll be fine," Durra assured the merchant, his bright eyes practically aflame. "See to your man."

Vahrem nodded and staggered uneasily to where Heydr lay.

The old scrapper's flesh looked almost translucent under the silvery light from on high. One ghostly pale hand rested on Siava's arm and squeezed it with what meager strength he had.

"You did good, boy," the older man said and managed a weak smile. "I saw you defeat more than a few of them."

Tears flowed freely down the young man's face and mingled with the blood that still seeped from his slashed brow.

"I'm s-so sorry," Siava replied, his voice choked as he fought back sobs, but Heydr chided him with a cluck of his tongue.

"None of that now," the old man said and shook his head, the motion uncomfortably limp. When he noticed Vahrem, a new smile crept across the scrapper's weathered features.

"Did you kill the giant, boss?" he asked and his eyes brightened for a second.

"Aye." He nodded as he sank down next to the man. "Although I had some help."

"I was only keepin' him warm for you, boss." Heydr chuckled, then winced and his body went rigid with pain.

"Maybe…" Siava began and his gaze darted frantically from the merchant to the dying man. "We can get him to the barracks still. It's not far and they must have a surgeon or something or even some healing tinctures. We could buy them if…if…"

The young man's voice failed him as he met the sad eyes of both men in turn.

"I'm past that, boy." Heydr nodded and squeezed Siava's arm weakly again. "This hook has torn me up inside and the fall burst something deep…ugh, deep in me."

"Rejoice," Vahrem said as he put a hand on the young man's shoulder. Tears welled in his eyes although his voice held firm. "Tonight, our brother goes to feast with the Shepherd."

"No!" Siava sobbed and twisted out from under the comforting hand. "No, there has to be something we can do!"

"There is," the old man said and his voice hardened as he locked gazes with his young friend. "There is something."

"W-what?" Siava asked and almost quailed before the fierce light in the dying man's eyes.

"Pray the Shepherd's Way over me," Heydr replied and his gaze refused to let the younger man go. "Let me go to his tent hearing a friend speak the Truth over me."

Siava sobbed again, but the old man's hand tightened around his arm.

"Come on," the old scrapper urged with a touch of a smile on his graying face. "Be a man for me only a little longer."

Vahrem rested one bloody hand on Siava's shoulder and the

other on Heydr's head. With a low hum, he began the accompanying tune for the prayer. Iyshan came to stand behind his master and added his wordless drone to the chorus. The young man sniffed and shook his head but when the caravan master nodded, he began to speak. His eyes were closed and his voice trembled but he spoke each word without fail.

"The Shepherd knows his flock and fetches them from field and fen

Although they are blind and walk into the lair of wolf and lion's den.

The Shepherd guards his flock from jackal without and snake within.

His watchful eye is keen, seeing all from beginning to end.

The Shepherd knew what must be done for those he loved and chose

So he walked the valley so black to the House of Seven Woes.

Came he from that place bearing wounds but gifts as well.

The Shepherd knows the cost of love and knows it well

So he calls his flock to follow him on his narrow, winding road.

For he has promised his flock a place, a sheltering abode.

So follow the Shepherd, seeking ever to heed his voice and know his Way,

Seek him while he may be found, to see his face one Great and Glorious day."

As Siava finished, Vahrem and Iyshan hummed the final note and all looked down to where Heydr stared heavenward with the same touch of a smile softening his hard face. The merchant drew the dead man's eyes closed and put an arm around Siava's jerking shoulders as the young man began to weep. Tears rolled freely down the caravan master's cheeks and into his blood-streaked beard.

"Someone's coming," Iyshan said thickly and one hand swiped across his face while the other pointed up the street.

A patrol of guards in the uniform of the Tin Quarter rounded the corner of Bite and Darning with lanterns in one hand and metal-wrapped clubs in the other. The caravan master gave Siava a comforting squeeze and rose shakily to his feet, suddenly very tired and hurting from a dozen bumps, bruises, and scratches he hadn't noticed before. He attempted to straighten his beard but his fingers brushed his nose and he cringed.

He would have to meet them as he was.

"Too little, too late," Siava muttered bitterly where he remained on his knees beside Heydr's body. "The party's already over."

"I don't think they're here for this party." Iyshan hawked and spat in disgust. "Look who's leading them."

Vahrem squinted past the glare of the lanterns and could barely make out the livery of the Gold Quarter royal guards and the sour-faced guard who'd summoned them.

"Do you see who's not with him?" Iyshan grunted.

"Alborz." He sighed and managed to say a quiet prayer for his old friend as he fought the urge to crumple and forgo any attempt to remain on his feet.

"Durra," he said quickly without turning. "You two will be protected from what comes next. They can't risk angering the clans by taking well-connected Wain Dwarves. I need you to get to Numi and find Alborz—if he can still be found."

The guards were closing in at a jog and their formation swept wide to encircle the survivors.

"And if he can't be?" Durra asked.

"Get the caravan out," he instructed and opened his empty hands as the guards closed in. "Get clear of J—"

"Every man here is under arrest," the frowning royal guard declared and motioned those under his command forward. "If you dwarves seek to impede us, you will be taken in as well."

The Tin Quarter guards swept in and rough hands snatched their weapons away and bound each man with leather cords.

Vahrem looked over his shoulder to where Asa and Durra stood to one side, their knuckles turning white as they grasped their Wain lances. He shook his head slightly as his hands were twisted behind his back and wrapped with cruelly tight cords.

"Did you have time to decide what we are being charged with on the way here?" Vahrem asked as he was hauled to join his group by the royal guard. "Or was that not worth the effort?"

For the first time, the man smiled, a cruel, ugly expression on his pinched, mean features. He drove a kick into his groin and the merchant's legs buckled, but the men holding his arms prevented him from sinking to his knees.

Iyshan and Siava snarled and struggled but both earned blows across the face and stomach.

"The charges begin with illegal possession of weapons of war under the Hasriiman Dictates." The guard sneered as he put a toe under Iyshan's scimitar where it lay on the street. "And end with sedition against the Jehadim and plots to overthrow the prince."

The merchant hung his head but knew better than to protest the absurd charges. His only hope was that Alborz was still alive.

"You runts had better claim whatever friends you have in this mess," the royal guard snapped at Asa and Durra. "Come first light, this whole mess is going to the rot pits, and what goes in stays in."

Neither dwarf spoke but their jewel-bright eyes shine with deadly intent under the moonlight. The royal guard spat again but turned away quicker than he needed to.

"Let's get these rebels into the pit," he called. "Move out!"

CHAPTER TWENTY-FOUR

"Eat it," the girl said after she'd swallowed a mouthful of cold arthropod flesh. "It won't get any prettier."

Ax-Wed stared at the ichor that dribbled from the corners of the girl's dainty mouth and then at the many-legged chitinous creature in her hand. It had stopped flailing and clicking its pincers shortly after Zoria had smashed its mandibled head into a pulp against the cavern wall. The child had even been kind enough to demonstrate how to crack the invertebrate's shell along seams in its glossy armor. Now, lobes of grayish flesh veined with traceries of blue and black lay before her and glistened in the dim blue light of a broken column that protruded from the floor.

This chamber seemed to have been an antechamber of the Gatehouse but during its disjunction from it had been thrown on the edge of an underground cavern where water from dripping stalactites pooled and created an alien ecosystem of sorts. Silvery blindfish no longer than a thumbnail darted about between algal blooms. Scuttling between the spongy pseudo-plants of the shallows were dozens or maybe hundreds of the elongated creatures that seemed to have been the girl's only source of food these last months.

Watching the slow, jerky motions of the living creatures as they raked through the blooms for cowering blindfish did nothing to improve the Thulian's appetite.

She had been a finicky eater as a child—one of the few weaknesses her mother tolerated—but since becoming a sell-sword, she'd learned to take food where she could find it.

But this…well, she was not even sure she would call this food.

"Hurry up, princess," her companion teased as she slurped a dangling spool of flesh. "It doesn't taste like much so pop it in and get it over with."

The warrior woman dug her fingers into the gaps in the carapace and tried to not think about the slurping wet pops that came from within the carcass. A few twisting tugs later, she let the forearm-long husk fall to the floor and held the quivering meat at arm's length.

"Oh, come o—"

"One more word," Ax-Wed warned with a growl in the back of her throat. "Only one and I'll shove this into your yapping mouth."

"Promise?" Zoria asked in a sickly-sweet tone.

She swore profusely and in several languages but when she saw that the girl was about to make another snide comment, she snapped her teeth into the cold, quivering flesh.

Her companion hadn't lied, at least. There was hardly any flavor to the mouthful that squelched between her chewing jaws. The flesh slid uncomfortably around her mouth, almost as though retreating from the teeth that burst the gelatinous lobes, but she pushed the thought aside and wolfed another bite. This was fuel for the madness that was about to come. She had nothing else so she would feed the furnace with this unclean flesh and hope her fury would burn it pure.

It took three more bites to eat the rest of the chewy flesh and when she finally came up for air, she heard the smack of a carapace upon stone.

Zoria had fished out two more of the creatures and was beating them on the floor.

"More?" Ax-Wed choked around a clinging chunk in her throat.

"Who knows how long it will take to reach this Gatehouse?" The girl shrugged as she laid the slain arthropods one beside the other. "We may need to eat again."

It was so sound and mature that Ax-Wed was glad for the darkness which hid the flush in her cheeks. She should have thought of that but the prospect of eating more of that unwholesome flesh was getting the better of her.

Fuel for the fire, she told herself as she tried to not look at the way the creatures' clawed legs slowly curled into the corpses.

"It's a good plan," she said and swallowed roughly. "I'm not sure how the Blind Spiral caused this but you're right that we might have to trudge along for a while."

Zoria turned to the water that lapped at the edge of the stone tiles which seemed to have flowed into tidal spirals as though they were sand and not more adamant material. Her small feet slid to the edge of the frigid water and she stood waiting for the ripples of her entrance to subside.

"So I understand," she said softly, her gaze fixed on the creatures teeming in the water. "You think someone messed up while closing this Gatehouse-thing and as a result, it threw the whole structure into the earth and left pieces of itself as it went."

"More or less," Ax-Wed replied as she took her dented helm from her belt and examined it. "I am counting on that, at least."

The girl frowned as the water stilled and the creatures that had retreated from her intrusion began to move slowly toward the edge where several algae tufts drifted.

"And this is possible how?" she asked, her whispering voice unable to hide her obvious consternation. "How does a building simply plunge through dirt and rock? And how can we expect any of it to still be intact?"

The warrior woman moved to the place where the rough stone of the cavern walls breached the twisted stone tiles. A few stalactites dangled low overhead that might fit the bill.

"First, we know some could be intact because we've already seen evidence of that," she explained as she drew her ax and with the raven beaked bill at the back of the head, began to take aim. "Second, a structure can do that when its whole purpose is to contain an entry to the Blind Spiral."

Zoria's hand plunged into the water and emerged with another two of the many-legged arthropods. The creatures clicked their mandibles and pincered toes as they squirmed in confused rage. The girl wasted no time and exited the water to beat the creatures on the floor and even against each other.

"Yes," she said, breathless with a mixture of damp chill and sudden exertion. "Can you stop assuming I know what you are talking about with all this Thulian sorcery? Until an hour or so ago, you were a ghul under the bed."

Ax-Wed swung out and the bill sparked against the stone. She had to dart away as a spear of rock plunged from the fractured stalactite and some of the shrapnel pattered against her armored back.

"What are you doing now?" Zoria asked as she laid her most recent catch alongside the other two she'd snagged.

The Thulian kicked aside some of the jagged chunks of rock before she bent to scoop up a spike of stone. She tapped it twice on the floor before she rose and looked at her companion.

"I'm improvising." She shrugged, slung her ax on her belt, and retrieved her helm. "Do you want to learn about Gatehouses or not?"

"Will I understand anything you are talking about?" Zoria asked and folded her arms over her narrow chest.

"It's unlikely," Ax-Wed muttered and settled on the floor with her helm and the blunt stone spike. "But I don't give up easily."

The girl rolled her eyes but nodded for her to continue as she set about wrapping the "food" in scraps of cloth and binding those rags to a makeshift sling.

"Gatehouses are constructions of both esoteric engineering and alchemy," Ax-Wed explained. "They are designed, placed, and constructed in a series of rituals that makes them conduits."

"Conduits of what?" Zoria asked as she tied a binding in place. "Magic?"

"Not merely any magic. Thulian sorcery." The warrior woman fitted the tip of the rock punch against the unwelcome dent inside her helm. "It is magic bound up in the Kingdom of Cacophony and its adjoining realms."

She clenched her armored hand into a knot of leather and metal and pounded the stone hard. Once, twice, and finally thrice, she struck like a hammer until the helm clunked in protest as the metal flexed outward. She set her impromptu tool aside and held her helm up for examination.

"It's good enough for who it's for," she muttered as she traced a thumb over the crinkled deformities running across the dome.

"What is the Kingdom of Cacophony?" the girl asked after she'd recovered from a reflexive cringe at the ramshackle armor repair. "And what does it have to do with the Gatehouse?"

Ax-Wed paused in preparing to don her helm.

"It is the un-realm," she said after a lengthy pause. "The place where old and powerful and utterly inhuman intelligences are in perpetual competition to subdue and consume. It is a hungry and godless plane of existence."

Zoria could sense that her struggle to speak was not only discomfort with the subject but a struggle to intimate what she meant. It was as though words—or perhaps her grasp of the trade tongue—were insufficient to convey the reality of the fantastical place. If the conversation had taken place before her abduction, she might have disbelieved or dismissed it, but after what she'd seen with the Thulian and horrors in the dark, the girl could only stare in glum silence.

What she would have given to make the world as she had once dreamed it despite the mortal horrors she'd faced so early in her life.

"My people learned to barter with the entities in the Kingdom for power," Ax-Wed said and held the helm in front of her, her copper eyes staring into the empty sockets. "That was how one island and one people subjugated most of the world all those centuries ago. I've read that even novice sorcerers with a few sacrifices at hand could use a Gatehouse to crush armies and break fortified cities but more than that, they could be used in even more powerful ways."

Zoria could hardly imagine what could be more potent than being able to breach a great city like Jehadim. What greater expression of power could there be?

The warrior woman raised her grim gaze from her helm and seemed to read the question in her eyes.

"It was said that the Gatehouses could connect two points in our world through a bridge across the Kingdom," she explained. "The Arcane Warlords of Thule could, within the Gatehouse, see any place, speak to any person, and even will bodies to pass along the bridge. If there was a properly made Gatehouse on the other side, it was said entire armies could pass with minimal…resources."

At first, the girl thought that while this sounded wonderful and frightening, it hardly seemed quite as incredible as consuming an army with sorcery or battering a city. She almost said as much when her companion returned to staring at her helm, dark thoughts of her homeland and people swimming behind her eyes, but then she had a thought.

What could a man like Behnam have done with such power? To see, speak, and reach out and touch any of them in the house no matter where he was or what they were doing. She shuddered as understanding dawned on her in the yawning silence.

Why crush an army or break a city when you could cow any of them with the utter certainty of your threats? Who would dare raise armies knowing that with a word, you could be found or worse, what you hold dearest could be found? What soldier would march to war knowing that no matter how swiftly he moved, his family would be slaughtered before he saw the battlefield?

"How were they ever defeated, then?" the girl asked.

"Time and corruption," Ax-Wed responded as she rearranged the mail aventail on her helm. "Negligence and Treachery."

She looked up from her work, her eyes shining as cold and hard as copper pennies in the queer twilight of the cavern.

"Thule defeated itself," she said, her voice flat and almost reproachful. "We damned ourselves for power, never realizing that the same lust would drag power from our grasp, one finger at a time."

The warrior woman donned her helm, buckled it into place, and let the veil of iron links descend. Rising from the stone floor, she stretched with a soft grunt and turned to regard the girl with her unflinching gaze. Looming over her with only the barest glint of her eyes within the helm's sockets, the Thulian seemed a deathless giant like a revenant titan risen to do battle eternal upon some hellish plane.

"Are you ready to go?" she asked as Zoria stared at her, dumb-struck. The large but faltering woman she'd first encountered was gone and in her place was a force of nature bound to the peculiarities of the female form writ large.

"So will we try to find this Gatehouse?" the girl asked as she drew the sling of dead arthropods over her shoulder. "And use it to escape?"

Ax-Wed nodded.

"But that means going deeper." She didn't bother to make it a question.

It drew a simple nod in response.

"There will be more of the gnashers down there," the girl warned and repressed a shiver. "I've heard them before—what sounded like tunnels full of them. And then there is the Voice and maybe other things too."

The Thulian's hand moved to the head of her ax in answer.

"We don't even know if you can use the Gatehouse," Zoria said and hated how she sounded but she felt as though she might burst if she didn't say anything. "We could sneak and fight and run all the way down there to the bottom of the world and the Gatehouse might be useless rubble."

Ax-Wed stared at her a second past what was comfortable to bear from those deep glinting sockets before she slid her hand to her belt and uncoupled her sheathed dagger. Turning toward the tunnel mouth, she pressed the weapon into the girl's hands.

"You'll need that," she muttered with barely a pause as she marched toward the exit.

Zoria felt her hands tremble and her mouth go dry but the solid weight of the dagger in her hands was a comfort. Her fingers closed around the hilt and she felt a fiery strength rise in her that could beat back the heavy chill of fearful doubt.

She turned to follow her companion and shook her head.

"You don't even know where you're going," she called, thankful to feel the crackle of defiance in her voice again.

"Then hurry and show me before I get too lost," the Thulian called as she was swallowed by the darkness.

CHAPTER TWENTY-FIVE

"I'll pull his guts up through his eye sockets."

Alborz grunted noncommittally as he made the last-minute adjustments to his office. While a fine leader and officer, he was not the most fastidious and as a result, he'd had to tidy things a touch. It might not matter but in his mind, a messy office was counterproductive when it came to intimidating a subordinate.

"I'll put a hex on him that will make him beg for death," *Mehk* Numi continued as she paced while her staff jingled softly with every step. "Caravans will carry stories by campfire from Verenvar to Narlish of what I'll do to him."

The *Argbed* stepped back to assess his office for a moment and nodded in approval.

"Will he beg for death before or after you extract his innards from his skull?" he asked as he moved to settle into his chair.

"This is no joke!" The dwarfess snarled belligerently as she rounded on the man. "Who knows what those faithless whoresons are doing to them?"

For all her thunder, Alborz could see it was fear and not fury that drove the elderly dwarf.

"Well, turnabout is fair play," he said with a grim imitation of a smile. "I have it on good authority from one of those whoresons that our men—at least those who survived the attack—remain unharmed and have even been fed, however meagerly."

That was far from enough to satisfy Numi, who threw a hand up with a dwarfish curse and resumed pacing. The *Argbed* decided that was just as well. He needed her to look angry.

There was a knock at the door and a voice spoke from the other side.

"Naiman Khani is here to see you, *Argbed*."

"Don't forget your part," Alborz said softly before he raised his voice to be heard in the hall beyond. "Enter."

Royal Guard Naiman Khani walked through the door, his face as pinched and sour-looking as ever. As the *Argbed* watched the man enter, at first scowling and then bug-eyed when he noticed the wizened dwarfess glaring at him, he felt a sudden sense of regret. He was not fool enough to believe that all the men under his command were good men—in fact, his faith in the teachings of the Shepherd made that a certainty—but he'd known that Guard Khani was rotten for some time. It was never much and only the little things—the looks, the half-caught remarks in the barracks, and other tiny details had always told the *Argbed* that the man was, even by men's lowly standards, a scoundrel.

And you did nothing about it, he berated himself as the guard stood uneasily before him. *There was always something else more pressing or some other duty more important than plucking the poisoned weed.*

The silence stretched but he continued to stare until Guard Khani practically squirmed before him while Numi seethed, one hand clutching his desk with whitening knuckles.

Should I have thrown him out? Alborz wondered as he steepled his hands in front of him. *Or would there have been a chance if I'd taken him under my wing and given him some attention?*

Khani glanced surreptitiously toward the window that over-looked the Citadel courtyard four stories below. It seemed more and more apparent that he wondered if a dive to the stones below would be preferable to standing before his commander's piercing gaze.

Either way, he was my responsibility and now, he is the reason a brother of the Flock is dead and my friend is in a dungeon.

He drew in a slow, leaden breath and realized too late that he might have been better served sorting his mind rather than his office.

"You were in the Tin Quarter last night when you were supposed to be on duty at the Citadel," the *Argbed* said, his tone cold and uncompromising. "You falsely delivered a message to Vahrem Kal'Stru's camp that I was waiting for him at the Tin Quarter barracks."

Guard Khani's mouth opened to object, but his tongue betrayed him as he continued to stare mutely at his superior.

"You delivered that message to ensure that the caravan master would be in the streets when hired thugs came to kill him," he continued. "When Vahrem and his men fought these attackers you—under the instruction of *Hazarbed* Guuhal—led a troop of Tin Quarter guards to arrest Vahrem and those with him."

"No," Naiman managed to rasp from his dry throat. "No, it—"

"Liar!" Numi shrieked and advanced on the man with her staff clanging like chimes in a whirlwind. "I saw your wretched face when you came and delivered that murderous message."

The guard recoiled and his jaw flapped as he tried to find the words to save himself, but all that emerged was, "No. No. No!"

"There is no question of your part in this," Alborz said and his voice cut through the babble like a flint knife. "The only question that remains is who gets to deal with you."

Naiman's features blanched until his skin seemed waxen over the bunched muscles in his jaw and face that all worked fruitlessly to compose some kind of argument.

"For betraying me and your brothers in arms, I could have you beaten to death in that courtyard," the *Argbed* said with a nod to the window. "You will be stripped, bound, and it will be the duty of every man you serve with to take turns striking you until you are a boneless heap before you are pitched into the charnel heaps."

"No," the guard mouthed and it seemed the power of speech had failed him utterly.

"Or I can hand you over to the Wain Clans." Alborz nodded at Numi. "I understand two of their clan were wounded in the attack and Vahrem's caravan was friends with their clan."

"Not only friends but clan-sworn," the dwarfess declared and glared daggers at the recoiling man. "A death of one of Master Kal'Stru's is a death of our own, and you will wish for something as sweet as being beaten to death by the time we are through with you."

The way her eyes gleamed with a terrible light, Naiman was not the only one in the room convinced of the elder dwarf's threat.

"Beware the vengeance of dwarves," the *Argbed* quoted, although until this point, he thought the proverb had been an exaggeration. "So what will it be, Guard Khani? Do you choose to die among us or the dwarves? I know which I would choose but you must go your own way as you already seem to have done."

Naiman stood trembling and looked from his commanding officer to the glowering dwarfess and back again.

"No," he managed to squeak, but even that effort seemed too much for him as he fell to his knees.

"If you will not choose, I will have to judge who holds the stronger claim," Alborz said, unable to keep the disgust from his voice as he looked at the man quivering before him. "I gave you the chance to choose your end like a man but it seems even that dignity is too much for you."

"No!" Naiman sobbed as tears began to roll down his face. "You don't understand."

"Don't understand what?" Numi all but snarled as she lurched forward and delivered a resounding backhanded slap across the man's face. "I understand that you are a traitor who lets good men be murdered in the street and drags innocent men into cells. What do we not understand?"

The guard tried to cover his finger-welted face but her hand struck twice more to split his lip and bruise his cheek before he could finally shield himself. In answer to that, the elder dwarf took the staff and began to rain blows on him with a ferocity that belied her age.

Alborz rose, uncertain as to what would happen first. Either Naiman would finally lash out or Numi would beat the man to death. His intervention wasn't required, however, as Guard Khani raised his voice in a despairing cry that froze everyone in place.

"It wasn't the *Hazarbed*," the man howled as he drew both arms up to guard his battered head.

A sudden, stomach-clenching silence gripped the room for a moment and Numi and Alborz shared a discomfited glance.

"You were seen leaving the inner court this morning," the *Argbed* said and struggled to keep his tone even. "Who else could you be reporting to other than *Hazarbed* Guuhal?"

He could guess the answer but he didn't want to believe it. If his assumption was true, it meant things became even more complicated and even more dangerous.

Naiman shook his head behind his hands and sobs wracked his frame.

Alborz stepped out from behind his desk like a rising thunderstorm. With one hand, he knocked the cowering man's arms away and with the other, he seized the front of his uniform.

"Who?" he roared with a blistering fury that made the man flinch.

"The p-p-prince," Guard Khani stammered, unable to meet his *Argbed*'s eye. "P-prince Tark-khind."

His left hand released the uniform and seized the man's throat.

"You lie," he accused in a voice so cold it could have frosted the air. "Do you think implicating the prince will save you?"

The look in his subordinate's eyes suggested that this had not even occurred to the terrified man.

"I-I've reported to the *Hazarbed* for months," Guard Khani confessed in a constricted rasp. "B-but yesterday, when I slipped away to make my report, I was told by Guuhal to go to the prince's solarium."

Alborz's grip slackened when strength began to leave his arm. He wished he could rally himself to choke the life out of the odious man but somewhere deep within, he knew it would do him no good. The truth would be the truth, Naiman or not.

"Prince Tarkhind gave me instructions on what I was to do even if Vahrem didn't come with me," the man continued. "When it was...over, I-I returned this morning to give my report that it was done. I don't think the prince expected me. He was meeting with Guuhal and they seemed like they'd been arguing. I gave my report and came back."

Alborz released him, sank back against his desk, and knocked the neatly stacked piles of parchment askew. One hand rose to massage his knotting temples while the other grasped the desk lest it too go out from under him like the rest of the world seemed to have done.

"What do we do now?" Numi asked quietly, her fury spent and ashen.

The *Argbed* stared into the courtyard and wondered what he would look like stripped and tied to a post. This was not what he'd planned for and not the battle he'd expected but Shepherd help him, he knew only one way—forward.

"You prepare the caravan to leave," he replied calmly as he continued to visualize his execution. "And I make peace with what comes next."

CHAPTER TWENTY-SIX

The deeper they went, the worse the stench became.

Even in the webwork of hidden tunnels that stretched through the sorcery-burrowed earth, the stink of the degenerates —or gnashers, as Zoria called them—was ever-present. Ax-Wed had assumed that eventually, they would become accustomed to the stench, but it was as if by some perverse scheme, the creatures had ensured that the intensity and nature of their vileness were complex and layered enough that there was always something more to turn the stomach.

A torch or candle might have burned away some of the stink but they'd known the light might not last as long as they needed and also that the scent would betray them to a snuffling degenerate. Instead, the Thulian had chosen to shave some of the alchemically glowing stone from a pillar and lace it onto strips of cloth that hung about their necks. The light was poor but sufficient and easily hidden under their clothing in a pinch.

"The smell..." Zoria wheezed as she slid a strip of cloth over her mouth and nose. "That might do me in before the gnashers."

The warrior woman nodded and held a hand up for silence.

They were approaching a junction point where they would

have to emerge from the hidden tunnels and would be exposed until they found the next panel that opened the path downward. Thus far, the degenerates seemed ignorant of the tunnels, which she found strange, but even Zoria, as clever as she was, had admitted that finding them was a happy accident.

Regardless, if they would have their expedition thwarted, a juncture seemed the most likely time and place.

Ax-Wed raised a finger and pressed it to her metallic veil in pantomime shushing before she moved with remarkable lightness to the panel.

She forced herself to take soft, shallow breaths, leaned close to it, and stifled a scowl of irritation when Zoria pressed in closer to listen as well. For several minutes, they hovered there but heard nothing but their heartbeats in their ears and the soft susurration of their breath.

"Is it clear?" the girl mouthed with a shrug, the borrowed dagger half-drawn from her sling.

The Thulian nodded but turned to prevent the girl from being the first one through the secret portal. It made sense that the one wearing armor and who was best capable of dispatching an ambusher went first, although if the creatures that dwelled there had set up an ambush, resistance would only delay the inevitable.

With her hand resting at the base of the Thulian sylver head of her weapon, Ax-Wed eased the panel a few inches to one side. The rush of foul air made her eyes water and gorge rise in her throat, but bloody-mindedness mixed with fear of what the smell portended helped her to not succumb.

From the seemingly absolute darkness beyond, she guessed that no torches were burning in the chamber, which might have seemed a comfort had she not faced a swallowing wall of blackness. The depthless expanse threatened to teem with a silent, crouching army of monsters, but she choked the dire imaginings as she tightened her hold on her ax.

She waited for a few moments and when no pallid claw or

malformed face rushed out of the dark, she let the panel slide gradually aside so the wan azure light began to play across the chamber. Under the tentative revealing glow, she could see the floor was different from what they'd encountered in other chambers. The rooms previous to this were dusty and perhaps streaked with the grime of unclean things passing through them, but the surface of this room was littered with refuse, all so moldering and mangled as to not be worth trying to identify.

We are getting close, she thought, the realization a heady mixture of excitement and terror. *Whether we die trying to escape or die hopeless could be moments away.*

The chest-tightening thoughts of trying to work the Gatehouse might have dominated her but as the panel slid completely to the side, her danger-sharpened eyes noticed something twitching amidst the detritus on the floor.

Ax-Wed immediately cupped a hand over the light at her breast and surrendered the room to darkness and in that strained stillness, she could faintly distinguish the sound of soft breathing. Something was alive in the room and she'd caught a glimpse of it moving. Had that been some kind of talon or claw she'd seen twitching at the end of an angular limb?

The Thulian chafed impatiently and her hot blood hammered through her veins as she waited in the dark, but she knew one misstep at this point could seal their fate. Rather than act in haste, she waited in the dark until she was almost certain the breathing she heard was the even drone of a sleeping creature.

Slowly, one finger at a time, she let the light seep out and little by little, it revealed the room again. Her searching gaze located the jaggedly-clawed foot—for that was indeed what it was, although it seemed poorly shaped for anything like what a human might call walking. The long, slack-fleshed leg it was attached to trembled and the claw shuddered as before, but that was all.

With her ax at the ready, she slid into the chamber and the

faint glow advanced before her. It was soon joined by Zoria's light as she followed with the dagger in hand.

The creature on the floor now bathed in shades of soft blue light was revealed to have a body akin to lumpy and deflated pouches of scabrous flesh gathered around a malformed and spindly frame. It took Ax-Wed a quarter of a minute—a hellish eternity of staring given the subject—to realize what she was looking at.

By the Watching Eye, she swore voicelessly. *It is a female!*

As she stood in morbid fascination, Zoria began to slide forward with dagger poised. She caught the girl's arm and gave the slightest shake of her head, careful to not let her mailed aventail clink.

Her companion responded with a scowl but relented when her grasp tightened fractionally.

She pointed to the walls and then at the panel they had entered through.

Zoria, still wearing her irritation across her brow, crept around the slumbering she-gnasher, mindful of the piles of filth and noxious leavings that littered the floor. She progressed carefully to the far wall under the warrior woman's watchful gaze and began to search for the next panel.

As the girl did so, Ax-Wed looked at the ruinous creature again, unable to avoid noting what the stretched and puddled flesh suggested. In that grim twilight, she believed she not only glimpsed a single creature but an entire bloodline of abominations wrought from catastrophe. If her theories of the Gatehouse had been correct—a vast complex stretched and driven through the earth that ran like water—couldn't the attendants have survived? And sustained by incestuous propagation, cannibalistic feeding, and liberal supplementations of sorcery and blasphemous rites, had they become something adjacent to the men they once were, twisted and regressed cousins to those offered to them? Was this troglodytic thing that lay naked in its squalid filth a distant relation to vaunted and dreaded Thule and even to her house?

The thought clung to the back of her throat like a hunk of putrid meat and threatened to make her gag.

She wanted to deny it and cast it off as some perverse fantasy but as she stared at this debased matron, could she deny that it made the most sense? And if she'd reached such conclusions, could that be what those in power of Jehadim above had learned? Was that ancient lineage why offerings were being made—blandishments to secure old knowledge or forestall ancient wrath? And where did the Voice in the dark enter into all of this?

Her foreboding thoughts were interrupted when Zoria stepped into view, the degenerate female sprawled between them.

"Nothing," she mouthed exaggeratedly as she pointed behind her. "Nothing."

Ax-Wed squinted into the dark and saw the girl's eyes wide with the fear that threatened to overcome her. If there were no more tunnels, they would have to brave the corridors—and the army of horrors that might be between them and whatever doom waited in the dark.

Before she could reply, the creature upon the floor stirred.

Woman and girl froze, hoping for a sluggish grumble as it tossed in its sleep, but one filmy eye slid open with mocking slowness. It beheld them in a moment and the eye flared to wakefulness in the ghostly light that hovered over it.

Zoria was the first to act and plunged her dagger into that eye, but not before a shrill squeal escaped the creature's throat. Even after the blade had penetrated, driven by all the strength in the girl's slight frame, it still thrashed and uttered gargled croaks while splintering claws raked at the filthy stone.

Frantic to silence the dying degenerate, the girl yanked her dagger free and careful of the flailing claws, aimed for its breast. Like a prospector's pick, the fang-sharp point of the weapon drove into the soft, pendulous chest but still, it would not die quietly.

Ax-Wed heard snarls and alarmed braying from the corridors to their left that led upward.

It's time to go.

With one long-legged stride, she moved around the dying, flailing creature and with the next, she dragged Zoria from her bloody work.

"Move," she snapped under her breath and gave the girl a slight shake as she did so.

A slight shake from her was enough to rattle her companion's teeth in her skull but it broke the girl out of her murderous trance.

"Where are we going?" she demanded as she fought to free herself from the Thulian's grip.

Ax-Wed released her hold as they began to jog down the right-hand corridor, which swept ever so slightly downward.

"Down," she declared and increased her pace, her ax held before her as she raced into the deep.

Winded and trembling, they ran down the corridor and rushed through three or perhaps four chambers before they finally staggered into a wide and peculiar room.

Rough columns of stone jutted from the floor like the trunks of fossilized trees that had sprouted between the tiles and lunged toward an eternally distant sky. The room bore markings and signs that suggested it had once been akin to the space where Ax-Wed had interpreted the bas reliefs for Zoria, but its carvings and artwork were fractured by the pillars that had split and splintered the fitted stones in many places.

Here, the two women stopped, puffing and panting, their path suddenly complicated by a mineralized thicket.

The warrior woman's weapon was splashed and smeared with blood that glistened black in the alchemical light. As they'd run through the dark, pursued by the hunting calls of the gnashers, a grasping hand or grimacing face had sometimes emerged but each time, her ax sang and their path had cleared.

Here, though, even Thulian sylver could not cleave so cleanly through what slowed their flight.

"Do you think we lost them?" Zoria asked as she leaned on her knees and panted.

The sounds from the corridor behind them were more distant than ever and seemed to be only the echoes of pursuit bouncing down the stone-lined walls behind them. That suggested hope, but even the gnashers would have understood that they were moving down, not up, so perhaps a vigorous pursuit seemed unnecessary.

Why hunt us when they know we'll run out of tunnel?

"I won't wait to find out." Ax-Wed grunted as she moved towards the stony forest. After a sigh that was as much a groan, the girl straightened and prepared to follow.

"It couldn't get any worse, I suppose," she muttered as she tried not to imagine gnashers creeping up on her in the dark with their filthy, malformed hands curled in anticipation of seizing her. The death-slicked dagger was still in her hand and her palms adhered to the hilt from the blood. She scuttled quickly and nervously to close the distance and walk directly behind her Thulian bulwark.

"Don't count on it," the warrior woman muttered as her head tilted to one side and her ears strained against the murmurs of pursuit and her thudding heart.

Three shapes detached themselves from the dancing shadows and stepped in front of them to bar their way. Another step into the azure light revealed the wardens of that treeless wood, creatures both familiar and yet strange. Although wrapped in the same tattered robes, they were clearly a different breed and stood upright and defiant with straight limbs and stiff spines. Their exposed skin was still translucently pale but far less pocked and marred by corrupting sores, except for their hands. These looked as though they'd been dipped in something noxious which now dripped from their claws.

"Blazphemerz!" the central figure declared in lisping old Thulian and raised its hooded head to howl, which was taken up by the others. The sound possessed a strange resonance in that place and to Ax-Wed's ear, she could almost have believed there was ghastly harmony in it.

Sensing the curdling presence of Sorcery in the air, she lunged forward and scythed the sylver head at the central foe. The creature raised its blackened hands over its head as though cowering and she smiled behind her metallic veil.

The smile vanished when her stroke did not part flesh and bone but stopped with a wrenching jolt up her arm. She gaped and ground her teeth against the strain on her limb and realized that the stained hands now grasped her ax-blade above the creature's hooded head.

It was the creature's turn for a black-toothed grin but she dismissed the taunting smile as quickly as her own with a boot in its belly. The dark-handed creature staggered back and rebounded off a pillar when its head clipped against the stone with a dull thunk. Its legs buckled and it fell on hands and knees.

"Stay close!" she called over her shoulder to Zoria as the other two closed in, their hands twisting and warping.

Something flashed at the corner of her vision and she spun away with a flourish of her ax. Like the scrape of stone on steel, one of the creature's hands—now little more than a nest of jagged spurs—grated against her weapon. The other hand swiped, having taken on a similar configuration, but the attempt was wasted as the warrior woman's deft footwork moved her clear.

The battle-wise Thulian might have seized the advantage of the squandered strike but the other attacked as her shoulder turned. Arms twisted into serrated appendages swept at her. Some rasped off her armor while others threshed only air.

One overreaching arm brought the attacker directly over her and she drove upward with the horn of her ax. To her relief, the point bit deeply into the creature's chest and the blade slid between the ribs. The unhallowed degenerate staggered back and suddenly, pale hands clutched the ax as something lightless and terrible sprang serpentine-like from the wound to latch onto the Thulian sylver.

Ax-Wed knew in an instant that the grasp would take more than a moment to break and when the enemy with the jagged arms made another attempt, she did the only thing she could. With a furious roar, she drove forward and thrust the ax deeper into the creature's chest until it backpedaled and made impact with a stony trunk. The head bit deeper into the stunned creature but she had no time to savor the victory as a spiny fist raked across her back.

The armor held but the blow unbalanced her as she spun to face her attacker. That blow was followed by two more. The unnatural spurs screeched and snapped off as she was pummeled to one side and reeled between two pillars of rock.

Her ears rang and the world threatened to keep spinning so she darted behind one of the columns of stone to escape the next few blows and orient herself.

She'd barely regained control when the unhallowed lunged after her.

The first swing slid over one shoulder and she ducked the second before she hammered an elbow into the creature's jaw and seized it by the head. Drawing upon every muscle in her shoulders and back, she shoved it down while her armored knee jerked up. Cartilage popped and bone cracked, but she wasn't satisfied. Her knee rose twice more before she let the degenerate slump on the floor.

As she drew in a steadying breath, Ax-Wed looked up and saw

what lay through the thicket of stone, and her breath caught in her throat. She scowled and her stomach twisted in a way that had nothing to do with the stink of the creature at her feet.

A sharp cry snapped her mind back to her immediate surroundings. With a low rumble in her chest, she moved around the stone pillar.

Zoria, her feet dancing in the air, dangled from the claws that had caught the Thulian's stroke at the onset. The unhallowed degenerate stood with the dagger protruding from its bloodied chest and its cowl filled with impenetrable shadow.

I am the Drinker of Life, the Voice thundered in her mind, each word a hammer blow inside her skull. *Wallower of—*

"Of Souls!" she shouted at the top of her lungs and beat the dark presence back with sheer volume. "Quencher of the Light! I know who and what you are, Atlacothix!"

The presence seething within the hood of the possessed degenerate seemed to twist forward like a bird cocking its head to one side in assessment.

"We were once known by that name," the Voice said in its sonorous tone.

She responded with a dry chuckle and took a step forward with the haft of her weapon held in a wide grip.

"You weren't only known by that name," she said, her voice wry and insinuating. "You were summoned by it."

Zoria whimpered as the dark hand that grasped the front of her ragged ensemble pressed a hooked nail to the side of her neck. The warrior woman's pulse quickened at the motion but instead of meeting the girl's terrified eyes, she looked at the dagger and the possessed creature's stained limbs.

"Careful, my enigma," the Voice warned and tapped the claw against the girl's throat. "This little rodent will be the first to pay for your arrogance."

Ax-Wed took another measured step and her gleaming copper eyes fixed on the darkness within the hood.

"Spare me your threats, *Tzitohn*," she retorted and the word came off her tongue with a chorus of unearthly whispers and the taste of blood. "An imp of the Resounding Depths has no business speaking to a daughter of Xhulth in such a way."

"Imp? Imp!" the Voice hissed and forced its puppet to take an unsteady step forward. "I was the first cohort of the Pazaul or have the children of Thule forgotten so quickly?"

If pressed, she would have had to admit that she'd never heard of Pazaul and her stab at the Resounding Depths was a lucky guess. The truth was that she remembered very little of the lower demon and his kind's history—*Tzitohn* in the sorcery-laden tongue of her people—but her mother had always insisted that when bartering with lesser demons, time was always on your side.

When she checked surreptitiously on the black speckled limb that held Zoria, the warrior woman confirmed it was true.

"You must have been long gone from the Kingdom to not know the answer." She laughed and stepped forward again. "Which is also why you do not bow to me rather than harassing my witless slave."

Despite the dire moment, she still noted how Zoria went rigid at the word and glared at her. She wished she could give her some sign to remain silent but her attention remained fixed on the demon.

"And what could there be to the house of Xhul that one such as I would even take notice?" the Voice asked haughtily but despite this, she could hear the desperate note beneath the surface.

"The House of Xhulth stands for Apotheos," Ax-Wed declared and her shoulders squared as she adjusted her footing.

Liar! Atlacothix screamed in her mind, forsaking the crude tongue in his fury.

"You have been severed a long time," she said as her grasp tightened on the ax. "Much has happened in the world above."

Lies! The Tzitohn wailed. *All lies.*

"Yes." She smiled within her mail-skirted helm. "But useful."

Thulian sylver split the air like a song and Zoria fell one way and the degenerate's arm fell another. The darkness on the limbs had retracted to the fingers before the stroke but with the severing blow, it immediately revealed the pale flesh and yellowed nail without a trace of the clinging stain.

The presence under the hood began to shrink as its vessel sank to its knees, a broken shell bleeding its contents.

"You will regret this," the Voice warned but its impactful voice had grown faint and less ominous. "You will regret the side you have chosen."

"Perhaps." Ax-Wed shrugged and her namesake parted more than merely air again. "But now, understand this."

The head landed with a soggy thump but still, the darkness clung like a patch of midnight inside the torn hood. She stared into this unlight as she kicked the head aside.

"I am coming," she stated a second before the dark vanished and the headless body collapsed to beat out its final shivers on the floor.

The Thulian watched the last spasm finish and turned her gaze to Zoria, who sat and stared at her with a combination of awe and dread. She began to squirm under the weight of the girl's frightened adulation and bent to haul her to her feet.

"Don't forget my dagger," she told her and nodded at the hilt that still protruded from the demoniac's chest.

Zoria walked forward shakily and began to tug the weapon free although her gaze never left her companion.

"Did you just intimidate a demon?" she asked and managed to pull the blade several inches before it stuck fast.

"A lesser one," the Thulain confirmed and began to stretch in a vain effort to ease the battered soreness in her back. "And it was more of a bluff to buy us time. It didn't have the power to animate the body much past death."

The girl stared at her protector in silence for a moment and with a grunting heave, dragged the blade free. With the dagger's exodus went the fragile aura of wonder that hung about her.

"So that was all an act," Zoria said and rose to point at her with the dagger while her other hand settled on her hip. "Especially the part about me being your stupid slave."

"I said 'witless slave,'" Ax-Wed corrected and shrugged. "It was the nicest thing I could think of in the moment."

The girl snorted in disgust as she cleaned the dagger on her ragged sleeve.

"Why not fellow adventurer?" she muttered in exaggerated irritation. "Maybe even companion in misfortune."

The Thulian chuckled and a moment later, her back gave a series of deep pops and she exhaled a grateful sigh.

"My, aren't we full of ourselves?" she groaned as she straightened and moved between the pillars of stone. "Come along, stupid."

"Bladebitch," Zoria muttered as she followed but then came up short when she looked into her companion's glaring visage.

"Guttersnipe," the warrior woman retorted and a smile twinkled in her eyes as she turned to walk away.

The girl grinned as she stepped behind her towering companion and the darkness seemed to not press in so much as she skirted the broken bodies of those that had almost killed them both.

That bright spark faltered and faded to extinction as Ax-Wed led her through the stone to stand and gaze at the vista the Thulian had beheld before the girl's capture by the possessed degenerate.

There, glimpsed like a mountain between the trunks of the fossilized forest, rose the sheer white spire of the Gatehouse, iridescent with a burning white glow.

Zoria might have thought the soft gleam from that structure would be a comfort in this dark place but the pale light only made the darkness that seethed at its heart seem all the more terrible. It conjured the feeling of the Voice—this Atlacothix—so close to her that it stroked her throat with a blackened talon.

She shuddered and her body began to shake and might have collapsed before that monolithic sight if not for a heavy hand that settled on her shoulder.

"One step at a time," Ax-Wed said without looking down, as implacable as ever behind her helm. "Battles are won this way—one step at a time."

The girl nodded, uncertain that her hopes could ever recover but thankful for the warrior woman all the same.

"Very well." She breathed deeply, the words threatening to stick in her throat. "Let's go."

CHAPTER TWENTY-SEVEN

Siava was not doing well.

When the guards had arrested them, Vahrem's urging that they have the young man's hand tended to was met with blows and curses. As such, rather than a cleaned and dressed wound, he'd had to make do with what bandaging he could accomplish as he sat in the communal cell they all shared, which was little more than a pit with a rusted grate over it. At his request, he and Iyshan had torn their clothes to provide as clean wrappings as they could manage but the ragged wound did not seem to clot properly, broke open at the slightest provocation, and soaked the bandages in moments.

As their time in the Tin Quarter dungeon stretched past mere hours, the caravan master watched the young man weaken as he grew paler and quieter. He and Iyshan had sought to exhort and fortify their young friend but the other occupants of the cell seemed determined to act like preening vultures over a sickening animal.

"It won't be long now, will it?" one muttered as he paced around the pit and watched Siava. "One more day, maybe two."

"Ignore him," Vahrem whispered in the young man's ear, his

arm around his shoulder. "Alborz is coming and even if he isn't, you know Numi will rally the Wain Clans to come for us. Stay strong, Siava."

"I'll trade you the next meal for what's left of 'is cloths," another scavenger croaked from where he squatted against a wall. "Two meals if he don't mess himself when he goes."

"Oh, he'll mess himself," the first vulture crowed with a cackle that showed rotted teeth. "I think he might have already. Can't yeh smell it?"

"Shut up." Iyshan snarled as he rose to his feet and his hand balled into fists.

The man cackled all the louder but everyone noted that his prowling ceased to stray so close to the three of them. Vahrem's manservant held his ground a moment longer and his burning glare turned to each one in turn in silent challenge. The wretched group in the pit suddenly found the floor and walls very enthralling.

"Alborz had best get here soon," Iyshan grumbled as he sank onto his haunches. "Or we'll have some real charges leveled when I finally lose my temper."

"Save your strength," the merchant said without looking up. "Even if we are rescued soon we'll have considerable work ahead of us."

The man responded with a low growl but fell silent and glowered across the pit at any who dared to meet his eye.

"More?" Siava asked and almost made both his companions jump. It was the first time he'd spoken since they'd been dragged to the Tin Quarter barracks.

"What?" Vahrem asked as he tried to process the question with a bemused expression stamped on his bruised and bloodied face. "No, not for you, Siava. You've earned a rest and a visit from the best healer-surgeon I can find."

"Those are mutually exclusive," Iyshan muttered. "Cursed needle-witches wi—"

The caravan master's immolating glare silenced his manservant, who studied the young man carefully. At the pitiful sight, his flinty expression cracked and he shuffled close enough to bump against the downcast young man's arm.

"The master will get you patched up," he said softly. "And a few days rest will see you playing your harp as sweet as honey and making all the girls smile, eh?"

Siava didn't respond at first and stared at his maimed and ripped hand before he shook his head slowly. The other two men exchanged a concerned look over the young man's bowed head but neither spoke for a time.

"Maybe we should speak to the Shepherd," Vahrem suggested, his voice as gentle as when he spoke to a frightened horse. "Set our minds on truth and light in this dark place."

Iyshan nodded readily and clasped his hands in front of him.

The merchant attempted to draw Siava closer but the young man pulled away with sudden violence. With a lurching shuffle, he rose to his feet and spun to glare at the caravan master.

"Maybe you should stop bleeding us dry for some pagan harlot," he snapped and his watering eyes shined with furious defiance.

"Easy boy," Iyshan said as his posture stiffened. His clasped hands trembled with indignation as his knuckles whitened.

"He's being a fool and we are all paying the price," Siava shouted before he swung to glare at Vahrem. "How much more for your heathen whore?"

The manservant was on his feet in an instant.

"Hold your—"

"It is all right, Iyshan," the merchant said in a firm but steady voice and stood from where he crouched with a heavy sigh. "Go ahead, lad. Say your piece."

The carrion-sniffer across the pit watched the drama unfolding with rapt interest, although no one had the first clue what exactly the new residents were discussing.

"My piece?" Siava sneered and ended it with a cutting, shrill laugh. "Where do I start? What about the fact that we shouldn't still be here or that every minute we stay here costs the caravan and damages our standing with the stables in Carnyxia?"

Vahrem nodded but did not argue, which seemed to only enrage the young man more.

"Or what about this?" he howled and shoved his bleeding hand almost into the older man's face before he moved his tearful, snarling face inches away. "What about the fact that Asa may be crippled for life or that Heydr is...he's...he..."

"Heydr is dead," the caravan master said softly.

Words seemed to fail Siava and he gaped at him. Then, with a fierce scream, he lunged. His undamaged fist landed hard on Vahrem's cheek, but the stout caravan master only rocked slightly with the blow while his battered face darkened with a fresh bruise. Iyshan started to surge forward, his hands outstretched, but his master seized an arm and drew him back.

The young man stood mute, his eyes swimming with a heady cocktail of horror at what he'd done and utter despair that dared him to care. Everything within the pit seemed to hang on the brittle tension which existed between the three men.

"Is there anything else?" Vahrem asked. His gaze hadn't flinched from Siava's the entire time.

A cold hatred settled on the young man's face and he darted forward with both hands extended to grasp the merchant's throat. A heavy-handed slap stung his face before his fingers and stumps could clutch their intended target and he fell before he realized that Vahrem had struck. The fall was arrested when the merchant caught him under the arms, although he tried drunkenly to shake him off.

"You bastard!" Siava groaned and shoved blindly with his damaged hand despite the pain while he drew his good hand back for another swing.

He never knew exactly what happened but before he could

make the attempt, the caravan master had spun him and sat him firmly on the ground. The young man had no time to appreciate the sudden change in his position before Vahrem's thick arms and legs snaked around his to both trap and cradle him. In a blind rage, he tried to thrust his head back into the man's face but it was pressed behind his shoulder and so thwarted him again.

"Damn you!" he screamed as he writhed in that iron grip.

"Shelter me, my Shepherd, my firm ground in deceiving sand," the merchant intoned, the words low and soft. "You alone teach me where my feet can stand."

The sound of the prayer seemed to stoke the young man to greater violence and his muscles strained as he fought to slam his head back.

"I hate you!" he shrieked. His teeth gnashed as his whole body contorted but he still could not break free.

"Your crook is never far and I know your rod guards me at rest," Vahrem continued, his breath coming heavier as he held fast. "Teach me to trust when I doubt your way is best."

"It's your fault!" Siava cried and his roar became a failing sob. "Heydr's dead and it's all your fault."

"Remind me, my Shepherd, for I turn aside and foolishly go my own way." The wagon master panted yet neither his voice nor his grasp faltered. "Your sheep needs your Word and your hand by night and by day."

"All...your...fault..." the young man muttered as the tension slipped from his trembling limbs and his head sank limply upon the other man's shoulder. "Your...fault."

Little by little, Vahrem let him slide to one side and placed him as gently as could be managed on the rough, grimy floor of the pit.

"All...for...her..." Siava sighed as his eyes fluttered shut. "Her..."

The caravan master rose to one knee and stretched to check the young man's hand. There was a second when he grunted in protest but his eyes didn't open, and Vahrem examined the mangled, blood-soaked bandages. With a muttered curse, he shucked off what was left of his tunic and began to rip off more strips.

From across the pit, one of the vultures gave a long, lilting whistle.

"Like I say, not long at all."

───────

"Vahrem Kal'Stru!" The rough call came a second before a cudgel rattled the grate overhead. "Vahrem Kal'Stru, on your feet."

The merchant, seated beside the young man with one hand holding his rebandaged hand on his chest and off the floor, didn't rise. His eyes were half-lidded and his lips moved with half-formed prayers.

"Vahrem Kal'Stru!" The guard above snarled as he struck the grate hard enough to send a shower of rust cascading into the pit. "On your feet."

"Vahrem," Iyshan said quietly as he placed a hand on his master's shoulder.

His eyes snapped open and he looked around sharply.

"Vahrem whoreson Kal'Stru!" the guard shouted with another crash of his club.

"I've got him," Iyshan promised as he pushed the caravan master gently to his feet. "Don't worry."

He looked up and squinted against the lantern light shining over the pit.

"I'm here."

"I can see that," the guard responded irritably and Vahrem had to shuffle back to avoid being struck by descending spittle. "Move to the center and stand still."

With his limbs still stiff from sitting so long on the hard earth, he was forced to undertake an undignified waddle to the center of the pit. Directly overhead, a hinged door had been worked into the grate and once he was in position, the guard drew out the bolt that held it shut and opened the portal with a squeal of protesting hinges.

"Secure this around your waist and clamp the shackles around your wrists," the man instructed in a bored yet irritated voice. "And you'd best make sure it's secure or the winch is liable to pull you apart."

A second later, an arrangement of stout chain and hard-edged manacles descended with one trailing tail rising to a pulley rigged to the ceiling. The feel of cold metal against his skin shook off the last vestiges of the not-sleep and with minimal rattling and grunting, the caravan master secured the chain as instructed and looked up for further instruction.

The guard gave a short whistle and rotated his arm at the elbow in a slow circle.

With a rumble, the winch, turned by two guards, was put to work and Vahrem rose out of the pit.

"Are we being released?" he asked as he cleared the portal and earned a painful backhand across his mouth.

"When I want your dung-mouthed breath fouling my air, I'll tell you," the guard snapped with his bluegum enhanced halitosis. "Now hold still and shut up."

His cheek stung and his hands clenched until his knuckles popped but he let himself be uncoupled from the thick winch chain. The shackles remained around his wrists and in short order, the guard ran a leather lead through the loops and yanked abruptly enough to make him wince when the metal cuffs clanked together.

"Up we go," the man said as he stepped to one side and pushed the prisoner toward the stairs with the end of his club.

Vahrem walked without protest, the cudgel never very far from digging at his shoulder blade as he was herded up the stairs.

He tried to stop himself from hoping that Alborz had come to free them but when he emerged on the barrack's ground floor, he couldn't help looking around in vain for signs of the *Argbed*'s men.

"Quit gawking and move," the guard ordered and jabbed the cudgel into his back.

They took another set of stairs that wound ever higher through the fortification until he began to wonder at his destination.

Would he be taken to the top of the barracks and given an ultimatum to either confess or be thrown to the street below in an "attempted escape?"

No, they had no issue with fabricating charges so why bother trying to extract a confession? He then wondered if they might be taking him to hang from the walls of the barracks, a crude but potent warning to the quarter. Not even a caravan master had the right or authority to question how the guards conducted their affairs.

Vahrem, despite his faith and convictions, had always struggled with the mystery of death but as he climbed yet more steps, he found he could not bring himself to be overly concerned with his possible end. There was sadness and even regret but when he searched himself, he discovered that it seemed centered solely on the fate of Ax-Wed, the mysterious, melancholy, and beautiful creature who had changed the trajectory of his life in one evening.

"Beautiful?" he muttered, past caring what the guard said or did. "Why is it that I can admit that only now?"

The guard's hand cuffed him across the back of the head and the club shoved him off the stairs to what must have been the topmost floor of the barracks. Vahrem had an instant to see a guard standing before a stout wooden door before he was pushed against a wall.

"Shut up and kiss the wall," his escort growled and shoved the club into his shoulder even as his cheek pressed flat against the stone.

The merchant heard the man at the door knock twice before he cleared his throat.

"The prisoner's here, sir."

Vahrem couldn't make out the muffled answer over the grinding of his teeth as the guard continued to push the club into his back.

"All right, give 'im here," the guard at the door said, his tone officious. "You can head down to the dungeon again."

"He's all yours." The escort grunted and tried too hard to not sound irritated at the other guard's superior tone.

To the merchant's relief, the club vanished from where it had bored into him but the hand that clamped around his neck like he was a mischievous pet was none too gentle either.

"One wrong move and I throw you down the stairs," the door guard rumbled in his ear. "I don't care who's come to see you."

Hope bright and brilliant filled Vahrem's heavy chest and it took everything in him to not burst into a broad smile.

Alborz must have come and instantly, he felt ashamed for ever having doubted him.

His wounds and aches melted away and the caravan master practically floated as he was led to the open door by the scruff of his neck.

When he entered, he saw the *Gondbed* of the Tin Quarter, a squarely built man with a curled mustache who stood at the desk and looked both very grim and very nervous. Seated at the desk was someone who was most certainly not *Argbed* Alborz.

Although it had been some time since he'd seen the man face to face, the caravan master was not likely to have forgotten the face of Prince Tarkhind of Jehadim.

He suddenly felt very hollow and very frail and the weight of everything seemed to crash over him as elation fled like a bird through the window that stood open behind the prince.

A breeze, not cool but gentle, rolled through the aperture, and he wondered if he would feel the grace of the wind ever again. He tried to focus on enjoying it although his knees threatened to buckle.

"You may leave us," the prince instructed.

The guard's hand left Vahrem's neck and he staggered forward a step. The *Gondbed*'s hand reached for the metal-wrapped staff that leaned against the desk but a raised eyebrow from Tarkhind stopped him.

"You may leave us as well, *Gondbed*," the ruler of Jehadim said icily.

The guard captain stiffened but said nothing as he walked woodenly toward the door. As he passed, Vahrem was certain he could hear the man's teeth grinding behind his elaborate mustache.

"Please, have a seat," the prince said and inclined his head toward a chair before the desk after the door thudded shut. "You look very tired."

"Thank you." The merchant sighed as stepped forward and settled gingerly into the chair. "I am very tired."

The royal watched him with a gaze whose intensity might shame an eagle. Nothing seemed to escape his notice and he wondered at the machinations behind those watchful eyes. As he mused about this and returned the stare, the caravan master couldn't help but notice the dull chords of gray beginning to streak his lustrous black hair and the shrunken aspect about his cheeks and eye sockets.

His dress was immaculate and his posture impeccable, but there was no hiding the fact that the young ruler was wearing thin under some incredible strain.

"You and your men will be released," the prince said and his scrutinizing gaze never faltered. "The two with you are being brought up from the dungeon and will be tended to, given water to wash with, fresh clothes, and a meal."

Vahrem shook his head, certain that he hadn't heard correctly.

"I understand one of them is injured. I've already had my apothecary prepare a selection of restoratives that will be offered to him. I understand that you are followers of the Flock so I'm not certain what is permissible for your faith, but I would not have the man suffer if I can help it."

A dark laugh threatened to bubble from inside the merchant and he wanted to ask if the apothecary had anything for Heydr, but he choked it back along with the bitter question as he cleared his throat.

"Eh…no, our confession does not prohibit the use of healing potions," he said and because he couldn't seem to help himself, added, "Nor do any of the orthodox confessions I've ever heard of."

The royal's eyebrow raised and Vahrem cursed himself silently for fatigue and fatalism loosening his tongue.

"Thank you, Prince," the caravan master said with a deep bow and his bruised forehead touched the manacles. "That is very generous of you."

For the first time, the royal's gaze turned away with a twist of his head as his aquiline nose sniffed sharply.

"No, I don't think so," Tarkhind said evenly despite his dark, piercing gaze that seemed to sweep suspiciously across the corner of the room. "You see, once you and your men are tended to, you will return to your caravan. You will have a day to deal with whatever business affairs remain but when Jehadim's gates close tomorrow night, you will be out of the city. I will give instruction that you will not be required to pay taxes on your business here to ensure your swift departure."

Vahrem felt like he'd known the knife that had gutted him when he'd first left the room was still lodged in him, but he'd forgotten until these words gave it a fresh twist.

"Am I forbidden to return?" he asked and tried to keep his voice steady but the quaver seemed inescapable.

Jehadim was the gate to the East. Banishment would make certain that this would be his last season in the East and would mean that he would have to start over somewhere else. That was assuming the rest of those sworn to him came with him. Whatever they might owe him, it was no small thing to ask families to leave everything they knew to start over with routes and markets their leader had never encountered.

"That depends," the ruler said and his stare returned to him like the burning sun from behind a merciful cloud. "If you leave promptly and without further worry concerning the fate of certain persons...well, I don't see any reason why you cannot return to Jehadim next year to conduct your business. My seneschal informs me that you have always done good trade in my city and never contested or evaded your dues, even after Hasriim."

"The Shepherd bids us be innocent of men, king or peasant," Vahrem said, his mouth dry and full of an acrid taste despite the holy words of his faith. "Pay what is owed yet learn with every exchange so as to not be made a fool and bring yourself to ruin."

The merchant knew it was a transparent attempt to buy himself time to process the offer, but to his surprise, the prince broke into a broad grin.

"A fine proverb," Tarkhind said with a nod and leaned forward to place his elbows on the desk and steeple his long, square fingers before him. "You seem well-versed in the common teachings of your faith, but are you familiar with the origins of it?"

The caravan master's brow furrowed and a slow, bemused noise slipped between his lips. Of all the things he had expected of this day, discussing the origins of the Flock with Prince Tarkhind of Jehadim had to be almost the last thing he could have thought of.

"Uh...yes, well...that is, I know what has been written by

founding scholars of our faith," he replied and tried to gather his thoughts.

Was this all part of a scheme or ploy to acquire his compliance through some kind of religious manipulation? He wasn't certain but the peculiarity of the situation put him on his guard despite his fatigue.

"So you know it all began in Jehadim," the prince said and his eyes gleamed strangely behind the profile of his steepled fingers. "That this city was where your Shepherd first established the Flock."

Vahrem drew a breath. He knew how foolish it was to correct royalty but when it came to matters of his faith, he suddenly seemed incapable of remaining silent.

"Well, the Flock is publicly recognized by the rest of the world," he said. "But technically, those he first called were from Khardalis—and not even Khardalis proper but Ez'Naveth on the southwestern slopes."

Tarkhind waved the correction away like a wayward fly.

"Yes, yes, I'm familiar with the Ten and Two," the ruler said quickly. "But Jehadim is where the Shepherd's bloodline began and where he kept coming back to, and it was from here that the Flock spread like an infection to touch every corner of the East—all after his disappearance, of course."

The merchant winced, not at hearing his faith described as an infection—which was tame compared to some descriptors he'd heard—but because again, he was obliged to offer a correction.

"You are mostly correct, Prince," he said and the words seemed to drag themselves out of him. "Except it is stated in both our writings and the words of Jehadim's senior scribes that the Shepherd did not disappear but rather—"

"I don't want to sit here and discuss minutia," Tarkhind snapped and his fingers interlaced into a white-knuckled knot.

Vahrem didn't feel the crux of his entire faith could be considered minutia by any reasonable person but the notoriously mercurial royal's first show of temper stoked his caution.

"Then what do you wish to discuss, Prince?" the caravan master said with bowed head and an attempt to keep his voice soothing. "I understand that my life and that of everyone in this city is in your hands."

The man threw his head back and laughed, the sound as sharp and hollow as a snake fang. He dared to look into the prince's gaze and what he saw forced a chill through his tired frame.

He'd once seen the same light in the eyes of a ragged man the caravan had come across in the middle of the Great Desert. The poor wretch had insisted that he was Hasriim the Great and the son of Myrnatt bound within one ragged flesh. They had tried to offer him water but he'd batted it away and claimed it was poisoned by his rivals in the celestial court before he wandered into the desert screaming profane euphemisms for the male anatomy.

Vahrem had never forgotten the same fevered light that now burned him from within the prince's eyes.

"Silence!" Tarkhind snapped and turned to the corner again with a withering glare.

The caravan master remained locked in place as though a coiled viper was at the desk in front of him and not the ruler of Jehadim.

The tension of the long silence stretched thin until the prince seemed to notice him out of the corner of his eye. His attention left the corner and returned to the present but for the first time, Tarkhind seemed at a loss and even embarrassed.

"You will go and take your people with you," he said and his gaze drifted down repeatedly in shame despite his attempts to remain composed. "You will not return until a year has passed. If you violate this, your life and those of any who aid you will be forfeit. Do you understand?"

Vahrem nodded slowly while his eyes studied every aspect of

the young ruler's face. He had been there like all of the caravan masters who frequented Jehadim when the prince was crowned and presented himself throughout a week of feasting. His gift had been a fine silver mare, one of his best, and the ruler had shown his gratitude by leaping upon the beast's back and prancing her about the royal plaza to the surprise of many there. He'd shown himself a very competent rider but more than that, Tarkhind had revealed that he was vigorous, fearless, and keen to show he would forge his own path.

Seeing this cold, troubled man before him, he could not help pitying him.

"What has a hold of you, Prince?" he asked and leaned forward despite feeling like he was offering his face to a serpent. "Men are snatching your subjects and sojourners alike and seem to be doing it with the approval of your *Hazarbed*. How can you allow this? What holds you hostage to such men?"

Again, that fanged laugh ripped from the prince but this time, the merchant did not flinch but leaned forward against it.

"Do you want me to change my mind?" Tarkhind asked, his voice suddenly hot and petulant. "With a word, I could have you and your men hanging from the walls, perhaps with *Argbed* Alborz at your side—a fine homage to Hasriim the Great, our glorious overlord."

Vahrem's stomach twisted at the threat but the words came out of him anyway.

"Does it have to do with Hasriim, then? Are those being taken part of his dictates?"

It seemed so mad to think of—what could Hasriim the Great want with night-snatched captives?—but nothing else seemed to make sense either.

"I suppose it had something to do with him at first," Tarkhind said with a strange high giggle at the back of his throat. "But then things changed, things were unearthed, and with that, they became so much more complicated."

The merchant had no idea what to do with the statement but something like honesty emerging instead of threats seemed miraculous enough. He shuffled to the edge of his seat and rested both manacled hands and forehead on the desk.

"Prince, I am simply a man trying to honor his commitments," he said, his brow still pressed to the wood. "I think we could help each other. You only have to help me understand what is happening in your city."

"No one—not even Guuhal—knows what is happening in my city," Tarkhind muttered, his eyes unfocused. "My city...my city..."

There was a knock at the door and both men jumped.

"My prince," a gruff but apologetic voice said through the stout planks of the door. "One of the prisoners refuses to be tended to until he has proof that his master is well. What do you wish us to do?"

"Iyshan." Vahrem sighed and wondered how such loyalty could ever become such a burden.

The two men locked gazes over the desk and both understood that the moment of frailty had passed.

"Go to your man," the ruler of Jehadim instructed with a wave of his hand. "You have until tomorrow."

The merchant struggled to stand, knowing what he must do, but he wondered if he should make one final attempt to sway the fracturing prince. Tarkhind, perhaps fearing what he might say, jabbed a trembling finger toward the door.

"I said go!" he all but snarled. "Or I'll have you sheared like all sheeple deserve."

CHAPTER TWENTY-EIGHT

The approach to the Gatehouse would have been taxing enough with the bizarre terrain to cover but when the baying degenerates finally poured in, the situation became something from a nightmare. The two women had begun to wade through the thicket of rock when their pursuers appeared and loped in after them. Had the cavern been an open space, they'd have been run down and overwhelmed in an instant but thanks to the maze-like division of the area, the hunters moved in roving splinters rather than a crashing wave.

Any splinter unlucky enough to reach them was met with a flashing ax and plunging dagger.

Still, Ax-Wed and Zoria were running again. This time, however, it was a nerve-wracking jog between the stony trunks in pale twilight rather than a blind sprint through the dark.

The Thulian could gauge that they were drawing closer to the iridescent structure by the way the light among the pillars grew, but given some of the blind turns toward dead ends they'd already encountered, she feared it wouldn't be long before they were cornered. The last group of pallid scavengers was still dying ten strides behind where she and Zoria now stood but soon, the creatures would gather in large groups for their safety if nothing else. If one of these larger packs caught them or worse, lay in wait for them, it would be over. The girl would be snatched first and the sheer weight of numbers combined with limited avenues of escape would guarantee that she would be dragged down eventually.

And death would be mercy too long in coming.

Not for the first time since entering the darkness, a creeping and half-formed thought of self-annihilation slithered through her mind. It was nothing so precise as a plan but it now insinuated that she could do the noble task of ending Zoria's suffering with one hard stroke before she finished herself. It would spare them a good deal of pain and toil, she reasoned, but something deep in her heart rejected the perverse idea. This combined with the gradual growing of the wan light kept her moving through the forest of stone, her head turning continuously while her gaze searched their surroundings.

Thanks to this desperate vigilance, she noticed something strange and a moment later, caught Zoria by the shoulder before a lethal footfall. On the floor of the cave was an expanse of darkness as swallowing and impenetrable as the space between the stars.

"What is it?" the girl asked and stared with horrified wonder.

"I'm not sure," Ax-Wed said although deep down, she was afraid that wasn't true. "But whatever it is, this close to the Gatehouse, we can't take any chances. Old evil like this corrupts everything around it."

The darkness stretched across the chamber, a flat anti-gloss across the stone. Beyond an expanse of perhaps a hundred paces, the outer walls of the Gatehouse rose in pearly luminescence. From where they stood, no path or bridge could be seen that would take them over the eerie dark-painted floor.

"How will we get across that?" Zoria cried and looked nervously over her shoulder.

"I'm not sure," the Thulian repeated as something close to panic tightened around her chest like a python. "I need a second to think."

"Time's up!" the girl cried in a terror-tightened voice. "They're here."

Behind them, a wailing war cry rose and they both spun to see a pack of degenerates bounding between the pillars toward them. At their heels came something like one of the shadow-handed unhallowed they'd faced earlier.

"I told you," Ax-Wed muttered as she hauled her companion around to pitch her against a stone pillar. "Keep stone at your back and stay behind me."

The girl drew her dagger and uttered a challenge profane enough to make the warrior woman blush.

"Yes," she muttered as she turned to face the tide of horrors. "What she said."

The first creature to spring forward was caught while airborne with a single swing that reversed to cleave the spine of the next degenerate that lunged at her legs. They fell, still gnashing their teeth and raking the air while thick blood jetted from gaping wounds.

Behind the fallen, the other creatures prowled like wolves at bay. They snuffled and snapped as they searched for weakness but found nothing but armored sinew and Thulian sylver to greet them.

"Blazphemerz!" the unhallowed screeched behind the pack.

"You certainly like that tune." The Thulian chuckled as she brandished her ax with a taunting flourish. "Maybe I'll teach you one of my own."

Pouncing with leonine force, Ax-Wed rushed forward and scythed her ax in a singing stroke. The degenerates squealed and their black eyes bulged in terror. Two of them were too slow and staggered back with their guts spilling from their split bellies. A lump turned its twisted arm into a crude hammer as one of the degenerates launched an attack but her ax haft swept up to check the blow and wrist bones shattered with a crunch.

Mad with fear or rage, the wounded creature lunged with its undamaged claw, but she caught it by the throat with one hand and threw it aside with contemptuous ease. Before it could even gnaw at her greaves, she stamped on it and her armored bulk crushed flesh and bone.

"Who's next?" She snarled and spread her arms in a challenge when the degenerates recoiled.

Her gaze swept the cringing remains of the hunting party and she realized that she'd lost track of the unhallowed degenerate. And why had she moved so far from Zoria?

Ax-Wed spun on her heel in time to see a degenerate collapse under a flurry of stabs delivered to its chest and belly by her companion. The creature—it must have crept behind Ax-Wed—sank to the floor with a whimper.

The girl gave her a bloody salute as ribbons of darkness streaked toward her from around the pillar. The curling strands of shadow were about to ensnare her but before the Thulian could scream a warning, she was knocked to one side by a sudden clinging weight. As she staggered to one side and rebounded off a stone column, she caught a glimpse of Zoria struggling against the entangling black tendrils that sprouted from the arms of the unhallowed degenerate.

Three of the creatures clawed and snapped at her armored hands and arms and had pushed her against the stone. They pressed their advantage and tried to snatch the ax in her firm grasp. With a feral growl, she heaved against their combined weight and they staggered back a step, but she was dragged with them when their claws clung doggedly to the haft.

They surged toward her and she planted her feet as she leaned into their onslaught. A fourth creature clambered over the backs of its fellows, a rag-wrapped iron spike held high for a fatal blow.

Somewhere in the dark, Zoria screamed in fear and pain.

Ax-Wed roared with a fury to set stone to trembling and drove forward, bowled the three that held fast to her ax over, and rushed through to the fourth with her weapon now free. Thulian sylver split its arm at the elbow before an armored brow butted into snapping jaws. The degenerate fell away in a shower of red spittle and shattered teeth and blood from its truncated arm splashed across the floor in broad arcs.

Two sharp chops took care of two of those fallen at her feet but the last swing bit deeply through ribs and lodged the blade in the dying creature. The third degenerate, a shrunken example of its malformed kind, scrambled to escape but she would not be denied. She used one hand as she pivoted to snatch a trailing arm.

Anchoring herself with her weight and the burdened weapon, Ax-Wed hurled the creature bodily over her shoulder. It tumbled through air and across stone and terminated its trajectory with a bounce into the blackness spread across the floor.

The would-be hunter uttered a pitiful scream, the closest thing to a human sound she'd heard from the degenerates, and raked with splintering claws as it tried to escape the blackness that lapped over it like an undulating wave. Its legs sank to a depth that was beyond the physical as spindly hands made of the same utter darkness rose to drag the rest of the unfortunate creature deeper.

The Thulian knew what would happen and even worse, what it meant but she couldn't turn away as she absently tugged her ax free.

The inky hands, unnervingly flat as though they only existed only in two dimensions, dug through flesh like it was pastry dough and elicited more screams. Trembling rippled through the papyrus-thin limbs like strings going taut and the degenerate was snapped into the swallowing darkness.

She attempted to shake off the shock at what she'd seen and her gaze searched for Zoria as her heart leapt into her throat.

Raise your eyes and survey my works, the Voice declared with a sudden intensity that made her wonder if her head was about to split.

Her eyes watering from the mental bludgeoning, she raised her gaze to the Gatehouse.

The unhallowed stood upon the outer wall with Zoria's limp body cradled in its stained arms.

"Not even the depths of the Kingdom will hide you if you hurt her!" the warrior woman screamed as she stormed to the edge of the blackness. "I swear by the Grim Maiden and the damned foundations of Xhulth that I will come for you. Not even the One-Eyed King will save you."

The unhallowed threw back its head but it was the Voice that mocked her. Atlacothix's stygian laughter echoed over and through the stone.

"I believe you," the *Tzitohn* called across the night-sewn expanse between them. "And I want you to follow me but now, I wonder why we should be set against each other?"

Ax-Wed thought the corpses of Atlacothix's children seemed a ready answer for that question but for Zoria's sake, she remained silent and watchful.

"I know why you seek this ruin," the Voice declared. "And should you be who you claim, perhaps we need not be enemies."

"Now he tells me," she muttered under her breath before she raised her voice. "What did you have in mind?"

The thoughtful silence stretched long enough that she checked to see if she was about to be ambushed twice before the answer came from the Gatehouse walls.

"Prove you are worthy to enter my tabernacle and I swear the child will live."

She stared at Zoria dangling in the creature's claws and lowered her gaze to the utter darkness that yawned before her. She guessed what was about to be demanded of her but she found time to pray to Morah that she was wrong.

"Show that the blood of Thule still runs strong," Atlacothix shouted to her. "Prove that you are indeed a child of the City of Gates and may cross in safety."

The hungry darkness, the swallowing unlife of the Cacophonic Realms spread before her in challenge. She shook off the image of flat hands reaching toward her and considered what it would cost her to refuse or to accept. Immediate damnation would be what waited for her if she failed but then again, what did she expect to find at the end of her days if she surrendered Zoria to the thing that called to her from the wall?

"I'd best get it over with," she muttered as she rolled one sinewy shoulder and then the other.

Ax-Wed stared at the challenge before her and the incantation rose in her mind unbidden. Her heart twisted violently inside her chest as she felt the layers of sign and signifier pile upon each other, almost eager to be drawn from the bound depths of her memory. The pressure began to build but she slowed its gathering as she raised her voice.

"Swear it!" she shouted as her body trembled with the choked flow of sorcerous power that eddied inside her. "Swear to her safety according to the Edicts of Contract."

After a moment of agonizing pause, the Voice, impressed and rippling with pleasure, answered her.

"By my name, this child will be safeguarded should you come to me."

She nodded in acknowledgment, a pained and jerky movement, as the energies approached their zenith.

"Now do it," Atlacothix demanded.

With a scream torn from her very soul, Ax-Wed enunciated the incantation in a rush of crimson motes that scattered from her lips.

Burning with the light of infernal stars in an alien sky, the sorcerous exhalation rolled across the blackness, which receded before the red lights. Recoiling like a living thing, the darkness slithered back, the excrescence of noisome realms held at bay by her blood infused with will and blasphemous rites. Papyrus-thin hands stretched toward the blood-born fireflies but when they neared the glow, blue flame kindled and they wilted away like burning straw.

Ax-Wed wiped her mouth with one hand and followed in the wake of the dancing lights, careful to stay in the center of the path they'd created. Her firm, armored steps were a steady cadence she leaned into like a weary soldier reliant upon the marching tune to keep in line and in time. She didn't dare to look behind her but felt the darkness closing in, although the thought of her standing in the midst of a sea of black oblivion was something not easily shaken.

From atop the Gatehouse walls, Atlacothix watched her progress through borrowed eyes.

The warrior woman was halfway across the expanse before the first of her lights flickered and was snatched out of the air by shadowy hands. There was a blue spark but it vanished so quickly that the only evidence of its existence was the afterimage that lingered for a heartbeat longer. Fighting the rising panic in her chest, she tried to gauge the power left in the spell and the ground she had still to cover.

She should have had the power to ford the plain of unlight but when she let her mind feel the flow of energy, she realized that the darkness was pressing harder against her spell the farther she went. Ax-Wed wasn't certain if this was a function of the unliving blackness responding to her, some kind of blind defensive reaction, or if it was something more sinister.

Her gaze wandered to the one watching her from the wall but in the same moment, she saw another of the lights wink out at the edge of her vision.

Doubtful that she had the strength and focus for another incantation and certain that she didn't have the time, she knew she only had one choice—run.

Driving the sorcerous wisps before her through sheer will,

her pace quickened as the path narrowed. The darkness seemed to sense the change and pressed harder on her mind and soon, tendrils of darkness twisted up. Almost all of them ignited and shriveled in a flash of cerulean flame but here and there, the stretched fingers pressed through and another red mote was snuffed out.

Three-quarters of the way across, her incantation was reduced to only a handful of lights. For the last dozen strides, she had three left and her heart pounded in time with her boots upon the stone.

By the time she set foot on the ground before the Gatehouse walls, the very last of the incantation hovered for a second over the dark before it was snatched into nothingness.

Her limbs trembled with more than only exertion but Ax-Wed forced herself to straighten and look atop the wall with her head high and shoulders square.

"Here I am," she called and wished she could have said something cleverer. She wasn't sure she had the breath yet, however, much less the nerve.

So you are, declared the Voice in her mind, a pleased purr behind the mental roar.

The Thulian watched, too breathless to scream, as the unhallowed who held Zoria took a step back and flung itself from the walls.

Still cradling the girl in its arms, it landed on the stone floor before the warrior woman. There were several sharp cracks that could only be bones snapping but despite this, the creature rose from its crouch as though it had hopped from the back of a wagon.

"I keep my promises," the Voice declared as it held the girl out.

Ax-Wed took her like a babe in arms but held her ax in one hand. No sooner had the possessed degenerate's claws released Zoria than she began to stir.

"W-what? Huh?" the girl murmured, her lids still heavy and her movements slow. "M-Momma?"

On an instinct so long buried it was almost foreign to her, she rocked Zoria in a firm but gentle embrace. As she stared into the oblivion-thick hood of the unhallowed, soft shushing sounds came from her tightening throat.

"Shh, I've got you," she whispered softly. "It'll be all right. I've got you."

As the girl roused slowly, Ax-Wed could feel Atlacothix's attention bearing down on her and with that pressure, the softness slipped from her voice and she glared in response.

"So what's next?" she demanded as her rocking motion stilled and her hand tightened around her ax.

"Now," the Voice declared with a flourish as one hand became a cluster of black hooks, "we see if we can help each other."

With serpentine alacrity, the nest of barbs raked across the degenerate's throat and blood spilled across its chest in a bubbling rush. The hook became fingers again and with those blood-drenched digits, it turned and stepped closer to the walls. With horror-numbed wonder, the Thulian watched the dying creature daub sorcerous sigils upon the walls using its lifeblood as ink. Blood still ran freely from its torn throat and dribbled down sodden robes and legs until it began to spatter and splash on the floor.

"Welcome to my home." Atlacothix sighed as the last sigil was completed and the body crumpled.

The spiral of symbols glistened with a profane twinkle and the luminescent stones of the Gatehouse wall ran like wax.

Ax-Wed took a steadying breath as she stared through the fresh portal.

Beyond lay a courtyard and within it would lie their only hope of escaping.

Still bearing the lethargic Zoria, she stepped over the melted stone.

CHAPTER TWENTY-NINE

"You can't be serious!" Numi cried as she ambled after Vahrem and her staff chimed discordantly.

He clambered onto the bed of a wagon and began to rifle through its contents.

"With Iyshan's help, you should reach Carnyxia without a problem," he continued as though he hadn't heard her. "If I don't reach the steppes by the time your business with the beast-riders is done, carry on to Arukahm. We'll eventually catch up."

"We?" The dwarfess groaned as she shook her head in bewilderment. "Please tell me this is some kind of gallows humor."

"I wish," Iyshan muttered as he stood to one side with folded arms and a seething scowl. "But he explained it all on the way from the barracks and won't be moved."

The merchant dragged a trunk from the bed of the wagon, threw it open, and removed a jingling pouch and a curved jile dagger of Scadish design.

"Take this," he instructed and tossed the bag to his manservant. "Govad will be finicky about sealing the deal for the mares without me there. Start laying down coin until he takes his hands off his belt and puts one on the table, then wait a moment and add one more. Can you remember that?"

The man didn't bother to hide the glare he directed at his master.

"I know how you conduct your affairs, *master*," he replied as he tucked the bag forcefully into his belt.

Vahrem looked up from the chest, a wounded expression stamped across his bruised face. He looked ready to gather himself for an argument but he let the words go with a deflated sigh and snatched another pouch from the trunk. The container was shut, latched, and shoved into the depths of the wagon before he clambered down to stand before the man.

"That's good," the caravan master said and looked directly into Iyshan's angry eyes. "If you complete the run and we still haven't arrived in Scadish, then you are unbound and the new master of the caravan."

Iyshan gaped as the merchant took his hand and pressed the other pouch into his numb grasp.

"You'll need to deliver this to the Scribe of Trade to confirm the transfer of mantle," he said. "Don't lose it."

The other man's fingers closed around the balding velvet bag which held Vahrem's seal. Beside him, heavy tears began their slow roll down Numi's weathered face.

"I...I can't run this caravan," the manservant protested in a choked voice. "You can't ask me to do this."

A smile hitched one side of Vahrem's face, the other side too swollen to comply.

"Yes, you can," the merchant said softly. "And I'm not asking. You aren't unbound yet."

Iyshan's hand clenched around the pouch until his fingers ached and his dark eyes roiled like a storm about to break.

"No...you can't... I won't...I—"

The caravan master raised a hand and settled it on his hard shoulder.

"If this is the last time we speak in this world," he said and paused to draw a steadying breath. "Then I would have it be as friends bidding farewell, not as a master commanding his servant."

Iyshan looked around for a moment but only saw Numi weeping openly. Blinking back tears, he straightened and gave several long sniffs before he met Vahrem's eye and nodded stiffly.

"Very well," he said with a gulp that clicked in his throat. "Shepherd keep you until we embrace again, b…brother."

"Until that or the Glorious Day," the merchant said and pulled his dearest friend into a crushing embrace. "Shepherd keep you, brother."

The man's arms moved like they were made of wood but they embraced the caravan master and he pressed his face into a broad shoulder. He drew small comfort that his tears might be hidden and the single sob which escaped his throat was muffled.

Vahrem didn't bother to hide his tears, even when they drew apart to an arm's length.

"All is as the Shepherd wills," he said with a sad smile.

"And I…" Iyshan began but was forced to pause to gather himself. "We must go where he calls."

Vahrem wished he could have seen them through the gate but he knew he couldn't run the risk of the prince's forces seeing him.

So, after making sure preparations were made with Julo and Jalen's father, he scrambled over the stockyard wall and hurried into the city a few hours before sundown, then meandered down alleys and side streets to make certain that he wasn't being followed. Twice, he was sure that someone was dogging his steps but each time he'd whirled around to try to catch sight of them, he'd been rewarded with nothing but an empty alley.

"Shepherd guard me," he whispered before he decided it was time to set off for his actual destination. The sun was burning low in the bruising sky and he didn't expect that he'd want to spend much longer in the Tin Quarter after dark. A lone man almost limping as he was in his current condition would probably seem like ripe picking to the snatchers.

The thought of the human fiends made him settle his hand on the dagger inside his cloak and a deep fury trembled in his chest.

"All things in their time," he said through gritted teeth.

He ducked his head and passed through the gate that separated the Tin Quarter from the causeways that crossed the royal canals. His heart hammered as he passed beneath the eyes of the royal guards who manned the gate but the traffic through it was brisk and he was one of many. Those who tended the palatial estates in the Gold Quarter during the day slid wearily past those bound to attend the city's elite through the evening. Servants and laborers shuffled past entertainers, courtesans, and nightwatchmen, and each offered grudging respect to the drudgery of the other, however spare it was. In such a rolling, flowing assembly, he was merely another soul shuffling to attend to the needs of his betters.

As he moved across the causeway with the swift waters of the canal murmuring beneath him, the caravan master remembered when he'd first dreamed of selling his mantle to an aspiring entrepreneur and settling amongst the wealthy of Jehadim.

For years, he'd tended his profits and investments carefully, his mind set upon making certain that when he finally retired from his wandering ways, he would have fortunes such that he and his children and even his children's children would know nothing but comfort amongst the perfumed and alabaster halls of the ancient city's premier families.

He'd since come to the Shepherd and knew the warnings of material prosperity that snared a man in the world that was but he'd told himself there was nothing wrong with being frugal and wise as he'd counted coin and plotted new ventures.

Still deep in thought, he stepped off the causeway and eased away from a group of entertainers he'd been walking beside. Looking about as surreptitiously as he could, Vahrem checked to make sure he hadn't garnered any particular attention before he ducked down a lane that ran between two iron-fenced gardens. The air was thick with the scent of jasmine and lavender, while the nightly trill of songbirds rose from the manicured bushes and curated trees.

The caravan master didn't know exactly when he'd shrugged off his deep longing for a garden to sip tea in as he watched the sunset but now, it seemed almost perverse that it had been his objective. The Shepherd had set him on a road and given him a people and a responsibility, and he'd learned that it did not end in an estate with scarlet ibises striding around a decorative pond. If he was honest, he wasn't sure if his road was very soon about to end hanging from the palace walls but moving among these monuments to wealth and power and position, he would have traded a score of them for the caravan at his side, a fine horse beneath him, and the Shepherd leading him on.

"Let's hope I haven't traded all that on a fool's errand," he mumbled softly as he saw the Citadel looming before him. It was one part palace and one part fortress and without a doubt, the bastioned heart of the city where his friend and last hope for a certain Thulian lay.

Vahrem reached the edge of the gardens and leaned his head out to look up and down the avenue that stretched toward the Citadel like an arrow.

"I'm not sure if this is anything but foolish." The merchant sighed and tried to remember exactly what he thought he could accomplish. He'd been forbidden to see Alborz but perhaps if he could talk to his friend, he could determine what he could do.

The briefest rustle of cloth was followed by a sharp hoot like an overeager, not a float. He had managed a quarter turn when he felt a sharp sting in the back of his neck. Halfway through the motion, his muscles began to cramp and burn. By the time he completed it, he was listing to one side and a moment later, his whole body gave out beneath him.

He caught a vague impression of two men advancing on him as he fell on the paving stones, his body in utter rebellion. He landed hard enough to compel a cry of pain but his venom-locked throat only permitted him a constricted whine. The pain of the impact was soon utterly consumed by the utter burning agony that closed his mind inside his skull. Helpless and struggling to even draw breath through his grinding teeth, he watched as the two men approached with cruel grins stretching the width of their faces.

"Oh, I think you were more than foolish, friend." The sibilant chuckle of the smaller of the two men was chilling. "It was downright suicidal."

"You should have left when you could," the bigger of the two rumbled as he bent and gave Vahrem's cheek a few sharp slaps. "But Crim said he knew you wouldn't. You're not smart enough for something like that."

The merchant watched impotently as a hand was thrust into his robes to yank the jile blade roughly from his waist. After inspecting it for a moment, the brute shoved the weapon into his belt and then drew out leather cords.

"You've been looking to get your friend back." The smaller man tittered as his gaze darted around the deepening dark. "That's the word about why you're such a special acquisition."

The bigger man cinched the cords tightly enough that they cut into his flesh even through the wracking pain of the venom.

Another strangled hiss of breath escaped his lips but this only provoked more stinging slaps.

"Don't you worry now," the big man said and punctuated each word with a slap. "You'll get to see where we put her soon enough."

CHAPTER THIRTY

The smell of salt, blood, ash, and rot were all heavy on the air as she moved into the courtyard. Her stomach twisted into spirals and her heart beat a mad drummer's tattoo.

"Come in," the oceanic voice called to her. "Come and take your ease in my home."

The air rippled and the smell vanished as she emerged from the darkness of the molten tunnel and stood not in a courtyard but an exquisitely furnished solarium similar to what her family had possessed overlooking the Bay of the Broken. Through open doors, she could hear the sea rolling as the setting sun painted the floor in shades of scarlet and crimson.

A rush of memories threatened to overwhelm Ax-Wed but Zoria stirred in her arms with a groan.

"You're crushing me." The girl grunted as she twisted in her grasp. "Put me down."

She forced her hold to loosen with more effort than it should have taken and lowered her slowly to the floor.

The girl looked at her and rubbed her eyes before she snapped to full wakefulness and gazed around her.

"Where are we?" she asked and her pitch rose in excitement. "Are we out?"

"You could be," said a familiar voice although it was gentler and richer now. "Very soon, this could become a reality."

A tall silhouette appeared in the doorway to the balcony, slender yet strong and with long, almost delicately tapered limbs.

The Thulian stepped forward and both hands tightened around the haft of her weapon as she moved to stand between Zoria and the figure framed in the dying light.

"At what cost?" she demanded and bared her teeth.

"Vengeance," the Voice said with an outward sweep of its arms. On the cliffs below, the waves crashed with a thunderous roar.

"I'm right here." She snarled and slid one foot forward as her weapon rose into the third position in the Handmaiden's wards. "You're welcome to try."

Atlacothix threw back its head and laughed, a resounding, buttery sound that despite herself, she couldn't help but like.

"Not for me, little lioness," it answered as its outstretched arms sank slowly to its sides. "The death of my children is nothing so terrible. It is their honor to do so but as I said, I am not speaking of myself. My price will be you wreaking your vengeance upon those who have wronged you."

She narrowed her eyes to slits within her helm and her mind roiled with very early memories, warnings of the treachery of *Tzitohn* and their ilk. While not true lords of the Kingdoms, they were still cunning and dangerous and ever eager to take advantage of desperate humans.

And they were indeed desperate.

"I don't understand," she said without lowering her guard. "Speak clearly or my ax will start answering for me."

The dusk-framed figure shook its head.

"So hostile and so brutish." Atlcathoix sighed as though with an old and heavy sorrow. "I remember a time when the keepers of this Gatehouse would bid me sit and sup with them, offer me a slave to possess should I desire it, and even be willing to accommodate me in other ways. There was communion and even friendship between your kind and mine."

"And I remember what that communion results in." Ax-Wed snorted and twitched her head over her shoulder. "The last one you communed with isn't cold yet."

"My children are not what they once were," the Voice said as the silhouette shrugged. "Debasement and our compromised situation have resulted in something...less than ideal, but they have still proven useful. They've kept me strong despite my exile and have now driven you to me."

"They're monsters!" Zoria snapped and leaned around the warrior woman to glare at Atlacothix. "Filthy beasts!"

"They are what they have had to be to suit my purposes," the Voice replied coolly. "But I make no excuses for them. Their baser needs and desires have only grown more needy and odious as time wears on."

A demon's words are webs, Ax-Wed recalled as she stared at the figure. *The longer you speak, the more easily they ensnare.*

"Back to the matter at hand," she said with a slight rise in her voice and sharpness in her tone that would brook no argument. "Speak your offer plainly, *Tzitohn*, or prepare to test the edge of Thulian sylver."

A slow, rolling chuckle rose and fell away like an answering tide.

"Very well." Atlacothix sighed again. "The fact is that I have not remained in your realm out of my over-fondness for your kind but rather because of what lies above us."

One long finger unfurled to point upward.

"Jehadim—or more precisely, the royal line of Jehadim—has garnered the protection of one of the *Cherubash* and this has inhibited my effort to escape this prison. I need you to help me by killing the prince, who happens to be the one who is to blame for you being here."

The Thulian gaped, for the first time utterly at a loss.

"What is a *Cherubash*?" she asked and disliked how foolish the question made her feel but also knew that not asking would be even greater folly.

A pause stretched on as the Voice seemed at a loss for words.

"You are a daughter of Xhulnth, aren't you?" it demanded. "You can't tell me you know nothing of *the* Enemy?"

"Enemy?" Ax-Wed said with a shake of her head. "Enemies of Thule?"

"The Bright Host?" Atlacothix pressed. "The Long War? The reason the king only has one damned eye!"

She shrugged and fought the urge to laugh. While she knew she should have been worried about what this ignorance would do to her chances of escape, seeing the ancient evil so out of sorts was more than a little funny.

"But you do know Thulian incantations," the Voice said and almost seemed to speak to itself. "Which I suppose is all that is necessary."

"What is a *Cherubash*?" she repeated. "If I am going to go up there and kill the prince, I need to know what I'm up against."

That drew another laugh from Atlacothix but this one was cold and mocking. All the former warmth vanished.

"You're not going up there you little fool," the Voice declared with a sneer. "You will use the Gatehouse to turn Jehadim to dust."

Zoria gasped and the blood drained from Ax-Wed's face.

"What?" she asked softly. "Why would I do that?"

Another silence followed, this one angrier and tenser as though the Voice was taking its time to formulate a calm reply.

"Because if you destroy the entire city, you get the prince and his meddlesome guardian will leave," Atlacothix said with openly forced calm. "I, as one of the glorious Kingdom, cannot work the

Gatehouse and even if I were to try, the *Cherubash* would stop me the same way it thwarted whoever you called on when you first arrived and attempted to make a sacrifice."

Something twisted painfully in her chest as she recalled the plunging dagger and the great wings and the denying voice.

"What is he talking about?" Zoria asked and something strained and skittish edged her voice.

"She was dying," Ax-Wed said as she turned halfway to regard the girl. "I was granting her an end to her pain before those creatures came back. She asked me to so I gave her Morah's peace."

The girl stared at her and for only an instant, the Thulian saw something which cut her deeper than any blade—disappointment. It was only there for a moment before the girl's face hardened and her eyes were merely glossy jewels set in a pretty mask.

"Morah is not *Tzitohn*," she declared and hated the trembling in her voice as she turned to glare at Atlacothix. "She is a goddess, patron of the Handmaidens."

"We can bother with a lecture on the circles of influence within the Kingdom some other time," the Voice replied irritably. "What I need to know now is whether you will help me by incanting the spell which will destroy Jehadim and thus set me free."

Her stomach churned as she thought of what she was about to say—to even consider what it would mean—but as best she could tell, there was no other option.

"So we destroy Jehadim. Then what?" she asked and steeled herself with each word.

"Ax-Wed, no!" Zoria cried but the Thulian refused to face her.

"Quiet, girl," she snapped and deliberately avoided the eyes that bored into the back of her helm. "You will make a compact with me to promise us safe transport to the surface—me and the girl."

"I don't want any part of this!" her companion shouted but neither of the negotiating parties paid her any mind.

"Of course," Atlacothix answered smoothly. "With the *Cherubash*, it will be a small matter to use the Gatehouse to place you wherever you like. I could even deliver you both to the very steps of your family in Xhulth if you wished."

Ax-Wed shook her head at the suggestion.

"Mahliknet will be fine," she replied. "So how do we do this?"

"How can you even talk about this?" Zoria sobbed.

She whirled to look at the girl and seemed to loom as tall as the specter in the doorway.

"When did anyone above ever do anything for you?" she asked in a rumbling voice. "When its rich men made you a whore while still a child or when its streets made you like an animal searching for scraps? When has great and beautiful Jehadim done a damned thing for you?"

The girl stood defiant. Tears streamed down her cheeks but she could not find any words to speak. Despite the silence—or perhaps because of it—Ax-Wed deflated as her shoulders sagged and her head lowered.

"Please." She sighed and the mailed veil tinkled as she stretched a hand toward the girl's shoulder. "Please trust me."

Zoria twisted away from the outstretched hand and the rejection drew a low groan from the warrior woman that she beat back with a growl.

She'll understand before the end, she told herself as she turned toward Atlacothix.

"Let's get this over with."

"Excellent," the Voice all but purred and added quickly. "I'm afraid I'll have to drop the comforting glamours to avoid disrupting the magic but I'm sure it's nothing you aren't used to by now."

There was a sound like a storm wind blowing up from the sea but rather than the fresh, cutting scent of tempest-tossed sea spray, the smells of blood, corruption, and soot blasted across her senses. Behind her, Zoria gagged and then became sick at the sight that emerged when the seaside solarium vanished like a mirage.

Ax-Wed stood upon the alchemically enriched stones, her mind overlaying the memories of her father taking her on tours of the old Gatehouses in Xhulth. The basic layout seemed to be the same with an altar stone rising out of the center of a stone basin a dozen strides across and a single arched walkway leading to this angular assemblage. Over the altar on chains of bronze hung the Eye of the King, the black disk through which potent sorceries were worked and the Kingdom contacted. But where the other Gatehouses had seemed pristine places, so sterile it was hard to imagine slaves being offered on the immaculate stones, this courtyard was a slovenly abattoir.

Scattered everywhere underfoot were charred bones, putrefying meat, and other things less distinguishable but no less foul. The white walls were spattered and smeared with effluence, and where the stone didn't seem cracked or crumbling, there were spans of indentations that suggested great raking claws. The basin seemed filled with blood mixed with a tarry substance that thickened and streaked it with black veins. These dark seams glimmered with malevolence as the blood sloshed slowly in a sacrilegious tide. Overhead on chains, green vagris where they were not blackened with soot, hung the Eye of the King, its black perfection riven with several deep cracks.

Rising out of the putrid pool was an abomination of the deep, its swollen body wrapping down and around like a vast eel. A mouth lined with rows of fangs as long as her hand twisted into a leering smile. Atlacothix, the Wallower of Souls and Quencher of Souls leaned forward. Its fetid breath drew tears from her eyes and with an ungainly flex of its bulk, it rose behind the altar.

"Come now, daughter of Thule," the oceanic voice called to her, the beauty of it all the more perverse for its source. "Let us do great and terrible things together."

CHAPTER THIRTY-ONE

"This ends tonight," he said softly as he took the badge of office into his hands.

Though he'd reached some level of comfort with the heavy staff, Guuhal's hands still longed for that offered by lance and saber. He had wielded the staff of the humble guards of Jehadim since Hasriim the Great's victory but his fingers had not forgotten the honest strength of good steel or stout war shaft. Like many of the disbanded Lancers, he'd entombed his weapons in a cave a few miles out from the city and he now told himself that if he survived this night, he would go to that abandoned armory and see if anything was still serviceable before he took to the road.

"They couldn't save Jehadim," he muttered as his gaze swept up and down the length of banded wood. "But perhaps you can redeem what is left."

The *Hazarbed* turned and looked across his room. He knew that whatever happened this evening, it would be a long time before he slept in such a fine bed or enjoyed such excellent wine. Not for the first time since he'd reached his decision, he wondered if he had what it took to live outside the Citadel. He'd kept himself trim and vigorous, but he knew it demanded more than simple fitness to survive outside the world of courts and the nobility. After so many years in the palace, he wasn't certain he had what it took but for all that, he was certain of one thing. Prince Tarkhind had to die.

First the strange excavations, then the bartering with the creatures and using the likes of Crim to meet their demands, and now this business with using more miscreants to try to kill caravan masters and clan princes. And all the while, the ruler of Jehadim seemed to slide deeper into madness, ranting at things that only he seemed to see.

"I hope you can forgive me, Turlihnd," Guuhal whispered as his hand tightened about the staff. "But the son you left the throne to is gone and if Jehadim, is to survive he must join you."

He closed his eyes for a moment and inhaled the scent of his clean linens one last time before he took the first steps that carried him out of his room and into his mission.

The *Hazarbed* knew that with no heir, the city would be thrown into chaos but also that there were enough cousins and the like. He was certain that when the dust settled and the knives were tucked away, a new prince would sit upon Jehdim's throne and things would return to what they had once been. For half a moment when first considering what he must do, Guuhal had thought about trying to ascend the throne but had dismissed the thought quickly. Not only would it sully his motivations for what he must do but given his preferences in affection, he'd be unlikely to ever produce an heir and his reign would thus not bring stability to the city.

No, it was the gallows or the road for him after tonight.

With no hesitation in his stride, he swept down the corridor and his long legs carried him down the hallways to the prince's chambers. Still, he attempted to harden himself with every step. He would make it a quick blow or maybe two. That would be all it would take.

"Hazarbed!"

Guuhal froze and his heart seized in his chest with the certainty that his thoughts had somehow been heard. He whirled and his feet slid into a strong stance as he prepared to go down swinging. But instead of a flurry of vengeful blows, he only saw Naiman Khani scuttling toward him, his eyes watering and his face a mass of bruises.

"Hazarbed!" the sniveling royal guardsman repeated. "You need to come quickly."

His heart was still in the process of trying to catch up the beats it had missed, but he turned away from his informant and tried to force his voice to remain even.

"Not right now," he said. "You can make your report tomorrow morning."

"Tomorrow will be too late!" Khani cried, his voice on the edge of cracking. "Tonight—"

"Whatever it is," he cut in, his tone icy. "It can wait."

Naiman gaped like a fish and his trembling lips twitched as he stared with huge, tear-filled eyes.

Something like pity rose inside him at the sight of the man he'd used and was now casting aside to face whatever shameful fate waited for him as an exposed spy among his brothers. With a growl in the back of his throat, he buried those weak thoughts and turned away. His feet struck the polished floors with a determined stride.

He'd only taken three steps before Khani's voice rose, strident and panicked.

"Alborz is starting a rebellion!"

Guuhal halted and stood for a moment as he tried to force his mind to accept the intrusive, world-altering information.

"Alborz was removed from command and placed in the dungeons of the Gold Quarter barracks," the *Hazarbed* said slowly as though attempting to jog the man's memory. "The *Gondbed* is keeping him in custody until the prince can decide what to—"

"Don't you think I know that?" the frantic guard interrupted. "Every last guard of the Citadel is already heading there to free him and from what I hear, more than a few of the *Gondbed*'s men will join them. Even in the Gold Quarter, people have heard about what is happening."

He felt as though the floor was about to slip out from under him and he would be spun toward the ceiling. Using his hold on his staff as an anchor for his senses, he forced himself to think.

"Well then," he muttered and his brow knotted as his free hand drew out a pinch of bluegum and tucked it into his lip. "So they spring Alborz. Then what? They storm the Citadel and capture the prince?"

Khani blinked rapidly and shrugged helplessly.

"Damn you, Naiman, think!" Guuhal roared. "They must have said something or at least given some indication of where they were going after Alborz was set free."

The royal guard's face bunched into an even less attractive contortion of bruises but the pensive contortion didn't yield anything but a fearful shake of his head. He was ready to give the man a fresh contusion across the side of his head when Khani suddenly looked up and something besides terror shined in the man's eyes.

"Evidence!" he said and at first, he spoke so quickly that the *Hazarbed* struggled to understand him. "They said they would need evidence for the trial. That's why it had to be now—tonight —because this was when they could get that evidence."

A mad laugh rose in his chest. Surely Alborz wasn't so insane as to think he could put Prince Tarkhind on trial? But was that any more insane than the commander of the royal guard assassinating the ruler of the city in his bedchamber? Could it be that this turn of events would be a way to save Jehadim and not send a reluctant *Hazarbed* to avoid a noose by living life as a vagabond?

But what evidence? Guuhal suddenly remembered what was bound for the Citadel this evening.

"Bring the prince to the eastern postern door," he instructed as a plan formed in his mind. "Tell him it is a matter of his safety and if that isn't enough, give this to the men guarding him and have them drag him to the postern."

When Khani balked, the guard commander drew out a small golden disk from his robes. If it weren't for the material and lack of a printed numeral, it might have passed for the latest batch of clay tokens he'd handed Crim a few days earlier. He pressed the token and seal of his authority into the informant's hands and met his terrified eyes with a gaze as stern as steel.

"If you want to survive this night you will do exactly as I say," Guuhal said. "And do it quickly."

Without waiting to see if he'd be obeyed, he strode away from the royal apartments and toward the eastern wing of the Citadel. A second later, he heard the rush of Khani's feet running in the opposite direction.

Alborz waited with his men—and more besides—in an alley that opened to a view of the eastern wall of the Citadel.

He would have liked to spend time with a washbasin and a mirror after his release, but his men, the bold fools that they were, had been right. There was no better time to put an end to this madness.

"They are coming." The whispered report came from a man at the mouth of the alley.

The informally reinstated *Argbed* nodded and rolled wrists that had not so very long ago worn shackles.

"Remember," he said in a low voice that carried to every ear around him. "We need everyone alive, both the abducted and abductors. We do this quickly and cleanly and ensure that we have as many options as possible for interrogation. We're pulling this all up by the root and that means we need to know everything."

The guards around him nodded and every gaze he met showed him that they understood exactly what was at stake. They were all traitors now, and the only way they could emerge from this with any of their honor intact and their necks unstretched was if they could prove their case.

It seemed inopportune to mention the fact that he wasn't yet sure what that case was. The word of the prince's involvement had come with barely enough time for him to give instructions to his men in preparation for this moment, but from the time Guuahl had come with the entire Gold Quarter barracks at his back to the moment to when his men arrived to set him free, he hadn't come up with a single plausible explanation for why the prince was the will driving this.

Of course, even while in chains, he'd heard mutterings that Tarkhind was becoming increasingly erratic, but at the beginning, at least, this hadn't all been madness. It had started so small and so measured that the *Argbed* struggled to believe it was all the design of a mad aristocrat. If the prince had possessed the good sense to take such measures, why begin in the first place?

The creaking rumble of a wagon drew his attention back to the moment and with a slow, measured stride, he led the men toward the mouth of the alley.

"Quickly and cleanly," he whispered. "Shepherd, hear my cry and know me. Quickly and cleanly tonight."

The donkey-drawn wagon rolled into view and Alborz's lips parted in a grim smile.

Crim sat at the front of the wagon next to the driver. He picked at his fingers, utterly confident and unconcerned. The *Argbed* hadn't asked for this additional blessing but Shepherd knew he would take hold of it with both hands.

The wagon had turned toward the narrow causeway over the moat before it forked into one ramp to the eastern postern door and another that ran down to the under canals beneath parts of the Citadel.

"Move in!" he shouted as he broke into a jog. At his side, his men raised their voices and their metal-shod clubs.

Crim's sharp face whipped around the side of the wagon and his eyes bulged in the moonlight when he saw the guards descending on him in force. Alborz could barely make out the abductor in chief shouting at the driver, and the wagon made a lurching acceleration toward the ramp to the under canals. The haste was short-lived as a knot of royal guards raised the portcullis to the lower portal and marched forward in close order. The draft beasts seemed to understand that there was no hope for escape before their frantic masters did and brayed in protest before they stopped a few yards short of the downward slope.

The guards were on the causeway and rushed forward when Crim hopped down from the wagon and walked toward them. The villain peered over the low wall which guarded the edges of the causeway and the *Argbed* wondered if he would choose a watery death over what was probably coming next. He hadn't thought of the ruffian as one with the stomach for such an act, even in spite, but he had learned much about how much he didn't know men's hearts lately.

When Crim reached the back of the wagon and drew out a clay token, Alborz was glad to see that the abductor wasn't yet ready to throw himself into the rolling water.

"Alborz, my good friend," he said silkily as he leaned against the rear of the conveyance. "I'd heard you'd retired but I am glad to see that the Citadel is still under your watchful eye for the moment."

This close, the *Argbed* could see the bound figures they hadn't bothered to cover this time in the back of the wagon. In the poor light, he couldn't make features out but there were at least four poor souls and one of them looked small enough to be a youth of a dozen years or so.

"I told you this day was coming, Crim," he reminded him coolly. "It didn't come fast enough for my taste but Shepherd be praised, it's come at last. You're done."

The man's lips twitched as he fought to keep his smile and he cast his gaze at the force brought to bear against him. Like a fox with his tail in a snare, he smiled all the wider.

"Oh, maybe you should have retired, Alborz, my dear friend," he responded pityingly as he brandished the clay disk for all to see. "You once again seem to forget all about this little token here."

He looked at the graven seal and raised his eyes to meet Crim's gaze.

"That won't save you now, Crim."

The corner of the abductor's eye twitched but his smile held, however brittle it now seemed.

"Is it simply a matter of inflation?" he asked and slid a hand into his shirt to draw out two more seals. "Because there's more where this comes from."

Alborz didn't waste his breath with an answer and instead, let the man see his collapsing world reflected in his relentless eyes.

Fear, both feral and petty, flashed across Crim's face, but before he could give the order to seize the abductors and free the abducted, there was a commotion at the postern door overhead. The heavily fortified door swung inward and out strode *Hazarbed* Guuhal.

To say that the *Argbed* was surprised to see him would have been a gross understatement, but the fact that the guard commander emerged alone and strode confidently down the ramp was beyond credulity. If every man on the causeway wasn't staring with him, he might have assumed he was seeing things.

All stood in rapt silence except for Crim, who spared a

moment from staring to loose a particularly venomous smile at the castellan.

"It looks like your superior is here to remind you about the way the law works in Jehadim."

Alborz didn't answer but instead, attempted to steel himself for what might happen. Before the business of the snatchers, he would have willingly said he respected the *Hazarbed* and although they didn't always see eye to eye, he would have said they were both true comrades in service of Jehadim. Now, though, they were men standing on opposite sides of a battlefield and he knew what that might require of him, no matter how much he disliked it.

"What is going on, *Argbed* Alborz?" Guuhal asked in a strong voice worthy of the parade-ground.

He paused for a moment, somewhat disconcerted by the guard commander using his supposedly stripped title. Alborz told himself it was probably a slip brought on by force of habit as he forced himself to reply.

"Arresting criminals, *Hazarbed*," he answered in his field voice. "These men have been caught kidnapping those within the walls of Jehadim."

Crim stepped toward them and held two clay disks up in one hand.

"See, that is where the good *Argbed* must be confused, oh wise *Hazarbed*," the abductor stated smugly. "He seems to forget that because of these lovely things, there can be no arrest because there can be no crime."

Guuhal looked at the tokens for a long moment and gave the man a small smile before his staff swept down. The clay disks along with a few of Crim's fingers broke with a crack and the abductor screamed in shock and pain.

"Carry on, *Argbed*," the *Hazarbed* instructed over the shrieks.

Alborz was taken aback but not willing to let the Shepherd's good grace go to waste, he nodded and called to his men.

"You heard him, lads," he shouted. "Bind these two and secure the victims."

A hearty cheer went up from the assembled guards as they rushed to do the duty so long denied them. Before he could twist away, Crim was seized and forced to his knees where he was bound quickly, although he snarled and spat like a cornered animal.

The driver proved faster than expected and with the graceless speed of the mortally desperate, scrambled into the back of the wagon and seized the first bound victim at hand and produced a long-knife from inside his tunic.

"Get back!" he screamed and flashed the blade before he rested against the bound man's neck. "Get back now."

The royal guards halted but did not retreat, their gazes torn between watching the desperate driver and looking to their *Argbed* for guidance.

Overhead, the skies rumbled and the wind picked up as if all of nature was stirred by the drama of the evening.

"This will not end in any way you want it to," Alborz said in a firm but gentle voice. "There is no reason to make thi—"

He halted in mid-word when he realized that he recognized the bound man with a knife to his throat.

"Vahrem?" the castellan muttered and the shock chased all sense of what he'd been saying out of his head.

"Ihfwamhsluuhcifhgfoohgoo," the caravan master replied through the gag packed and bound over his mouth.

The driver seemed confused by what was happening, which was probably fair to say of most who were present. His gaze darted suspiciously from his hostage to the *Argbed* and back again.

"Stay back," he said and a tremor of uncertainty threaded through his voice. "One step closer and I slice him open."

"Oh, Shepherd, be merciful," Alborz said and chuckled. "I'm

merely going to tell you right now that you'd be much better off if you threw that knife away and quickly."

"What?" The driver grunted and squinted at the castellan. "What are you talking about?"

"Dhiz!" Vahrem growled through the fabric as he twisted his whole body to drive his head into the side of his captor's face.

The man dropped the knife with the force and shock of the sudden impact and before he could recover to defend himself, the bound merchant lurched forward and powered his head into him. Blood exploded from the driver's crushed nose and he staggered back and tumbled over the side of the wagon into the waiting grasp of Alborz's men.

"Told you." The *Argbed* shrugged as he turned from watching the bloodied man being firmly bound to looking into his old friend's battered face.

"Shepherd love you, brother." He chuckled. "How does this keep happening to you?"

"Ifhwa—" was all Vahrem could manage before his bound feet lost their balance and he flopped into the wagon with a pained grunt.

Laughing, Alborz climbed up the back and began to untie his friend as other guards reached into the wagon to do likewise for the remaining three captives. The bindings were secure and not the easiest to loosen but within a few moments, all four were standing, stretching, and generally doing their best to get feeling back into their limbs.

"I was looking for you," Vahrem explained as shook his legs out and flexed his fingers. "That's what I was trying to say."

Alborz chuckled again as he threw his arm around him and patted his broad shoulder.

"Well, you found me."

Both men began to laugh but were interrupted by a sharp voice calling from the postern gate.

"What have you done?"

Every eye followed the voice up the ramp and there, flanked on either side by royal guards, was Prince Tarkhind. He looked as though he'd been dragged from his bed.

Above them, the storm flashed lighting that threw the prince's face into stark contrast and each and every vein seemed to bulge against his skin. Despite this, *Hazarbed* Guuhal was the first to answer.

"It seems they are arresting criminals," the guard commander declared, his shoulders square and head held high.

Another fork of lightning ripped across the sky and a second later, a blast of thunder seemed to make the causeway rock. Even after the last rumble died away, Alborz felt the structure beneath them shake.

"You idiots!" Prince Tarkhind ranted and spittle frothed out of his mouth as he turned a wild, baleful look at everyone in his presence. "This is your fault! You fools have ruined everything. You've killed Jehadim!"

CHAPTER THIRTY-TWO

"This will be utterly delicious." Atlacothix hissed with pleasure as it shuffled closer to look over her shoulder while she studied the symbols carved into the begrimed stones of the altar.

"Do you have to be so close?" Ax-Wed asked and swallowed the urge to retch by force of will alone.

The fiend chuckled softly as its huge head nodded, inky ichor dripping from its fangs, but it made no move to shift its bulk back.

"I am sure the enormity of my woes is lost on you," it continued and its slick, corpulent body shivered as it spoke. "But after the failed attempts to shelter the Gatehouse in the earth, I was wounded and weakened and unable to repair the Eye to return to the Kingdom. It took time and sustenance, which was... limited, but as the years passed, my strength returned but also ensnared me here even more within this crude physical *existence*."

Ripples spread through the gelatinous mixture within the pool with each word, but the last one spoken was like a dire curse and the ripples grew to splashes. Despite the concentration needed to bind the incantation to her mind, she spared a second to check that Zoria was close at hand.

The girl seemed broken. She stood a stride away and her head hung and her entire body drooped.

I hope she'll understand, the warrior woman thought before focused on the inscription on the altar again. *At least before this is all over.*

"By the time I had the strength to repair the Eye, that blasted bloodline was established above and my children below were no longer capable of sorcery." Atlacothix hissed as he turned jet-black eyes to the ceiling. "Then that *Cherubash* was always hovering overhead and I could do nothing but sit here in this pit and wait for something to change before the end of the Long War."

"Do you have to talk so much?" Ax-Wed grunted as she traced the curl of a sigil with one gloved finger. "This isn't easy."

"I would apologize but it's not as though I've had much conversation in the past millennium," the fiend explained and brushed her complaint aside with a toss of its wide head. "Before the prince finally found me, I hadn't had anyone worth talking to for centuries and there was too much at stake with him to spend any time in idle chatter."

She quieted her next protest at the mention of the prince and hoped that the chatty demon would find a reason to speak more on his connection to the ruler of Jehadim.

Fortunately, it continued with a deeply amused rumble that stirred deep inside its throat.

"I had hopes that my manipulation of him would result in the *Cherubash* finally forsaking its duty, but even with an accelerated timetable, the chasm between the mortal and his divine guard dog seemed to be crawling if it's widening at all. True, the little vermin has been losing his mind as humans understand it, but it seems that was of little consequence to the cruel guardian. For a time, I thought I might despair. Yet, as the True King always says, 'The victory of the Kingdom is assured,' and lo, there do you come, my salvation from the days of old delivered by my ingenious efforts."

And you almost had me killed several times, Ax-Wed thought as she surreptitiously finished her examination of the last sigil. *But keep believing it was all meant to be.*

"And now we'll kill a whole city to kill one man," she remarked dryly as she made a show of still examining the symbols.

"I know. Isn't it thrilling?" the fiend said with an appreciative grin. "Although to be honest, this will hardly be the first time one of your race has done so or at least something of this magnitude. Truly, your people were perhaps the greatest accomplishment of our labors. A grand society of materialistic sorcerers with a dedication to reality and its subjugation that rivaled our own. While I grieve to see their grandeur so faded, I'm glad to see their spirit, however diminished, remains with your kind."

Uncertain of how to respond to the backhanded compliment about her damnable people, she settled for a slow nod and turned to look into the ghastly face that hovered over her.

"All right, I think I understand," she said as she shuffled a half-step from the altar. "The first incantation will gather the power for the spell and the second one will direct it."

Atlacothix nodded so vigorously that strands of black slime were slung into the air.

"Yes, yes," it agreed enthusiastically and rearranged its coils to look at her from across the altar. "But be very precise as the damage to the Eye makes it a mite touchy and I'm certain I won't have to tell you that channeling such power will hurt a great deal."

"I'm quite aware," the Thulian replied before she turned for a soft word with Zoria. "Stay close to me. This will be scary."

The girl nodded but gave no further response.

"Are we ready?" the fiend asked and its entire body shivered with anticipation.

Ax-Wed knew it was a distraction she could not afford, but she thought of Jehadim above, of its high walls and the proud Citadel, and the market squares and plazas teeming with people from across the East and beyond. She recalled the faces of some she had seen passing her when she entered the city—an old man with twinkling eyes and a young woman with braids like a water-fall of black gold. Then she remembered Julo and Jalen, their eyes huge and curious as they watched her by firelight and this opened a flood of faces—Numi, Durra, Iyshan, and Vahrem.

Why was his face so hard to picture? She remembered it well but at first, the mental image seemed like a weight she didn't have the energy to lift. Despite this, the memory of the caravan master wracked with care as he looked heavenward with a dusting of moonlight on his dark beard drew her in. She saw the sweep of his broad shoulders and wondered if perhaps there would have been room for her to rest her head there. Could those heavy arms have held her even when she thrashed with nightmares? But it was too late now.

She put the thoughts aside and hoped that Vahrem and his caravan were far from Jehadim.

"Let's do this," Ax-Wed said with a nod and let the first incan-tation take shape in her mind.

"You've doomed us all," Prince Tarkhind screamed as he lurched toward Alborz.

Guuhal stepped forward and extended his hand to block his path.

"My prince," the *Hazarbed* said softly. "You are not yourself."

Tarkhind looked into his face and his mouth twisted with a snarl.

"You are part of this!" the young ruler shrieked. "You and these traitors have killed us all!"

Alborz stepped to Guuhal's shoulder with Vahrem a pace behind him.

"What is he talking about?" the *Argbed* asked and felt the confusion and tension spread through his men like the crackles of lightning in the sky above.

"Didn't he tell you?" Tarkhind shouted over the guard commander's unmoving shoulder. "Didn't he explain why we had to offer sacrifices?"

"Sacrifices?" Alborz repeated as an anxious murmur rippled through the assembly of guards. He didn't like the energy in the air that infused the expressions of the men when they looked at each other. Emotions were running high and things could get out of hand in short order.

"What sacrifices?" Vahrem demanded as he pushed closer to the prince and even shouldered past Guuhal to reach him. "Those you took? What did you do to them?"

Prince Tarkhind's fury crumpled before the burly merchant's accusing glare. He looked into eyes ready to ignite with a terrible and righteous wrath and he recoiled. Reflexively, he looked from face to face and found no comfort or support.

"I...I did what was necessary," he said slowly and tried to draw himself up and away from those who should have knelt before him. "That is the burden of leadership, of ruling."

"That's not good enough!" the caravan master snapped and advanced a step, his fingers curled into thick claws that seemed eager to rend royal flesh. "What happened to those you took?"

The royal retreated a step but the guards who had brought him to this treasonous assembly prevented him from retreating further. He turned and realized that those before him—not only Alborz, Guuhal, and Vahrem but every man on the causeway—had stepped closer and now pressed in with hard faces and narrowed eyes.

"Don't any of you understand?" he shouted but his voice

cracked as he started to fold into himself. "I did it to save this city!"

Vahrem lunged forward, seized the slight royal by the front of his dressing gown, and began to haul him toward the edge of the causeway.

"You start making sense or you won't have to worry about Jehadim!" the caravan master warned.

"Vahrem!" Alborz shouted but stopped short of rushing forward when the merchant heaved Tarkhind onto the lip of the wall. "Don't, please. We need him to face trial."

"You can have him when I'm done, assuming there's anything left," he responded shortly and his gaze remained fixed on Tarkhind's bloodless face. "Now speak!"

The prince didn't look at the dark water rushing behind him but instead, his eyes turned upward to stare at the fury-riven skies.

"They won't believe me," he whined in a small and brittle voice. "They won't understand."

Vahrem's brow knotted as the royal continued to stare skyward until another peal of thunder broke the spell. He shook him roughly and one of his slippered feet scuffed at the edge of the wall and his heel slid over empty air.

"No more lies and no more conspiracies," he rumbled with a voice that matched the tumult in the heavens. "What did you do?"

Tarkhind's eyes seemed to go out of focus for a moment and he thought the prince might have swooned but with a shudder, the young man came back to himself. Sharp, hard eyes glared at the merchant before the prince threw his head back and laughed.

"Don't you remember?" he sneered. "It all started with Hasriim the Great."

He scowled but his hold upon Tarkhind remained firm.

"My father, the Sentinel, stood watch as Hasriim the Great neutered and shackled Jehadim," Tarkhind explained bitterly. "After all, where are our lancer cohorts and why do our guards bear clubs and staves instead of spears and blades? It's all because of Hasriim's boot on our neck but unlike my father, I wasn't content to let this indignity stand. I knew that once the broken old fool was gone, I would do everything in my power to see Jehadim free and strong enough to deny the tyrant and anything he brought against us."

Several of the men on the causeway shuffled uncomfortably but something akin to defiant pride flared in the eyes of a few of them. It seemed the prince wasn't the only one who chafed under the bonds of the Hasriiman Dictates.

"Yet how could I do this with my father allowing Hasriim to cut our balls off? I turned to old stories of what had once stood where Jehadim is now and when secrecy was all but assured, I had the lower reaches of the Citadel excavated in search of the ancient means to unleash ruin not seen since the days of the Thulian Empire. It proceeded slowly at first but in time, we saw the fruit of our labors when we found tunnels that led deep into the earth, remnants of the mighty people who once built their fortresses to house weapons of terrible power. We continued to dig, sure that salvation was beneath the next layer. Then, we found Him."

The skies bellowed and Tarkhind winced as though struck.

"He was a monster, a demon or perhaps even some ancient god who had waited, restless and unslumbering in the dark. He told me that he indeed possessed the weapon I desired but he required sacrifices before he would part with it. I offered the workers who had unearthed the depths, who were all criminals and slaves anyway, but it soon became clear that his appetites were larger than that. I enlisted Guuhal to find someone to acquire more people—those who wouldn't be missed like the workers—but as more were given, it became clear that he would never be satisfied and I tried to refuse him. He threatened to turn the very weapon I'd sought upon Jehadim! What choice did I have?"

All stood in horrified silence, some of them unable to meet the prince's wild stare.

"And that is what has become of your sell-sword and every other soul sent into circles carved deep in the earth," the prince said with a defiant glare at Vahrem. "Kill me if you want, but you'll merely make me a martyr for Jehadim exactly like her."

The merchant's arm trembled with rage and for a moment, no one on the causeway dared to move. Then, with a howl like a wounded beast, his whole body flexed in a violent twist and the royal was thrown back toward the center of the causeway. The young ruler fell at Guuhal's feet and shook his head as though surprised to still be breathing air.

With a defeated sob, the caravan master sank to his knees and rested his elbows on the low wall at the edge of the causeway.

"Nothing," he whispered. "She's been gone all this time."

Alborz appeared at his back and placed strong hands on the bowed shoulders.

"I'm sorry, Vahrem," the *Argbed* said, his throat tight but his voice gentle.

"Nothing!" Vahrem roared to the sky, which answered with its titanic echo. "All of it! Nothing!"

Alborz's voice betrayed him when his mouth opened to speak. He shook his head, remained silent, and simply stood with one hand on his friend's shoulder.

"Bind the prince," Guuhal instructed the closest guards. "See that he comes to no harm."

Still on the ground, Tarkhind cackled like a reeling drunk.

"Oh, it's too late for that!" He giggled. "None of us will live long enough to escape this city. He'll make sure of that."

Nervous glances were exchanged among the assembly of guards until the *Hazarbed* struck his staff on the stone and launched another parade-ground address.

"Royal guards of Jehadim, to your duties!" he bellowed and with a start, the men hurried to obey.

They'd dragged the prince to his feet when the heavens resounded with a tremendous crash and a fury unlike anything they had witnessed before. Every gaze rose to the tumult in the celestial vault. As a result, every face was etched with a searing glare as a bolt launched from on high to stab through the heart of the Citadel like the burning lance of God.

"It's coming!" Tarkhind screamed, his cry barely audible through the tremendous sound of ancient fortifications splintering apart. "I told you!"

Lost in all the roar was the faintest impression of great wings beating.

"Yes!" Atlacothix roared. "Excellent!"

Ax-Wed screamed as the power coursed in and around and through her flesh. It threatened to consume her as her whole body went rigid and sparks spat from her eyes and fingertips.

"Quickly!" the fiend called over the crackling roar that filled the chamber. "The *Cherubash* is coming. Strike before it destroys us all."

Three potent syllables were all she needed to annunciate—*hal'kah'qua*. They would send the gathered sorcerous energy surging upward to reduce Jehadim to a lifeless crater. Three small sounds would be all it took and she and Zoria would be free of this nightmarish place forever.

"Ax-Wed!" the girl cried, her voice almost lost in the thrum of the energy that threatened to tear the Thulian apart. "Please! Please don't!"

"Do it now! It's almost here."

Every muscle in her body screamed in protest as Ax-Wed lifted her head and opened her mouth to scream.

"*Qua'kah'hal!*"

The pain that surged through her was beyond screams,

beyond bodily spasms, and beyond any understanding. She felt the very fibers of her body and soul come unspooled as arcs of power slammed into her from impossible distances.

"You fool! You—"

Sorcerous power, not simply heat or light but raw, unnatural fury, launched out from the Thulian's outstretched hands and ripped through everything it touched in a cascade of ruin. Stone erupted like tufts of chaff as tendrils of snapping, undulating light burrowed and chewed through anything in their erratic path.

Her eyelids drawn painfully wide in the glare of the sorcerous onslaught, she watched as arcs and rays of the unleashed power buried themselves in Atlacothix's flesh to release noxious clouds of black vapor before they punched through to the other side.

Traitor! the terrible voice howled inside her head but it was a distant cry compared to the storm that raged in her.

Wave after wave poured through her to flense stone in great molten curls or open fresh ichor-leaking wounds in the demon's flesh until, with a final exultant cry, she threw her hands upward and a final blast struck the fractured Eye that hung overhead. For an instant, the black disk held and drank in the earth-shattering power, but fissures like torn veins soon appeared amidst the jagged expanse. There was a crack like the spine of the world breaking and the blasphemous icon sundered to rain burning shards of stone onto the fiend and cause the fetid pool to boil.

Steam and curls of smoke rolled off her body as Ax-Wed collapsed onto her hands and knees. In a single heave, she tore her helm from her head and knelt upon the floor, in too much pain to do anything but force one breath in and one breath out.

All around her, the tortured stones groaned as they ground against one another, shifted, slipped, and prepared for the inexorable collapse. She knew that her life could be measured in seconds.

Slowly, she turned and beheld the ruined form of Atlacothix

where it lay spent and flaccid in the bubbling pool. Its fanged maw gaped wide and a dribble of ichor seeped steadily into the liquid. She stared at the fallen hulk and a smile stole across her lacerated lips until the perforated body uttered a quavering rasp and quivered slightly.

"When you reach the darkest pits of the Kingdom," Atlacothix wheezed as its remaining eye turned toward her. "I'll be waiting for you."

Then, like a punctured wineskin, the *Tzitohn* deflated in a rush of putrid foulness too dark and turgid to be blood. An oppressiveness so subliminal it seemed natural left the chamber and for the first time since being thrown into the dark beneath Jehadim, Ax-Wed drew in an untroubled breath.

"Zoria?" she called in a hoarse voice, rose stiffly to her feet, and beat the pain back with a fatalist's final elation. It was almost over.

A small sound behind her made her turn and she saw Zoria curled in a ball on the floor, as white as a sheet but otherwise seemingly unharmed. Every movement a little easier than the last but all of them exquisitely painful, the Thulian shuffled closer to the girl and with a long groan, sank beside her.

"Come here, girl." She sighed, her arms outstretched. "I've got you."

Zoria let herself be gathered into Ax-Wed's arms as the first chunks of stone broke free from the ceiling and splashed into the pool.

"You didn't destroy the city," she whispered as she pressed herself against her armored chest.

"No, I didn't," she agreed softly and tugged one gauntlet off to run scarred fingers through the girl's silken hair.

"But that means we'll die down here." The words were untouched by fear but resonant with sadness.

"Sooner rather than later, I'm afraid," Ax-Wed said and did her best to speak around the lump forming in her throat. A larger chunk of stone split from the ceiling and struck the floor a few paces from them, but she continued to stroke Zoira's hair. There was nowhere to go and nothing else to do.

"I don't want to die," the girl stated almost matter of factly and a single tear traced along the scar on her face.

"Me neither," she agreed with a swallow that gave a soft click in her throat.

Zoria looked up and smiled at her, the expression sad but sincere. "But I'm glad I'm with you," she said before she rested her head again, still smiling.

The walls groaned around them and began to buckle slowly.

"Thank you," Ax-Wed said with a sniff. "I'm glad I'm with you too."

Neither of them bothered to look up at a deep and ominous crack overhead.

"I suppose this is the end then." The girl sighed.

The pulse of a heavy wing beat between the grinding cracks of stone almost seemed like a dream and both felt a thrill when a voice, deeper and purer than Atlacothix could imagine, whispered at the edge of their awareness.

Not quite yet.

CHAPTER THIRTY-THREE

"It's over! There's no escape."

Prince Tarkhind's dire proclamations rang unchallenged as those on the causeway scrambled to retreat from the collapsing Citadel. Great sections of the structure twisted and fell free from the bones of the venerable fortress and plunged in a spray of debris and a cloud of dust.

Vahrem and Alborz ran side by side and ducked flying chunks of masonry as they raced to clear the causeway which had already begun to buckle behind them. The wagon, its team of donkeys, and the rear guards had already been claimed and when the caravan master stole a glance over his shoulder, he saw that *Hazarbed* Guuhal raced barely ahead of the crumbling stones with the mad prince thrown over one shoulder.

In that moment and by the Shepherd's grace, he forgave the guard commander before he focused on his own escape.

He and Alborz reached the street seconds before a cloud of dust from the imploding building enveloped them and the world became a choking phantasm of moonlight on crushed stone.

Staggering and colliding with others in this bleary nether-world, the merchant was soon separated from his friend and he staggered forward, blinking like an owl in daylight. For a time, there was nothing but one foot moving in front of the other and each particle-choked breath rasped through his raw throat.

"Nothing," Vahrem muttered as he lurched past a half-glimpsed figure in the dark miasma. "All for nothing."

Songs and poems, the lifeblood of his faith, rose to his mind to remind him to trust the Shepherd but the ache in his heart would not be soothed.

"Nothing," he repeated after he stumbled over a fractured bit of masonry. "All for—"

But a wool be knit, so the Shepherd works his will.

The words rose in his mind but they seemed to not be in his voice.

So take heart, dear Flock, and in your aching be still.

"Be still." He breathed and coughed as dust coated his throat. "Be...uh, be still."

Slowly, his feet dragged to a stop and his hands rose to cradle his head.

"Shepherd, keep me," he whispered, so lost in prayer that he remained ignorant of those who staggered past him like ghosts in the muffling cloud. "I am lost and afraid, and I doubt. Forgive me. Keep me."

With his eyes pinched shut and his hands over his face, Vahrem was taken completely unawares when something butted up against him. In surprise, his hand clamped down on a narrow shoulder, the slight support exactly what he needed to keep his balance. He tried to dislodge clinging clumps of dust while he squinted to inspect the small figure under his hand.

"Child, are you lost?" Vahrem managed to croak before a grasp like iron seized his wrist.

"Let go of her!" A leonine roar was followed by a sharp twist and he was driven back until his foot turned on some debris. He had an impression of a tall figure coming towards him before he toppled and landed with a winded grunt.

Confused and struggling to gulp polluted air, he looked up with bleary eyes to see his attacker standing over him with a bright-edged ax that gleamed despite the dust. Yet, even with the doom that grin of steel foretold, it was the executioner's face which seized the caravan master's attention.

Burning copper eyes set in a face strong and proud glared at him. One side of the face was graven with scars.

"Ax-Wed?" he choked out as he tried to rise while he slipped and slid on more debris.

The ax rose to strike but the Thulian's eyes narrowed and then widened in surprise.

"Vahrem?" she cried and her face knotted with confusion and concern. "What are you doing here?"

The merchant didn't know whether to laugh or cry as he finally managed to find his feet and take a staggering step towards her. Some part of him refused to believe it could be true, convinced that any second now, he would realize he'd struck his head or he was looking at some other towering, warrior woman with a bright and terrifying ax in her hands.

Hands that he very much felt the urge to take and kiss, if he were honest.

"L-looking for you," he stammered as he drove the distracting and intrusive thoughts back.

Ax-Wed smiled and something strange and potent flashed in her eyes as she looked at him. Vahrem wasn't sure what it portended and when the look lingered, he felt a flutter of panic in his chest. Despite this, he couldn't deny that he didn't want her to stop.

"Make way!" a voice shouted from somewhere in the dust cloud. "Make way for the Prince of Jehadim!"

This was answered by a series of angry shouts and sounds of fighting somewhere ahead.

"Well, that didn't take long," he muttered and spat out a mouthful of dust before he turned to Ax-Wed again. "Come. I'm not sure what is going on—demonic wrath or civil war or who knows what else—but regardless, Jehadim seems like a less than ideal city to be in right now."

She nodded and her gaze scanned the obfuscating whorls of dust for threats.

"I'm with you as long as the girl can come along."

"Girl?" Vahrem asked, then realized that the small figure he'd grabbed was still standing behind the Thulian. The caravan master blinked away more offending dust and confirmed that the rag-wrapped creature was a girl child probably very close to Julo's age.

"I'm Zoria," she said with a stiff nod of her head as she gave him a sidelong stare. "Big and ax-happy's with me."

Ax-Wed snorted softly in the back of her throat but didn't argue.

"Zoria, you are most welcome to come," he said and bowed in return. "But I'm afraid you'll have to ride with her."

"Ride?" they asked in unison, which drew a chuckle from him before he led them off at a brisk pace.

Julo and Jalen had seen the bolt of lightning arc into the Gold Quarter from where their father had told them to wait at the thoroughfare, and it had taken all their wits and will to keep the two silver-coated mares from trampling them or running off in the wake of the tremendous boom that followed.

After the horses were quieted, they had listened anxiously to sounds of further chaos, stones cracking, men shouting, and great crashes from within the city's grandest quarter. Neither of them had the first idea of what was going on in Jehadim but both could tell that things were unsettled in the worst possible way, After their encounter with the snatchers, neither of them had any desire for further disruption.

"Do you think it has something to do with the snatchers?" Jalen asked and stroked his mare's mane nervously, which the trembling animal allowed reluctantly. "Like maybe they caught them and there's some kind of execution going on in the Gold Quarter?"

Julo shook his head as he chewed his lip and watched the thick cloud rising from the area toward the moon overhead. Quietly he wondered if the cloud would be enough to blot out the moon and then realized that would mean he and Jalen would have to walk home in the dark.

"An execution by what? Lightning?" the older brother snapped with a ferocity meant for his fears, not his brother. To his good fortune, Jalen failed to notice as three figures jogged down the thoroughfare toward them.

"I think they're here!" he exclaimed as he moved to lead his horse out to greet them.

"Wait, stupid!" Julo snapped and reached a hand out to snare the back of his brother's shirt. "How do you know it's them? Pap said it'd only be two."

"Geroff me!" Jalen snarled and twisted futilely in his brother's grasp before he leveled a finger at the most conspicuous member of the advancing group. "When else did you see a lady that big, stupid?"

Julo let go of his brother and his knees went watery and his stomach began to romp about like a dancing bear at the sight of the towering warrior woman bounding toward them. He took hold of the horse's lead in both hands but his legs refused to move. He'd hoped beyond hope that this moment would come and had prayed to every god he'd ever heard of—even Master Kal'Struh's odd Shepherd—but now that the moment was there, he didn't know what to do. He supposed going out to present the horses as his father had instructed would have been fine but for some reason, his body seemed to have other ideas.

"Julo, come on," his younger brother called over his shoulder. "Remember Pap said they were in a hurry."

He took a deep breath and mastered the squirming in his guts as best he could as he moved forward with the horse in tow.

Vahrem, Ax-Wed, and a pretty girl around Julo's age came to a slow, loping halt and took a moment to try to slow their panting breath.

Julo stared at Ax-Wed, convinced she was the most beautiful and frightening thing he'd ever seen in his life. He had known what he wanted to say to her when his Pap had told them why they would be minding horses along the thoroughfare that night but suddenly, his voice seemed to have deserted him.

Jalen, on the other hand, seemed to have no such predicament.

"Hey, big lady!" he shouted and waved a hand in eager greeting. "Thanks for keeping me from getting snatched."

Ax-Wed, still panting heavily, found the energy to break into a smile.

"You're welcome," she said and when she turned her flashing eyes to Julo, she added, "You both are."

His face burned from his cheeks to his nose and he held the lead for the horse out to the Thulian.

"I-I wanted to thank you t-too," he began and tried to not forget the words he promised himself he'd say if he ever had the chance to see her again. "I've never met a woma—uh, I mean a lady, of such strength and bravery and...uh, b-beauty before, and I doubt I ever will. Thank you for being so wonderful and for saving me and Jalen."

She took the lead from his shaking hands before she sank to one knee in front of him. Even like this, she was a little taller than him.

"You are most welcome," she said softly and before he could respond, she leaned forward and kissed him on the forehead.

Jalen giggled and Julo felt he might burst into flames from

embarrassment. At the same time, however, the spot on his brow tingled in a way he'd never known could feel so good.

"I saved your life," she said as she rose and placed the girl with her on the mare's back before she mounted. "And now you two save mine."

He could take it no longer and stared at his feet as they scuffed the cobbles.

"Well done, boys, and thank you," Vahrem said from the back of the mare he'd taken from Jalen. "Now get home as quickly as possible. There'll be no more snatchers tonight, but Jehadim is still not safe and in fact, you should tell your father for me that I recommend he find a reason to travel for a few weeks."

"Will do, Master Kal'Stru." Jalen saluted with a serious scowl, which prompted the merchant to reach down and ruffle the lad's hair before he set off at a trot.

"Take care, boys," Ax-Wed said with a wave. "May we meet again in better times."

"Good luck, kids," the girl sitting with the warrior woman called. "Thanks for the horse."

Both boys stood waving farewell as the mares bore their riders toward the gates of Jehadim, where their father had arranged for the gates to be opened for a short time to allow the riders to depart. They had heard Father say it was good money and given that it was Master Kal'Stru who was asking, he knew it was a good cause even before mention was made that he'd be helping the woman who'd saved his sons.

Now, those sons turned to head home and both hoped, if perhaps for different reasons, to see the riders again someday.

EPILOGUE

They'd ridden hard through the night and had crested a rough dune that overlooked the caravan's camp as the sun was coming up.

None of them had spoken much during the ride, each of them bound in their thoughts concerning the travails they'd all endured during the last several days. Yet, when they saw the tents and fresh cooking fires below where their horses stood, it seemed the silence could no longer hold and Vahrem turned in the saddle and looked at Ax-Wed, his face earnest.

"I know so much has happened and most of it I won't understand," he began and guided his horse to walk directly beside hers. "But I want you to know that the offer to have you join the caravan still stands."

She had no ready answer to that and Zoria looked expectantly at her.

"I understand if you want some time to think about it," he added quickly when he saw her discomfited glance. "We are bound for Carnyxia first, by way of Mahliknet and the Girdle, so if you want to, you could come with us as far as that and then make your decision there. If you don't want to take up with us, I'm sure there's work for someone like you there."

The Thulian nodded but continued to stare at him as they moved slowly along the brow of the dune. Vahrem began to say something else, thinking she wanted some other assurance, but thought better of it and waited quietly.

"Why?" Ax-Wed asked at last. "Why did you stay behind for me?"

The caravan master considered the question for a moment before he answered, his brows knitted pensively over a thoughtful stare toward his camp.

"You were part of my camp that night and I didn't keep you safe," he said at last. "I couldn't leave you after what happened when you were under my protection."

"In leadership, everything is your fault," she quoted with a nod but he could see that she wasn't entirely satisfied with the answer. Neither was he.

"Was there any other reason?" she asked, her voice softer than he'd ever heard it.

"Perhaps," he said and turned away from her gaze at the last second lest she see something there he wasn't ready for her to see. "Would you like there to be?"

"Perhaps," she answered and turned to look at the camp.

The silence stretched between them again until Zoria could no longer bear it.

"You know what I would like?" she said, seemingly to no one in particular. "Breakfast. A hot breakfast from something that had at most four legs."

Vahrem raised an eyebrow at the leg specifications but remained silent when he noticed Ax-Wed mouthing, "Don't ask," before she shuddered.

"I think breakfast is a fine start," he said with a courteous bow to Zoira before his gaze drifted to meet the warrior woman's. "What say you?"

She looked at the camp, then at him before she smiled and spurred her horse over the crest.

"I say let's race!" she shouted over her shoulder and Zoria responded with a wild war cry.

Dear Reader,

Thank you for coming with me on this new journey.

When Mike reached out to me and asked me if I wanted to do a sword and sorcery tale I was practically falling over myself to accept (which as a bigger guy wasn't safe for anyone let me tell you). As you might have guessed from my acknowledgments, the likes of Conan, Kull, and Bran Mak Moran loom large in my youthful imaginings and the chance to create a series in such a line was the chance of a lifetime. Once I'd cleaned up the mess I'd made and thanked Mike for the opportunity, I immediately set to work.

You are now the recipients of that work and I hope you've enjoyed it. If you came here from Skharr then you might have been surprised and hopefully not unpleasantly so. While Mike has created a rollicking and rambunctious world of adventure in the West for the likes of Skharr and Cassandra and others, but the East... the East was mine.

And true to form (and much to Mike's chagrin), I took Mick Jagger's advice and painted it black. So you'll find it quite a bit darker and grimmer and prone to the sort of fell wonders akin to what you might find in spider haunted Zamora or shadow-guarded Stygia. It's a land of blood and intrigues, of secrets and sorceries. Ancient horrors lurking in the depths but it is perhaps men who seem the most capable of doing far worse.

Hither came Axe-Wed of Thule, blue-maned and fierce eyed... too much. Like I said, I really love this stuff, and it is my great hope that you will too, because I've got a lot more in store for you. Wind-blasted plains, frigid mountains, and enough monstrous foes than you can shake an axe at.

And if it's not your horn of mead... well I guess Mike gets to say I told you so.

Regardless, I appreciate the time and chance you've taken on me and Axe-Wed.

Until next time dear ones,
Aaron D. Schneider

P.S.

Okay I've got a little more to say, and it comes from my heart (crooked thing that it is) and I hope it comes through loud and clear. It all starts with one word: Dissatisfaction.

That is the word I'd speak to you today. I would have you be dissatisfied with this book, indeed dissatisfied with every book. Hopefully not because you didn't enjoy it, and if I may flatter myself, not because it isn't a good book. I want you to be dissatisfied because I'd never want to see settled and satisfied with what this world has to offer, and yes I am including myself in there in case you are wondering.

Now, you may ask me how I, as a Christian, could exhort people to dissatisfaction, because doesn't that Book I care so much tell me to be content?

Content; most certainly. Satisfied; never, at least not this side of the dirt.

Now in an age when everyone seems to want to redefine

words and what they mean I'm not looking to add my voice to the throng, but I feel this is important. Contentment is to accept what comes without worry and resentment, but to be satisfied… well, that means to have all you could need, all you could want. I'd never wish that for you, because that is not what this world is for.

To quote my beloved Professor Lewis:

"Our Father refreshes us on the journey with some pleasant inns, but will not encourage us to mistake them for home."

This world isn't your home, hasn't been for some time, and I beg you to never buy the lie that you must be satisfied with it. Yes, find the "inns" along the way, even build them as I hope this book of mine can be, but never, ever be satisfied with them.

You aren't home here, and woe to you if you want it to be. He empties that He may fill, dry bones to living water, hearts of stone for hearts of flesh, but He won't fill what is already satisfied in itself and the petty bits of rubble and straw we gather around ourselves.

Seek while He may be found dear one, for His dissatisfaction is a finer, higher, better thing than this world can offer (and yes I'm again including myself in all that).

But regardless, content or satisfied, empty or filled, I hope you will continue to walk with me as we follow Axe-Wed on her ashen road, looking ahead to a day when something good and green will grow.

Regards,
Aaron D. Schneider

AUTHOR NOTES - MICHAEL ANDERLE
WRITTEN JULY 14, 2021

Thank you for not only reading this story, but these author notes as well!

When I conceived of Skharr DeathEater, I was excited to bring more stories than I could write into the Sword & Sorcery arena. In order to accomplish this goal, I reached out to Aaron to discuss a story about a new character living in the same world but nowhere near Skharr.

He's a barbarian, she's a royal outcast.

In this one Aaron wanted to write a story where his character was action, but with a pain filled past. A past that catches up with her and a future that she needs to carve out for herself.

Aaron's prose is amazing. I love his writing and know that his talent far outshines my own. While I might suffer a bit of professional jealousy, what do I have to complain about?

My name is on the cover, too!

Aaron and I share a love of stories, but we somewhat differ on the tone of the stories that we enjoy.

My writing leans towards fun and frivolity, while Aaron tends to be a bit more somber and dark. Frankly, I think Aaron's writing is closer to Robert E. Howard (the creator and author of the Conan™) stories than anything I can create.

(Those of you who have provided reviews on my Skharr DeathEater series and mentioned Conan, please do not go back and revise them. I love those comments!)

For those interested in the world's story, think of the Skharr DeathEater series as the 'far left' (or Western United States) geographically and the Eastern United States where Axe-wed story is located.

However, the true history lesson comes from across the oceans (approximately near the Mediterranean area geographically.) Way over there something happened centuries ago which pushed the spread of magic and those wielding magic to move west.

Or die.

We will touch on that area in a forthcoming series called Myth of the Dragon, coming out in Hardback, paperback, and ebook late 2021.

For those who enjoyed the first Axe-wed story, we have two more lined up! Go ahead and push the pre-order button and have the next story all queued up ready to deliver as soon as it is released on Kindle.

It's a good one!

See you in the next Sword & Sorcery book.

Ad Aeternitatem,

Michael Anderle

For those who read the Skharr DeathEater series, Skharr will be returning in book 08!

OTHER BOOKS BY AARON D. SCHNEIDER

The Warring Realm Series

War-Born

War-Torn

War-Sworn

Rings of the Inconquo

(with A.L. Knorr)

World's First Wizard

(with Michael Anderle)

Witchmarked (Book 1)

Sorcerybound (Book 2)

Wizardborn (Book 3)

BOOKS BY MICHAEL ANDERLE

Sign up for the LMBPN email list to be notified of new releases and special deals!

https://lmbpn.com/email/

For a complete list of books by Michael Anderle, please visit:

www.lmbpn.com/ma-books/